THE CODEX

THE CODEX

Helen McCabe

The Piper Trilogy Book 3

Published in 2016 by Telos Publishing Ltd
5A Church Road, Shortlands, Bromley, Kent BR2 0HP, UK

www.telos.co.uk

Telos Publishing Ltd values feedback. Please e-mail us with any comments you may have about this book to:
feedback@telos.co.uk

Cover Design: David J Howe
Cover Art: Iain Robertson

ISBN: 978-1-84583-923-9

British Library Cataloguing in Publication Data. A catalogue record for this book is available from the British Library.

ACKNOWLEDGEMENTS

I would like to thank the following for their help and support in the preparation of this book: my agent, Hazel Latus, for her continued support; Lucia Contaldi, for her enthusiasm and her helpful suggestions in the translation of the earlier volumes of the trilogy; Dr Keith Nash, for a careful reading of the manuscript; and Dr Keith Bromley for his helpful suggestions.

1

Oxford, England, January 2024

At about 11.30, the trio – two teenage boys and a girl – left the venue outside Oxford.

The night had been a success, and Olga wanted it to last forever. Like Spencer, she had told her mother that she was going to play at the orchestra's New Year's concert, but not that she would be going on to a club afterwards. Her mother would have forbidden it. One of the club's attractions for Olga was that Klaas Honen was coming with them. What neither she nor Spencer had expected was that the usual flautist would be taken ill at the last minute and Klaas would take his place. It had been a double whammy for Olga. Almost as if it was meant to be.

Klaas was lucky in that he didn't have to tell anyone. He could do as he liked.

Spencer walked to the car and waited for the others to catch him up. As they approached, Klaas had his arm around Olga. Spencer was puzzled by their relationship, because as far as he knew, no guy except Klaas fancied Olga, and Klaas didn't usually bother with girls. He had always been too much of a geek, amongst other things.

It had caused a stir at school when Olga had told her friends that she was going out with Klaas. He had left St Willibrord's by then, as he had finished his exams much sooner than anyone else. Klaas was 17, a year younger than Spencer, but he was a genius. He was already studying at the University in one of the best colleges. He was good at everything, but lots of people had been relieved when he had left the school. Strange things happened when you were Klaas's friend. So most people kept away from him.

Olga was a swot too, so they probably suited each other. She wasn't Spencer's type. She was tall and a bit too slim and pale. He had never looked into her eyes properly, because she usually wore glasses, but he thought they were brown.

Olga, like Klaas, was clever, a scholar, and she didn't fit in. She wasn't a boarder, and she kept herself to herself. There was an untouchable quality about her, and Spencer had never even considered her company, although they were both in the orchestra. The only reason he was with her now was that Klaas had given them both a lift. It had saved Spencer's dad picking him up, because he didn't like driving on winter nights and often complained that he was a free taxi service for his son.

Spencer had been surprised when Klaas had offered to take both of them in his car, though. Klaas didn't do things like that. He had been the first one in Spencer's year at school to have a car. And it wasn't a heap of junk. His mother worked in the American Embassy in London, and he never mentioned his father, but he was wealthy. How or why Klaas had picked up with Olga, Spencer wasn't sure, but he suspected it was not only because of her intelligence but also because she was a dedicated musician. Klaas could play violin and piano as well as being a demon on the flute, which was Olga's instrument. Maybe he was giving her lessons?

Now Olga and Klaas were standing beside him, and he felt guilty for what he'd been thinking.

'Wanna drive?' asked Klaas, tossing over the car keys.

Spencer could hardly believe his ears. Who wouldn't want to drive Klaas's car? Most of the guys Spencer knew had old vehicles, and the insurance was punishing. Another reason why he hadn't got a car was his parents thought he would crash it. Spencer had only passed his test six months ago. Klaas had an American licence, which allowed a kid of 16 to drive in the US.

What would happen if Klaas was caught by the police for driving so young here, Spencer didn't know.

'What's on your mind?' asked Klaas, fixing him with his strange black eyes.

'Nothing.'

'Are you scared?'

'No,' lied Spencer. Whether he meant of driving, or of him, Spencer wasn't sure. Maybe it was both.

'I know what you're thinking,' said Klaas, grinning.

For a moment, Spencer believed it was true that Klaas was reading his mind, but then he shrugged it off. 'Fuck off!'

Klaas's smile disappeared as he indicated the keys. 'Get in. I've things to do.' He grinned at Olga. She was holding his hand.

'Sure.' Spencer was embarrassed. If he'd been Olga's dad, he wouldn't have let her go out with Klaas. Besides, she was under age, and Honen was taking a risk! Trying to appear cool, and not too eager, Spencer got in, and the other two jumped into the back. Seconds later, the engine was running.

'Go fast,' said Klaas, leaning over his shoulder. Spencer heard Olga giggle. His mum said the quiet ones were the worst. Then Klaas gripped his arm. It hurt. 'Well, get going!'

'Okay.' When Spencer accelerated, he felt the power beneath his foot as the speed increased ...

Outside the city, patches of black ice had turned the road surface into a slippery means of death. Although lorries had been spewing out their loads of grit before midnight, the traffic had already sent the pebbles rolling into the gutters. Now, the January night was still.

In the small lay-by outside the village of Woodstock, the evil eye of a yellow speed camera had preyed on motorists a decade ago. Now, its sophisticated replacement peered out, hardly noticeable from the protection of menacing dark trees except for its slim antennae. At the foot of this check-in station, a black-booted rider sat astride his powerful BMW motorbike, waiting for his next victim.

Traffic policeman 'Marty' Marshall was regarded as a maverick by some of his colleagues, but those few who were his friends admired him for his success with motoring offence convictions. He regarded the law as the means of reward for his unconventional way of policing. So far his behaviour had not brought him to the notice of the Police Complaints Commission, although he had been warned once or twice by his superiors that his conduct needed revision.

That night had not so far produced any nut who regarded his life as cheap. He had called in several times, but the girl on the switchboard he usually joked with had been exchanged for some miserable cow who didn't appreciate his banter. All of this meant that Marshall was not in a forgiving mood. His expression was sullen and boredom was making his temper short, meaning that any motorist passing at even a fraction over the speed limit was facing a penalty. A single man, he had worked over the holiday not out of any sense of good will towards his colleagues who had families to celebrate Christmas with, but out of a desire for the overtime.

He looked at his watch. Half past midnight. He grimaced. A moment later, though, he heard an engine approaching and slammed down his helmet visor. His patience had been rewarded. He was ready!

Spencer was nervous on a couple of bends, but when they reached Woodstock, although he slowed right down as he passed the police station, he increased his speed on the village limits. He couldn't wait to reach the main road, which had a long straight stretch ahead. He wanted to see how fast the car would really go! So he revved up.

'Shit!' A moment later, he saw red and blue lights approaching him from behind. He was tempted to accelerate more, but by then the police bike had caught him up, and he had no choice but to pull over. He felt very scared and glanced into the mirror. Olga had her head on Klaas's shoulder, but

Klaas was looking straight at him.

'Relax,' said the boy. 'I'll handle the cop.' Then he grinned again.

Spencer didn't think it was funny. His dad would kill him if he got a ticket! He wanted to scream at Klaas, *It was your fault for making me drive.* But he choked back the recriminations. He didn't want Klaas getting nasty. It wasn't worth it.

The wing mirror went black, filled with the bulk of the policeman. Spencer looked up at him. The man was pushing up his visor. He had a grim look on his face as he motioned Spencer to put the window down. The lad was sweating as he activated the electrics and the glass slid down.

Marshall smiled. A car full of kids. Exactly what he'd been hoping for. 'Get out,' he said. No *please* or *sir* for them.

Spencer opened the door, conscious of the fact that neither Klaas nor Olga had moved. It wasn't fair. Now he was the one who'd be for it.

'You're not S Honen?' The direct question caught Spencer by surprise.

'Erm … No … I don't understand,' he stuttered.

'You don't own this car, do you?' The Automatic Number Plate Recognition system had done its work. The problem was, the car was Diplomatic.

'No, but …' Spencer struggled with the dilemma of lying to the police or risking Klaas's anger. He felt heat rising, not only in his face, but from deep inside. What gave Klaas the right to put him though this? Then the voice from behind made him jump.

'I'm Klaas Honen and the car belongs to my mother.' Klaas sounded recklessly arrogant. Spencer was shocked. His mother's!

'What's this lot then?' asked Marshall, ignoring the statement and staring at the music cases on the front seat. 'Where'd you get them?' His tone was accusatory.

'They're music cases,' Klaas sneered. 'Mine's the flute. We couldn't fit in the piano, but that's a violin.'

Marshall stiffened. Evidently this lad had no respect for the police. He'd met youths like that before, and dealt with them. 'Get out,' he ordered.

He watched as the back door opened and the lad sprang out. No cowering there! Honen straightened as the moon revealed itself from behind clouds, which had obscured it for hours. It drew the boy's long shadow into a crooked shape, which dwarfed the side of the car and was broken only by the roof line. When the policeman shone the torch right into his face, the boy didn't shade his eyes. Instead, he fixed them on Marshall. *This is a cool one*, the policeman thought.

The boy was very tall. For a second, Marshall's brain flickered with the memory of when he had first joined the force. He was only five-six, and some of the lads had taken it out on him. They had called him *short arse*. The nickname had stuck for a time. No-one dared to use it now. He squashed the memory. He didn't know why he was thinking about that now. All at once, he felt unsettled. Edgy.

'So, you're *Klaas* Honen?' He studied the information. 'Licence?'

'Here.' A flourish and it was in Marshall's hand. He scrutinised the document. It was American. This kid had a licence – to kill. James Bond was in Marshall's brain now. What was the matter with him? He wasn't doing his job. He wrested himself back.

'Insurance?' Honen drew it from his pocket with one stroke, like a conjurer. The arrogance of the gesture couldn't be ignored. It was as if the kid was trying to rile him. The policeman scented trouble. Drivers rarely carried all their documents – except their identity cards, which had become compulsory due to terrorist threats. He scrutinised the insurance document, turning it over several times. That kind of gesture usually spooked people, giving Marshall the upper hand.

'You've got a US licence. This is the UK.'

'So?' said the kid.

Marshall's mouth was tight. He was on shaky ground here, because he didn't know whether Honen could drive on it or not.

'You need to check?' It was like Honen was reading his thoughts.

'You think you're smart,' Marshall retorted.

Honen smiled. 'Yeah, I'm a genius.'

'You don't say!' Marshall's tone was sarcastic.

'I just said so.' His attitude was really getting to the policeman.

'Who do you think you are, you little …?' Marshall stopped before *prick*.

'Really, officer. You should mind who you're talking to.'

Marshall thought he was going to burst. He would have smacked the boy in the mouth, but he knew what that would mean. Besides, Diplomatic meant above suspicion. He turned instead to the driver, who looked fair game. 'Identity card?' he asked. The boy produced it, and Marshall turned it over and over, pretending to scrutinise it officiously. The lad was shivering. 'Licence?'

'Yes, but not on me.'

'You'll have to bring it in.'

'Yes.'

Marshall walked towards the back of the car. 'You in there,' he said. A shaft of moonlight streaked across the seat and lost itself as the clouds drew their curtains once more.

'Yes?'

He could hear the girl's accent, but he couldn't place it. He shone his torch into the darkness, revealing her trying to shade her eyes. 'Out,' he ordered. He could see *she* was scared, which cheered him up. Fear brought out the bully in him, and females were no exception.

As she moved over and he caught a glimpse of her, his first instinct made him think she was a gypsy. But as she stood up and faced him, he realised she was too refined. She was wearing a long, black evening dress and her hair was sleek and dark. She had high cheekbones and looked class. But she was definitely foreign. East European, he thought. Maybe Polish or Romanian? No, not Polish. Looking at the way she carried herself, it was unlikely she was an illegal.

'Your identity card, miss,' he said.

She bent over and pulled out her bag from the back seat of the car. He watched her every movement. She wasn't his type, but she had a nice little arse. After rummaging about in her small evening bag, she produced the card. She was Romanian. He felt pleased with himself.

'You're not 16 yet,' he said, fixing her with stern eyes. 'What are you doing with these two?'

'We've been to a concert.'

'A concert. Where?' Marshall was enjoying himself.

'We've been playing in Banbury. That's why we're late.'

'Taking the long way round, eh?' She didn't answer, but began to sidle over to Honen. The policeman looked again at the American. 'Identity card.'

The boy produced it immediately, and Marshall inspected it. 'So, you're all students? He looked at the three of them. 'Which school?'

'Spencer and I are at St Willibrord's in Oxford,' said Olga. Her voice shook.

'Rich kids, eh. And you?' He turned to Honen.

'Not me. I'm a college boy.' He had assumed a Yankee drawl, which annoyed Marshall immensely. Everything Honen said insulted with its arrogance. 'I told you I'm a genius?'

'Which college?'

'Norris.'

'The University, eh?' Marshall was even more wary.

'Well done.' The lad grinned.

'I'm not taking any more of this crap!' growled the policeman. The other two looked scared.

'Why did you stop us?' asked Honen.

'The ANPR clocked you.'

'How much over the speed limit was he?' Honen gestured at Spencer.

Marshall had to tell. If he lied, they *would* have had something against him. 'Twenty,' he growled.

'For fuck's sake,' said Honen, laughing. 'You must be kidding.'

'*You* won't be when you get the ticket.'

'Just send it to the American Embassy. It's in London. My mother will settle the bill. Mrs *S* Honen.' He was taunting Marshall.

The policeman stiffened. You could never tell who these foreign shits knew. 'Yeah, I will. And a duplicate to your college,' he snarled.

'Cool,' said Honen. His tone was cold, and Marshall knew he didn't believe the lie. Not least because only the driver could be ticketed. 'Come on, you two,' Honen told his friends, gesturing towards the car. 'It's late.'

'You're driving, Honen,' said Marshall. It sounded like an order. 'And keep your speed down. The road's a death trap!'

'No, Spencer is. He'll bring in his licence.' Honen turned to Spencer. 'You're doing great, Spence. Come on.'

A moment later, the girl was scrambling into the back of the low car. Spencer went round to the driver's side, but he couldn't look at Marshall, because he was still shaking.

'I'll remember you,' said the policeman to Honen.

'Ditto,' the boy replied, getting into the back. Then he stuck his spiky head out of the window. He was grinning. 'Hope to see you again – I don't think.' And the window slid down.

Marshall watched them drive off. 'I hope you fucking crash,' he said. The trees above creaked in the wind, which was stirring up the still night. The policeman snapped down his visor and shivered. It was the first time he'd felt so cold for a long time. *Maybe I'm coming down with something*, he thought.

Ten minutes later, Marshall decided it was time to move. He was feeling even colder, and was convinced that something really was the matter with him as a shivery feeling had gripped him. He felt sick as well, and thought of those lucky bastards who were off shift. Sniffing, he looked at his watch. It was nearing 1.00, and he wished he hadn't spent so much time dealing with those kids. Remembering the American's arrogance made him swear under his breath.

As he revved up the bike, a lorry passed him, and the camera clocked it as going way over the speed limit. Marshall's icy feeling was quenched by the thrill of the chase as he accelerated out of the lay-by. He could see the lorry's tail lights flicking on and off in the distance. It was veering from side to side. This driver was a real nutter. And probably a drunk. However heavy it was, driving a vehicle at that speed in this weather was crazy. The driver was a danger on the road.

He blinked and came off autopilot. As he followed the tail lights, he could feel himself sweating. No accident had ever seemed as bad as the first one he'd seen. He was experienced at dealing with death now, but the memory was sharp enough to pierce the hard shell that he'd built up round himself for years. The sweat was running down his face. *What the hell* is *the matter with me?*, he thought. This was no time to be dwelling on unpleasant memories. He was a copper – and he would have gone mad if he had made a habit of this. Death was part of his working life.

The policeman's powerful headlights blazed against the thick red dust covering the back of the lorry as he drew closer. Through the murk, the blue strip and the 12 stars of the European Union lit up. He blinked at the white plate with its black registration. RO. Romanian. Then, with a shock, he realised he was dangerously close. A second later, the driver slammed on the brakes!

In that moment of helpless recognition, Marshall tried to take evasive action. He screamed. But it was too late. Paralysis spread through his body as the powerful bike crashed into the back of the massive vehicle. For a second, it hung there like a squashed fly suspended in the air, then it dropped to the road. A second later, the BMW's smashed frame, mingled with Marshall's mangled body, was drawn by the slipstream underneath and into the lorry's undercarriage.

Professor Pip Durrant woke in his Oxford rooms. He could feel the clammy coldness of sweat running down his neck and chest. *Another nightmare.* It took him some time to move, to remember where he was in this unfamiliar world of clamour.

Could he hear bells? Church bells? He shivered and kept his eyes closed. When the panic of his nightmare had receded, he opened them and looked round. No threatening shadowy figure stood by his bed, as it had done so many times in the past. He was alive. He was all right. Why the hell had he dreamed about being dragged under a truck? The old feeling of utter foreboding struck him. Fear seeped from every pore in his body. He put a hand to his head. He was soaking with sweat.

He settled back in bed to try to get some sleep, but then, although he had tried to avoid it, his earlier dream settled upon him once more. What had happened before he was dragged under the truck? Who were those people he had seen? He had trained his subconscious mind to view the whole scene with detachment, or at least provide a means whereby he could rationalise the horror that must come.

Come on, think, he muttered to himself, and tried to relax, to get those unknown travellers out of his head. Who the hell were they? But nothing worked for him, so he sat up in bed …

He blinked as bright flashes of light penetrated the tops of the heavy drapes. A storm? No! Fireworks. *New Year's Day, 2024. Another Piper Year.* The year he had waited for so long and, sometimes, thought he might never see.

In spite of all that had happened to him since, he still had the chance to follow the killer's trail; a quest that seemed to have ended in 2007, that dreadful year when he had quit Romania after stealing the box that contained Eisenmann's precious manuscript pages. He had committed the crime out of desperation to discover the identity of the man known as Grandsire, whom he was sure had slaughtered the children of Arva. The precious pages he had stolen from Eisenmann had furthered his quest, as he had known they would, but now he had come to a full stop. He shivered again.

He had been a wreck after the sinister German had tried to kill him. Every step he had taken, from then on, had found him looking over his shoulder. His instincts told him he was a marked man. So far, though, his fears had not been realised. Sometimes, when he remembered the shots he had heard inside the house as he escaped, he wondered if his enemy had died. The German had never once contacted him in the intervening years, as Pip had expected he would. The only mention of Eisenmann's name and business interests on the internet came in a brief Wikipedia entry, which gave no indication that he had died. He appeared to have vanished. Where could he have gone? That question haunted Pip, and fuelled his fear that someday he might be faced with a hired assassin lurking around some corner. If he had not been such a coward, he might have delved further and made enquiries of some official sources; but if he did that, and if it turned out that Eisenmann had indeed died, then given that Pip had been present in his house that day, he could have been adding suspicion of murder, as well as theft, to the Romanian police's dossier on him. Pip had been around too many unexplained deaths!

Pip had survived, unlike all the others, and he looked back at that short period he had spent in Eastern Europe in 2007 with regret and dismay. Yet, in spite of his friends' and acquaintances' deaths, Pip had convinced himself that what he had done had been necessary – if violent death could ever be classed as such. The age-old serial killer of Arva had to be stopped.

As to his own survival, he could only cheer himself with the prophesy of the old gypsy, Eva Kirchma, and the confident words of his friend, mentor and close companion, the late Professor Simu Dalca: *You were sent to us. You were chosen to be our witness and saviour* ... Pip had felt utterly miserable, and guilty too, on that day in the University library when he had read his dear friend's Simu's obituary in an international article published by PACE. He had thought the worst of Simu before, for failing to turn up to see him off at the airport and tell him 'something very important' that he apparently needed to know, and also for failing to accompany him to meet Eisenmann. Learning that Simu was dead had really spooked him – because Pip could never now receive that information he had been meant to hear from Simu's own lips.

Pip also hated himself for not keeping in touch with Ghita,

Simu's only child. He had promised to go back to Arva, to fetch her to America. His weakness in not doing so was his biggest regret …

As he again tried to settle back to sleep, his restless mind flicked to his flight from Romania in 2007, when he'd discovered a flash of white at the bottom of the box containing the manuscript pages. The small piece of paper had turned out to bear an address in Brooklyn, New York.

The man he had later found living there had proved to be one of the best leads he had been given so far; but like all the other threads he had followed, their meeting had had tragic consequences. Nothing had changed. Pip remained a thief, but no-one knew. Nor would anyone suspect that the middle-aged, bespectacled academic with the slight limp could be hiding a monstrous secret, which had haunted him every day since then. Pip's mind flicked back to that milestone meeting in 2007 with the gypsy man, Simionce …

2

Brooklyn, New York, 2007.

Pip walked along East 17th Street. Whoever was waiting for the box to arrive wouldn't be expecting *him* to come calling. Maybe Eisenmann had intended to make the visit himself. However, Pip couldn't give up the chance of discovering what the unknown contact knew, and so he had spent the day after he arrived from Romania carefully photocopying the stolen manuscript pages and placing the originals in his bank safety deposit box, which was the safest place he could think of for them at that moment.

All the way to the address, his mood was a mixture of anticipation and fear of what was likely to happen. He remembered how he had felt when he had faced the gun that Eisenmann's bully boy Muller had pointed at him. Luckily, and for some reason that Pip didn't understand, Muller hadn't carried out his boss's command to dispose of him. That last day in Romania was something Pip was never likely to forget, and now that he was back in the States, he was wondering if he should carry a firearm himself. However, he felt that wasn't the way. His father had shown him how to use a gun when he was a child, but he hadn't used one since; and he was concerned that even applying for a firearm licence might prove a dangerous thing, if Eisenmann's men were on his trail. His adversary had powerful contacts.

Pip had lived long enough in Brooklyn to keep safe, but who

or what was waiting for him at the address he had found beneath the manuscript pages he couldn't judge. The mystery contact was either one of Eisenmann's people, or one of his enemies whom he intended to eliminate. Pip preferred to think it was the latter. He, or it could be a she, must be holding something Eisenmann wanted very badly. Eisenmann, like Pip, would do everything he could to obtain it. Yet in Pip's case, violence wasn't part of the equation. Pip grimaced, imagining the probable outcome. Knowing Eisenmann's methods, whoever crossed him or held any useful information wasn't going to come out of it alive. Sweating, Pip walked on.

As he passed the Church of the Holy Innocents, his mind switched back to those helpless little girls from Arva, faced with their murderer, the ageless evil that they called Grandsire. Pip had visited that church once, a long time ago, and had admired its Gothic Revival architecture. The Catholic Church itself meant nothing to him personally, except that he hoped he would discover the part it had played in the horror that had befallen Grandsire's victims. Throughout his perusal of the Marcu Papers and the conversations he'd had with the unlucky priest at Arva, as well as his discussions with Dalca and the gypsy women, Pip had remained confident in the belief that the Church's murky involvement was unquestionable.

He began to hurry, glancing back several times. The entry to the street he was plotting on his mobile came into sight. *I haven't been down there before*, he remembered thinking. It looked quiet and ordinary, although his quivering senses were reminding him to be on his guard. Some houses were well kept, others run-down. Always imaginative, his brain was racing on, pre-empting the scenario. His arrival at the door of the house, the bell ringing inside. Someone – or maybe two or three – hesitating, waiting for trouble, peering out from behind the drapes. He squashed down the thought that someone in there might be armed. What was he going to say then? He didn't even know a name. He had thought he had a plan when he set out, but the old fears were rising. He pushed them away – but they hovered. Telling himself to calm down, he rehearsed the prepared opener:

'Good afternoon, I'm Dr Durrant from the New York Institute …'

It was ludicrous. It had sounded so much better in the privacy of his flat. Here, he was out in the open. He was a sitting duck!

He slowed down and looked up and down the street, trying to collect his thoughts. Several people passed him without a glance, but he noticed a swarthy man, who was sitting on the steps of a brownstone building further on, stare at him, then get up and go inside.

Pip's intuition kicked in again. Maybe he should leave it? At that point he did something he wouldn't recommend to any of his students: he changed his plan at the last minute. He crossed the road nonchalantly and looked up at other houses, although his eyes swivelled in the direction of the old brownstone again. The building looked like apartments. He walked on, staring at door numbers. The street seemed eerily empty now. He had chosen a time when most people were at work. He wouldn't have gone after dark.

Then he found himself facing the brownstone. His intuition had been right. It was the address on the piece of paper. But how was he going to find the right apartment? He walked slowly up the steps towards the imposing door, which hadn't been painted for some years, and stared at the list of flats. He could hear the sound of quick footsteps inside. He drew in his breath to calm himself as the door opened. No gun was pointed by the swarthy man facing him. He was young, maybe in his early thirties, with dark eyebrows raised in a gaunt face. There was no doubt he was of Eastern European origin, possibly Roma. They stood, then the man said, 'We have been waiting for you.' More men appeared at his shoulder, one holding a heavy weapon. Pip felt a host of hostile eyes boring into him.

Pip's immediate thought was, *I don't stand a chance. What the fuck have I got myself into?*

'Who are you?' The swarthy man's accent was thick.

'Dr Pip Durrant – from the New York Institute and – from

Cluj University. Are you Romanian?'

He received no answer – and they didn't shoot him. Instead, he was escorted across a broad hall dominated by a great staircase. The floor was littered with cigarette ends, torn envelopes and all the detritus expected to be found in an unloved building like this.

They walked along a corridor that led alongside the stairs and stopped in front of an internal door. He could feel the gun at his back. The swarthy man turned to him. 'We have been expecting your visit. Once inside, you will have to prove yourself.'

Pip nodded, wondering who needed that proof, and whom he was about to meet. His shirt collar felt tight and damp around his neck, with both fear and excitement. He was expecting to see the men's boss, perhaps another Eisenmann; but in that he was way off the mark.

The swarthy man went in before him. He could hear dull voices, then the man returned and held open the door. '*Puraddad*, Old Man, Granddad.'

A moment later, Pip stepped into a bright stuffy room full of trinkets, gleaming china and accoutrements of the same type he had seen in the Roma vans when he had visited Black Anya and Eva Kirchma in the company of Simu Dalca.

An old man was sitting in an armchair beside an electric fire, on the other side of which was a small wicker chair. He waved a trembling arm, motioning Pip to approach. His eyes, coal-black specks of pupils swimming in a bleary red-veined pool of viscous liquid, held Pip's unwaveringly. What he spoke then resembled what Pip recognised as the Roma language.

'I am *Puraddad*. Simionce.' The voice was weak but authoritative.

'Pip Durrant from the Institute – and the University of Cluj Napocka.' Pip held out his hand. 'Do you speak English?' The man's lashes flicked, and those old eyes closed. Pip added, 'I am sorry. I speak very little Roma, but can manage some Romanian.'

Simionce shifted in his chair. 'What do you want from me?'

he asked, this time in Romanian.

'Information!' replied Pip.

The old man smiled, his mouth disappearing into folds of loose skin. He held out his hand again and clicked his fingers.

'I have not brought you any money,' added Pip, bending forward to make him understand, 'because if you do have the information I am looking for, it is worth more than anyone can afford, and I believe it should belong to everyone.'

He felt a hypocrite, because he was carrying a wad of notes that he would have offered the informant if he'd had to. Then he was startled by a laugh that seemed to rumble up from that pitiful body. It was robust, even triumphant, and accompanied by a grin, which was ghastly but friendly:

'Now I know for sure you are not the German. Sit!' The old man indicated the wicker chair.

'Thanks.' The chair was small, hardly big enough to fit in. *Maybe it belonged to his wife*, was Pip's whimsical thought. He could feel heat rising in his body, not only from the fire, but from excited expectancy at what he was about to hear. He put his hand into his jacket and heard the door creak. He looked round and saw the men at the door. 'It's okay, guys. I am only looking for my notebook.' His words were followed by an unrecognisable tirade that poured from the old man's mouth. The door clicked shut. The old man rocked backwards and forwards, then nodded at Pip.

'My boys,' he said, 'they think you're going to shoot me.' Pip shook his head and grinned back. 'Now – what information could an old Roma give to a professor? We shall speak English.'

Pip nodded again, feeling the warmth between them, but still on his guard. He found his notebook and then, about to sit down, said, 'I am searching for,' he paused, 'the Grandsire of Arva.'

All at once, the room seemed to shrink and the trinkets to lose their brash brightness. He could feel nausea and the familiar crawling in his legs. Then the shiver began that always heralded the darkness followed by the light of a vision. He felt the sweat on his neck, and the familiar sensation that evil was close.

Christ, don't let me have a vision here, he prayed inwardly. A feeling of dizziness overcame him, and he almost toppled from the tiny chair. In a mist, he saw the grandfather wriggle and wrest himself, almost miraculously, from his slump. He sat up tall, stretched out his arms and steadied Pip. Pip slumped back. They did not speak for a moment as Pip fought for his breath. When he came to, the old man was waiting.

'I sense it too, Professor,' Simionce said. 'It happens to our folk.'

'Are you a seer?' asked Pip.

'Less brightly now.' The old man nodded. 'It is both a blessing and a curse.'

'You can help me, then?'

'Perhaps better with some *tuica*. It is restorative.' He was beckoning towards a wide cupboard. Seconds later, Pip hoisted himself out of the chair and went over towards the looming dark-brown cupboard. He opened it to face a tray on which was placed a bottle and two glasses. He stared at it, thinking of Eisenmann's potentially deadly offering at their last meeting. 'For friend not foe,' he heard Simionce say, and realised that the old man must be reading his thoughts. As he brought over the tray, he thought how far he had come, to reach an acceptance that such things could happen.

The first sip of *tuica* loosened Pip's throat and his memories, as that fiery burst of alcohol burned its way towards his stomach. It brought immediate regret as well as restoration. Those he had drunk with back in Romania – all he had questioned – were now dead.

'You miss them?' asked Simionce.

'Yes –' began Pip.

'They played their part. There will be others to come. Others who will help your quest.' The old man smiled and put a comforting hand upon his sleeve. 'Before we begin my story, I must tell you that I do not know all of it, and it is not written down. It is my burden to keep here – all in my head … This is the method we have always used to keep alive our culture.'

'I understand,' replied Pip, remembering past studies. Before him sat a *scop,* a teller of tales of valour and heroism. But could Grandsire's tale be one such? Maybe he was going to hear the story of a devil? Pip was almost shivering with excitement. 'If it is not written,' he added, 'will you allow me to record it, so that it is never lost? I promise never to divulge it, except if I need it to bring down the Grandsire of Arva.'

'Do as you will,' replied Simionce. His eyes held Pip's again. 'I shall not live to see it. If I should die, you must go to her. She knows more of the story.' His face was blank and pale.

'*Her*?' repeated Pip.

'I mean the one who gave birth to our common enemy. Eisenmann. She knows more of this story. She is one of us. Black Anya! The woman who has seen the evil one. Who mated with him.'

Pip shivered. 'How do you know all this?' he asked. 'Did she tell you?'

'She is part of the plan, as are all of us. She is waiting for you.'

'I know that I should go back,' Pip began, but broke off.

'Swallow your fear – and your pride. You must also find the Dalca girl. It is more important than you could ever imagine. Then talk to her gypsy grandmother if it is the last thing that you do. Or the story cannot be ended.'

'Go back to Romania?' Pip felt desperate.

'Listen to what I say,' replied Simionce. 'You are the only one who can find them.'

'I shall, when ...'

The old man shook his head. 'You will not meet them here.'

'You mean I should go back now?' Pip persisted.

Simionce closed his eyes. 'Don't ask me any more. That knowledge is veiled. The only thing that is clear is that you have been sent to us. You are a Christian?' The abrupt change of tone startled Pip.

'Yes ...'

'Then you should remember from your Gospels that a certain old man dwelt in a temple waiting to see his Lord.

Simeon vowed he would not die before he saw Him. This may seem like blasphemy, but I prophesy that you are the one who will deliver us.'

The air around them seemed so thick that Pip could hardly breathe. Simionce had just echoed both Eva Kirchma's words and Simu's. A shiver ran through him. He was no-one's Messiah. He had no desire to be a hero. Inside, he knew he was a coward, who was afraid of his visions and of the prophecies.

Simionce was staring at the bars of the electric fire. He looked as if he was sleeping. Pip caught his arm. The old man shook his head and looked away. 'My time is almost over.' The words were almost inaudible.

'No, no, don't go to sleep, please. You said you would tell me about the Grandsire. His history?' asked Pip. He was scared he had gone too far with his probing and that he would discover nothing. The old man's face had turned from pale to red and his breath was laboured. He looked heated and under stress.

'I am sorry if I've upset you,' Pip went on. 'Simionce, please …' The old man lay back in the chair and closed his eyes. Pip looked around. Maybe one of the men outside the door would help? But it was more likely that they would throw him out.

Then, all of a sudden, Simionce sat bolt upright and held up one hand as if to detain Pip from whatever he was doing. It was as if he had come alive once more. Pip checked that his microphone was switched on and connected to his laptop, which he had brought with him in its case. He had no wish that anyone else should ever find out what he was going to hear. He wanted it only for himself …

'The Saxonia are a savage race,' began Simionce, clearing his throat. 'They do not worship the meek Christian God, who hung on the Cross. They are bloodthirsty men who worship the Devil. He was such a one as these …'

If Pip had known what was to come, he would have not been so enthusiastic. The story was horrific. An hour later, Simionce was obliged to stop, as his voice was failing. When Pip finally left, the old man was near sleep; but Pip had already arranged to visit again the following day to hear more. He was shown out by a less-than-happy great grandson, who snarled 'You've worn him out!' and slammed the door.

Pip stood outside for a while, trying to take it all in, but he was getting so cold that eventually he had to move. How much did Eisenmann know of the story, or of what the manuscript pages meant? Maybe he had been ahead of Pip in wanting to find the Codex?

According to Simionce's story, Grandsire, aka the Piper, aka Nicholas, had set down in the Codex all his personal wickedness throughout history; a catalogue of wickedness that would cease only when the prophesied cycle was fulfilled. It was the Devil's unholy Bible.

Pip had to find out what the few pages he held represented. He also needed to know how Eisenmann had managed to get hold of them. He had believed he would be listening to a legend, but Simionce had told him more than that. Within the Codex was believed to be set down the natural progression of the cycle of evil from the year 800, when the Holy Roman Empire was founded.

Unlike some of Nostradamus's obscure prophesies based on astrology, the Codex was backed up by history, religion and mathematics. It was clear now that the knowledge in that book, if found, would be world-shattering.

The night after Pip's meeting with Simionce was troubled. His imagination conjured up the horrors that had been and were to come, and he woke up as if he had not slept at all. Yet although he felt exhausted, he was meticulous in his preparations for his second meeting with the old gypsy. His mood at that moment was almost too difficult to explain, even to himself.

After first torturing himself as to what revelation would come next, strangely he then retreated into the kind of man he had been when he first began work on the Marcu Papers: a sceptic who had doubted even his own visions and had been torn between reality and fantasy. At that time, he had wondered if Marcu had gone mad, setting aside all his training to exchange it for a belief that, as a rational man and a scientist, he knew could have no place in proper research.

As Pip packed his laptop case and prepared himself for what was to come, he began to be afraid that what had happened to Marcu's fine brain might be happening to his own. He thought of Ghita, whom he believed he loved, and told himself that he could never have her as she was with someone else. She had said she was going to marry Anton. Then he returned to his small sitting-room and flung the case onto the couch. He was near to panic. If he went back to Romania, then what had happened to Marcu could very well happen to him. He hadn't the courage to pursue a cause he didn't believe in. The thought that he might be the saviour of Arva was ludicrous. What could he do? He was only a present-day man pitting himself against the self-styled devil of a legend. A legend wrapped up in poetic words. Then the black period lifted, and he realised that if he didn't hurry he was going to be late for the meeting with Simionce. He told himself that the unfortunate deaths of those who had attempted to help him had all been rationally explicable.

All at once, Pip felt he owed it to the dead to hear the rest of a story that was going to come to an end some day. The illuminated pages he had in his possession were real enough. He had held them in his hand, and they were precious enough for Eisenmann to kill for them. Evidently the German had believed there were more of them, and had hoped to hear the very story that Pip had heard the day before. To discover proof for this horror would be mind-blowing. The thought dispelled those fleeting moments of self-doubt and disbelief.

He jumped up, grabbed his coat and laptop case and was about to go out of the door when his mobile distracted him with its jarring rhythm.

The voice was familiar; the heavy, broken accent, the faltering English. Simionce's great-grandson …

'Dr Durrant.' The voice was thick. 'Do not come today!' The tone was hard-edged. 'Do not come anymore to this house. If you do, it will be the worse for you.'

'Why? What has happened?' Silence. 'Has something happened to your granddad?'

'Ten minutes after you left,' the man growled, 'the Granddad called for us. His face was red. We knew he was ill. The room was hot. I am now going to speak in Romanian. Please, I cannot tell you in your language …' What Pip heard next would have been horrific in any language. 'I ask one of my brothers to call the doctor, but I can see that the heat is making the Granddad scream. I cannot go near him. He is burning. It is almost as if he is … I ran out of the room …' Pip knew the man was crying. 'He is dead. Do not come today. No more.' He hung up abruptly.

Pip walked over to his chair and sat down by the radiator. He had been getting decidedly shaky as the conversation had gone on. He leaned back in the chair; and then he saw the glowing ball, as clearly as he had when, years earlier, he had watched his brother Teddy playing with it near Kiefer Adams' storm drain. *Ball lightning.*

Rigid with fear, he watched it approach him across the carpet. The whole of his body felt like a band of worn-out elastic as he tried to spring from the chair but couldn't move. Then he could feel the heat from it, licking at his toes, burning his shoes. A second later, it leapt onto his knees, and he was scorching. Inside, he could feel his body fat melting, as if he were in a furnace.

He pressed his shoulders and back into the chair as the light hovered over his thighs, then felt searing agony as it flattened and crept through him, sucking his life into its gaping hole of a mouth as it curled itself into a ball again. He watched the tops of his legs descend into a lake of burning fat and he screamed, taking the fire into his mouth. He watched it reach his chest, then hollow out the cavity with hungry lips. The thudding of his heart in his ears ceased. A deathly quiet descended as his living brain considered its final exit from pain. He looked down. None of him remained, except for his smoking shoes, which were floating in his body grease … He lifted his eyes and gazed about the room. He tried to move, and no movement came. He reached out his arms, but found they were gone; and yet he retained every memory of movement, of everything that was familiar. He thought then that he was dead, and struggled to find some way back to the reality he remembered.

Slowly and painfully, he recovered from his vision; and when he did, he discovered something that terrified him. The chair beneath him was smoking. It had a charred patch where he had been sitting and the back was wet, not with water, but with a stinking, discoloured grease.

The realisation struck a brutal blow. He had shared the experience of Simionce's death. It was too much to take in. He vomited then, as he always did after one of his visions; not in the lavatory pan, but right there, in front of the chair.

Pip had the chair taken away and the carpet renewed, but the flat was never the same after the experience. When he was able to think about it calmly, which took some days, a shuddering fear took over when all the memories of his visions surfaced and marched in front of him. The horrors inside the Sunny Mead chalet; the Hamelin children and the rat; so many sights that had affected his life with their terrors. Except for one he didn't want to discard: the man with the smiling child on his shoulders. It had taken a long time to come out of it.

3

2024

That New Year's morning in Oxford, when Pip lay, eyes closed, praying for sleep, he was sure 'the burning' had been the last of his visions. He had always experienced them from childhood, but in the intervening years since 2007, he'd had none – save for a few premonitions, and many nightmares like the vivid one that had disturbed his sleep half an hour ago, where he was dragged under a lorry. It had been so real, and also terrifying, but not like his earlier visions, which had come both day and night.

In one way, he regretted their loss, as he had discovered later on that he had relied on them to open his eyes and help him understand himself, as well as his quest, which – in spite of all his former scepticism – was still the pursuit of a supernatural predator.

He had asked himself, so many times since, if he wanted his visions to return. In most of them he had been an unwilling bystander; but that last one he had suffered in 2007, after he had met Simionce, had given him a direct experience of what some might have called the fires of Hell. It had scared the hell out of him.

The local Brooklyn newspaper's lurid column had gone into the old man's death in close detail: *All that was left of him was a residue of grease, a heap of ashes – and his slippers. His legs and feet had burned off, but the slippers remained. The room was hardly damaged except for his chair, as all the fire had concentrated on the old-timer. He had burned up from the inside!*

Pip had known little of the phenomenon of spontaneous human combustion, but afterwards had researched it. He had read several scholarly articles containing bizarre and horrific reports of other unfortunates who had succumbed to such a fate. He had been desperate to find out for sure if he himself had experienced exactly what Simionce had. His feelings of guilt had weighed him down. It was as if he had killed the old man himself.

His own vision of death by burning had damaged him a great deal. He was still crippled by it, as he had been by his visions as a child, and now he couldn't progress with his own work on his quest. It had been a warning he would never forget.

It had changed his life. When he looked back over the past few years, he sometimes thought he had gone mad, changing his career and his academic work to concentrate on writing novels. Yet he had even come to a stop with that now. He knew the book he had just written was probably his last. That's why he had called it *The Last Vision*. He had begun the trilogy five years before, in the hope he might lure out the enemy he feared both inside himself and without. He had spread the clues carefully, hoping that one day someone or something would turn up in his quest for the answer to the questions posed in the Marcu Papers, which had led to the perpetual loss of his peace of mind.

Today, in Oxford, he was doing a signing for *The Last Vision*. Unknown to his colleagues, his fiction had become his real life's work. Yet he was still in demand at universities as a visiting professor, for his knowledge of psychology in relation to East European mediaeval history. So far, the present year at Oxford had been as useful to him as the Faculty hoped he would be to his students.

He realised very well that in the world of academia, his adventures in fiction were a source of some amusement, tinged with envy. He could have published more academic books, but at least his fiction was widely read, both in e-book and in print. How well his books had sold was attested to in his publisher's accounts and evidenced by his own good living. His peers saw his fiction as no more than an indulgent hobby, in contrast to their constant slaving over their next university publication. They had no idea that his work was as unpredictable as theirs, and that his writing was the only thing that kept him going.

Pip had built up an international reputation slowly and gained a good following of readers, who all waited eagerly for the next novel – and the next. What they didn't know was that he had allowed them into his real life. Now, near to exhausting his sources, he still believed that somewhere out there was the special reader he sought. Someone who knew what was meant by his past visions and dreams. One who had followed all his clues and might hold the answer in his quest to find the author of the Codex.

What he needed now was to gain another mentor like Marcu or Dalca or – the thing he craved most of all – to meet in reality those two 'friends', the man and the child, he had seen in his vision at Koppelberg's chalet in Sunny Mead, rising up from the fourth display case, when he was only 13 years old.

They were the two who had given him courage to carry on in the hope of meeting them again. They had made him feel brave. The smiling child must be grown now. Simply, Pip believed in them. He had asked them who they were, but they hadn't answered, although they had promised he would see them again – eventually! When they'd said that, his head had been filled with good memories, even in the stinking place of death that had been the Piper's lair. He had held that promise inside. They had seemed like his family. That man and that girl – part of him.

Finally, when they'd disappeared, he'd felt lonelier than ever before in his life; but it had been a good kind of loneliness. At 13, he'd thought he could wait for them to return; but now, in middle age, when he was at his worst, he asked himself how much longer he could wait. Sometimes, he had a feeling that they were very near, which kept him going a little longer – but even in his bouts of depression, he never lost faith in that vision.

Ever since 'the burning', however, he had recognised the true magnitude of the challenge he faced. The only weapons he held against the Devil himself were a few manuscript pages, and the horrific and fabulous fragment of a story that Simionce had recounted to him. He had read over his transcript of Simionce's words so many times that he knew them by heart. He had often thought grimly that he could have stood up in some theatre and recited them to his spellbound public.

My Christian name is Nicholas … By my calculations I am now 36 years old. At 13, I was pulled by my golden hair across the battlefield and taken as a hostage by the victor, the Frankish king, Charles. This year of 800, when I begin writing my own Bible, the unholy Codex, Charles, my oppressor, will be crowned Emperor by the sinful Pope of Rome at the Christian festival of Christmas and renamed by his people as Charlemagne.

The old man had managed to tell him only so much of the Piper's story. He had told him also to find 'The one who gave birth to our common enemy … Black Anya! The woman who has seen the evil one. Who mated with him.' But when Pip had overcome his cowardice and began searching for Ghita and Anya, it was too late. They had disappeared. He had come to the conclusion that if Simu Dalca's mother was indeed alive, she didn't want to be found. As for Ghita, he hadn't been able to find her either. She must have hated him for leaving her, for never getting in touch.

Pip had now exhausted all possibilities, just as Marcu had in Romania, and as Simu had afterwards, until 2007, when Pip had turned up. He and Simu had shared so much together. Now Pip was on his own, and it was 2024, the year when the Grandsire, aka the Piper, would return to Arva once more and take some unfortunate little girl as his victim; a child destined to grow old and die in the space of a week.

This was Pip's dilemma. He needed someone to bring him out of the wilderness, because his own visions had stopped. This was his last hope.

He had tried through his scholarship to learn more, and

finally he had turned to fiction to try to contact Ghita and Black Anya, who were the only two who held the key. This sabbatical he had been granted to work and study in Oxford could be the time. It had to be. In the summer, he planned to return to Arva and face the Devil himself, even though he might die doing it.

The last thing Pip wanted to do was to go back, but he had to prevent a child's murder if he could. He needed to stop being a coward and face the fact that one of the things that had dissuaded him from returning to Romania before was the risk that he might be identified and imprisoned by the authorities.

Since 2007, through the medium of the internet, Pip had watched the village of Arva change, year after year; but he had never dared set foot there. *Coward.* Even now, his heart continued to beat the word in his ears; but as far as he knew, no-one had ever connected him with the theft of the priceless pages that had belonged to Eisenmann. Pure fear had stopped him. But still, wherever he went, he searched for Anya and Ghita. And he intended to do the same in Oxford.

As exhausting as the quest was proving to be, he had a duty to go on with it, and especially in this Piper Year. As far as he knew, he was the only man still alive who held the key to the origin of the Arvan serial killer, whose imagined destiny was to be master of the world. And the only woman alive who could add to the jigsaw of the Piper story was Anya, a gypsy from that small, cursed village in Romania, the granddaughter of a fallen priest.

From Simionce, he had discovered that the Codex, in which the Piper's story was set down, contained a secret all men desired. It was unbelievable that Anya might know that secret, or part of it. Simionce had been able to recount only a fragment of the story in the manuscript, which had been handed down though the gypsy family for generations. To think that Anya was the next link in the chain, and that she might know the secret, was both exciting and terrifying. And if Pip could not find her, then the secret might be lost forever.

He realised now how important this knowledge had been to Eisenmann, who must have been searching too. If the German was alive, he must still be in the race. But Pip had reached

Simionce before him. So where was he? Pip banged his pillows with his fist in frustration. He needed to banish the night fears and get some rest, but it was no use. His head was full of complications, questions that tormented him.

The other burden that Pip carried was the knowledge of how many innocent people had perished in the quest. Dr Sacha Marcu had begun it all, discovering how the serial killings had stretched back through history. The young psychiatrist had died quickly. He had been luckier than his faithful aide, the nurse, Robert Riparu, who had suffered a lingering death.

The catalogue of deaths lengthened. The retired investigating police officer of the Arva crimes, Chief Inspector Valentin, and even Pip's greatest ally, Simu Dalca, were dead. Not for a moment did Pip believe that Simu's death had been an accident. He owed so much to Simu, who had known what risk he was taking personally, but who had believed in him and risked his life introducing him to his mother, Black Anya, and the hundred-year-old gypsy woman, Eva Kirchma.

Pip went over the other unnatural deaths in his mind: that of Father Joseph, parish priest of the village, who had been a terrified man in spite of his cloth; and that of Ghita's mother, the half-mad Emilia, gone like all the crazed schizophrenic women incarcerated in Burbor, the grim psychiatric hospital where Pip had visited Simona Murgu – who herself had died unnaturally.

Sometimes he had thought he would go mad, but the day of the gypsy funeral remained clear in his mind. He was convinced now that Eva Kirchma had seen his past and foretold his future in her scrying bowl: Pip Durrant, whom she had identified as a 13-year-old disabled boy, would grow up to be the one who would outwit the ancient killer of Arva's children. What had seemed ludicrous at the time, he had now accepted as a fact. The fears he had were dual: the supernatural entity who stalked him, and the associates of the sinister Eisenmann. But he felt he also had to make reparation for those senseless deaths. He owed it to the victims.

I have to work harder. If I can only find the Codex, I shall know the whole secret and when the whole cycle ends … Maybe the answer is here in Oxford …? He shook his head as if he couldn't believe it himself, then jumped as his mobile rang.

It was his sister, Mel. He felt a moment of real relief, then annoyance. But it was only just coming up to New Year for her! She had forgotten the time difference. *That's it for the night now,* he thought. Yet her voice was welcome. They had always been close. His other siblings, the twins Rose and Teddy, had been seven years younger.

'Happy New Year, Pip – and good luck.'

'What for?'

'The book signing!'

'Do you know what time it is?' He couldn't help himself.

'Sorry! I forgot you must still be in bed.' It sounded like an accusation. She knew he'd never been a party animal. He was a perpetual loner.

'Yes. And you aren't?'

'No, I shall be sitting up. I am *so* tired.'

'Is Ryan giving you a bad time?' His nephew knew how to party.

'The usual.' He imagined her grimace.

'You know he'll be all right. He's young!' Mel spent a lot of time worrying about her son.

They chatted on for a while about family things. Then the conversation ended and Mel rang off, with a warning to Pip not to forget to call their parents.

He'd rung them already. They were enjoying their retirement, although his mother still missed her 'kids'. He kept in touch, but Mel was closer to them, in every sense. He had always lived far away, as if he didn't want to go home. Whenever he did visit, he often felt 13 years old again. He couldn't help but be reminded about the time he had got his voice and his legs back. 1988. The year it had all begun for him – but not for history.

He threw off the bedclothes and made for the bathroom. On the way back, he walked to the window, almost afraid to look out in case he saw a shadowy figure watching him, as he had so many times before. He drew back the drapes and stared down at the emptiness. The moonlight was as hard and brittle as the frost. Then he heard rattling below. It spooked him; but it was only a swinging window that someone had forgotten to close.

The college quad lay quiet under the ice of a hard winter. The roofs of the small mediaeval houses along one side turned briefly rainbow-like in the artificial light of a nearby firework, which mingled with the urban glow as it shivered its way upwards into the dark sky. Somewhere below, he could hear the raucous music of a party deep inside the building. Although Hilary Term at Oxford didn't begin until the seventeenth, there were students around. And dons. But not him.

He closed the drapes and went back to bed to think some more – and hope, as always, that Anya or Ghita would finally make contact with him. A copy of his new book lay on his bedside table. He stretched out his hand, settled himself against his pillows and began to leaf through it, not to look for typos as he had done so often, but to convince himself it really was to be his own last vision.

Then he began to torment himself. Was it likely to produce the result that he craved so much? Not queues of readers waiting to have him sign it, but a response to its veiled message. He flipped through the pages. In fiction, his hero now dared once more to stir up the Devil in an attempt to lure him into the open. With Simionce's story in mind, Pip had found this the only way to characterise the fearful monster whose identity he was seeking in reality. Many of the characters in *The Last Vision* had paid the ultimate price for their daring, just like his friends had.

He had introduced his readers to this personification of evil and the fictional ancient rite enacted every year in a remote corner of Eastern Europe, which was the gateway to Hell. No peasant knew the evil entity's origins, or when it would strike. So far, the ritual's source had eluded the investigators, who were scholars, doctors and the police; but Pip's hero was getting nearer to the truth in every book.

Frustrated instead of satisfied, he decided he'd had enough of looking at his novel. He yawned and began to close it, but then his thumb got caught between the pages! It felt as if something was pushing the covers together with tremendous force. He winced in agony, but his thumb was trapped. Using his other hand, he tried to prise the book open, while his conscious brain told him this couldn't be happening. As he tried to free his thumb, he found that now all of his fingers were caught between the pages of the hardback. He felt like a mouse in a trap. Panicking, he swivelled his eyes from side to side and upwards, then felt something creeping down his upper lip. His eyes went down, and he could see blood, splashing blots onto the book. His blood?

'I'm dreaming.' His thought came out in words. The blood was heavier now, dripping onto the bed, and his hands were helpless. 'Let me go!' he yelled, his face near to the book's cover. But his hands were stuck fast.

Then, like a miracle, the book snapped open, hitting him sharply in the face. He gulped, drew back, and wiped his nose with his tortured hand. He tasted blood in his mouth and throat. At the same moment, the pages of the book began to flutter and rise, until they fell open in a particular place. The words were raised like giant letters, dancing in front of his eyes. One word in particular: *NICHOLAS*.

'What the fuck!' He leapt out of bed and staggered against the wall. He was awake. He knew he was! He looked across his bloody counterpane, and the book lay quiet now. His fingers ached, his nose ached, everything about him hurt. He slumped there, staring – until he heard a rustle beside him and a familiar noise – a noise he hadn't heard for a long time. A scrabbling followed by squeaking! He'd known that noise all his life: it was a rat. The whispers in his head were louder now, warning him … He drew in his breath, then turned his head a little, instinctively screwing up his eyes like a child.

The rat was huge and black – and it was crawling up his duvet, holding on with its pink claws until it sat on his bed. It lifted its head and looked at him; and not in the way his pet white Cass had done. Instead its small, vicious eyes were staring at him, its whiskers quivering in anticipation.

'Get off! he yelled. He tried to lunge at it, but his legs wouldn't obey. He was helpless as he watched it bend its head and sniff his blood. It paused, then began to gnaw the pages of his book …

Then he heard another squeaking; high-pitched, like a digital hearing aid, or a bow being scratched across fiddle strings, or a raw amateur on a tin whistle! He recognised the cacophony of sounds that assailed him. It reminded him of the dinner party where Stella Drury had choked, and where … He closed his eyes, swallowed … began to pant … to pray to the God he had thought he didn't believe in.

He found himself slipping down the wall onto the carpet, where he crouched shivering and sweating at the same time, his brain alive with the sickening memories of that terrible day in Sunny Mead … He kept his eyes shut; frightened to open them in case *he* was there. Koppelberg.

Then the noise stopped. Silence. He waited for something to happen. Nothing, except fear. Finally, he dared to open his eyes and lifted his head level with the bed. His book was lying there open, and the rat had gone. He was on his knees now, and he carefully put out his hand and reached for the book, grimacing with pain. It was still lying open. He couldn't see any blood. He touched it with the tips of his fingers, then drew back, scared.

The pain in his hand was telling him that what had happened had been real. He made a fist and it hurt. He hadn't been dreaming! The realisation made him feel sick; but, inside, a tiny spring of relief mixed with apprehension was trickling. His visions were back. He had been hurt again, but that was all they could do. What he wanted to know was what the phantoms had done! He pulled himself off his knees and sat down, staring at the open book. He needed to look, but he didn't know what he was going to find … Maybe a photo of Koppelberg? Like the one he had seen staring back at him from his computer screen, when he'd started on the Marcu Papers!

He looked. No face. The two pages were normal … *except* … he squinted … for a tiny river of dried blood that had run along the spine in the middle, but that could be explained by a nose bleed. He put up his hand, and his nose felt stiff and sore. He felt as if all the life had been dragged out of him. Yet his mind was weighing up all the possibilities.

Was it possible that the black rat, Snipe, the fantasy that had tormented his teenage dreams, had paid him a visit? He needed to look for any signs of damage, just as back in 2007 he had examined the chair in his Brooklyn flat and found it was burned.

He picked up the book carefully. The hardback's cover had been ripped, apparently by a row of scissor teeth. Pip drew back. He had seen enough. There was no mistake. It was the type of damage a rat would cause.

There was no question about it. His visions were back and … harder to believe … he had been paid a real visit by the Rat and the Piper. The sickness he had been feeling earlier suddenly became urgent, and a second later he was leaping off the bed in the direction of the bathroom.

He sat on the lavatory for some time, watching the door all the while. That's what he'd done always when he was a kid. When he got up, he screwed up his eyes again as he went over to the basin to wash his hands, determined not to look in the mirror. He had looked in too many mirrors that had scared him with the sight of what was standing behind him.

The warm water soothed his bruised fingers, but he was still scared. It had been like 'the burning'. He tried to console himself with the thought that while the Piper might be able to hurt him, it seemed he couldn't kill him. He still didn't look in the mirror – just in case. He backed away, and stretched his hand out for the towel; but as he touched where it should have been, he jumped as though he'd had an electric shock. His fingers had touched fur! He knew the feeling. Rat fur. He could hear his heart in his ears. Like a kid, with eyes only half-open, he peered out from under his eyelashes. No familiar towel hung there, only a long cape with a hood. He retched.

The hood was disgusting, made out of a stuffed rat's head; the animal's eyes in death were still bright, and its body hung down the back of the cape, its thick, hairless tail extending limply towards the waist. Pip turned back to the toilet. This time he did throw up. When he dared to look again, the cape was gone. He ran out and searched his other rooms. Finally he ended up in the corridor outside. Nothing lingered there at all.

He hurried back and looked out of the window. A dark figure was crossing the quad, almost floating along in the eerie light of dawn. Pip watched it disappear, and rested his head in his hands on the window sill. He was battered, broken. Whoever or whatever had visited him had as much power to terrify him as always. Once more, it was a warning. How many times would it be, before it was borne out?

All he wanted to do was go back to bed, but he wouldn't get in. He needed the linen changed before he would – if ever. He hated himself for the way he was, most of all because he couldn't rationalise it. So far, he had survived, but now he was really on his own – that was, unless he was able to find the right person to help him. He walked into the kitchen, where he switched on the kettle. He was shivering, so he took a throw off his armchair and wound it about him.

After he'd made himself a black coffee, he sat down and thought of his new hardback lying on the bed, and what had been done to it. Maybe all the marks of his night visitors might have gone by now? His courage began to return. If the marks still remained, the book would be evidence – of his sanity, at least. After all, the rat had only nibbled it and not destroyed it. And he hadn't been eliminated, only terrified.

He felt calmer now, ready to believe his unearthly visitors didn't have that power. Once again, he returned to Eva Kirchma's prophecy that he would survive. Maybe he wouldn't be able to hold his pen and sign the copies very well with his aching thumb and hand, but the Devil hadn't got him yet! He was ready to see his book out into the world now. It was a means to an end. He was ready for *them*.

His book's worldly success was immaterial to him, because if this last fiction was successful on his terms, he might find Anya and Ghita again, redeem himself, and put an end the horrors of Arva.

4

Pip sighed. His university rooms were snug on that cold January lunchtime and he was loath to go out and do his duty. Besides, he'd had a sleepless night, with the New Year's bells and the vision. He breathed in slowly to relax, then sat down under the lamp and began to read. He was on edge and couldn't concentrate. He sighed again, thinking of his predicament.

He couldn't settle, so he stood up, straightened his tie and studied his reflection. He looked so calm, but he was churned up inside, because he was about to reveal his work once more in the public domain. Every time and every book, he asked himself, *When will I find the answer that Marcu and his predecessors died for?* He didn't know what he would do or how he would feel or even if he was worthy, but he held on to the instinct that 2024 would be the year. Though not a religious man, he prayed this date would mark the latest turn of a cycle of evil that had existed from the 9th Century. Then he might be redeemed.

'Time to go,' he said out loud. His agent, Larry, was meeting him at the venue. He'd already reported that they were expecting a good crowd. Pip had had a well-publicised launch in London at one of the major bookshops, but he was a professional and still remembered the days when hardly anyone had turned up. Now it was time for him to encounter his Oxford public. He hoped the signing wouldn't go on too long, because he still had work to do for the new term. As a visiting academic and successful author, who had been invited by Norris College, he needed to live up to his reputation. However, as he went downstairs and closed the front door behind him, he was thinking back over his climb to outward success. Much of it was due to hard work and persistence; but his public face was far different from the one he wore in the isolation of his mind.

On the way to the signing, Pip stepped off the pavement to avoid a group of fascinated Chinese tourists, who were not listening to their guide but watching a procession trailing along the pavement of Broad Street, at the end of which was one of the most well-known bookshops in Oxford. A line of altar boys, their faces red as their cassocks as the cold nipped them, were swinging brass censers, while behind, a robed priest and his congregation chanted in Latin on their way to some mysterious ceremony. This was a sight that would doubtless have caused a stir in the ordinary inhabitants of any other provincial city, but in Oxford was regarded as just another eccentricity.

As Pip attempted to pass the group of tourists, one of them stepped back, causing him to lurch out further into the road. As he did so, a bicycle almost caught him. He jumped out of the way and swore. The cyclist, who had no helmet to cover a dark head with hair spiked into barbs, turned and grinned at his near victim. Pip hadn't been in Oxford that long, but he could see the lad was a student, as he was wearing a gown. Pip felt uncharacteristically angry for a moment, but then realised that the near accident was his fault. He had been lucky, because if he'd stepped back any further, he might have been knocked over. Bicycles were still *de rigueur* in Oxford, although other traffic was no longer allowed – except for a host of small, ugly driverless cabs, in which he had no faith.

Pulling himself together, he followed the procession in the direction of Blackwell's bookshop, which had been taken over recently and undergone a facelift, spreading itself into a vulgar expanse of front window. Devotees of the shop had campaigned in the hope its original frontage would be left alone, but to no avail, and now the ground floor had lost all its former charm. Yet he was happy to see that it still welcomed the printed book, which had managed to survive the digital onslaught. Real books had lasted, in spite of general fears for their fate at the beginning of the Digital Age.

In the past, 1 January had been a public holiday. Now things had changed. People were working harder – and dying younger, in spite of past forecasts to the contrary. Stress had taken its toll on the population and a general malaise had followed, owing to world events and the environmental changes to which Man had been forced to adapt.

Reaching the window, he glanced at his book display, wondering how much the publisher had paid for the privilege. But even after two other successful novels, he still had an unsophisticated thrill when he saw his work in print.

As he walked inside, he could see that Larry had been right. A lot of people were wandering about, looking around expectantly. In front of him, a woman was blocking the gangway, turning over his novel. 'Excuse me,' he said.

It would have been so easy to have tapped her on the shoulder, said something inane like 'Hope you're going to buy it,' and laughed. But that wasn't his way. As Mel had pointed out too many times, he was a loner. The woman was reading the blurb now. Her dark hair under her funny little beanie hat was falling over her face. Then he caught her perfume, clean and appealing, and for one stupid moment he almost reached out to touch her hair's long silkiness! She didn't look at him, just removed herself. She put down the book then, and walked off. Another uncharacteristic impulse assailed him, as he almost grabbed a copy and pursued her. Then Larry was hurrying towards him.

'Pip, you've a good spot. Over here. I would have complained if you hadn't, of course.' His agent was very good at his job, and they made a good team. All Pip wanted to do was write, while Larry was a born PR man.

'Of course,' said Pip as he was led to a prominent table close to the foot-flow.

An hour later, his signing was going well, although his hand hurt more than usual and the after-effects of his night experiences precluded too much chat.

Occasionally he wondered if the woman he'd seen when he first came in would turn up now that she knew she could get a signed copy. For some reason he felt attracted to her, although he had not seen her face. It was almost as if she was familiar. He thought perhaps she might have been at one of his lectures. Otherwise, he didn't know any women in Oxford – yet. He'd had several e-mails from Oxford fans keen to come to his signing. One, a woman in fact, had been in touch with him for some time, begging him to come to the city, and had promised that she and her friends would turn up and identify themselves, although so far that hadn't happened. Maybe the woman he was interested in might be one of those?

The queue was shortening now and he sighed, relieved that there was an end in sight to the boring round of requests for personal dedications and responding enquiries from him as to what the customers would like him to write, and in a few cases how their unfamiliar names were spelt. He was still a psychologist, and knew that things like that mattered to his readers!

'Phew. I think we've done okay?' he said to Larry, putting down the special pen he used for signing.

'More than that,' Larry grinned. 'I'll go up and sort out the coffee.'

'Okay.'

Then a voice behind Pip said, 'I've read all of your books, Dr Durrant. Would you sign mine?' He turned in his chair. It was the woman he'd seen earlier. She was standing at an awkward angle, holding out his book while at the same time staring at one of the bookshelves beside her. He smiled and stretched out his hand, was about to take the book from her, but then failed to do so as a severe nerve pain shot through his arm.

'Ow!' He collapsed back into the chair.

'Too much signing?' she asked.

He didn't look up, as the book was level with his face. He ignored the quip, seemingly tinged with sarcasm, took the book and put it down on the table. He reached out for his pen, feeling such an idiot that he couldn't immediately put it to the paper. His arm hurt so much! What was the matter with it? He felt bewildered.

'What would you like me to say?' he muttered, head still down, waiting for the request, while all the time the pain was growing worse. In fact, his hand didn't seem part of him, but frozen into a rigid mess. He was in a cold sweat. What the fuck was the matter? He was getting angry. Where was Larry?

'Just write your name, please?' she answered. Her voice was so low he could hardly hear her. She was still turning sideways, looking at something else; as if she didn't care about his suffering. *Have the courtesy to turn round, woman,* he thought.

'No big deal then,' he muttered to himself. He forced himself to begin, then stopped, horrified as the expensive biro formed the first character with a flourish … 'N'. He dropped the pen. It was burning his fingers. It rolled away and off the desk, glad to escape. But *he* couldn't. He stared at the mocking black letter.

No, he screamed inside, *I won't write your fucking name!* The woman was standing in front of him now. He could see the hem of her coat and the beginning of her boots.

'What's the matter?' she asked.

'Nothing. Just my pen,' he mumbled.

'It's all right. I have one.'

He looked up, ready to apologise, and she was holding out the biro, staring at him in a strange way. He stared back.

Ghita Dalca. He felt his nose running and a drop ready to fall, when he came to and caught it on the side of his good hand. 'Sorry, he said, wiping it away. 'Arthritis.' He took a deep breath. The image that he had held fast to in his memory for all those years apart, raced back. *But … but maybe it isn't her,* he thought, trying to fix her face in his memory. His mouth had gone dry. She must be 36 by now!

'Ghita?'

'You still know me then,' she said. He began to get up, but his knees felt weak with emotion as well as shock. 'It's not an accusation!' she added.

He finally managed to stand up. 'How could I forget you? What are you doing in Oxford?' he asked, trying to get himself under control.

'I thought *you* were in America?' she flashed back.

'No, I'm teaching here.'

'So am I. Imagine – me, a teacher.' Her English was near-perfect, far different from all those years ago when she was only learning the language. 'We can talk in Romanian, if you prefer.' She looked both mischievous and quizzical.

'I'm a bit rusty,' he admitted. They were going through the niceties as if they had been nothing to each other.

'You look older,' she said. 'I'm sorry you have arthritis.'

'You don't look any different. And it's okay now,' he replied. 'Don't let's mention it anymore.'

'Sorry. I suppose you're shattered after that long queue.'

'Something like that,' he replied. 'I'm sorry that I didn't recognise you straightaway … but …' He was trying to find the right words without being clumsy. ' … but not because you look older. You were at the door when I came in, and even from the back you seemed … familiar …' He knew he was bumbling.

'You haven't changed, Pip,' she replied, and her eyes soothed his awkwardness. His panic was disappearing, although in the back of his mind he was terrified it might come again. She said his name like she always had.

Until then, he hadn't noticed anything except her face. She was as trim as ever, dark hair, dark eyes full of fun, teasing him like the day he had first met her seated at the Dalcas' breakfast table.

'You don't know me really,' he replied, hoping it didn't sound pitiful. He looked down at her. 'Coffee?' He could see Larry hovering.

'What about my book?'

'I'll do one for you in a minute, if that's okay.' She nodded. He couldn't go through that again. He turned. 'This is my agent. Larry, Ghita Dalca. I used to know her in Romania.'

Larry shook hands with Ghita. Pip, who knew him well, could see he was weighing up the situation. 'Oh, right,' he said.

'You're going upstairs?' Pip knew the question implied, *Shall I get rid of her?*

'Yes. We both are.' Pip ignored the raised eyebrows. 'Okay?'

'Yeah, I'll finish up here, then I'll join you.'

'I might be quite a long time.'

'Fair enough,' Larry nodded. 'I'll ring you later.'

'Great.'

'Goodbye – Miss Dalca?' Larry was a quick learner. She smiled, acknowledging the inference as to her marital status. Then, with a nod, Larry walked off.

'He looks after me,' explained Pip.

'So you still need looking after?' she said, as he indicated the lift to the first floor where the old coffee bar, with its squeezed-in tables and chairs, had metamorphosed into modernity.

'Let's use the stairs,' she said. A small crowd was gathered at the lift, some of them holding copies of Pip's book.

'Great.'

In a moment, they were through into the lobby. Pip's mind was computing. Was it coincidence – which he'd never believed in – or fate – that the woman he'd deserted was here now, about to climb the stairs ahead of him? At that moment, he wondered how he could explain an absence of 17 years – and his cowardice. Simple. He couldn't.

The once-intimate coffee bar on the first floor was now combined with a restaurant, which catered for a clientele drawn from the cosmopolitan mix to be found in a city housing one of the greatest universities in the world. It was not the place for revelations of the kind that Pip was now facing. He felt, rather, that his confessions should take place in some secluded and shadowy place that reflected his present feelings. Somewhere where he could whisper his reasons to Ghita and be forgiven. But he knew that wasn't possible. As they searched for a table, he was almost ready to turn and walk away.

Could anything be left between them, given his past behaviour? The woman who had meant everything to him and who, together with her family, had been through so much. When he had said goodbye to Ghita, she had been 19, a girl about to marry a man Pip knew she did not love. And yet, it seemed as if the years had disappeared and she was with him again. His confusion and foreboding seemed to have driven all the sense out of his head, because here she was, the woman he longed for and who might hold the key to everything he desired.

'Come on,' she said. 'Look, there's a table vacant – by the window! There, where that woman's getting up! We're lucky!' The petite young woman in sunglasses and headscarf was on her mobile phone and picking up her bag. She didn't look at them as she pushed past.

Ghita sat down. 'By the look on your face, you need coffee as much as I do.'

He nodded and turned away, glad to push into the press of people, wishing he could disappear. He was served far too quickly for him to be able to gather his thoughts. He returned and sat down opposite her. She was already opening her purse with those deft fingers he remembered. He waved her away. 'No, it's all on the house. I have a tab when I'm signing.'

'I'll come with you again,' she said, but her face was solemn.

Pip had reached the state then of despising himself even more. He couldn't make anything up. He had to tell her he'd disappeared for 17 years to save his own skin.

'You don't have to worry,' said Ghita, her eyes focusing on his. 'I'm not blaming you. But why did you stay away? You didn't even answer my letters ...' she paused '... and I think I would have understood if you'd let me know.'

He was shocked at her directness. It was as if she was reading his thoughts. He just nodded, considering how he could begin. Excusing himself would be unforgivable. In the past, he had always been someone who chose his words carefully before he committed himself. Facing Ghita was different. The words were in his head though. He wanted to blurt out that he was a thief and he'd deserted her because he was scared of going back and being accused of something he hadn't done, or even being killed.

He would have been even more worried if he'd looked across the room and seen the woman in the silk headscarf, sunglasses and brown suit who had given up her seat for them. She was watching their every move, her mobile phone still to her ear.

'I would have understood if you'd only explained,' repeated Ghita. 'If you hadn't wanted to see me anymore, I'd have been angry probably, but I'd have gotten over it. As for my father … She stopped and shrugged her shoulder in a hurt gesture. She lowered her voice so much that he strained to hear her. This time she was speaking in Romanian. 'My father cared about you – and his work. How could you do it?'

'I know,' was all his stupid mouth could produce. He moistened his dry lips with his tongue, then remembered he had coffee to produce that result. He took a mouthful and sputtered.

She was staring at him as he recovered. 'Burned yourself,' she said. It was almost an accusation.

If only she knew, he thought, as he shook his head. Then she put out her hand and touched his.

'Don't worry. It was a long time ago,' she added. 'You're famous now.'

That made him feel a bit sick. What could he say? *Only so that I could find you*? He chose to skirt the problem. 'Seventeen years,' he replied, which produced a challenging half smile from her; the kind he remembered, faint, almost mocking. He leaned back. He could handle accusations and harshness, but not her pity or her mild reproach when he deserved a beating. He needed to direct the conversation away. 'You haven't changed,' he said. 'Did you and Anton get married?' It was such a facile question – and he needed the answer to be negative, selfish as that was.

'Anton was in love with me. You know that. And after *Tăta* died, I needed someone.' All at once he remembered the diminutive she had used for Simu. He felt a sudden rush of sadness at what had happened to them all. He, not Anton, should have married her! Then she added, 'We split up in the end. We're divorced.'

'Oh.' It was all he could find to say. He stared down at the table. She was looking out of the window as if he wasn't there. If he'd been a different man, he might have said, *Did you split up because of me?* But he had no right.

In 2007, Ghita had revealed her feelings about marriage, and what she had said had shaken him. Coming from another person, it could have been some careless teenage remark made for effect or to gain attention. He knew better. He'd never forgotten her words, which had been born of the terrible secret that all Arva women carried: *I have made up my mind about something. I shall never have children.*

At that time, she hadn't known the likelihood of the sacrifice she might have to make, because until she married, her mother wouldn't share the age-old secret that had been handed down between Arvan women for centuries. She herself had 'gone up' as a child and nothing had happened to her; but she didn't know if any girl she bore would be destined to be the Grandsire's next sacrifice. No woman knew the secret until they married.

He had been desperate to find Ghita, and now 2024 was here. She was his past and only real love, whom he had lost. No other woman before or since had provoked such feelings within him. When he had been with her, it had felt as if they were meant to be together always; but he had left her without explanation, had ignored her letters and had cut himself off.

He had selfishly told himself it was for her own good; that she might become embroiled in his mixed-up life; that she might recognise him for the coward he was and consider him responsible for her father's death.

The day Ghita had said those fateful words, she had affirmed that she did not want any child of hers to suffer like she had. Nor did she want to end up a tormented schizophrenic destined to be incarcerated in a Romanian psychiatric hospital like her mother, and her mother before her. He shivered.

A few moments ago, she'd said he was famous! Little did

anyone know that he was literally living the trauma of his novel, *The Last Vision*. He had done what he needed to in his fiction, and he would have to pay the price in reality.

2007 had been the most wonderful and most terrible year of his life. In spite of all the shocking things that had happened, he had fallen in love for the first time; but after he had committed the theft at Eisenmann's home and deserted his love, Ghita, he had been able to see no salvation for himself.

She was sipping her coffee when he looked up. At that moment he had to know if she had stuck to her wild statement! He was cold and trembling inside. 'Do you have any …?

'I have one child,' she said. He breathed in. 'A girl. I called her Olga.'

'Olga? How old is she?' He tried to sound normal, but he was squeezing the words out to mask his horror.

'Almost 16.'

Pip swallowed. He was calculating. So, even back then, she and Anton had been more than just friends … He didn't want to think about it.

'I only wanted to mourn my father,' she said. 'I was a mess. Did you know my father had died?'

'Yes, but not the details. I …' He could hardly bear to hurt her any more. Then he forced himself to add, 'I read about it. I'm sorry!'

'You read about it?' Ghita regarded him, and he hoped she wouldn't see his hand tremble 'I wrote to you to tell you.' She looked incredulous. 'Didn't you open my letters?'

He shook his head, miserable enough to crawl away. 'Only a few. I'm sorry.'

'So am I! He was going to meet you at the airport. You left me a note.'

Pip swallowed. He remembered every detail of what he had written to Ghita. He had been over it enough times. He recalled those first long nights apart, when he had seen her mobile number on his call display and had wanted to pick up the phone, but had resisted doing so, until finally her calls had ceased. The commitment she had naturally expected had been renounced in that final note he'd written and had never forgotten. But one thing was true. He'd never forgotten her, either.

Dearest Ghita, I want you to know I'm thinking of you. I have had to go back to the States to sort out something urgent with my supervisor. Dare I say that as your mother is so ill, maybe you won't be tying the knot for a while. You don't have to, you know. If, for any reason, I can't get back, although I expect to be there only a little while, if you change your mind, you could always come over and see me in New York. This is my phone number ... I shall miss you.

Screw you, Durrant, he screamed at himself inwardly. During their last conversation, he had even pretended he hadn't heard from Dalca that Emilia had died.

'Finally, I believed you'd forgotten me, or for some reason you didn't want any contact,' she said. 'In time, it didn't hurt, and what had happened between us became a memory, which I pushed to the back of my mind. They say, "You'll get over it." I had to – until I started reading your books!'

'I wanted to keep in touch, Ghita,' Pip replied. 'Please believe me, but ... I can't explain – yet.' He didn't know what else to add, but the whole time he was thinking, *How can you be so forgiving? But if I tell you why I didn't keep in touch, I'll have to tell you all of it!* He couldn't bear what she would think of him, if he explained. She must despise him already. How could he have left her to Anton, when he knew she loved *him* instead?

She sighed and finished her coffee. 'As I said, don't worry. I got over it.'

They talked about trivialities after that. Finally, Pip looked at her and asked, awkwardly, 'What are your plans for this evening?' Not for a long time had he wanted to be with a woman so much.

She shrugged. 'I'm going to go home and read this.' She picked up his novel and turned it over, leafing through the pages. She looked up at him. 'Maybe you might get it right this time.'

'I've tried, but I need help. The real thing is here, Ghita.'

She looked him up and down, and smiled. 'Maybe I'm not interested in the real thing.' But her eyes told him otherwise, and he knew he was right, because she added, 'Anyway, what are your plans?'

'I'm not sure.' He didn't dare hope.

'Where are you staying?

'In one of the colleges. I'm a visiting Professor.'

'Impressive, but not that comfortable, unless, of course, you …?' She stopped.

'No, there's only me.'

She nodded. 'Same here, except for …' She broke off.

'Olga?'

'Yes, but she mightn't be in. Teenagers, you know.'

It was his turn to nod, but he didn't know about anything like that. He just wished he did.

'Why don't you come home to mine then? I could cook something.'

'Great!' Her invitation stunned him. He didn't deserve anything. In fact, he had been wondering how he would be able to cope if she simply walked out of his life, like he had hers.

She was picking up her coat now, and he rushed to help her. It was then she turned and looked him full in the eyes. 'I was hoping we'd meet,' she said. 'That's why I was hanging around. Usually, I don't go to signings.'

The absent fan flashed into his mind. So it hadn't been Ghita. How could he have thought it might be! 'Neither do I, but I can't get out of it.' It was a half-lie. How many boring hours had he spent travelling on tour and forcing a smile? How many books had he signed, hoping one day, she would appear? After he had returned to America, it had been a very long time before he had been able to convince himself he would never see her again. But as Pip looked at Ghita now, he knew his feelings hadn't changed, even though he was a coward and that, sooner or later, his cowardice would be exposed. Whether or not he would be able to tell Ghita the whole truth was another matter.

As Pip and Ghita left the shop together, the small woman in the silk headscarf and glasses was standing in an alcove, still on her phone. If they had been near enough to her, they would have heard her say in a clipped American accent, 'Yes, they are leaving together now, darling. Yes, I have that. I'm glad you're happy. Speak to you soon.' With that, she closed her phone and walked off quickly in the direction of the river bridge.

Pip and Ghita walked all the way down Beaumont Street and turned right at the junction. Skirting the imposing perimeter wall of Worcester College, Pip found himself in a maze of unfamiliar streets. Oxford had changed a lot since he had last been there. The place was meant to be pedestrian-friendly, and the city plan had succeeded. Only people and cabs. He noticed that at the bottom of the street they were now entering was a rank for the small, driverless vehicles, which travelled slowly and were evidently deemed to be of little danger to people walking. At the other end of the street, Ghita stopped in front of a terraced house.

'Come on,' she said, and pushed hard on the gate. 'It has a habit of sticking,' she joked. 'Don't trip over the path. I'll have to do something about that sometime! Never get round to it, I'm afraid.'

He helped her. The tiny garden in front was not trim, but had been well looked after by someone. The earth was white under the frost, and a sad-looking collection of twigs that had been a bush in the summer was trailing over the path's edge. Once they were through the awkward gate, Ghita opened the shabby front door with her key, which kept sticking in the lock as well. She grimaced. Pip had already recognised that the exterior was in need of some repair. 'That's the problem when you own a place,' she said. He nodded his head. His only experience of the housing market was a rented apartment – far removed from a terrace. 'Don't look so surprised,' she added. 'It has an extension. Extra room and full of junk. It was meant to be my study, but I never got round to it.' He wondered then how Simu had left her financially, and remembered the Dalcas' house in Arva, which had looked as if it was falling down when he'd first gone there. Simu must have seen Ghita all right, though, as prices were ridiculously high in Oxford, especially in the city. A moment later, they were in.

'I'm back,' she called as she hung up her coat in the small hall, then flicked him a small smile. No reply.

So we might be alone, he thought. 'Maybe your daughter's out,' he said.

She shrugged. 'It's early yet. Come on into the kitchen.'

As he followed her along the book-lined dark corridor towards the back of the house, he couldn't help his eyes lingering on her slim frame. Then a familiar smell came wafting through. A sharp memory stabbed him of the time when he had followed Simu down the corridor of the Dalcas' crumbling, cavernous house and been led into the kitchen, where Simu's wife, Emilia, had sat motionless, staring into the fire, oblivious to a large pot of stew bubbling away. The shock of that same cooking smell was now very strong. *Mamaliga!* The cornmeal mush that substituted for bread in the farming communities of that part of Romania. He blinked himself back to reality as an elderly woman, who was bent over the table, turned and stared hard at him. They held each other's eyes in shock.

'Anya. This is Professor Durrant. The author I was going to see. I've brought him home.' Ghita smiled at Pip. 'Anya looks after the house for me. She's also the best friend I have.'

Pip's heart lurched in his chest. Friend! It was Black Anya! Ghita's grandmother – and it seemed Ghita had no idea. He felt like a criminal for knowing.

The old lady got up from the table with difficulty. He could see that living in a van on a derelict gypsy site most of her life had not done her much good. The erect bearing he remembered Simu's gypsy mother possessing had disappeared. She stooped as she came slowly forward. But her gaze was still piercing from under her hooded brows. In her eyes he detected an unspoken warning. The glance said clearly: *Do not betray me*. It figured that Simu had not disclosed the truth about his origins to his daughter. It would have set her apart. Yet how could he not have, if Anya was with Ghita in Oxford? They shook hands, but their palms were clammy as they stood there, facing each other, their minds full of guilt.

'I am the housekeeper,' said Anya in heavily-accented English.

'He speaks our language,' explained Ghita, and Anya nodded, her eyes following his every move.

'This is marvellous,' Ghita said. 'And Anya is *not* the housekeeper. She is one of my mother's distant relations. I never knew her before. You remember how difficult it was to get anything out of Mother. Anya turned up at my father's funeral, and I was so grateful. I still am! Are you cold? The stove is a bit low.'

'No, I'll do that,' replied Anya, and Pip could breathe again as she turned to stoke the fire.

'Please, I'm fine,' he remonstrated. 'I have my jacket under my coat.'

'Not as cold as Romania, but you look cold,' said Anya, turning.

'It's all right.' He took off his coat, and Ghita held out her hand for it.

'I'll go and hang it up. Then I'll put on something more comfortable. You two can practise your Romanian while I'm gone.' She grinned.

When she'd left the room, they stood looking at each other. Anya's high cheekbones, which had once been a striking feature, now jutted out, dominating her face. The hooded brows, which had not been so noticeable then because of the expressive, dark eyes beneath, now overshadowed them. They too had sunk, and were now only slits in the skin of a face, too drawn to be wrinkled. He remembered when he'd first seen her at the gypsy camp. Then, Anya had been an extremely good-looking woman in her sixties … She must be eighty now, he thought. What a miserable life she'd had, shunned by her own people. She was the mother of two boys: one who would not acknowledge her, or she him; the other, loving, who would have looked after her in her old age, now dead.

'So she has found you at last, Philip Durrant,' she whispered in Romanian. 'She's missed you.' A reprimand flashed in her eyes. Naturally, she didn't want Ghita to know about their earlier acquaintance.

His tongue curled slowly into the language again. He had imagined his fluency lost, but he found, with surprise, it was returning. 'I have missed her too,' he replied. *Every day since*, he wanted to add.

'Have you forgotten our history?' She touched him on his arm, and he shook his head. 'My son always said you were to be trusted. That you were the one.' The atmosphere was as thick as the bubbling soup. 'May God never forgive the devil who killed Simu!'

Pip felt goose pimples rise. The gypsy's curse! 'I haven't forgotten,' he said. The anger in her eyes softened to a wariness that he understood.

'How many times I have thought of my son lying burned in the snow – but we have no snow here yet,' she said, 'although I sensed it was on its way.'

He nodded, thinking she was speaking of his coldness of heart in not contacting Ghita for so many years. 'I shan't hurt her again, Anya,' he replied.

She put a hand on his arm. 'I knew you would come, Philip Durrant. I have seen it,' she whispered, touching his cheek. He stiffened and felt her cold fingers withdraw. 'So much older,' she added. 'As we all are.' Then her hand was on his sleeve, her fingers digging into his arm. 'Do not let Ghita know I practise the art.'

'I shan't. She must suspect something, though?'

'I tell her some things I feel I have to, and she calls it my "nonsense",' she replied. He looked towards the door. 'You've no need to worry. She is still upstairs. Come, sit down. Here, by the stove,' added Anya, 'then she won't think anything is wrong.'

He took the offered chair and stretched out his legs as if everything was normal. *How am I going to keep this up*, he thought. *How am I going to explain anything to Ghita now?*

Once he had believed fortune-telling and other such practices were mumbo-jumbo, but now he knew better. His scepticism had long gone, although he still questioned how such things could happen. He had never wanted to be involved. All his scientific beliefs had been shaken, or hidden like dirty secrets. Now, when he looked back to the past, he realised that strange things had been happening to him all his life; but back then, he could not or would not recognise anything that could not be explained by reasoning alone. He had met those people now, to whom such happenings were a way of life.

Anya's grandmother, Eva Kirchma, the old gypsy who had read Pip's future in her scrying bowl, had been a seer, like Simionce. Anya, who bore a striking physical resemblance to the ancient woman, whom he'd met only once, and who had related her chilling history in that small, snug trailer, had just told him she had inherited her grandmother's talents. Why had he been surprised?

The future Eva had foretold for Pip had been difficult to take on board; but, in later years, the prophecies were starting to be borne out. The vision she had conjured rose into his mind.

That day with Simu, Eva had seen him as a child lured by Koppelberg into that small chalet in Sunny Mead. There Koppelberg had shown him the glass cases he kept, housing foul beings like the Statue Man and the evil rat. How could Eva have known what Pip, as a young boy, thousands of miles away, had been thinking? *The horror that he himself had conjured up.* Eva had told him that she had seen his future too. It made him shiver. She had indicated that amidst those horrors in Koppelberg's last-but-one case, two people had arisen who, in some future time, would stand like saviours between Pip and evil. Why hadn't he believed her from the beginning? Why shouldn't he now believe everything her granddaughter, Anya, might be ready to tell him? Why should he, a visionary himself, think it strange that destiny had reunited him with Ghita and Anya in Oxford?

He could hear Anya clattering the cutlery, but reality meant nothing to Pip in those moments. All he could think of then was the man and the child he had seen in the case. Who were they? Where were they now? Once he had believed they were only in his mind, but now he felt they were real and they were waiting for him. Could they be in Oxford too? How long would he have to wait? Should he ask Anya? Maybe she knew? If only he could see them again, as he had in that childhood waking dream, he would be helped, and the evil that dogged him, and had done ever since then, would be erased.

'Are you warmer now, Professor?' The voice broke into his frantic inner questioning. Anya was staring down at him. 'Ghita will be down in a minute. She must be taking a long time getting ready.' There was a tiny, knowing smile on her lips, which all at once was replaced by urgency. 'We have to talk privately. I'll send you word when. Don't tell her! Please!'

A moment later, Ghita came through the door. He breathed in. *Did she dress up like that for me*, he thought. He'd never been big on clothes, but to him she seemed illuminated. It wasn't just her clothes, although she was wearing an attractive white fluffy fitted sweater that showed off her waist and tailored black trousers; nor her hair, which was loose and in which he had a sudden mad desire to bury his face. It was her expression. Lit up. Should he say she looked nice? He couldn't.

'You must have warmed up by now.' Ghita's eyes were mischievous. It was as if the years between them had disappeared. 'Wait until you taste Anya's version of *mamaliga*! *Tuica* after; you can get a cab home.'

'Maybe mine will not be as good as you're used to, Professor Durrant,' Anya interposed. 'I shall keep some back for Olga and …' She returned to stirring the stew. Pip waited for her to finish the sentence. He wanted to know who Olga was bringing home.

'So you're expecting another visitor?' he asked. Ghita shook her head. 'Oh, I thought Anya said …' He wasn't given time to finish. He caught the warning glance between the two women. Evidently it was something they would prefer him not to know about.

A moment later, Ghita said, 'I think Anya's got the wrong day.' Anya nodded.

Pip knew now they were hiding something, so he switched the subject back to the soup. 'I haven't eaten *mamaliga* since …um …' he replied. He couldn't finish that sentence either, but Ghita did for him. They were still evident, those secrets that had always stood between them.

'Pip was brought up on it when he stayed with us, Anya.'

'Oh, yes,' Anya replied. 'I forget some things easily these days, Professor Durrant, but not all. I remember Emilia telling me that Ghita could not cook. She was right.'

The joy drained from him … More secrets … That earlier moment of magic had gone. All at once, everything seemed wrong, in spite of his recent optimism.

Ghita cut in, 'That's not fair. I can make … coffee.' They forced a laugh.

'Coffee!' Anya grimaced. 'Outside, we are English, Ghita, but in this house, Romanians. Come over to the table both of you. You have a lot to talk about.' Pip wondered what she meant. He was afraid he was going to hear more lies. Anya looked straight at him as if she was reading his thoughts. 'Ghita is very worried these days,' she added. 'Perhaps you'll be able to help us?'

Pip glanced from one woman to the other. Ghita was staring down at the table, while Anya had her eyes fixed upon him. How could he help them? *Our saviour and our witness*, Simu had said. Pip knew he was not worthy to be called that. Yet he also knew that this was the only place he wanted to be, and it was *he* who needed *their* help. Instead, he answered, 'Of course I'd like to help. What's the problem?'

5

'The past. Things have not changed, Pip,' Ghita said. He smiled at her use of his nickname. As Anya ladled out the soup, the thieving night crept up and stole the light. Then Ghita got up and switched on the comforting lamps and drew down the blinds, dispelling the gloom.

'You asked earlier on who might be coming to dinner,' Ghita went on. 'Olga will be with her friend, Klaas.'

'Her boyfriend?' asked Pip.

Ghita nodded. 'And I hope she won't be too late tonight, considering what happened on New Year's Eve.' Pip was going to ask what, but decided to wait for her to open up. 'She's practising hard for a school concert,' she explained, 'but she has exams to prepare for. She's an extremely good musician.'

'Not as good as he is,' Anya said. 'He plays the flute like the devil himself!' Her expression was hard. Pip swallowed, and his mouthful of soup nearly went down the wrong way.

'Anya doesn't like him,' retorted Ghita. 'Do you, Anya?' The old woman didn't reply. Ghita laid down her spoon. 'She thinks Klaas is a bad influence, but if Olga likes him, then I think we shouldn't try to put her off him, or she will only like him more. He is a very persuasive young man.'

'But is he a bad influence?' asked Pip, thinking *What I have walked into here tonight?* Why did they want to involve him? How could they, after all he had done? Yet, he was remembering Emilia and her troubled relationship with Ghita.

Evidently Olga was her mother's daughter. But still Ghita was prepared to give her some rein. A smile flicked across his face. How could he forget how Ghita had been at that age? She had been such a feisty girl.

'I'm not sure – yet. You might see him before you go back to the college. That's if you'll stay?' Ghita's eyes told him it was what she wanted. 'He's very bright. Well, more than that. Some call him a genius.' She glanced at her watch.

Pip studied her face. She was worried, he knew that. His eyes flicked away before she noticed. As to her question – he would like to stay all night, but he squashed that thought.

'Is Klaas a student at Oxford?' he asked.

'Yes, a brilliant one. He's 17 and he's already in his second year.'

'Which college?'

'Norris.'

'That's mine. Maybe I've seen him. What's he reading?'

'History, I believe. But I'm not surprised you've never met him, as I've heard he doesn't go into college much. Maybe only when it suits him. But I am surprised you've never *heard* of him.'

'Probably not been here long enough, and I'm only on sabbatical. I'd like to meet him. Maybe I'll learn something,' he quipped, but she didn't smile.

'He'll probably find *you*,' Ghita replied.

Anya was still frowning, her black brows almost meeting. 'Shall I fetch the meat?' she asked, beginning to clear away the bowls.

'Please,' replied Ghita.

Pip watched as Anya busied herself at the oven. Then he asked, 'How does Olga know Klaas? Isn't she still at school?' He was determined to find out about her boyfriend.

'She's a day girl in the sixth form at St Willibrord's. Klaas was there too, but as a boarder. He was doing his A Levels at 13.'

'A child prodigy, then?' Pip grimaced.

'I think so,' replied Ghita.

'They have – what you say – things in common.' Anya looked up from carving the meat, knife poised.

'What?'

'Their music,' replied Anya.

'What instrument does she play?'

'Violin mainly – and …' began Ghita.

'And flute,' added Anya. Her tone said everything. Pip was with her on that. He had never liked flute players since … *Koppelberg.*

'Yes. That's where they are now. At a concert in the city. Last night, they were at one in Banbury with the Youth Orchestra. I don't know how it went, because Olga was strung up when she came in. I just didn't have the energy to say anything about her being out to that time in the morning. Klaas is the soloist tonight. Sometimes …' She hesitated. 'Sometimes – I feel she should put as much energy into her other subjects as she does to her music. But then, she always reminds me that she is doing Music at A Level, and what can I say?' Ghita sighed and, reaching over, handed Pip a plate. 'Now, how much meat?'

Afterwards, carrying two mugs of coffee, Ghita led him into the sitting room, which seemed more a home for books than for its owner. They were stacked everywhere on tables and even chairs. He had to help her clear a place on the coffee table to set the mugs down.

'By the way, did you want some *tuica*?' she asked. 'Anya sees it as a restorative. Like my dad. I find it too strong!'

'Coffee is great, thanks.' He was thinking about the last time he had agreed to have some *tuica*, at Simionce's. Almost passing out wouldn't be a good idea now.

She looked around. 'I'm untidy,' she grimaced. 'I don't know what my father would have said to see how I treat books. His library was …'

'Pristine? I know. The first time I met him in Cluj he gave me a lecture on how to look after books. He was scared of letting the sun in on the covers.'

'Anya calls all this my clutter. She drives me mad sometimes when she tries to clear up.' Pip glanced at her. He wasn't keen on the word, 'mad'. He had seen too much madness. 'Did you ever hear anything about Anya when you were back home?'

'I don't think so. Your father never discussed personal matters.' He decided on a half-lie, although it wouldn't do him much good when she found out the truth.

'My father never told me either,' she replied. 'I suppose he was just secretive. I've no idea why. I would have loved it if he had told me that I had a relation on my mother's side. But I think there had been some kind of feud on her side of the family. Anyway, Anya didn't want to talk about it, when she turned up at *Tăta's* funeral. Or since.' Pip remembered again how close she and her father really had been. 'I wish my mother had told me the reason. It would have made all the difference. I felt an orphan when both my parents died; that is, before I met Anya.'

Pip stared at one of the books on the coffee table and picked it up. As he leafed through, he said casually, 'Didn't your father ever tell you about his family?'

He cursed himself inside for not blurting out all he knew. But it was too big a secret, and it wasn't his to tell. If Anya did not want Ghita to know, then Pip would go along with it. Simu too had had things to hide. Both of them he had shared with Pip. The secret of his own lineage was one he had taken to the grave. It was only over the last 17 years that Pip had started to unravel the other: the danger that women and their children had to face in Arva. He found himself hoping that when Ghita had married Anton, she had discovered 'the secret of the marriage bed'. Her mother had died before passing it on, of course, but maybe someone else had told her? At least, if they had, she had managed to get away from Arva and its horrors. Ghita showed no sign of the mental illness that had plagued her mother and all those other women before her. Was that why she and Anya needed his help? Did they want to know what else he knew, that they did not? Or were they worried only about Olga and her boyfriend, the *Wunderkind*, Klaas? He had a feeling he was going to find out in a minute though … She was staring at him now.

'My father and I were very close, Pip, but I feel there were several things he didn't tell me that he might have told you?'

He stared back in mock surprise.

'He left me a note before he died.' Her glance was meaningful.

What was she expecting him to say? *What did you tell her, Simu?* he thought. *Whatever you wrote, it wasn't fair on me.* 'What did it say?' he asked. He hoped he sounded calmer than he felt.

'He told me that he was going to Someşini that night because he had something important to tell you. Something about you and me, which he wished he'd said to me earlier. In that note he promised that he was going to tell me too. He also added that, in case he never came back, you would let me know ….' Ghita hesitated. The relief Pip was feeling inside made him sweat, even though the night was cold. Then she added, 'Why would my father say he mightn't come back, Pip? Did he know something was going to happen to him? And what did he know about you and me?'

'That he'd found out we'd been to bed together?' They looked at each other. Inside, Pip was praying she would believe him. He knew it must have been more than that for Simu to have come to some decision and rush to see him before he left.

'No! I don't think so. Do you know how he died?' Tears were bright in her eyes.

Pip shook his head. 'Only that he'd been involved in a road accident.'

'The accident, as you call it, was very strange. If another driver had been involved it would have been different, but the police said my father drove over the edge of the mountain. I went to see the place. Before he hit the bottom of the ravine, the roof of our car was ripped right off. I hope he was dead before the fire. He knew that road well, Pip. He wouldn't have taken any chances in the snow.'

'Fire?' Pip breathed in to calm himself. A *modus operandi* he knew too well … That was why Anya had said a few minutes ago that Simu had been burned, lying in the snow. He was glad he hadn't asked her to explain.

'Yes, the car set on fire. You look shocked. I'm sorry. You can imagine how I felt, especially when I began to wonder if he took his own life!'

'No! Simu wouldn't do that. He cared for you too much. You were everything to him.'

'I wanted so much to talk to you after he died. But I gave up in the end. You should have got in touch, if only to find out about him. You and my father discussed everything. You knew what he was working on – and no way did I ever believe that you were only studying history. What do you know about my family, Pip, that I don't know?' she persisted.

'Is that why you brought me here, Ghita? Is that why you want me to help you?' He fixed his eyes on her face. She looked down, and her voice was soft as she answered.

'Partly. It was never Anton, you know.'

'I care too.'

'What were you and my father searching for?'

At that moment, he wondered how the hell he was going to get out of relating the obscenities that had been revealed to him in the gypsy camp. 'I …I …'

At that moment, they heard the door slam. Ghita jumped up. 'That's Olga!' She turned her head to look at him as she reached the door. 'You're not getting away until I know.'

'Give me some time to think. Please.' He was ashamed of such a pathetic excuse to save his neck. They stared at each other.

'That's not good enough. We'll talk about this later. If you want to stay?'

He nodded in response. She hurried out, pulling the door to behind her. He could hear raised voices. The door opened again and he stood up. It was Anya.

'They have gone upstairs,' she said. 'Well?'

'I've said nothing.'

'Good. That's better for us both. At least she got rid of the boy.'

'What's he done, Anya?'

'He's dangerous.'

'Dangerous,' Pip repeated, staring at her. 'In what way?'

'Trust me, Pip, he may be only a boy, but he is bad news. For both of them.' Her voice was strong now, like a young woman's.

'Have you seen something, Anya?' His voice cracked. He turned and took a swig of his coffee, which was as cold as he was. 'Tell me.'

'Some things you cannot tell – only feel. You have to do something about it.'

'Me?'

'That's what Simu wanted most of all. To protect his family. Why do you think I have lived so long?' Her voice trembled, and she looked like she was going to collapse. Pip caught her arm, and for a brief moment she was leaning against him for support, then she shook her head. 'I shall protect them as long as I can, but I know it won't be long before I am gone.'

'Gone? Where? Are you going back to Romania?'

'To my ancestors.' She smiled. He had not noticed before that she had lost so many teeth. He felt a shiver run through him.

'Anya! Have you seen your own death?' She didn't answer. 'Tell me!' He caught her arm, but she pulled away.

'Now you are here, you will take my place. Later, you'll know why. You'll understand. Before that happens, I need to speak with you. You need to know what Simu was going to tell you, before he was killed.'

'Killed? You believe he was murdered?'

'Yes,' said Anya. 'Are you surprised? The beast that killed my son must be destroyed before it can take Ghita and Olga. They are very dear to me, even though they do not know me for who I really am.' She sat down. He had not seen any colour in her cheeks before, but now a dull flush had spread over her cheekbones, which did not enhance her features but made her look older. He crouched down beside her.

'Don't upset yourself,' he said. 'I will do my best to look after them.'

'Shhh, they are ready to come down.' He didn't ask how she

knew. 'I must talk to you!' He felt the urgency in her voice, as if she had no time left. Pip produced his business card from his wallet.

'Here, for you, so we can arrange a time to meet and talk in private.' He could only be thankful that he had gone to his book signing that day. He might never have encountered Ghita otherwise.

The old lady regarded him as he handed her the card. She had a faint smile on her face as she added, 'You had to be there today, Dr Durrant.'

'You knew that as well, I suppose?'

She nodded and slipped the card into her apron pocket. A moment later, the door opened and a girl came through. Pip caught his breath. Olga! With a pang, he realised that she looked exactly like Ghita, except she wore glasses and had a serious air about her, which had been absent from the girl that her mother had been the first time they met. There was *something else* about her though – as though he had seen her before. Ghita followed behind her.

'I guess this is Olga,' he said

'Hello, Professor Durrant.'

He held out his hand. She took it, but as they touched, a sharp zing of electricity passed between them. They jumped apart.

'I got a shock,' she said, staring at her palm.

'So did I!'

'Olga is always complaining of getting shocks off things,' said Ghita. 'Even door handles.'

'Well, I could do with some of that energy,' replied Pip. They all laughed.

'And the car door handle,' she said.

'I didn't know you had a car,' Pip remarked to Ghita.

'I don't,' she replied.

'I mean Klaas's car, Mum,' Olga said. 'And don't look like that.' Ghita didn't reply, but Anya snorted. Olga stared at them both, then turned to Pip, 'You're the famous writer, then?' The awkward moment was over and she was cool again.

'I don't know about famous.'

'Why are we all standing up, except for Anya?' Olga yawned. 'God, I'm tired. Sorry! I shall tell the girls at school that I got a shock off the author who wrote *The Last Vision.*' She laughed. 'Or maybe I won't.' She yawned again. Ghita exchanged glances with Pip.

'Have you read my books, then?' Pip asked.

'Sort of,' she said. She went over to Anya. 'Are you all right, Anya? It looks as though you've done too much tonight.'

The old lady waved her away. 'No, but I *feel* tired, like you.' She started to get up, but tottered back.

Ghita sprang forward to help. 'Olga's right. Are you going up now? If so, I'm coming with you. Those stairs are steep. We don't want you falling.' Pip stood by awkwardly. 'Olga will keep you company, Pip. That's if she can keep awake.' Pip was thinking of his sister Melanie as he looked at Olga, whose expression at that moment was pure teen. Anya turned to him and said in Romanian, 'I shall see you again soon, Professor?'

'I hope so,' replied Pip.

Olga was staring. They watched together as her mother and Anya went slowly out of the door, then she turned to him. 'You speak Romanian?'

He nodded. 'Do you?'

'Yes, but I'm not very good. My mother insisted, and so I try.'

He grinned at the honest answer. 'So do I.'

'How do you know it? Were you over there?' she asked.

'I studied under your granddad at the University of Cluj.'

'Cool! Will you tell me about him? Mother never says anything about the past.'

As they were chatting away, Pip tried to avoid anything that might prompt any awkward questions. Yet he kept thinking how this girl would have felt if she had known anything of what had gone on before she was born; of how much different her life might have been if her mother and Anton had stayed together in Arva.

He shivered inside at the thought that if she had been living in the village she was now exactly the age to 'go up', as the villagers called it. She would have had to go through the obscene ritual; unless, of course, Ghita forbade it, but … the possibilities were endless …

'Hey,' she said,' I don't want to be rude, but you were telling me about my grandpa. Where did you go? Thinking of your next book?'

'Nope, this one's my last.'

'You can't do that,' she said. 'Think of your fans.'

'Maybe I'm just tired of writing,' he said.

'I'll let you into a secret,' she replied. Pip wasn't sure what he was going to hear. 'I haven't really read any of your books. Mum is crazy about them! She's a real fan. It's so great to meet you. Really.' He was faced with the most enchanting smile. His insides ached for Ghita again. Olga was looking at him in a strange way. 'Anyway, tell me some more. I wish I'd known my grandpa. He sounds cool.'

'He was, but there's not much more to tell.'

Then Olga yawned. 'Sorry. I had a late night – and it wasn't all good.' Her mood had changed. 'You know we – that's Klaas, Spencer and me – we were pulled over by this policeman after the concert. Don't tell, will you?'

He was touched that she was confiding in him. He shook his head.

'Spencer was driving Klaas's car, and he has to go and produce his documents at the police station.'

'Bad luck. Where was that?'

'Just outside Woodstock.' She looked upset. All of a sudden, he wanted to put his arm round her and cheer her up. Then he remembered that he was getting old, and that this pretty teenager was not her mother, who'd had a bad relationship with her own parents and seen their marriage degenerate daily. This had nothing to do with him.

'And my mum is going to go mad and … There's something else …' She hesitated. 'I was walking outside the paper shop today and I saw something about a traffic policeman getting killed in the early hours of the morning. So I went in and bought the *Mail* and – I think it might have been the policeman who stopped us. He was dragged under a lorry. It was horrible,' she said.

The news hit Pip right in the stomach as his dream came back. He felt a bit sick.

'What is it?' asked Olga.

'Nothing. Probably too much *tuica*,' he lied. 'Anyway, why do you think it was the same man?'

'I just *feel* it was,' she said. 'Is that silly?'

He shook his head, and for the next few moments they didn't speak. That was the 'something else' he had felt when he had met her. It wasn't only that she looked like Ghita, but that he had seen her and her friends in his nightmare.

'Shall we sit down?' she added. He was glad to.

'Your mother tells me you're a musician,' he remarked, changing the subject. All at once, it seemed the most important thing in the world to find out Olga's likes and dislikes.

She grimaced. 'I'm Grade Eight at the flute, but I wouldn't call myself a musician. Not like Klaas. I could never be a concert artist.'

'Did you want to?'

'No way,' she said, shaking her head.

'Music runs in my family,' he ventured. They chatted away about his mother, then his sister Melanie and his twin siblings. When there was a break in the conversation, Pip turned to the subject of her boyfriend. 'Your mother mentioned that Klaas was a musician.'

'What has she been saying about Klaas?' Olga's tone had changed to defensive. Pip's psychological training kicked in. She was really sore about the fact Klaas wasn't welcome in the house, and Pip was intrigued about the guy.

'Nothing, except that he's very bright. Gifted.'

'He's fantastic,' said Olga. He could see her eyes light up when she spoke of him, and he thought of Anya's opposite description of Klaas. 'He's at the Uni already and he's only 17. He took his exams at 13. Did my mother tell you that? She ought to be proud. He's not like other boys of his age. I don't know why nobody likes him. It was the same at school.'

'I can see you are – proud, I mean. Maybe the rest of the kids think he's a bit too intelligent?'

'I think that too, but I'm not jealous. You know, they said awful things about him.'

'What like?'

'That he's strange. Not – normal. He's …' She stopped. 'He's … I don't know. Nobody understands.'

'Try me?'

'I can't tell you a lot about what happened. Anyway, I don't want to believe it. I know the others were telling lies! Klaas and I have always got on really well. He helps me with my homework.' Defiance had leapt into her voice. Pip could see Olga wouldn't be easy to persuade. She was like her mother.

'Well, I think he must be a good guy if you like him so much.' Years of psychological training had led him to make a manipulative statement. But he wanted to find out as much as he could about Klaas, because he respected Anya's judgement. Yet he felt almost protective towards Olga. Though he didn't know why.

'Thank you,' she said. 'I'm glad my mum knows you.' The serious look had been replaced by a smile that made her face come alive, which made Pip feel ridiculously happy. 'You're a good guy as well.' They were laughing as Ghita came in.

'I'm glad you're getting along so well. Did you get any homework done, Olga?'

'Mother!' Olga turned to Pip. 'See? Mum doesn't understand me.' She turned back. 'You know I want to pass my exams, and I wouldn't do anything to jeopardise that.'

'Except stay out all night,' was Ghita's sharp retort.

Olga sighed. 'See,' she said to Pip. 'Anyway, I'll tell all my friends about you, Professor Durrant. And I hope to see you again too.'

'You can drop the Professor,' he said. 'Call me Pip.'

'Pip? Like out of *Great Expectations*?'

'That's me!' At that moment, he glanced at Ghita. He couldn't place her expression. Perhaps she thought he was flirting with her daughter?

'Well, bye – Pip!' Olga looked at him. He held out his hand. She shook her head. There was mischief in her dark eyes.

'No, I don't want to get shocked again!' A moment later, she was gone.

'She's …' He was going to say 'enchanting' but changed his mind. '… great.'

'She used to be such a lovely kid. Now, I think she wants to get away from me,' replied Ghita. 'She goes about these days as if she has the world on her shoulders.'

'Teenage angst. Remember.'

'Yes, I know. I wish I hadn't given my dad such a hard time.'

'So did I.' If only she knew.

Ghita crossed over to the couch and gestured to him. 'You'll stay for more coffee, won't you? Besides, what we were talking about before, I want you to tell me.'

He glanced at his watch. 'I can't stay any longer, I'm afraid. I have to go now and catch up with Larry. Believe me, I would like to! It's been one of the best days I've had in a long time, because of meeting you. I knew I would, one day. Or I was hoping I would, so that I could tell you …' Every sentence he said was not what he wanted to. He needed time with her, to explain – although he was scared that if he did, she wouldn't want anything to do with him. 'I'll be back, I promise. I'm not going away again.'

'I hope not. Just one thing, though. Did Olga mention Klaas?'

Pip was guarded in his reply. 'She didn't give much away.' He didn't add that he could see Olga was smitten with the guy. Did Ghita know that she and Anya weren't alone in their dislike of the student? That even the other schoolkids thought he wasn't 'normal'? Pip didn't like the word. It didn't figure in his psychological vocabulary. But in this particular case it worried him a lot. Maybe something serious was the matter with Klaas? But he couldn't judge unless he met him. And he wanted to, a lot!

'She won't say anything to me – and, besides, it's driving me mad what they might be doing.'

He understood. Some kids started having sex early. But Olga didn't look the type. He smiled inwardly then at his own naiveté. He didn't even know her. In any case, it must be hell for parents if they were the type who cared. Since he'd never had any children, he could only imagine how Ghita felt.

She looked so upset then that the last thing he wanted to do was leave. But it was probably for the best – because, if he stayed, he might go too far. And he didn't want to spoil things with Ghita. That would drive him mad too. He could almost feel his arms round her, making love to her in that dingy little room in Cluj after the Halloween party. It was as fresh as yesterday in his memory! But he couldn't bet on it that she was feeling the same. He had to go. How could he think about making it with Ghita after what he had done to her?

'In spite of everything that's happened,' she said, 'I'm so glad you're here – and so is Anya. She told me. She says it's a miracle. That it's meant to be, and that I shouldn't think of the past. Only the future.'

'That's why you were upstairs such a long time, then,' replied Pip; but, inside, he was thinking, *Oh, Anya, you know how to play it, don't you?* She nodded.

They looked at each other and he stepped forward. He could hardly keep his hands off her. He wanted to pull her into his arms. She held out her hand and he took it, hoping she couldn't feel his trembling. He had not felt like that with any woman for 17 years. He wanted to kiss her so much – and this time it wouldn't be a one-night stand. He could hardly believe she'd been only that. One stolen night, which he hadn't seen coming.

Ghita probably felt the same as he did, but things were changing in the world. Recently, there had been a tendency to turn away from promiscuity. Prostitution had been made legal, but rape crimes had increased. People were careful now. Everything had become more dangerous. English police carried guns, and you didn't cross them. No, it was better that he and Ghita got to know each other again – and he would have to put up with it. She had to make the first move.

'Thank you, Pip,' she said. 'Would you like the number of a

cab?' She reached for her mobile.

'No, thanks. I'll walk.'

'Norris is right the other side of town. It's freezing out there.'

'It'll do me good.' He needed to cool off. The mad moment was almost over. 'Thank you. For everything. I'll ring you – soon.'

'I hope so,' she said.

'I don't want to lose you again,' he dared reply.

'See that you don't, then. I'll be here. We've a lot of talking to do.'

'Just one thing before I go,' he said. 'It worried me a bit.'

'Yes?' Ghita stopped.

'Anya told me – that Klaas is dangerous. How? What did she mean?'

'Oh, take no notice. I'm worried about the boy, but I wouldn't go that far. It's a family joke, really. Olga has a new white carpet in her room and she makes people take off their shoes before going in. Imagine! Klaas keeps leaving his trainers near the top of the stairs, and Anya keeps moving them. She says they'll be the death of one of us!'

'Oh, right!' He smiled and followed Ghita out into the corridor, thinking it didn't seem like a joke when Anya had said it. He cursed himself for never being able to trust anyone, even Ghita. For instance, he'd always wondered what had really led Simu to risk everything by driving to the airport in that foul weather. Why hadn't his friend simply used the phone to talk to him …?

Ghita unhooked his coat from the rack.

'Thank you,' he said. 'It's been … most enjoyable.' Then he bent and kissed her on the cheek. It was burning.

'Yes, it has, Pip.' She was smiling again.

'I'll ring you. I promise.' He could still feel the hot touch but, in the street light, her face looked small and wan as she closed the door behind him. He stood there for a moment, acclimatising to the cold as it stung his face. Then he turned up his collar, went through the small gate and shut it behind him with care. He paused, looking up at that little terraced house. It had been like a good dream, which he'd been over so many times in his head. As he walked along, he was thinking how it might have been, and imagined Ghita hand in hand with him, leading him upstairs, across the landing into her bedroom.

Whether or not that would be possible ever again, he didn't know, but Anya's earlier warning was already dispelling the magic of the evening. Somewhere, tragedy was waiting for the woman he still loved. And now he had met her daughter, he was doubly sure that he would do all in his power to try to avert it.

Once he and Anya had had a chance to meet and talk again, the danger might become clearer. He also knew that becoming reacquainted with her here was the fulfilment of Simionce's prophecy. Tonight had seemed a brief respite from his continual obsession with his quest, but it shouldn't have, because he felt he was nearer to success now than he had ever been before. His novel had led him to Ghita and Anya.

Later, as he passed along the broad avenue lined with ancient colleges and stopped at the entrance to Norris, he had a sudden premonition that turned his stomach and made him sweat. He felt that someone else who would be another vital link in his research was very near. He looked around and upwards to the blank, ornate windows above. Nothing, no-one. Yet, at that moment, he knew that sooner or later he was going to meet this other person, who would be either for him, or against him and on the side of evil.

Pip was relaxed the following morning – in spite of the humorous grilling he'd received from Larry about Ghita, when his agent had rung him first thing. He'd had no nightmares, and felt clear-headed enough to take some 'thinking time' – which meant he was going to sit and look through whatever book or file was the most important to him just then. *The Last Vision* was out of his hands now, and he would have given anything at that moment to experience a vision of his own future. He had seen other people's, but never his own. It had been only the old gypsy, Eva Kirchma, who had prophesied that.

He was in no hurry to do anything for work. All he had to do was prepare his first lecture for the Psychology Department at Norris. He thought of the student, Klaas Honen. Ghita had said he was reading History, which was a big subject. He wondered what the guy specialised in. But he would find out. Forewarned was forearmed, in this case.

He glanced toward the kitchen. He had promised himself that he would prepare a special breakfast if ever he found Ghita. One to compare to a condemned man's last meal! Usually, he was a 'no breakfast and black coffee' man. But when he thought of the implications of the night before, he decided against it. He now had a day to do as he liked – until Anya, or maybe Ghita, rang him. The growing excitement within him made him restless, but he took himself in hand. There was no need to worry. He wouldn't lose them again. He would rather die.

Being on sabbatical, Pip could do as much or as little as he liked. He told himself he had earned the rest, and he aimed to return to New York in the fall. One of his early plans had been to stay in London, where he could have continued to promote his book while pursuing his current research into mediaeval history by making trips to the British Library and the capital's various museums. However, a growing instinct had caused him to argue with Larry that he ought to base himself in Oxford instead. Now he knew why he had had that instinct, and was glad he had trusted it. It had been a premonition; but not like the dark ones that caused him to repress everything inside for days on end while he waited for disaster to follow.

By trusting those good feelings, he had found Ghita again. That early January morning of another Piper Year, Pip had come home in his heart, whether he deserved it or not. A meeting with two women from his past, one with whom he was still in love, the other who could offer him a way to pursue his obsession with exterminating an evil that had brought death and madness to many innocent people.

He now had a new impetus: getting to know Ghita again. That was something else he had hoped for; but he had not expected that he would also find his next lead, Anya, who was obviously ready to unload her burdens on him. He hadn't felt so hopeful about his quest in a very long time. He had spent many years writing fiction out of desperation. It had been for him a hard slog, even though he had been feted as 'a writer of extraordinary and original books', as his publisher's PR company liked to describe him. That wasn't how he saw himself; only as a crazy man bringing out glimpses of light from a tormented mind, a man who could see an outcome far too horrible to contemplate, not only for himself but for the whole world. In those moments of desperation, he remembered far too clearly the desolation of the Piper's last display case in that disgusting chalet in Sunny Mead, depicting a world of nothing, like those images captured in the aftermath of Hiroshima; a landscape violated by some cataclysmic event that had reduced it to oblivion.

Sighing, he caught a glimpse of the *Oxford Mail* on the coffee table and took in the same lurid headline Olga had mentioned: *Hit and Run. Policeman Dead. First casualty of the New Year.*

What a start to anyone's New Year! Killed on the road! As he read on, and the report went into detail about the manner of death, his happy mood faltered and the images of the night overtook his mind. It chimed exactly with his nightmare. Being pulled under a truck. He moistened his mouth, which had dried. The three kids! What had they to do with it? The girl with the two young men. Olga and her companions. He remembered her now. Beautiful, sensitive, bright – like her mother.

He squashed the cruel idea that kept stabbing at his brain. This was Oxford, not a backward village in Romania. Olga wouldn't have to go through that. A sudden throbbing in his head reminded him that he needed to keep focused on the day in hand. He walked over and looked at his calendar. It had taken a while for him to find a calendar of that nature in Brooklyn, but although he had no real faith, he had retraced that walk to Simionce's house and called in at the church he had passed. It had done something to alleviate the guilt he felt for the old man's death. Inside, he had donated to a mission in

Africa, and had received in return a wonderful calendar of saints.

Today was 2 January. St Berthold's Day. Pip was interested in every saint in that calendar. To him, a feast day usually meant something. St Berthold was hard to pin down. What was known about him came from various sources. One stated he was not in fact a saint but Berthold V, Duke of Zähringen, who according to legend went hunting and on his first expedition killed a bear, from whom he named the city of Bern or Berne. But another told that St Berthold was the great Crusader Saint, who founded a noble and holy order of monks. Ninth Century monks were Pip's province.

But no day was as precious to him as 22 July, dedicated to St Mary Magdalene, the patron saint of, amongst others, reformed prostitutes and sexual temptation, which really fitted into his research. If he had been only a researcher, it would have been marvellous. He was far more than that, according to Professor Dalca.

But the mission Pip had been chosen to undertake was personal rather than grandiose or vainglorious. He was very near to finding out Grandsire's identity, when previously the trail had gone cold, as it had for his predecessors. However crazy it sounded, Pip believed he now had evidence that the Arva Grandsire was also the legendary Piper of Hamelin; the kidnapper of a pair of American twins in 1952; and the flute-player Diep Koppelberg in 1988. He was also constrained to follow a pattern that Pip had been working to discern for many years.

Koppelberg's power to enchant by his music and his beauty, which masked the evil inside, was no fiction. He had appeared as a real person in several documented cases – and, as far as Pip knew, still did, or perhaps lived on in people known or unknown. The world was full of Koppelbergs and Pipers, and Pip wanted to know what made them tick. *Psychology and history*, Dalca had said. An explosive mix.

With Simionce's story under his belt, he had discovered that the Piper had existed in 800 AD, and what had happened then had sparked off the atrocities he had committed, according to the cycle prescribed.

Soon, Pip might hear more from Anya. He felt confident that her coming story would at last put him on an equal footing with his earthly and supernatural rivals.

The idea excited him so much that he couldn't settle, and half an hour later he was sitting at his desk, staring at the notes he had made from his meeting with Simionce. He had needed no more than an overview for his fiction; but now he must be ready to add Anya's input, which would be a vital contribution to the true transcription he intended to make of the Piper's own story.

6

Pip thought back to when he had last met the unfortunate young man Otto Werner in his own flat in Brooklyn. Werner had become another innocent victim in the search for the Piper.

Pip had been told about the post-grad student by his former supervisor at the Institute, where he had been out of favour after his recall from Romania 'in disgrace' – which was how he liked to describe the situation he had found himself in when he returned to New York in the fall of 2007. He had trusted his old professor not to ask him why he needed a good translator of Old High German texts. Otto was his man, according to Pip's superior. Brilliant, but unreliable, in that he was liable to suffer – the Professor had sniffed and paused then, looking around as if someone was listening, lowered his voice, tapped his head and said – '… mental problems. But that shouldn't worry *you*, because you know all about that, don't you?'

'I assume you mean because I'm a psychologist?' Pip's tone had been level but cold, although he had been seething inside. The Professor had assumed, like so many other people, that a mental illness was something to be ashamed of. But Pip's tone had clearly been noted, as the Professor had corrected himself with his next speech:

'The poor guy has been asked to leave several good universities – unsteady but brilliant, I'm afraid. He is looking for some private work, I know. Pleasant young man, though!' And he'd sniffed again and started on another subject …

The Professor had been right about Otto's brilliance. Pip had been more worried about his ability to keep secrets, as allowing someone who might be unstable access to his stolen manuscript pages had been a huge risk. So he had decided to use only the photocopies in the beginning.

Otto had seemed the last person who might be of interest to Eisenmann and his cronies. His gaunt face had lit up when he realised what he was being asked to do. They had got on extremely well from the beginning. Pip had fed Otto well as he examined the copies of the manuscript pages with the pleasure that any researcher or academic would have felt to have such a task in front of his eyes. Yet the day did come when he had asked Pip how he had managed to have the pages copied. He had recognised one or two of them, in fact, telling Pip where they were held. Pip had fielded the question well, but in the end had been left with little option but to take Otto to the bank, under the promise of utter secrecy, to see the originals.

Otto asked no questions. He thought either that Pip was a crook or that he was a millionaire.

As Pip unwrapped the pages from the strongbox and his gloved hands laid them out carefully, Otto was already quivering. He made a noise like a small, frightened animal as he examined one of them.

'What is it?' Pip asked.

'I don't understand,' replied Otto. 'This is not the same as the photocopy you showed me. The text maybe, but the picture – the picture is …' He stopped and his voice quivered. 'The picture has been bastardised … But it looks,' he was peering at it, 'authentic!'

'What do you mean?' Pip's voice had gone so weak he could hardly hear it in his head. All he heard was a buzzing, maybe a faint laugh, which he had heard so many times in his nightmares. What had happened to his glorious manuscript pages? His whole body had gone cold as he came to the table and looked.

'Here,' said Otto, 'and here.' He was turning over the other pages. 'These look exactly right, but they are not what I have seen before at your home. I hope that you have not paid a great amount of money for these? They must be another version or … And who is the man?' He handed him the pages.

Pip took the magnifying glass from Otto and examined each manuscript page. The pictures showed a succession of Popes. But a new figure, only half visible, had appeared in each of them, staring over the Holy Father's shoulder. The haggard face was one that Pip knew well. That straggling hair; those light-blue eyes, like a wolf's kindred; and that sinister smile, which on careful examination revealed pointed incisors.

Pip felt sick. Who could have changed his beautiful manuscript pages? *Or had they changed themselves?*

Otto sat there, looking down to the table. His hands were clasped together in front of him, cupped as if ready to catch his tears. There was no way that Pip could explain. He could only fold the manuscript pages, with their leering addition, into their protective tissues and replace them in their strongbox. Inwardly, Pip was cursing Koppelberg. Wishing he would die! But, like all his alter egos, he would not … Pip was churned up with hate at that moment, consumed with it. He felt as if he had lost the battle …

Otto looked up, his face sympathetic. 'It has been so good to work with you. I have enjoyed the experience. And, may I say, I have no knowledge of who that person could be, or of how he could fit into the history of the manuscript. Maybe I could find out for you?' He hesitated, when Pip didn't answer, then added, 'I am not good at revealing my feelings, but I think we have become friends? May I say … although I don't understand … I realise this has been a shock to you too. I suggest you still use the translations to go with the copies and –'

'*No*, Otto, you must not look for this man or his face or anything about him.' Otto was surprised by the vehemence of Pip's words. 'What I want you to do is forget all about this. I can't explain why, except to tell you it is better you do.'

'Can I say something more?' Otto asked. 'Or at least …. I would like to do this …' Pip was very surprised when the reserved Otto hugged him in a spontaneous manner that so belied his character. After he loosened his grip and they stood face to face, Otto added, 'One other thing I must say, which I should not. You have been my employer and paid me well. I am happy that you did not steal those pages, because I feared that you had. Now I know you are a good man.'

They parted with the promise to meet again. Pip was not going to discard Otto, even though the young man had now completed his assignment. He had been touched by the true expression of his friendship. Through Otto's hard work, he now had a translation of the Old High German that verified what he had found out already about the Piper and where the trail might lead; back to where he and Dalca had thought it would: to the founding of the Holy Roman Empire and the crowning of Charlemagne as Emperor.

Pip leaned back in his comfortable chair in his Oxford rooms on that cold and sunny January morning in 2024. Somewhere, a book was hidden that would reveal the crimes of this man or devil. Was it still in Arva? He needed to find it, whatever happened to him. And it must be this year. He would be too old when the cycle came round again. 2060 – a long time. But now he had been promised more help. Anya. All at once, he was afraid that something might happen to her. But he would guard her well. She wouldn't be lost to him.

However, Otto had had no such escape.

The poor post-graduate's subsequent death had not fitted into the *modus operandi* of the other murders. He had been simply frightened to death. The memory distressed Pip a great deal. He believed that if Otto had not met him and offered to put in all those hours of work, he might be alive today. The medical examiner and the coroner had each had their own explanation for the death. However, Pip was the one who really knew …

He could still remember clearly the evening when Otto had called him at home and begged him to go as quickly as he could to the man's small flat in a less affluent part of Brooklyn. It was not far from the church that Pip had passed on his way to meet Simionce.

That evening, he did not want to go to see Otto, because he himself was suffering from a headache, the kind that he now believed comparable to the one Dr Marcu had complained about in those neat, handwritten notes to be found in the Papers that bore his name. An unearthly ache that had almost a tune within it, attacking his ability to think. It troubled him, because he felt he should know the words to the skinny-string reediness that crept through his skull and stuck like a hapless insect in his memory web. It had been insistent all day, and had disabled him in the usual way; he could do ordinary tasks, but even the thought of pursuing some reading or research provoked the idea that his head might burst open with the mental effort.

Otto's voice, that night, had had none of its usual strength. It quavered like the voice control on Pip's mobile. 'I need to see you,' he had reiterated. 'Something has happened.' By the time Pip had queried what, Otto's tone had changed to frantic. '*No, I can't tell you on the phone!*' The last sentence had been as near a scream as anything Pip had ever heard. Then Otto had hung up.

Pip knew very well what crisis sounded like. When Otto had been working on the translations, he had shown no sign of the crippling mental illness cited by the Professor, although he had been far from what could be described as normal. When Pip had first met him, he might have taken him to be on the fringe of the autistic spectrum. But after they had been in each other's company for a while, he had revised his opinion, suspecting that Otto might have some kind of schizophreniform disorder - something Pip was familiar with in past patients. It could be helped enormously with certain techniques in the psychotherapeutic field.

Otto had never asked for Pip's help, though, and as Pip had not been practising as a psychologist, and at that time had no wish to do so, the question had never arisen. However, Pip had never been someone who would ignore a cry for help. Asking for help in a crisis was a sensible thing to do. Yet, Pip had hesitated for several reasons when he had reached the door of

Otto's flat. His headache had been no better either.

He had wondered, as he had climbed the narrow stairs, what he would do if Otto was so incapacitated that he could not come to the door. He had also had Robert Riparu fresh in his mind. Riparu had died from rabies – and had been dying when Pip had called in to see him, received no response and gone away again! That was not going to happen with Otto.

Having to face whatever had tipped Otto over the edge was a very unsettling prospect. However, Pip gathered his nerves and knocked on the door, and a few moments later it opened to reveal the student standing in the corridor beyond.

Otto was alive – but not well. Pip's eyes were drawn to the untidy bandage round his head. He had evidently wound it about himself. His eyes were expressionless at first, then changed to an agonised expression as he adjusted the bandage with pitifully trembling hands. There was no blood though. Pip considered that a good sign.

'What's happened, Otto? Have you fallen down? Banged into something? Let me look.'

Otto backed away, and immediately Pip could see raw fear replacing the anguish. The young man sat down hard in his computer chair, which protested with a loud squeak, making Pip jump. He could see Otto had been working. He looked around for another chair for himself, but couldn't see one. Had Otto been fighting? Been attacked? Pip's quick eyes also noted an upturned side table, some papers strewn on the floor, and one or two cups that were on the floor too, and definitely out of place there, as Otto was painfully tidy. There was an atmosphere too, as if something serious was about to happen. He found a chair in the small bedroom and brought it in. Otto now had a hand to the bandage, as if he was afraid it would slip. Pip's breathing had shortened. He knew he was getting worried. Things seemed unreal. It flashed through his mind that he himself might not be all right. That … He didn't even want to think about visions.

'I can wait,' Pip said, 'but I'd like to know what's happened. Why did you call me? You sounded frantic. Why hang up,

Otto?' His friend's eyes were closed now, as if he were asleep. In fact, he didn't seem to be in pain. He seemed peaceful.

Pip approached him, thinking *Maybe he's unconscious …?* Yet, as Pip bent over him, Otto's lips drew back in a kind of ugly snarl, which flicked on for only a moment and then disappeared. Pip jumped back.

The young man put up a hand and wiped his mouth, as if he wanted to wash away the grimace. 'Don't take any notice. I didn't mean it,' he said, 'but *he* made me.'

Pip stiffened at the strange words. He was beginning to think things were worse than he'd supposed. 'Who made you? I don't understand. Has someone hurt you? Is it – because of what you did for me?' Pip's own head was not clear either.

'He didn't like it.' Otto's voice had changed. It sounded almost like a threat.

Pip stood back, but insisted, 'Who?'

Otto stared in the direction of the computer. Meanwhile, Pip was considering his next move. Otto's behaviour was far from ordinary – whatever that was – but he had never given any indication he could be even slightly threatening. Pip's former training was clicking into place.

'You got mixed up in something? A fight?' he repeated, indicating Otto's head. The student was shivering now. His teeth were chattering and he seemed to be trying to control himself, to put a brake on what was happening. 'You can tell me,' Pip probed, but it was gentle probing. He needed to find out, but quietly. Carefully. Yet, a little voice in his brain kept prompting, *What's the matter with his head, you idiot? Look for yourself. There are no tell-tale signs. No blood.*

Otto was now trying to shake his head. The fear was in his eyes again, and they glittered. *Drugs*, thought Pip. *What had he taken? Maybe it's his medication? That's if he takes any …* The list of possibilities was endless. Where to begin? Then Otto leaned toward him.

'I saw him,' he said. His words were robotic. Then he repeated it.

'Where. On the computer? Who did you see, Otto?' asked

Pip. He could feel a clear pulse drumming in his own head. He began preparing for the worst, because he couldn't forget the day he had seen Koppelberg's picture replace Eisenmann's on his own laptop screen. 'Just take it quietly now.' He backed away from Otto and walked over to his knapsack. 'You want a beer? I got one.' He looked inside. 'And I brought food. Just in case you –' The last sentence was broken into by a violent yell.

'I don't want this!' Otto's voice, usually so measured, was staccato, rasping and ugly. He struggled with the bandage and pulled it away from his forehead.

'Christ!' burst out Pip, thinking he couldn't be seeing what it revealed.

A hole had appeared in the centre of Otto's forehead. Neat as a rat bite! He'd been shot! Pip stared. It was a bullet wound. But the man should have been dead as soon as that bullet entered! It was deep. As he continued to stare, the skull bones seemed to part before his eyes, like a sinkhole appearing, and what was inside was unravelling.

Still no blood. Only a river of ooze …

Pip felt himself go dizzy. But the rational part of his brain was trying desperately to separate fantasy from reality. He was seeing things now. But a voice inside him accused, *And it's all your fault.*

It isn't, screamed this thing inside his consciousness. Otto's lips were moving. *Yes it's me, Pip, I'm here …*

Otto pulled the bandage down again, and the voice stopped. He looked near collapse, falling sideways in the computer chair. Pip was shaking all over, trying to control himself. Returning to himself again, now that the obscenity was covered.

'It came on suddenly,' gibbered Otto. 'I thought my head was going burst with a migraine, Pip, and then it did, and I could see him in my mind.' He made a dive toward Pip and grabbed him, pulling him down onto the floor with him.

Otto indicated his head, not touching it, only stabbing the air with his finger, while Pip tried to get away from him. 'He's in here, the man we saw in the manuscript. In the vault. I shouldn't have seen him. Why did you let me? '

Pip was struggling to get free of Otto. He could smell that old familiar scent of raw earth. He was fighting back belief in what was happening then, trying to find reality again.

'This isn't real,' he shouted to Otto, whose arms were now a tight band holding him to his chest, taking his breath, arms so tightly fixed that it seemed they would never let him go. 'Get off,' Pip screamed, kicking at him in any part he could until the student went flying on his back across the laminated floor. 'We're hallucinating,' he shouted. 'Both of us. I know!'

Otto didn't speak. He lay silent. An exhausted Pip crawled over to him, his eyes averted from the bandage. Otto was panting, but quietly, like an anguished animal. The room was silent except for the heavy breathing of the two men.

'Listen, Otto, it's a joint hallucination!' Pip fought back the bile in his mouth. 'Listen. Just lie there and listen. Don't touch me again.' His stomach was churning now. 'Are you listening? *He* isn't really here. Nor in there.' He pointed to Otto's head. 'He wants you to think he is. He hasn't taken over your body. He hasn't broken open your head. You're in charge. *I'm in charge.* He can't hurt you. He's been dead for hundreds of years. Don't think of him. Concentrate on anything but him. Think about me. I'm a psychologist. I'll help you. I'm going to look at that hole and it'll be gone. He'll be gone. We will have won together. He won't win. He will never win.' Pip was frantic, gabbling himself to exhaustion; but he was going to keep on doing it, because whoever they were in the past – Grandsire, Piper, Koppelberg – they wouldn't triumph. Pip wouldn't let them!

He had finished crawling. He sat up on his haunches, stared at the bandage, summoned up all his courage and whipped it off!

Otto Werner's head was not split open, but a deep black mark remained where the hole had been; an angry impression radiating from a depressed dent in the skull. Pip wasn't going to touch it.

'Otto! Otto! Speak to me. It's gone. He's gone. You're okay.' All of a sudden, Pip spewed up on the floor. He had given everything of himself, but he had won. Their adversary had been overcome. But the Piper's tune remained in his head, and his headache came back with such force that he was as disabled as he'd been when he was a kid. Along with the tune there was the noise of raucous, squeaking laughter, so strong that he thought it came from behind him. He was on his knees now, too weak to get up, so he looked through his legs. The room was empty.

Otto was motionless. Pip crawled back to him and lay down beside him. Holding the shivering student to him in his arms until his trembling ceased.

Later, much later, the two of them cleaned up. An hour after that, Pip told Otto as much of the Piper story as he felt the student could take, and he stayed the night there in the flat, lying on the couch. Otto seemed calm when he went to bed. However, in the morning, when Pip made coffee and went to wake him up, he discovered to his horror that the man who had become his friend, and for whom he felt responsible, had overdosed on sleeping tablets he kept inside a bedroom drawer.

It was a victory no more. The Piper had claimed another victim. Pip called an ambulance, but it was too late. The presence of the mark on Otto's forehead led to a post mortem and an inquest. Both revealed that Otto Werner had been suffering from a malignant brain tumour. The verdict was that he had probably harmed himself by trying to combat the terrible pain he would have suffered.

Pip was questioned closely by the police, but he had his story ready, and that was the end of the matter. The guilt remained, though, along with the memory of that dreadful night, when he had been offered more evidence of an evil power at work. At least Otto would suffer it no longer.

All Pip had to do now was make sure that if Anya helped him, she would never face such a terrible fate. He had also realised that his visions were becoming more dangerous. He had to take care to defend himself, too, from what he dubbed 'the Otto outcome'.

He checked his mobile phone. No message yet. Maybe she'd changed her mind? He turned once more to his notes to refresh himself with a story he already knew almost by heart; his compilation of Simionce's fragments as to the origin of the Piper.

<u>Dialogue 1. Compiled from fragments of an oral tradition related by Simionce. Brooklyn. Winter, 2007. Recorded and collated by Philip Durrant, PhD.</u>

<u>The Life and Origin of the famous Nicholas of Saxony, a royal hostage, flute player, seer and magician who was first converted to Christianity by St Alcuin and reverted to the Dark Arts. His story has been handed down by one who knew him, a descendant of 'the Wicked Gypsy' of the Eastern regions, to his tribe and his descendants for posterity.</u>

The scurrilous fellow, hardly a man, whom I once called 'friend', begins my story. He is known by his tribe as a descendant of the Wicked Gypsy, and is a wanderer through the world. A small, black, gibbering thing, akin to the monkeys in Charlemagne's menagerie.

This monkey of a man – a gypsy as he called himself – was a great favourite with the ladies of the court and became of much interest to me, a lust-filled young prince, when daily he recited his disgusting habits; one of which was being suckled in the bosoms of wet nurses, highborn ladies and dames. I was so much above him in stature and in mind that it pleased me to have him trail behind and make me laugh. He is given to hanging in my cloak, even though I forbade the practice.

As for me, I was a man filled with such vengeance that it tore me apart. I vowed vengeance on their odious god, who hung meekly on a cross for three hours and died, leaving behind his followers, who have the effrontery to claim true divinity for him and his supremacy as the one, true God.

Oh, my own god of vengeance, bring me justice for what has been done to me. My Christian name is Nicholas, but I am and shall always be the handsome prince who was taken as a boy hostage into Charles's household after he captured me in a fierce battle with his Christian army against my own tribe, the Saxonia, whom it took thirty years to bring to heel.

We are a savage race, who worship not the Christian God but the powerful gods of the earth and sky, who roam through the world crying 'Havoc!' and 'Death to our enemies!' We are pledged to devilish practices and dance with the Master of Darkness himself. But those sweet rites and battle days are over, and now we are cowed after thirty years of war. Inside, we seethe and long to rise against our conquerors.

By my calculations I am now 36 years old. At 13, I was pulled by my golden hair across the battlefield and taken as a hostage by the victor, the Frankish king, Charles. This year of 800,when I begin writing my own Bible, the unholy Codex, Charles, my oppressor, will be crowned Emperor by the sinful Pope of Rome at the Christian festival of Christmas and renamed by his people as Charlemagne.

I call this Pope sinful because, last spring, his own people attacked him and attempted to blind him and cut out his tongue for his wrongdoing, but he fled to Charlemagne's camp, then returned to Rome with the King and crowned him Emperor in St Peter's. This weary ceremony I was forced to attend.

How many times have I counted on an abacus those wearisome years since I was taken? I wished to die on the field of battle, but I was saved to do a monk's bidding, and taught how to read and write with the children of the palace, the **pueri paladini***. We were an aristocratic crew. Though I was hated by the youths, I was loved by all women, including a high-born lady close to the Emperor, who had borne him a daughter. They gave her a title: Princess Hildegarde. From this, much of the hate originated.*

My cursed master Alcuin was adviser to Charlemagne and a stern punisher of the boys in his charge. I was whipped by him often for my vanity, but secretly, at nights, I dawdled through the cloisters and delighted in my handsome image in the pool where the great fish lie. Now Alcuin has been replaced by another, made in his likeness.

Alcuin was the one who thrust my head under the water thrice and baptised me. I was given the name Nicholas. I laughed when I discovered Nicholas was one of their Christian saints, the patron of children and prostitutes. I have always debated why those two are put together under one sainthood! The monk, Alcuin, was and ever will be my deadly enemy, since he forced me into that Christian baptism. I cursed Alcuin then, and I curse him still, even though he is gone now, as I sit on my stool working on my leaf of parchment. By day, I spend my time copying the Christian Bible, for which I have no respect. No more do I hear the old legends of war from the lips of those slavish monks, but the message of forgiveness holds no attraction for me, who have sworn revenge on my masters. I have been taught my scripture, but in my head I have secretly devised my own creed. It is my own sacrilegious Bible, the Codex, in which I stamp my image. My book is hidden, but one day its secrets will be revealed. Secrets born of visions and hate.

These days I am strong and lustful, with no Christian God to curb my desires for drink and women. I am now made a clerk of the chapel, as I am possessed of a wondrous talent for music and a superb singing voice. I have been forced to be celibate.

As an unredeemed hostage I slave still, but I have kept my hair and have not suffered castration like other sweet-toned boys that I have heard of. No tonsure for me, as my golden hair still falls full on my shoulders, so different from the bald ugliness of the monks. I have the Princess Hildegarde's mother to thank for that, because I know more about her lustful desires than does her husband.

I have been taught that lust is a sin, but that lady must sin every time she looks at me! But I have always told myself, I would rather lie with the Devil than with a Christian hag.

The first time I met the Princess Hildegarde, who until then I had seen only from afar, was when she approached my master to question him about me. I, who have ears as keen as a hungry wolf's, listened, smiling inwardly. We had seen each other from afar for many years, but had been kept apart lest our desires got the better of us.

'Who is the fair one?' she asked the master of the monks who has replaced Alcuin, who is gone to die in Tours. The master smiled fondly at her, and in my heart I reviled him, as I knew he

lusted for her childish body too.

'That is Nicholas, your Highness. The hostage prince from Saxony. He is trained to scribe in my household and sing in the choir.'

'Yes, I have heard of him,' she said. 'He was once my fellow pupil. May I see what he is writing?'

'You shall, Highness. But I must make him fit before you may approach him.' In other words, he meant to threaten me, to dissuade me from uttering words that might make the Princess blush. I should have been beaten, I admit, because the 15-year-old with her golden braids and her lissom child's body promised much to a young man whose tastes were no longer those of an unformed boy. She had learned how to work on parchment too, but I think as a female she had less wit than I. She had attended school by the order of Charlemagne, who spent his time at war like a proper man. He loved war, as we all do, but some of us have no chance to pursue this noble calling anymore. I am a hostage and kept away from the battlefield, where I would happily die rather than be imprisoned here in the scriptorium.

From then onwards, I had hot dreams of becoming Hildegarde's tutor; but even her mother will not allow that. I am still as much a slave as I ever was, hated by all in the Chapter, because I am favoured by that noble mother, who was once less faithful to the child's father! I know that is the truth.

Yet that day, when the child princess leaned over me, I put my cool hand over her little hot one, and the master stepped forward, his eyes blazing.

'No, let him, Fr Abbot,' the princess said. 'I have never seen such beautiful script. Look at the angel.'

I had been working on depictions of an angel and the Virgin Mary, and had meant to let the lady's dugs slip out of her dress. It would have been the finest initial letter that a man had ever seen. But it had been noticed by the master of scribes, who had carried it to our master, and he had had it painted out and beaten me for sacrilege. Thus, the Virgin was still sickeningly demure.

'I wish I could do that, Fr Abbot,' Hildegarde exclaimed, staring first at me with wide blue eyes. I had made the angel in my own likeness, but crowned it in gold, rather than dark like

my idol, Lucifer. Then she looked up with awakening knowledge that the image was mine, but my eyes told her not to speak. She understood, but her round cheeks were flaming. I traced with her small be-ringed hand – dwarfed by a mighty cabochon, as befitted a lady of her rank – the shape of the letters on my parchment. I knew how she felt at my touch, and as for me, I felt hers for hot nights after, when I lusted for this living virgin. The odious little creature in my cloak, that wicked small gypsy, was doing things to me also, too lewd even to tell.

And the Princess came to see me again and again until she was enchanted. Most nights now, I play my swan-bone flute, its song drawing Hildegarde to me, making her toss on her silken bed. And now at last I know she will be coming to me like a pretty moth caught in a spider's web. But her killing will be not by sword, but by coupling.

Now, daily, she is brought to me by her maids on the pretence of learning my art. Her women giggle and point at me, until I pierce them with my wolf-blue eyes. My master always calls for a stool to be brought for her to sit beside me and watch me work on Revelation. I admit I have the nimblest fingers in the Chapter, which comes from playing the flute and holding the goose pen. In dreams I feel her sweet breath on my face in the hot of the night and imagine her pretty shoes and what is underneath her skirt, and I will my pagan gods to reveal her maiden secrets to me.

One burning eve in the middle of July, a storm was brewing inside me, reminding me of those hot nights when we Saxonia called up the Devil and danced with him in the forests at home. I have always been a seer, even as a child, lying in my hard little bed, conjuring up the spirits of sleep, who floated forth from the grave to obey me. Now, as a man, I am more powerful.

So, with the promise of the Princess within my grasp, I called up my visions and felt a great heat come upon me. That night it was my fate to have her. She bent over me before she left with her maids, her scented rope of hair brushing my lectern. Her little hand was as hot and plump as ever, while I was hard as a rock.

'Come and play your swan-bone flute for me tonight,' she whispered; and although I knew she was an innocent, her

mother's blood ran in her veins.

'What about your maids?' I whispered, and she blushed.

'They will gather to sleep in another chamber. They are afraid of storms. But I ...' She blushed again. 'I wish the storm would come, so we can ...'

Her voice was low and sent thrills through me. I felt very wicked.

'Walk in the forest?' I asked.

'Not so far that we are lost?' She looked alarmed.

'I know the forest well, Princess.' I had good cause for saying so. There were many I consorted with at the Court of Charlemagne who were not as holy as the Emperor. Unfrocked priests and servants, slaves like me and wild gypsies like my dark companion, who came from the East and wandered the world. Many of these would meet in the moonlit forest the eve of 22 July, which is the Feast of Mary Magdalene. They gather in remembrance of what that holy woman was before she became a saint.

Holy monks like my master insist they do not believe in sorcery and try to convince men of their errors. But I was brought up with pagan rites and have no patience with the hypocrisy of priests.

Such monks promise vengeance and punishment to men and women who serve demons, who cast spells and interpret dreams. But they will never root out these magical practices, which have been within me since my birth. The Princess was staring at me now.

'I am afraid of the forest deeps,' she said. 'Wild animals roam there.'

'Ay, Princess,' I replied. 'Does not your father go there for sport almost every day to kill those animals? They would be afraid of the Princess Hildegarde.' A delightful giggle followed my lie.

'That is for sure,' she said, and I smiled with her. 'But what if there really is a storm?' I felt her shiver. Her luminous eyes were fixed on me, and I knew she was entranced.

'I shall command it to cease,' I replied. She put a nervous hand to her mouth, so I assured her that I was not blaspheming, *but was making a joke. It did no good, because she was taken in completely.*

'Are you one of the tempestarii? *They who command the storms? Please tell me.' Many gullible folks believed these spirits conjured up magical storms, sailing between the clouds in strange vessels.*

'I promise you I am only a man. I do not ride in the storm clouds. And the tempest will not hurt you. I can play my flute for you in the moonlight. I know a glade where you can sit on a great stone and listen. There is even a chapel there to guard you.'

'But what if my mother finds out?'

'You mother will understand. Nor will she tell your father. Remember, I have been brought up in a godly atmosphere.' Women always said my lop-sided smile was very attractive. 'After midnight, I shall come for you.'

'Very well,' she said. I saw her maids' eyes flick toward me, then turn away. They realised I knew what they were thinking, which is an art of mine. A moment later, she was gone. She would be mine that night, and no-one would stop me from what I was about to do.

Every time he read this, Pip was tantalised. He could only imagine – a dangerous thing in a researcher. He sighed. The notes he had gleaned from old Simionce's words had ended. He would know no more until Anya enlightened him. His fear was that she would know only the same. He had been crazy to discover what had happened that night of 22 July, when the 15-year-old virgin princess had been lured away by the killer in monkish habit. He would never know how much had been lost in the oral handing down through successions of gypsy generations, nor what elaborations had been made to the material for an enthusiastic audience.

He had also researched as much as he was able the monkey-like gypsy shadow of the Piper. That this reviled being, who was the stuff of legends, was supposed to be one of Ghita's predecessors was a sobering thought ...

Some things were beginning to be clear in his mind though. He was mulling them over when he was startled by a sharp knock at the door. He looked round the dim room. It was getting dark and he had not noticed. Stretching out an arm, he touched the light panel. Nothing happened. *Must be a power cut,* he thought. Daylight on tap was something he'd come to expect in his American city home, and technology had provided it, but Oxford was not as advanced. There was no spy hole in the sturdy door that led into the corridor. He had heard no creaking of footsteps on the aged floorboards outside. He hovered at his side of the door, like they do in detective movies.

'Who is it?'

'Olga.' The voice wasn't as girlish and gentle as he remembered. He opened the door tentatively, to reveal not Olga but a tall, unfamiliar youth with his hood pulled up.

'What the hell?' Pip looked down the corridor. Empty. 'Who the fuck are you? How do you know Olga?'

The boy was grinning. 'She's my girlfriend. Pretty good at her voice, aren't I?'

Pip tried to slam the door shut, but the boy's strong body was in between. Pip had his hand in his pocket before he realised his mobile was on the table.

'It's all right, I'm not a hoodie!' said the kid. 'Okay, I'm sorry I said I was Olga, but I sensed you wouldn't see me …' he hesitated, ' … if I introduced myself as Klaas Honen …'

'You're Honen?' So this was the boy whom Anya thought dangerous, and with whom Ghita's daughter was smitten.

'American but Germanic in origin.' The hood was off. He was a striking-looking kid, sleek brown hair, dark eyes. He had an edge about him. He was one you wouldn't mess with. One the girls would go for. 'I'm not dangerous. I'm not popular in certain quarters, either …' He grimaced in a mocking fashion.

'So I've been told. What the hell have you come to see me for?'

'Because I'd like some help.'

They were still standing in close proximity. Pip stepped back. The kid nodded – and waited. He didn't try to push the door any further open. From what Pip had heard, he wasn't the kind who asked for help. There was something wrong with this. *No*, thought Pip, *you have another motive for coming here, Mr Honen. Maybe you think you'll get me onside?*

'Oh, well, this isn't the way to win my approval!' said Pip. A smile flicked around the boy's lips, but he remained silent, and Pip realised that this bumptious kid felt he was getting the upper hand here. He wasn't looking for approval. No, it was more than that – and Pip really wanted to know what it was. 'You'd better come in then, Klaas,' he added, stepping back again. With a tiny gesture of his head – possibly instead of thanks – Klaas walked through. For some reason, Pip was worried about his open notebooks on the desk, so he overtook him and closed his work. 'Sit down.'

'Sir.' Surprising, thought Pip. A moment later, Klaas's long, jean-clad legs were stretched out from his easy chair.

Pip came over and sat at his desk, swivelling his own chair round after he had closed his laptop. Something inside told him it would be better to hide what he was working on from this 'boy wonder', as he had been labelled.

Klaas was silent, so Pip began the conversation. 'Whatever you've really come for, I'm not sure, but I don't care for deceit. Of any kind.'

The boy acknowledged this with a nod in the easy, dismissive manner that Pip had seen in so many truculently arrogant adolescents. 'I think in the end it will be worth it, though. For both of us,' answered Klaas, with no hint of remorse. Confidence exuded from him.

'Let me be the judge of that,' said Pip. 'I had an idea you were going to push your way in. Maybe you were?'

'I thought about it, Professor, but – nope. Why would I? I was sure you were going to let me in; and, besides, I've been longing to meet you. I admire your books.'

Pip ignored that. 'How did you get into this building?'

'Yeah, well, let's say I have contacts here.'

'I'm not impressed. And I'm not susceptible to flattery, either.'

'As it happens, neither am I,' said the kid. 'Come on,

Professor, this is heavy.'

'Nor wheedling. I'm busy.'

'I think you have just finished what you're doing, though.'

Pip blocked Klaas's desktop view with his body. Then he wondered why he had done it. What harm could the kid possibly do to him?

'But I can see you have important things in hand,' added Klaas. 'I won't be here long. Promise.'

'No, you won't. What I want to know is why you're here at all. I don't usually allow students in to see me unless I've invited them.' Pip wanted to find out how brazen this kid could really be, and what Olga saw in him. He didn't seem her type.

'That figures.'

'What do you want? I'm not going to be teaching you.' Pip's mind was wandering. Even the kid's haircut was challenging, dark and spiky.

'My mother won't like it,' was the surprising result of Pip's appraisal. 'I take after her. She can get in anywhere.'

'I don't know her, but I assume she waits to be invited.' Inside, he was thinking, *You sound like on old fart, Durrant. You want to know what makes this kid tick, so say so!*

Klaas shrugged. 'I came here because I knew you'd be interested in what I have to say.' He leaned forward and added, 'Yeah, definitely, you are an interested party, because you really needed to meet me.'

'To meet you? What gives you that idea?'

'I think you don't want to see Olga hurt?'

Pip looked away, then back at him. He felt uncomfortable. It was like the boy was reading his thoughts. He didn't like it.

'Why should I think that? I hardly know your girlfriend!'

'You know Ghita. You've been looking for each other for years.' Klaas shrugged.

'Olga told you that!' was Pip's immediate response.

'She tells me everything!'

'She also told me you were clever, but you are going the way to really upset me.' Pip looked at his phone. Then his watch. 'I could report you for coming in here like this.'

'Cool,' replied Klaas. 'No-one will be surprised if you report me. This kind of thing has happened before. They don't want to lose me.'

Pip frowned. 'You're saying you don't care if you're reported to the Provost? You think it's cool to be reported? You're playing with fire.'

Klaas seemed startled. 'No, I meant your watch, Professor. It's cool. I saw one like that in an antiques shop. I guess your dad gave you it?' He jutted out his chin and lifted his perfectly-shaped eyebrows. Underneath, something in the darkness of those eyes gave Pip a jolt of recognition, and he had no idea why. He felt wary, even uncertain, faced with such instant deviousness.

'Am I right?' said Klaas. Pip could see all this was a game to him. He was already a master of cross-purpose. He wanted to get Pip rattled. 'Your dad did give you that watch, Professor,' he persisted. He was maddening.

'Actually, he did,' replied Pip, as coolly as he could muster. 'I guess now you'd better tell me why you're really here. Let's stop playing games, because we're wasting time. Okay, we'll talk – for a while. I have things to do, but I think I can stretch to a cup of coffee. You?'

'Cool.' The sarcasm was obvious.

At that moment, if Pip had possessed the true gift of prophecy like Eva Kirchma or Simionce, he would have known this first meeting of theirs was not only a milestone on the journey to his ultimate goal of defeating his evil adversary, but the key to his long search; both embodied in this arrogant youngster, who was not only a polymath, but also an extraordinary visionary.

7

As they sat, regarding each other, Pip thought of his first meeting in 2007 with Simu Dalca at the University in Cluj. What had brought it into his mind, he wasn't sure. Maybe it was because this time he was the Professor and Klaas the student. It had taken a long time for Pip and Simu to reveal their secrets to each other. Later, he had realised it would have been better for both of them if they had done so much earlier. And one secret he still didn't know was what Simu Dalca had been coming to the airport to tell him, in that mad dash that had resulted in his death.

He dragged himself back to the present and discovered Klaas staring at him in silence. One of them needed to speak, to make the first move. Yet Klaas's expression was blank. Even Pip, a practised psychologist, could not read anything in it. The calm that surrounded the kid was eerie, given the atmosphere of the last few moments. It was as if he had shut down, causing that restless energy he had created in the room to subside.

Klaas seemed to be waiting for him to speak, but Pip's need for instant gratification had passed. He preferred to give the boy time to explain the real reason for his visit – and, hopefully, to be unguarded enough to give a clue as to the secrets he was hiding.

It would be better for Klaas if he did, because, as Pip had told himself when he first met Dalca, *Secrets bring terror, and the result of terror lasts for a very long time. It doesn't go away.*

What was the boy scared of? And, more worrying, why was Pip unsettled by him? In 2007, it would have been unheard of for Pip to be giving advice to a man of Dalca's stature and experience. Now, as the older man, his inner voice was warning him it would be puerile to try to offer wisdom to Klaas. As yet, Pip, who had dealt with a variety of students in his professional life, had not worked this out.

Maybe this is wisdom. To keep quiet, he thought, wishing he had been wise all those years ago. Maybe then Simu might have been spared. He continued to wait. The unspoken request in his eyes for Klaas to begin was ignored for a moment, until finally the youth broke the silence. Now there was no verbal fencing.

'I was waiting for *The Last Vision*,' said Klaas. 'I read it straight off, and ...' Pip caught his breath. ' ...and I can supply some of your answers – but you mightn't like them.' There was no hint of uncertainty in the statement. Just a confidence that could belong only to someone of that age. Black and white.

Pip was trying to decide whether this kid was a fake with an enormous ego or the real thing, with something to say that would be in his interest to hear.

'Note, I didn't say "think", Professor. I know.' Klaas was studying him with those curtained eyes, drawing them into indecipherable darkness. This was no time to offer some platitude, or challenge him, or even mock him.

'Okay,' replied Pip, 'I'll go along with you. Fire away then.'

Klaas frowned. 'You don't think I'm serious? I thought better of you, Professor. I've seen that look before. Disbelief. I'm disappointed. I thought I could trust you.'

'You can, but you have to take into account how I feel,' replied Pip. 'Although this is not common knowledge, my books were written with a specific purpose. To find someone who would say to me exactly what you have just said, and then back it up. Someone who would come with a reasoned explanation. Not just appear at my door and enter my world without warning.'

'I think you've had too many warnings,' replied Klaas.

'Explain that,' demanded Pip.

'This is not easy for me. I don't want you ...' Surprisingly, he seemed to struggle for the words. 'I don't want you to think I'm crazy!' He grimaced. 'Yeah, that's got that shit out of the way then.'

'Has somebody else told you that, then? Do you think I would say it to you? If I thought you were, you wouldn't be sitting in that chair. Is it that – or your pride – that's holding you back now? Just tell me how it is, and I'll listen. '

'I thought you were busy.'

'Not too busy for this. You have to realise that saying you have answers that I've been searching for since 2007 – answers that good men and women have died for, men who were good friends of mine – is going to make me jumpy. Doubtless you have a fine brain, but this ...'

Pip broke off, got up and pulled the curtains on the dreary darkness of the afternoon. Then he paused in shock. The frosty roofs below had an unearthly glow, and he caught his breath as he saw a tall figure standing in the doorway to his building. He jumped back before the man looked up, and to his embarrassment found himself sweating. He turned to Klaas, who was watching his every move.

'It's hot in here. Were you telling me the truth when you said you came alone?'

'Why? Is there someone down there?' replied Klaas, unwinding his legs and standing up.

'He's probably gone now,' answered Pip.

'I'll check?'

Pip nodded. As Klaas passed him, the kid had a strange look in those expressive eyes. 'Is it a friend of yours?' Pip asked. Long experience told him it wasn't, and that someone would pay for it.

'I don't have friends.' Klaas looked down, then turned away. 'But the same man visits me too.'

'You mean the man with the hood?' Pip felt little shivers run through him as he tried to take in the possibility. 'You mean you know him? Who is he?' He heard the urgency in his tone, which he couldn't suppress.

'I was right to come to you.' Klaas was staring at him, which made Pip angry. Why couldn't the goddamn kid answer the question? He was cross at himself for feeling like he did. At the student's mercy.

'You're playing tricks,' he snapped. 'What does he do, then, this man with the hood?'

'Let's say his visits spook me out. I can see they do you.' Klaas's tone had changed too. 'Believe me, Prof, I see him too. He has been with me for a long time.' As he spoke, Pip was struggling with himself. If it was indeed true – and he wanted it to be, and not to be – unknown possibilities presented themselves.

'With you for a long time?' repeated Pip. 'How?'

'I hoped you'd want to know. You don't know how much.' It was the first emotion Klaas had shown.

Pip remained silent. To commit himself would draw him in to what was perhaps a fantasy dreamed up by some clever kid, who just wanted to get him rattled – and he didn't want that; he wanted to be an observer, to be in control as he always had been. Klaas's strange eyes were fixed on him as if he were reading his mind.

'I have read all your books, Professor. Academic and fiction. You picked a good title for the latest one, because I can tell you, *The Last Vision* really will be your last if we don't join forces.'

Pip stared at him. 'Who do you think you are?' he asked. 'Do you think I'm an idiot? What you just said – what was it? Some kind of threat? I've had experience of dealing with kids like you.'

Klaas's half-smile curled at the corners of his mouth. Then his expression changed to ruefulness, tinged with sardonic amusement. 'I'm a 17-year-old student of history, who has never wished to be ordinary, and has always succeeded.'

'Cut the crap,' responded Pip. 'I'm not going to feed your arrogance. Let's go back to the question I asked. I can assure you I am not an idiot. You want me to join forces with you, because you think that a hooded man lurking outside has something to do with me. You think I need you. Why should I?' He stopped, then looked at him, trying to divine his motives. 'What do you really know about me?'

'I've read your books, and it seems to me, Professor Durrant, that you need help too. And it's all in here,' said Klaas, tapping his head. 'Before I forget it. And unless I get a response from you, I shall go on to another life. To Olga.'

'For Christ's sake, why did you pick on her? Leave her alone – and her family!' The outburst was spontaneous. He thought of Anya saying the boy was dangerous.

Klaas was shaking his head. 'I wouldn't hurt Olga. She's already part of me.'

Pip felt cold. What did that mean? Had he been sleeping with her? All at once, it really mattered, but before he had time to say anything, Klaas was on his feet. Pip got up too. They faced each other.

'I wasn't going to say any of this,' Klaas went on, 'but you drove me into a corner.' All of a sudden, he seemed just a scared teenager, the kind Pip had been treating on and off for years. 'What I mean is, I wasn't expecting to go so far. Listen! You can help me. That's why I came here tonight.

'Professor, I have dreams – but they're not dreams. They are …' He grimaced as if it hurt. 'They are real – I have found that out. They lead me and I follow them; and I know this sounds crazy …' he hesitated, then swallowed as if the words were stuck, '… just crazy, but sometimes, I think I am that shape down there in the quad. He's me …

'You look scared. I'm scared too, because then … then I do bad things. But, believe me, they are not my fault …'

'What things?' Pip couldn't help thinking of Ghita, Olga and Anya.

'I said what I did, because I do think you're like me, like this. That you have dreams too. I can smell it on you – the fear …' He was becoming agitated.

'For Christ's sake, stop it,' interrupted Pip, his mind weighing up the possibilities. Was Klaas unbalanced – or could he be genuine? Pip thought back to when he had been 13. He hadn't been ill, only locked in a prison he had made for himself. And he hadn't been crazy. Was this kid like that? The things he'd just described would have seemed impossible to most people – but Pip knew they were possible. Hadn't he himself been looking for something, someone to tell? Maybe, just maybe … He stood, silent. Then he heard the little voice of intuition inside, prompting him: *Listen to the kid!*

'And this is why you turned up at my rooms? To pretend to give me hell? But you really wanted my help?' asked Pip. He could see Klaas was returning to the calm that he had probably built around himself – to protect him. Pip wanted to believe that, but he was wary.

'Olga knows that I'm here. She told me to come. She said she was certain you'd help me.'

Pip shook his head, torn as to whether or not to believe him. It could all still be a trick. 'Olga doesn't know me either!' he accused.

'She said she feels she's always known you.'

Pip stared at him. This was the kind of fantasy liars built for those who wanted something badly enough to believe.

'I've been to a shrink,' offered Klaas. He turned away. 'To a guy like you as well. The shrink couldn't help me. I'm here, and you know what I'm talking about. I know you do. You're one of us.'

'One of us? For Christ's sake, that's enough,' ordered Pip. To his shock, Klaas stepped toward him with fists clenched. He braced himself, expecting be attacked. Klaas was as far into his personal space as any patient had ever been. But Klaas wasn't his patient!

'Give me a chance, Professor, for fuck's sake. I don't believe in God. I'm split – in here.' He tapped his head again.

'Move away,' said Pip. The kid withdrew. 'Have you been diagnosed as schizophrenic?'

'No.' The tension eased.

'Okay, let's sit down again, shall we?' Pip indicated the chairs. 'No more about you needing my help and me needing yours. I'd like to ask you a personal question, Klaas.' The boy nodded. 'Why does Anya dislike you so much? You talked about doing things. What have you done to her?' He felt he was back in control and Klaas had regained his self-possession.

'What do you think? She thinks she knows what I am.'

Pip made a mental note: the kid hadn't said *who I am*. 'Okay, just for the record, what do *you* think you are?'

'She hates me.' Pip's question had been ignored, but Klaas wouldn't get off that easily.

'You may think that, but could it be something else maybe? Is she scared for Olga? Does she think Olga's too young for you? That you're not good for her?'

'No!' The reply was vehement. 'I know she wants me out of their life. If she could kill me, she would.'

'Hold on there …' Pip regarded him, then ventured, 'Anya wouldn't kill anyone. She's afraid for Olga.'

'Afraid of me. I have never done anything to Olga.' Klaas sprang up from the chair.

'Now, earlier on, you said … "I do bad things"! Do you think that's what she meant? What have you done, Klaas?'

There was vehemence in the way Klaas shook his head, dismissing Pip's words. 'Maybe it is what the old lady thinks she knows that scares her. But it isn't about *that*. People only *think* these things. They're just – scared of me. She knows …' He hesitated, then continued. 'As they say here in England, *It takes one to know one*.'

'So, you're telling me that you are like Anya. In what way?'

'I know what game you're playing, Professor. We're wasting time. I'm the same as you – and her,' he reiterated.

'And how could I be like Anya?' Pip was determined to know what the kid thought he was.

'Do you want a demonstration?' was Klaas's amazing response.

Pip forced himself to keep control. To be professional, be ordered in what he was thinking. Emotion mustn't come into this. 'That would be very interesting. But, no, not at this minute.' He thrust away the thought that the boy might be crazy enough to try something.

Klaas shook his head. 'That will come soon enough,' he answered. 'When you get to know me. To believe me.'

'I'm not saying I don't believe you,' Pip pandered to him. 'But back to my earlier question. Please sit down. What do you think you are, Klaas? A mind-reader, a magician or …?' He paused and waited.

'I am a seer. A visionary. Call it what you want. I see things.' Klaas's face was a sombre mask.

Pip felt a shiver run through him. He had not expected it to be put so bluntly. What he would have given to have spoken with such confidence himself! Years ago, he would have told the kid to leave and slammed the door behind him. Now his mind was open to all possibilities. He was a changed man. But he would not allow himself to be overawed by this 17-year-old.

'I have read many books,' Klaas went on, 'and it is the only answer. I said this to a shrink once, and he asked me if I was a druggie.'

'And are you?'

The response was a shake of the head.

'Do your parents know about you being a *seer*, as you call it?'

'My mother is happy with it.'

Pip filed that away mentally. 'And your father?'

'I don't know him – and I don't want to!' The answer was passionate.

Add *dysfunctional*, thought Pip. 'And you think you can control these visions?' No reply. 'Where do you think this power of yours comes from? Is it innate? Natural? Supernatural?' The boy was silent. Not a good sign.

Then Klaas burst out, 'You don't know what I can do! *Or do you?*'

'No, we don't want to discuss that again.' Pip was calm. 'Not now, anyway. I think we should leave it there?' He could see the kid getting agitated again, and he wasn't ready. He had to think this one out. To formulate a plan as to how to proceed. He needed to protect himself.

'Okay, Prof. Why don't you ask someone who knows me?'

'Maybe I shall,' replied Pip. His tone was measured but, inside, he felt as shaken up as the agitated young man in front of him.

'Ask Spencer James. He doesn't like me. Olga knows him. I was at school with him.'

'I'm looking for the truth, not lies.'

'Oh, he'll give you that. He's too scared not to.'

'I shall ask him.'

'Then I can come back? I can pay.'

'No need for that.' Pip lifted his hands. 'Just informal talks. I have plenty of time. You're a very interesting young guy to talk to, Klaas.'

The boy got up again and walked over to the door, his face pale under the thatch of unkempt dark hair. At that moment, he seemed very young and vulnerable. Pip followed, blaming himself for putting the screws on him. He held out his hand. 'Please don't think I don't take you seriously, Klaas. I just wanted to make sure we know where we stand.' His offer of peace was implicit.

To his consternation, the kid's resulting smile was of pure satisfaction, if not triumph. A moment later, he took Pip's hand with a grip like sealing an ancient bond, followed by: 'Please tell Anya when you meet her to be careful.'

'How do you know I'm meeting her? What are you going to do?' Pip asked. The old shiver that had returned was now replaced by a cold anger as he realised how easily he had fallen into Klaas's trap.

'Nothing. I'm only anxious,' Klaas replied. 'Like I told you, when I'm upset, things happen.'

Next time, you are not getting away with this, thought Pip. 'Okay, I'll tell her,' he responded, mustering up all the presence of mind he could. 'I'll also be in touch. And don't come uninvited next time.'

Klaas nodded, pulled up his hood, bent his head and made for the door. Once again, he looked like any miserable student leaving his tutor's rooms – though that was certainly not the case.

Pip shut the door behind him and secured it, then hurried across to the window and waited to see the young man come out of the building. He watched him cross the quad – alone, as expected. No other hooded figure accompanied him, and Pip realised he wasn't in the least surprised.

Pip went over to the cupboard, pulled out a bottle of spirits and swigged a mouthful. This was the most stressed he'd felt since … He considered the last time, but that didn't make him feel any better.

Later, he sat down in the friendly glow of his living room to consider his first impressions of Klaas. Were they what he had expected, based on what Ghita and Anya had told him earlier? His interest in the young polymath had been first awakened when Ghita had confided that she was worried about Olga's coming exams. She had felt that her daughter's chances of success was being hindered by her obsession with her boyfriend. Following that had come Anya's vehement revelation that not only did she not like Klaas, but she thought he was dangerous.

In Pip's opinion, the two women were both justified in their fears. With the story he had told Pip, whether true or false, the kid had shown the power to enrapture. Pip could see how a 15-year-old teenager like Olga could be obsessed with him.

As for danger? Pip felt sure that Klaas could be dangerous, although as yet he had no proof. The boy's sinister assertion that 'things happen' could be looked at in various ways, from a psychologist's perspective. All he had to go on at that moment was Klaas's defence of his own assertion, in the form of the name of someone who could supposedly back it up. Pip couldn't wait. He reduced this challenge to a note on his mobile: *Check out Spencer James (Olga's friend). Find out as much as possible about KH.*

It was certainly worth doing. He had to know whether the boy was a criminal or not. Maybe he wouldn't find any proof, and Klaas would turn out to be delusional, or perhaps just a first-class boaster and liar? He remembered that air of vulnerability and thought how easy it would be to be taken in by it. The kid could probably turn it on at will; and even Pip, who was used to such ploys, had been taken by surprise and almost convinced. It hadn't worked on Anya, though.

Klaas's hints that he had some kind of supernatural gift and would be willing to demonstrate it, followed by his suggestion that Pip would be the beneficiary, now seemed even more bizarre. Even so, the seeds had been planted, and they were presently germinating in Pip's mind, telling him that Klaas *might* be able to do what he claimed. He had discovered in the course of his quest that he had to be prepared to suspend disbelief, however unwilling he might be.

As yet, Pip had no real idea as to how he could help Klaas. But instinctively he felt that he wanted – even needed – to meet the boy again and dig further into the morass of a truly fascinating mind, unbalanced or not.

However, Klaas's confident statements of power, and the threats he had followed them with, were unsettling, and made Pip afraid that he might be open to being taken in by a criminal or a charlatan. Pip himself had been careful to hide any hint of supernatural involvement for as long as he could, as had the late Marcu ... and he knew that if Simu Dalca had been with him now, the Professor would have warned him to take it easy, to be careful, as that 'quagmire' of Klaas's mind, which was no doubt brilliant, could be confused and muddled, however confident he appeared.

Pip considered the dilemma. Assuming he came to believe Klaas, would he ever be able to trust him with the information he held? Yet, inside, he was awakening to the fact that, on the strength of one meeting, he was willing to take the risk to investigate what Klaas was offering him. Pip had always been a risk-taker.

Whoever the kid really was, he didn't know, but in spite of any earlier misgivings, Pip told himself he needed to find out what this 17-year-old could do; for his own sake, as well as for those he loved, and those he had lost.

Pip received the call he had been waiting for the following morning. Anya's tone told him she was nervous of anyone overhearing the conversation. Little did she know his mood matched hers.

'Can you meet me at the café in the square by the bus station at 2.00 pm?' she asked, with a tremble of fear in her voice. 'In the corner. We can sit at the back. Olga has gone out and Ghita is working late. I've prepared their dinner.' She paused, as if that were the most precious function in her world – which it probably had been, since they became a family. Pip felt guilty as well as nervously elated. 'I …' she went on, then hesitated …

Pip waited, scared she was going to change her mind, then got in first: 'Great!' His enthusiasm was entirely real. 'Are you sure that's okay?' He knew he'd made a mistake the moment he said it. He had meant her choice of the café, not her suggestion to meet. When she had told him the venue, he had felt that somewhere more private would be preferable for him to hear whatever dark secrets she had to disclose. She didn't reply straightaway. Had she changed her mind? Had he lost her? Then she began again, and this time her tones were measured, less afraid.

'Don't worry, Professor, I shall be there. Many people in and out. Much talking. No-one to listen.' The last words came out in a rush, then tailed off. He imagined her looking over her shoulder as she spoke.

'Why should I think otherwise, Anya? I meant, wouldn't you rather go to a hotel, which would be more comfortable …'

'What would I do in a hotel? No. The café. In the corner of the square. I go there when I am out.'

'Yes, okay, that'll be good. I'll be there. At two,' he said.

He was hoping his voice sounded firm; that it would give her courage. The thought of what Anya might be able to tell him had provided him already with a taste of something he recognised, something he hadn't felt for a long time – save for when Klaas had left his rooms the night before. That meeting had reminded Pip that the gods were on his side. He hoped it would still be so.

As Anya had indicated, the café was the kind of place where no-one would notice them.

Pip arrived first and wandered about outside, glancing up and down. He was anxious. When he saw her approach, her words came back into his head. *What would I do in a hotel?*

She was wearing the customary headscarf of the elderly Romanian woman, heavily patterned jumper and pleated homespun skirt. She would have been very out of place further up the road, seated in a curtained alcove at The Randolph. Yet, Black Anya was very precious to Pip. She was in possession of the thing he desired most of all – another piece in the puzzle of the Piper's story.

He thought about other planned meetings on the same subject when his contact had never appeared, and was relieved to see no harm had befallen Anya. She was leaning on her stick, her gait far removed from the lively step he had known 17 years before, when he had met her at the gypsy settlement.

He hurried to open the door for the stooped figure and followed her into the café, conscious of the glances of the elderly man at the counter and the swarthy young man waiting on tables.

Anya sat down, her stick dropping with a clatter beside her. As Pip bent to retrieve it, setting his laptop case down beside his own chair, he noticed those once-bright eyes were dull and had almost disappeared under the thin crepe veil of her eyelids.

'I'm glad you made it, Anya,' he said. 'Would you like coffee, tea?'

'Nothing,' she replied, but the young waiter was coming over.

'Just coffee for me. Latte, please,' said Pip.

'Extra large, large or standard?'

'Standard.'

The man sniffed, and turned to Anya. 'And you?'

'Nothing.'

The man shrugged and moved away.

Anya was smiling. 'You were always the gentleman, Pip Durrant. More than some. But you do not always say what you mean.'

'Thank you. It's a defensive habit.'

'We all have something to fear.' In her smile, he recognised a vestige of the strong woman he had first met outside her van in the gypsy camp.

'Some more than most,' he replied. She nodded. 'I'm grateful you came,' he added.

'I keep my promises,' she said. She looked round, as if she was afraid someone was watching. 'Sorry,' she added, 'it is a habit. Please, Professor, I would like to speak in Romanian.'

'All right – but not too fast. I'm rusty.'

'You did well enough the other day,' she retorted.

'I surprised myself,' he replied, 'but that's fine.'

A little shiver of excitement crept along his shoulders, but then he remembered how many times he'd felt like that, and the unpleasant consequences that had followed. He watched her lean forward and fumble around her neck. What was she doing? He could smell the mustiness from her woollen clothing. A moment later, the fumbling had stopped. He tried to draw back, but she put out her hand and detained him. A chain was hanging from her loose-skin neck, its fastener close to an old-fashioned memory stick that had been concealed beneath her heavy jumper. He stared.

'Unclasp it,' she whispered. She withdrew her hand and nodded, her unkempt eyebrows rising above eyes that were watching his every movement. 'It's for you. I have kept it a long time. Put it away as soon as you have it in your hand.' He was clumsy unfastening the clasp, and he heard her murmur of impatience as he fiddled with it. 'Oh, let me!' Some more fumbling, and then she had the chain open and the memory stick was in his hand. Her expression had changed from impatient to urgent, appealing to him to conceal it quickly.

As he transferred it to his jacket pocket, his eyes swivelled round to see the waiter staring at Anya with a warning look. The young man had noticed the operation, certainly. Maybe he thought they were passing drugs? Pip grinned and said in English, 'Thank you, Grandma. I don't deserve to have your locket. I've always liked it though.' He saw the waiter turn away.

They relaxed and sat back. It was ludicrous that she had been so keen to remain inconspicuous, when the result had been just the opposite.

'What is it?' he asked quietly.

'It belonged to Simu,' she replied, 'and I know he was killed for it.'

'Killed?'

'On the way to the airport. But, the One,' she crossed herself, 'he knew! He murdered my son, my Simu. There was nothing wrong with his car. And he was burnt in the fire.' Anya's lips trembled. Pip put his hand over hers.

'I know. I am so sorry. How did you …?'

'Simu made me this copy. He was very clever.' She was still trying not to cry. 'You know, Professor, he thought something might happen to him. He made a very big sacrifice – for you.' Pip nodded. 'But he said to me, "If I die, then you must give this to Philip Durrant. Guard it with your life. He will come back. I know he will, because he has not finished what he started."'

Pip was feeling the kind of guilt that had plagued him constantly since the first death of one of those who had helped him – and now, his suspicions were being confirmed. It had happened to Simu as well …

'He loved you, Pip Durrant,' said Anya. 'But he had been looking for information like that,' her eyes indicated the position of the memory stick, 'all his life. Therefore, I cannot blame you. I can only blame myself. I am far more guilty than you are. I should never have borne that monster. I knew what he was from the first.'

'You think Eisenmann …?

Anya shook her head and put a swift finger to her lips. 'Do not say his name!' The old voice had grown in strength. 'Someone will hear! He will exterminate anyone who stands in his way.' She looked around again.

'Anya, listen, no-one has heard anything from him for years. I have looked for him. On the net. Everywhere. Do *you* know where he is?'

Anya shook her head. 'No, but I know he is still alive. I feel it – inside. I feel him and the One he is part of.'

'You mean the Dev–'

'The One,' she interrupted, with a warning glance. 'He feels – near!' Her voice was low and rasping, almost as if someone was strangling her. This time, Pip's shiver was not from excitement. At that moment, he felt the least brave he ever had. He'd had 17 years of watching his back, of thinking an assassin was near. The cowardly thought came to him as a surprise, *Why don't you give up? You're fucked. He'll get you in the end.*

The waiter was coming across again. Pip glanced at his watch. Then he realised Anya was struggling to her feet. 'Sorry,' he said, as the waiter arrived, 'my grandma wants to get home. How much?'

'You pay at the till!' snorted the waiter.

Pip followed him, while Anya stumped past and out through the door.

'How much money did you give him?' asked Anya, when they were both standing outside the coffee shop. 'He didn't deserve it.'

'Come on,' he said, 'I'll walk you back.' At least he had some information, even if it wasn't the Piper's story. As they waited to cross to the road to the new West Plaza, she put her hand on his arm and looked up at him as if she were a small child.

'They will not be home yet. I have promised I shall tell you the story you were really hoping to hear. Then it will be done. I could not do so in that place, although it was my intention.'

'That would be amazing!'

She crossed herself again. 'I shall tell you my part, which has been a burden to me since I was born. Those words I have never forgotten, even in my wickedness. Yet my God knows whatever He has planned for me, I have done my duty and my penance. I shall go to my rest believing that *He* will take pity on me for spawning that monster. Then it will be up to you, Professor, to play your part.'

Pip nodded, then smiled, although he didn't feel the least like it. 'Come on, Anya, don't say that. You'll be okay, now I'm here. Nothing is going to happen to you. Remember what Eva said all that time ago? That I would save you all? You loved her – and you trusted her words. She won't let any harm come to you.'

Pip didn't know what else to add. He wasn't used to playing the priest. Fr Joseph, the only cleric he had really profited from, had been scared as hell of dying, as well as the Devil – and, in a manner of speaking, Pip had put him in his grave. So who was he to comfort an old woman? The idea dampened his excitement as he felt Simu's hard little memory stick in his pocket. The contents would doubtless be in an outdated file format, and would have to be extracted using a special program. His mind wandered as he wondered how he could proceed if that didn't work.

Yet, as they reached Ghita's, he had already regained his spirits. When Anya unlocked the door, the smell of *mamaliga* seeped into his nostrils. It was like being back at Simu's house again, when he had first met the Dalcas in 2007. Almost like coming home. He hovered on the doorstep, giving Anya time to go up the corridor, then he closed the door on modern Oxford. Now he was ready once more to face what was awaiting him; the murky darkness of the pre-mediaeval world.

8

'Would you like some *tuica*?' Anya asked.

'Do you think I'll need it?' asked Pip, then felt sorry for the flippant remark. It was his way of shaking off his feeling of foreboding, but Anya didn't know that, so he lied, adding: 'No thank you, Anya. I had too much to drink over New Year.'

At that moment, he remembered how he'd felt after he'd heard the first part of the Piper story from Simionce. Maybe it had brought on the feeling he'd experienced of an impending vision. That would be the worst thing in these circumstances.

'I shall,' she replied, reaching down for a bottle in a cupboard near the sink. She poured herself a small amount of the liquid. 'Professor, I want you to forgive me.'

'What for? The *tuica*?'

'No, for breaking your good mood.'

'Sorry. It's just that I'm feeling excited and …' He was digging himself a hole. To change the subject, he said, 'Have you any objection to being recorded? I need to make sure I don't miss anything, and then I …' She held up her hand and stopped him.

'Do what you want. I understand your excitement. You're a young man.' She sat down in the comfy chair by the stove, which was unmistakably hers, and settled the cushion behind her.

Pip shook his head and lifted two hands. 'No, no … I apologise. I'm using this. Is that all right?' He produced his powerful wireless microphone from his laptop case and switched it to unidirectional; only one of its functions, but the best for capturing speech. The quality was as good as being in a recording studio, and it was so different from the old ones, as it cut out any extraneous sounds. How he wished he'd had one of these in the past, to record the words of Simionce.

'What I am going to tell you, is not pleasant,' she continued. 'Whatever I say, please remember it is not me that is speaking. It is part of the oral tradition of our tribe, handed down for many generations.'

'I shall,' he replied, 'but who do you think is going to be speaking?'

She looked around the cosy English kitchen she had made her own and shook her head. 'The words have been carried down through our gypsy tribe, woman to woman, for over 1,200 years. And I believe that we, our generation, my grandmother and my mother, escaped the horrors of the concentration camp at Transnistria for that very purpose.'

'But your mother died early.'

'Yes, but not my grandmother, Eva. These words are never lost. Mouth to mouth they come – and have never been written down by us. Don't look like that. You think they may have changed in the telling, Professor. You're a clever man. But these are no fairy stories.'

'But why woman to woman?' asked Pip. He suspected why, but he wanted her to tell him.

'Because it is always the woman who is injured, as it was in those days – and still is, although you may think that is not true, Professor. I am not a modern woman. Nor was the Princess Hildegarde, who was the chattel of the Emperor Charles.'

'Of course,' he said, noting that she didn't call him the Emperor Charlemagne. To the gypsy, he was still Charles!

'She was also the innocent daughter of an adulterous mother, a trusting child who accompanied that devil into the forest on the eve of the feast of St Mary Magdalene, the sinner, in the year of Our Lord, 800. All poor women,' she sighed, looking into the stove.

Pip was thinking then about her life, and her mother's and grandmother's as prostitutes, and how much psychological damage it must have caused them. 'I understand,' he said, 'and thank you for explaining.'

'Some more to explain, Professor, before I begin.' She took a deep breath. 'We come from a tribe of gypsies that is much maligned even by our own kind. The reason for this springs from an ancestor of ours, a certain gypsy who travelled from the East with the Three Wise Men, or Kings, as you probably call them. It is said this gypsy, known to us still as "the Wicked Gypsy", learned his art of telling the future from them, also that he tried to kidnap the Christ-Child from his crib. His descendant, a midget, accompanied the devil, Nicholas, to the evil happenings in the forest, and was the witness to his cruelties.'

'Yes, I've heard of the Wicked Gypsy, and also of his small descendant,' interjected Pip. 'They were in Simionce's account –'

'Please, Professor, no more interruptions. The quicker I can get this out of my head, the better. Besides, we have little time.' She glanced at the clock.

Of course, thought Pip. *Ghita and Olga might come home!* 'Sorry, Anya. It's just … that I'm excited.' It was such a childish thing to say. Pip regretted it immediately, then settled. Anya sighed again. 'I'm sorry if I've offended you.'

'You haven't.' She stretched forward and put her hand on his arm. 'We have only a little time. This is the beginning for you and the end for me.'

'What do you mean?' he asked, thinking of the fate of all his other informants. Maybe he should never have asked her.

'I mean that when this is out of here,' she tapped her head, 'I shall have done my duty. As far as I know, there is no more. The rest will be up to you alone.' The words came like a blow. 'We, his descendants, have our own cross to bear. We are forced to watch this cruelty throughout the ages, but not to take part, thank God – and because of this, we share no guilt of the terrible crime that is committed at Arva … But, wait, I am going too fast. Let me begin where I should … First, I must prepare myself.'

Anya leaned back and closed her eyes. Her lips moved without speaking, and Pip realised that she must be praying. Her eyes were closed now and her body stiff. She raised her hand in the manner of the *scop,* a pose he recognised from the pictures he had seen of the old Anglo-Saxon and Norse poets.

Pip watched, fascinated, as he waited for the account that was to be transcribed as Dialogue 2 – Anya's fragment of the story of Nicholas, the Piper.

It was a terrible story. Pip could hardly wait to return to his rooms and transcribe it, and he felt cold with horror as at last he knew why the Grandsire, aka the Piper, returned periodically to Arva to commit his brutal crimes.

Anya fell asleep in her chair by the stove immediately after the session, and as Pip was packing up his equipment, he heard the key turn in the front door lock. He was both glad and sorry. Although he was eager to return to his work, he wanted to see Ghita again. But what would she think about him calling uninvited? His quick brain was computing a variety of excuses.

Stuffing everything into his laptop case as quickly as possible, he picked up the large ladle from the table and began stirring the pot of *mamaliga,* which was simmering on the stove. The action helped him mentally to prepare for what could be an awkward situation, as well as affording an adequate cover for more lies.

'Anya?' called Ghita.

'Don't worry, it's only me,' he replied, coming to the kitchen door. 'Anya found me wandering in town and insisted on me coming home with her. Sorry. I'll go if you don't want me.' He drew in his breath at her loveliness as her wide eyes stared at him.

'You. Goodness! Whatever are you doing?' she asked, looking from the stew to Pip. He took off his glasses and rubbed them, as the steam had almost blotted out his vision. 'Is Anya all right?' she added. She went up to the chair and peered into her face.

'She just fell asleep,' replied Pip, replacing his glasses, 'and I think supper is ready. I didn't want it to burn.' Her bright directness was already chasing his ancient ghosts away.

'It's good to see you,' she said, 'as well as a nice change! Will you stay – again!' They laughed. 'Wine – or *tuica*?' Her eyes were on the bottle of spirits beside Anya, and her expression changed to puzzled. She turned away and looked in another cupboard. A moment later, she produced two bottles and showed him. 'White or red?'

'Okay, red please – and I wasn't drinking *tuica*.'

'And Anya? I've hardly ever seen her drink in the afternoon.'

It was strange how he remembered little things about Ghita. In this case, her knack of sniffing out the truth. He wasn't going to lie to her anymore – if possible. 'We were talking about Romania,' he said.

She nodded. 'That figures. She gets very sentimental sometimes, especially when she talks about my father. Were you –?'

'Yes, we mentioned him. She misses him.' Inside, he was calculating how long it would be until he made a slip and she found him out. He didn't want that. He watched her pouring the wine, and again his eyes were drawn to her bust under the white shirt, which was accentuated by the belt, making her shape under the smart trousers look even trimmer. She caught him looking.

'And if you're thinking I usually get out the wine as soon as I come home, forget it,' she said. 'Look, there's dust on the bottle!' They laughed.

Pip noticed Anya was stirring in the chair. What should he do? Ghita went over to the old women and smiled at the drowsy eyes turned up to her face.

'Are you okay?' she asked. 'Anya?'

Anya's eyes opened wide. She looked straight at Pip, then at Ghita. 'I brought Professor Durrant home,' she said.

'And you found him wandering in Oxford. I know. But I don't believe it. Now, both of you, tell me the truth.' Ghita perched herself on the arm of Anya's chair.

'He asked me if he could come over when I told him I was making a stew,' was Anya's glib reply.

'Sounds more like it,' replied Ghita. 'Pip was never a very good liar.' She regarded him under her lashes with a look that tugged at his conscience. 'He prefers to disappear.'

Pip looked down. Instead of keep on with the subterfuge, he said, 'Actually, I would like some of that stew, but then I shall have to go. I have work to do tonight.'

By then, Anya was hauling herself up from the chair. 'I'll see to it,' she said. 'I don't know what I was doing, falling asleep like that. My apologies, Professor.' He shook his head at her. 'Now get out of my kitchen, both of you, and go drink that stuff.' She indicated the wine bottle. 'Give me a home-brewed concoction any day.'

'You mean that?' countered Ghita, going over to the *tuica* bottle and replacing it in the cupboard. She frowned. 'You look really pale, Anya. Let me see to the supper and you go and lie down.'

'No!' Anya said firmly. 'I shall have plenty of time to do that when I am in my grave.' Pip felt his mouth go dry.

Ghita frowned again. 'Come on, Pip, if she's going to be silly. And you're not getting away yet. Bring your glass with you. I'll bring the bottle.'

He glanced at Anya as he started to follow Ghita out of the kitchen. She indicated with an imperceptible jerk of her head that he should go.

'She's been tidying up again,' said Ghita as they entered the sitting-room, 'and I won't be able to find a thing. Seat?'

She indicated the big armchair, when what Pip desperately wanted was sit on the couch beside her. He just couldn't help himself imagining making love with Ghita. He wondered if she felt like that, even a little bit. They settled themselves.

'Right, what's all this about, Pip?' she asked.

'What?'

'You know what.'

'Not really,' he shrugged. 'Did you mind me talking over old times with your – Anya,' he corrected himself just in time. What he needed was to read the old memory stick before he really put his foot in it. Also to put what he'd heard earlier out of his mind.

'My what? Anya is my great aunt.'

'That's right,' he said, feeling able to breathe again.

'But it isn't, is it?' she said. 'I can smell a rat!' The words sent a frisson of anxiety through him. 'Did you – no, let's get this right.' She screwed up her eyes in the way he remembered. 'I think – that you knew Anya already, didn't you? Don't lie to me, please.'

He sighed. 'Okay.' He gave a little shrug. 'Did you ever think of joining the police, Ghita?' he joked to alleviate the tension. 'Yes, I met her once when I went out with your dad. But I hardly remembered it until I saw her again, and I thought it wouldn't be, I dunno, right to say something after we hadn't seen each other for so long. I thought it might upset you.'

'Bravo, Professor.' Her sarcasm hurt him. If she only knew why he was doing all this. 'You and he were so good at hiding things from me, weren't you? Like when you told me you were my father's student and it didn't turn out that way.'

'That's a long time ago – and if you think I'm hiding something this time, you might be partly right. But, at present, it's for the right reasons. For Christ's sake, give me a chance, Ghita?' he appealed. 'I promise that I'll level with you soon – and then we'll talk it all out. Do you believe me?'

'I don't know,' she said, finishing her wine. 'I hope so, because otherwise we can't –' she stopped.

'Go on.' It was amazing how those few words put back the life in him.

'Forget it,' she replied.

'I won't be able to. And that's the truth.'

'Well, remember it then, and level with me, if that's what you call it.' She looked at her watch. 'I don't know when Olga will be back. Not too late, I hope.'

'Do you mind if I'm here when she comes home?' asked Pip. He wanted to see her daughter again. There was something about Olga that interested him. He rephrased that mentally. It wasn't 'interested' he meant, but …

'Why should I?' asked Ghita. 'You seemed to like each other – and I'm happy about that. My daughter doesn't have that many friends, unfortunately.'

'Why?'

'It's a long story,' Ghita replied, 'and not one I intend to go into now.'

'I would like – to add something there,' said Pip. A plan was forming in his mind. 'How long do we have before she's here?'

'Why?' Pip could hear the alarm in the question.

'Well,' he said, 'I wanted to say something about Klaas.'

'Have you found something out about him?' Alarm again.

'No, it's nothing to be scared about. Not about him and Olga.' He shook his head. 'It's just that last night I got my wish. You remember when I said I'd like to meet him? He came to see me last night.'

She stared. 'Klaas came to see you? Why the hell would he do that? You've never met him. I don't understand.'

'I didn't either.' Pip wasn't going to tell Ghita about the kid's pretence. 'Maybe Olga mentioned me – and he was in college. But I found him extremely interesting. He's very bright.'

'You knew that.'

'He's …' he considered his words, '… unusual. Very interesting indeed – and he told me that he cares a lot for Olga.'

'He told you that? But you're a stranger.'

'We got on. He wanted me to help him.' Pip waited for the response. Ghita sat back against the couch and let out a sigh of disbelief.

'What does he want you to do?' She was frowning again.

'He's worried about his – image and – wait, listen, Ghita – he wants to improve it. He thinks everyone is against him, and seeing that I'm a psychologist, he thought I'd be willing to give him some advice.' Pip really despised himself for playing Ghita like he was, but he had no option. He couldn't tell her why the kid had really turned up at his rooms, or what he really thought about him. Not yet, anyway; not until he had discovered exactly what made Klaas tick; whether he was only a troubled kid, or whether there was actually something more sinister about him.

'I can't believe what I'm hearing,' burst out Ghita. 'He's the most arrogant young man I've ever met. I know he's convinced he cares for her, but as for caring about other people's opinions, I would say that's completely out of character. Well …' She poured herself another glass of wine, then leaned back and sipped it, feigning calm. 'Go on then …'

'Nothing much to it at the moment. He and I are going to meet again, but I don't want you to say anything to anyone, even Anya.'

'I wouldn't. She hates him,' came the vehement reply. 'Klaas is too clever to make a fool of himself. There must be something behind his behaviour. I wonder why he came to you?'

'Why not me?'

'Why not to his student counsellor or tutor? That should be his first port of call.'

'He mentioned that. But they don't get on.' Pip wondered what Ghita would have said if he'd told her that Klaas had seen a shrink in the past, and that the treatment hadn't worked. He also wasn't going to tell her anything about the more alarming things Klaas had claimed for himself. She would have been so scared.

'He doesn't get on with anyone, I've heard,' she said, 'except Olga.'

'Ghita, I'm telling you this because you're Olga's mother and you want to keep her safe. Okay?' She nodded. 'I'll keep an eye on the kid – and if there is anything, anything at all, that I am worried about in Klaas's behaviour, I'll tell you, and we –'

'We?'

'Sorry, I mean *you* can do something about it. This is really why I'm here tonight. I was going to ring you anyway, and then I met Anya by chance and –' he shrugged '– and here I am.' She nodded. He felt even guiltier when he saw her expression.

'I have been really worried, Pip. Olga is only 15, and Klaas – he's like no-one she's ever known. In fact, I've never known anyone like him. He has a bad reputation.' Her lovely eyes fixed on his, and he brazened it out.

'Yes, he told me – and I'm going to find out what I can about that. He said I should ask Spencer about him.'

'Spencer James?'

'Yes. And I intend to find out – with your permission to play the detective. What do you think? Will you let me?' Pip watched her take a deep breath – and waited. The little voice inside him was calling him *a fucking liar, a snake in the grass*. Asking him how he could fulfil his own wants and needs at the expense of another innocent. Telling him to shut up now and not make things worse by saying that he knew he was nothing to her and that she didn't have to be grateful – because all he wanted to do was *go to bed with her; to comfort her and alleviate his own guilt*. He watched her struggling to keep her feelings in check, and didn't make a move.

'Thank you. And you'd do that for us?' she said.

'Of course.' Inside, the little voice of his conscience was laughing at his mock sincerity. 'For old times' sake.'

She smiled. 'Thank you,' she repeated. 'And you'll tell me as you go along? I've never asked for anyone's help …'

'You didn't,' he soothed. 'I offered.'

'Dad always used to fix things for me – and you reminded me of him for a minute,' she said.

'I hope not,' he quipped.

'Of course not, but you know what I mean. Since then, I've had to be strong for both of us. Anton was no good at anything like that. I should never have married him.' She seemed to be talking to herself. 'But I didn't ever think that Olga would pick up with someone like Klaas Honen. I confess that I am out of my depth with him, and I suppose I just want to keep her close. She's only 15. She used to be so quiet and work so hard, and now …' She trailed off.

'Well, my guess is that you've done a good job, although I've only seen her once.' He smiled and continued, 'Yes, I think she's done pretty well so far, given what I know about teenagers. If it's any help, Ghita, I've treated quite a few mixed-up ones in my time.' At least that was the truth.

'I suppose you have,' answered Ghita, 'but – will you have time?'

'I have a very light timetable,' Pip replied. True again. 'I do also have my research, but I'll put this down as some more, so you can stop worrying. Nobody is bothered what I'm doing as long as I fill my lecture quota.'

'Is Klaas going to pay you? He should. I know his mother is very wealthy,' she said. 'And that's something else. I worry about that – which seems ridiculous, but I do. I want Olga to do well in her exams and have a career. Not end up with nothing except a rich playboy for a boyfriend.'

'I agree. One thing again. Please don't talk this over with Anya. I know I shouldn't ask, but I have a feeling she wouldn't be that happy.'

'No,' Ghita smiled. 'She'd stick a knife in his ribs if she could. She watches them like a hawk. In fact, she reminds me of – oh, never mind.' Pip knew that Ghita had been thinking of her own mother Emilia when she said that. 'It's mothers, I suppose,' she added. Pip nodded. 'Are you still going to wait until Olga gets back?'

'No,' he said, getting up. 'I'll just go, if you don't mind, now that I've run the idea past you. I suppose you don't have this Spencer's number, do you?'

'Of course. It's on my phone. Well, his mother's is. Is that okay?'

'Great,' he said.

They stood together as she searched her mobile, and he could hardly stop himself from taking her in his arms and kissing her. Then he was putting the number in his own phone.

There was no awkwardness about them now as he followed her through the corridor to the door.

'Thanks for everything,' he added; and, next moment, she threw her arms about his neck and hugged him. Her body felt so good against his that he could hardly breathe.

'Sorry, probably shouldn't have done that,' she said, withdrawing. 'Thank you so much. Will you let me know as soon as you find out anything?'

'Of course – and it's been great seeing you again. Explain to Anya I had lots to do and that I have nothing against the *mamaliga*! Next time, perhaps. Shall I ring you?'

'Any time,' she said, and a moment later, his arms were empty.

He couldn't have explained his feelings at that moment as she closed the door behind him. He had regained her trust by lying to her again – half-lying perhaps – but now he had an open invitation into her arms, as well as her permission to investigate her daughter's boyfriend – who, in Pip's eyes, was not only that. His conviction was increasing that the strange American kid who'd gate-crashed his rooms was someone else who was going to fit into the equation of his long search for the Grandsire of Arva. How or why, he didn't understand yet.

Also, he now had in his possession Anya's story, and Simu Dalca's memory stick. *You lucky bastard*, he said to himself, squashing the mean little voice of his conscience. *What you make of this is gonna put you right on top.* He stood on the doorstep for a few seconds and stared up into the orange night sky, the city lights having blotted out any stars that might otherwise have been visible. As he breathed in, the cold air cut into his chest and he began to cough, which was unusual for him. He couldn't remember when he was last sick. *Must be coming out of a warm room*, he thought. He couldn't be bothered to check the temperature on his phone, but he could feel that it had dropped and could see the fog drifting toward him. *That's weird*, he said to himself, as he walked coughing along the pavement.

All at once he saw a small yellow-and-red driverless cab in the distance, coming out of the fog toward him under the streetlights. Strangely, it appeared to have no passenger. He waited for it to draw closer. *At least it knows where it's going in the fog. I'll hop in it back to Norris*, he thought. He was so full of his recent successes that he didn't notice that the cab was moving faster than usual. It was only when it veered to the right-hand side of the safety bollards that he realised something was wrong.

Then he saw to his amazement that the driverless vehicle had a driver after all, a hooded shape hunched low over the wheel. *That can't be right*, his mind was saying as it came closer.

Seconds later, he froze as the cab accelerated toward him along the empty street, veering from side to side on the yellow lines, while the driver remained motionless, oblivious. *But there shouldn't be a driver at all*, was all Pip could think as the vehicle mounted the pavement of the narrow street and headed straight for him. His brain finally got back into gear when the cab was only about 150 metres away. He needed a means of escape. So he turned back toward Ghita's and ran, with the crazy little vehicle gaining on him. He could feel the wind, which had risen now and was fighting him, trying to push him back in the direction of the cab.

The vehicle was almost on him, and he had no option but to dive headlong into Ghita's gate. It gave away under his weight, and next moment he was lying flat on his face on the uneven stone paving. In his ears came the sound of mocking laughter, which was picked up and carried off by the wind. Pip's spectacles were askew, and when he put his hand up to try to right them, he found to his cost that one side of the frame was pressing sharply into his nose. It seemed stuck into his flesh. He thought for a moment he was going to faint, but the feeling went off. The rest of his face was crushed and sore, and he didn't dare move yet. He couldn't remember another time he had fallen so hard or so awkwardly against stone.

He lay there, running his hand down the side of his leg to feel if he'd broken it. It hurt a lot. Then he put his other hand up to his face and felt the wet. He stared at the smears of blood, almost dark green in the violent orange light from the streetlamps. He had to get up. He tried, but lay back down, then tried again. He thought his sight had become blurred, but then realised his spectacle lenses were cracked – and he couldn't see properly without them. His other pair was in his laptop case. Where was it? He looked around a zig zag world, realising that he had dropped the case and fearing that it might have burst open and spilt its contents. He needed to move!

A moment later, he heard the noise of running feet, and fear produced a cold sweat that ran down the side of his nose. Whoever had attacked him must have come back to finish him off! He had to get to safety. The footsteps were already thuds in his ears as he struggled to his feet and geared himself up to retaliate. Then a pale hand came down and touched his face. The blur that was his sight picked up the small white face in the harsh orange light.

'Professor! What happened? Hurry up, Klaas.' More footsteps. Pip struggled to sit up. He was dazed. Another face was peering down at him. The dark eyes were expressionless, the hair slicked back. Two strong male hands dragged him up into a sitting position and propped him against the wall. Then Klaas was squatting beside him.

'Too much *tuica*, Prof?' The voice was slightly mocking.

'Don't be horrible, Klaas. He's hurt himself. I'm going to get Mother.' Olga's voice was full of tears. Then he heard the door wrested wide open and the frantic yell. 'Mother, Anya, where are you? Professor Durrant's had an accident. He's outside our door.'

With a deep sigh, Pip tried to collect his thoughts. He felt like an old man. Klaas was still regarding him with a bemused expression, devoid of sympathy.

'My laptop. My papers,' Pip groaned. 'Where are they?'

'All here, Prof. I brought them in off the road. You took some tumble. Who was chasing you?'

'No-one,' snapped Pip, but his heart was thumping. 'And stop grinning,' he exploded.

'Hang in there, sir,' the kid replied in an insolent tone, which riled Pip. 'I guess you'll need some new glasses, though.'

A moment later, Pip grabbed at Klaas's arm. 'Which way did you come? Did you see the cab? The yellow-and-red one. Someone was driving it. I don't understand, because … But …' He stopped. 'But it was chasing me, really chasing me. I had to dive through the gate.' He put a hand to his head and tried again to get up. Next moment, with Klaas's help, he was struggling to his feet. 'Sorry, I guess I'm shaken. *And I've not been drinking.*'

All at once, the whole household were around him, *oohing* and *aahing* all over him, and he began to feel like a fool.

'Were you mugged? Do you think you need an ambulance?' Ghita asked anxiously.

'No way,' said Pip. 'I'm okay now.'

'We didn't see anyone outside, did we, Klaas?' noted Olga.

'It was an accident,' said Klaas. His voice was hard, almost authoritative. 'I guess we should get the Prof into the sitting-room and patch him up. I'll bring him. You go on in.'

The sounds faded. Klaas and Pip stood together. To his annoyance, Pip realised he was leaning on the kid. But he was shaky. The night was silent around them.

'Come on, then,' Klaas said. 'Let's get inside.' His mouth was very close to Pip's ear as he added, 'The guy, the hoodie. I can identify him for you. He had bright yellow hair and he was *not* good-looking. I've seen him before, though. Unless I was dreaming.'

'You saw the cab? And the driver?' Pip couldn't move.

'Yep,' said Klaas.

'Why didn't Olga?' Pip started to shiver.

'Well, let's say she doesn't share what you and I do,' Klaas whispered. 'And let's keep it to ourselves, shall we, Professor? For now? Come on, and watch your step.'

Later that evening, when they had patched him up, Pip went over the incident again and again in his mind. Not only because he had a black eye and had messed up his glasses, and so couldn't see properly, nor because his face and his jaw were aching, but because of the experience itself. One of the most unsettling things was that he'd been in danger again, and hurt, and also that someone else – Klaas – had apparently seen a being that only Pip knew, and that couldn't really exist because … He couldn't explain why, not properly.

In spite of their protests, he had assured Ghita and Olga he didn't need to go to hospital or to call the cab company; and as for the police, what could they do?

'I just don't understand you,' said Ghita, her eyes flashing. 'If those cabs aren't safe, they need to be told. It's an offence. Say

… say it had been someone else, someone vulnerable, and they'd been killed? No, Pip, I'm definitely going to ring the company in the morning if you won't.'

'Okay, if you want, but I'm fine now.'

'You don't look it – and you're staying here. I insist. '

'Those cabs always seem such sweet little things,' Olga added. 'I can't believe it went out of control like that. I've never been in one, and now I don't want to.'

The next debate was where it had gone. All the time, Klaas was sitting in the armchair with his legs sprawled out in front of him, contributing nothing but occasionally flicking his eyes toward Pip with a knowing look. Then he chipped in, 'Anyway, I guess that cab must have run out of juice soon' – which was the most logical thing anyone had said for a long time.

If it hadn't been such an unsettling and painful experience and Pip hadn't been feeling so sorry for himself, he wouldn't have dreamed of letting his feelings be known. For some reason, that night he felt vulnerable and hardly recognised himself.

'I don't know why everyone is making such a fuss,' he declared, then felt guilty at the clamour of protestation that followed. Part of his mind was reasoning it out. He liked being the centre of attention, especially when Ghita was ministering to him.

'What about your parents … your fans?' she asked.

'Well, Larry, my agent, might miss me,' he replied, smiling, then grimacing because it hurt. 'He'd have lost his source of income. Okay, I agree, someone might care …' Then he saw Klaas's wry expression. The young man had already checked his watch, several times.

'Hey, Olga, we need to get on,' he said.

'Oh, sorry,' she apologised. 'I'm coming.' She turned to her mother and added, 'Klaas is helping me with one of my essays. Can I take some soup up for us?'

'Fine.' Ghita glanced at Klaas, and with a meaningful expression added, 'But don't keep her up too late. She has revision.'

'That's what we're going to be doing, Mother.' Pip

recognised the mixture of indignation and annoyance in Olga's tone.

Ghita sighed, then looked at Pip. 'I'm sorry, but we go to bed early here. I have a lot to do tomorrow.'

'That's fine. I really should get going now anyway – again.'

'No, I've told you that's the last thing you're going to do. If you stay here, you can go to the opticians in the morning and sort out your specs.'

'I don't need to go to the optician. I have a second pair back at Norris,' he lied, knowing that they were actually just in his laptop case.

'You can't go back to Norris tonight. I can only offer you the couch,' added Ghita, 'but it's a bed-settee. We have only three beds in this house! If that's all right?'

She seemed agitated – besides which, he realised he was in shock – so he decided to give in. 'More than all right,' he replied, although he wanted to say, *I could share yours!* Instead, he added, 'I suppose I am still a bit shaky. Thank you.' And it was true. He didn't want to be alone.

Olga and Klaas were standing by the door, fingers linked.

'Goodnight, Professor – sorry, Pip,' Olga corrected herself. Klaas nodded to him, his mocking eyes holding his, annoying him. Pip could imagine him and Olga laughing as they went upstairs, and Klaas saying something like *The Prof sure wants to get laid* … And what would Olga say? Pip's imagination was about to answer when he forced himself to stop, to be reasonable and professional about this young man, who had forced himself under his skin. But it was difficult, because try as he might, he couldn't stop feeling that Klaas was playing with him and manipulating his thoughts. Nobody else had done that since Koppelberg, and … Pip went cold. That was who Klaas reminded him of! Diep Koppelberg and his ability to set one family member, one friend against another. He felt his legs shaking now.

'Remember the time, Olga,' said Ghita.

Olga nodded. 'Don't keep on, Mother! We were only waiting to say goodnight to Pip.' She turned to Pip. 'I hope you feel better tomorrow.' She looked at Klaas, who nodded in mock agreement. Pip squashed the sudden urge to tell Olga to watch herself. He didn't want to be a hypocrite, because he wanted to sleep with her mother just as much as they wanted to do whatever they did.

Next moment, they were off. Ghita looked at him. 'See what I mean? Why I'm anxious?'

'Don't be,' he said. 'He knows how old she is. And she's got sense.'

'I hope so. I only wish –' She broke off. 'Never mind. I'll go and get your bedclothes. I'm glad you weren't really hurt. I was so worried.'

'Were you?' he said.

She nodded. 'I've only just found you again and … we have to have that talk you mentioned. I want to tell you things too.'

'Yes, and I have to get on with my work, so I can explain,' Pip replied.

'I hope it's not too bad.'

'What?'

'What you have to tell me,' she said.

'It'll be fine. Everything's going to be okay, Ghita.' Those stupid words rolled out of his mouth like they did in disaster movies when the world was going to blow up any minute.

'Thanks!' But she didn't make any attempt to hug him this time. 'By the way, I have some aspirin. You look as though you need to take a couple. Do you feel like eating? Then you can take them.' He shook his head. 'Why don't you have some soup? I can bring it in here. In fact, we can sit together and have it on our knees?'

She was back soon and made up the couch, while he tried to help. He was hopeless at it. He stood back.

'Great.' He looked down at his bed. 'Everything's great,' he repeated. 'But I can't eat much. I feel a bit sick.' The thought of them sitting on the bed eating soup together was almost too much for Pip in his circumstances. But he wanted to.

The meal turned out to be a misery for him. He could see she had no thought of becoming intimate with him; and even if she'd rolled into his arms, he would have been too tired and hurt to do anything. *Serves me right*, he thought.

Finally she took the bowls and stood looking down at him. 'You look like death,' she said. He nodded. 'Good night then. The bathroom's upstairs on the left. I'll leave the hall light on.'

'Thanks,' he replied, wondering if she was contemplating a change of heart and asking him to go upstairs with her.

All at once, Ghita had that old mischievous smile on her face. 'You look a mess. Maybe you'll feel better in the morning.' He couldn't think of an answer. 'Oh, by the way,' she added, 'sometimes Anya gets up in the night, but don't take any notice.'

'I won't.'

He waited until she had gone, then sat down, going over and over what had taken place. He was an idiot even to hope Ghita might forgive him. He might as well forget it.

He was worried too about what had happened earlier on that evening. How would normal people – if anyone could be seen as normal – act if such an 'accident' had happened to them? There was no answer to his hypothetical question, because it wouldn't have happened to anyone else. His earlier fears were being borne out. Things were changing in his world.

He had to face it. The cab might have been one of his visions. He'd been hurt again. He remembered Otto then, and Simionce's transferred death by spontaneous combustion. He shivered. What was happening to the safe world of his imagination, and his 'dreams' where no-one could touch him? A place where he saw terrifying things and even became part of them, but never came off worse. He'd always felt guilty about the others' deaths, but now he was becoming like them. Vulnerable. How long would he last? He lay down and huddled under the blankets. Once, he had thought himself invulnerable. He hadn't cared what he did, but now … He thought of Klaas. He said he had seen the vision with its hooded driver. Olga hadn't. She'd said, *We didn't see anything, did we, Klaas?* He was going to make sure and check it out with her. Ask where she and Klaas had been when he had hit the gate.

What did she think Pip had done, to be lying there on her path, half-dead? Had Klaas been meant to share this experience with him? Or had they imagined it together? He put his hand to his head.

When the house was quiet, he went in his stockinged feet up the steep stairs. They led to a tidy landing, and on the left he found an equally tidy bathroom. *Probably all Anya's influence*, he thought. He could still hear faint talking and laughing. What Ghita called late for Olga, he didn't know, but he would be surprised if Klaas went home now. He wasn't sure why, but the idea of Klaas sleeping with Olga upset him again. He could see Ghita's dilemma, but her daughter was 15, and lots of 13-year-olds slept together, although a new age of moral puritanism seemed to be flourishing. If Olga had been his daughter he wouldn't have been happy either.

When he was back in the sitting-room, he checked he had all his things safe; but in spite of eagerness to find out what Simu Dalca had wanted him to know, and to transcribe Anya's narrative, he said to himself, *I'm too tired to do anything else now.*

However, as soon as he lay down, the image of the sinister hooded face framed by the straggling yellow hair returned to his mind. He turned over and over on what was not an ideal mattress, trying to dispel it. He needed to think of something good instead of Koppelberg and Eisenmann and the Piper and all the dead people who came flooding in to him afterwards …

He fixed his thoughts on Ghita, cuddled up in bed. He remembered so clearly that one precious night they'd spent together in Romania so long ago, and marvelled at how the memory could store the tiniest thing it wanted to. Yet the regrets of what might have been welled up from deep within him. *Stop it, you fool*, he told himself. *Remember how things were with her on the first day you came here. At least there is a chance you might be forgiven now.*

Staring up at the ceiling, he wondered again what the teenagers were doing, then tried to block out the image in his mind, because he knew he was being unfair. Besides, it was none of his business. Why it mattered to him what happened to

Olga, he didn't know, but the idea of Ghita's daughter being so close to a guy as spooky as Klaas, filled him with revulsion. Then he fell asleep.

Around 3.00, Anya woke up and lay there in her bed, the duvet pulled up around her neck. She didn't know why she was cold and wished she had her own heavy woollen blankets around her as in the past. She pulled the duvet up under her chin. She had never been keen on the down-filled piece of nothing, but finally Ghita had persuaded her that duvets were modern and saved a lot of trouble.

She reached out to switch on her light, but accidentally knocked it down between the chest and the side of the bed. She couldn't pull it up, and she needed to see to go to the bathroom. She would have liked a candle in her room too, like they used to have, but Ghita said it was dangerous if she didn't remember to blow it out. Anya had a habit of getting up at night and wandering around. She hadn't done it lately though. She grumbled at the half-buried light, which produced an eerie glow, throwing the curtain's shadows over the ceiling. Strangely then, she thought of that cosy little van she had shared with Eva Kirchma, and lay back against the pillows. She remembered only so much of the past, but there were some things she would never forget – for example, her rape and the birth of the little golden-headed monster she had given away. She shook her head. All these memories were bad and liable to return in the darkness before dawn. Anya couldn't share any of them with Ghita, because Ghita didn't know who she really was.

The old lady screwed up her eyes, but dared not go back to sleep, as she needed the bathroom more, and she was also worried that the bedside light might set the house on fire. She looked over toward the door and started to heave her body up. She stopped. A faint light was coming into the room through the crack between the door and the frame. There must be a bulb still on somewhere in one of the other rooms. She sniffed. Ghita wouldn't like that. Olga was probably still working or had fallen asleep with the light on.

She groaned as she put a foot out of bed and the pain in her arthritic joints hit her. She waited to gain her breath. Then she thought she could hear low laughter. She panicked. That evil boy must be with Olga! He was probably in bed with her. She would go and turf them out. Throw him out. Picking the sleep out of the corner of one of her eyes, she finally managed to prop herself on the side of the bed in the half dark, reaching for her stick. A sudden burst of anger rose from deep inside her as her fingers curled around the handle and she cursed Klaas Honen.

'A few thumps of this would do you good, my lad,' she muttered. 'That'd keep you away from our Olga!' Her anger provoked an effort that hurt her body too much as she reached for her dressing gown. She couldn't put the garment on. She felt useless. Then a sharp little pain struck her in the side of the head, so she moved. It was like the room was swirling about her. She came to again. She'd been told by a doctor that she had high blood pressure. Rest more, the young lady had said. She was nice enough, but looked hardly old enough to be a doctor.

Yet, soon, Anya was up again and hobbling across to the bedroom door. Her arm hurt as she pulled the door open. She paused, overwhelmed by a pulsating noise in her head. Then a sudden extra thud sounded in her ears, as if someone was downstairs. That couldn't be right, could it? Then she perked up as she remembered that Pip was down in the sitting-room. Immediately across the landing she could also hear a snuffling and snoring sound. Or was it her own heart in her chest? She didn't know!

Maybe it was Simu? But he never snored. Then Anya remembered Simu was dead. She felt tears prickling behind her eyes. Her dear son had been burned in a fire by that monster.

She stood there, trembling, looking over toward the toilet door. She didn't want to wake Ghita and ask for help. The girl worked so hard. Anya's feet felt cold and heavy, but although they did not seem part of her, they obeyed her brain, propelling her toward the door on the left of the stairs.

Again, she heard the noise below. With the help of the wall, she pulled herself along to the very top of the stairs and looked down. To her amazement, what looked like a bundle of old rags was lying on a stair half-way down.

I never left that there, she thought. *It must be something of Klaas's!* She was filled with anger toward the young man who had come into their lives and made everything so complicated. How dare he leave a bundle on her stairs! It was probably his shoes – he had a habit of leaving them lying around.

Then her old eyes widened in shock. The bundle was moving. Wriggling. *What is it*, was her first thought.

It wriggled and struggled on, then a moment later it was sitting up on its end, propped against the banister like a – her memory stirred. Like a baby in a shroud? Her cold hands were clammy now and she was squinting. Her mouth went very tight as she watched the bundle shuffle up onto its bottom.

Then she discovered her arm was too useless even to make the sign of the cross. The thing was alive. 'Go away!' she said. 'I don't know you.' Her lopsided mouth couldn't form the words properly.

'You did,' replied a child's piercing voice; or at least she thought it was a child's. Anya began to feel tremors all over her body as the bundle unrolled itself on the stairs. She tried to turn away, but she couldn't. An icy hand was holding her feet to the floor. Saliva trickled from her mouth down her nightdress.

Below, the bundle was growing before her horrified eyes and the rags were falling away. A shaft of light from nowhere struck its bright golden hair as it threw off its rags to reveal a child, staring up at her, its large, luminous eyes boring into her skull. Then it began to crawl upstairs, stair by stair.

Anya couldn't even bring her foot off the ground as the thing started its ascent. She was transfixed with horror, *'You,'* she screamed, but no sound came, and the house slept on.

God have mercy on me, she screamed again in her head. *Release me from this nightmare!* But the child was getting near now and beckoning her. She shook her head, but found she was moving. Her feet were being forced to move toward it, as it held out its small arms. She tottered on the first stair and stopped, but it was no good, because the child's arms were growing, ready to draw her in.

As Anya tried again to turn back, she felt her feet fly away beneath her. Then she was falling into a void and she couldn't stop. As she lay at the foot of the stairs, her last terrified sight was of the yellow-haired man whom she knew from her dreams. His mouth, full of sharp white teeth, smiled coldly as he drew his rat-tailed, fur-trimmed cloak around him and faded away from Anya's failing sight.

The loud noise of Anya's body hitting the floor woke Pip. He shook the sleep away and looked around the unfamiliar room. Then he remembered where he was. He had gone to sleep in his jacket, but he had to scrabble about for his jeans, which he pulled on as quickly as he could, and then made for the door. He couldn't open it. He pushed and pushed, but Anya's heavy weight was jammed against it.

Outside, he could hear the noise of running feet and a woman shouting.

'Ghita, what's happened?' he shouted back. 'Let me out!' Silence. That moment seemed to last forever, until he heard Klaas's voice.

'Here, let me!'

'Don't move her,' screamed Ghita.

'What's going on?' Pip roared. Silence again. Then Klaas's voice came again, flat and clear.

'Anya has fallen down the stairs and is jammed against your door. I can't move her. I'm calling an ambulance.'

'Is she alive?' shouted Pip.

'Don't think so,' was the calm reply.

'Fucking well look then! And get me out.'

'I can't. You'll have to wait, Prof.' Pause, then … 'I think she's dead.'

Pip sat on the couch. He had never felt so useless. A moment later, Ghita called, in a voice he hardly recognised, 'Pip, Klaas has sent for the ambulance. We shouldn't move her. I can't get you out.'

'I'm getting out through the window,' he shouted back. Afterwards, he thought it had been a stupid thing to do, but at that moment, he felt he had no choice. He hurt himself again as he jumped off the sill into the garden, but all he wanted was to be with Ghita. The front door opened and she let him in, and the next moment she was clinging to him. He didn't ask how it had happened, but let her sob.

When the ambulance came, the police followed, and the rest of the night was taken up by question after question. It wasn't until all the photos had been taken that he discovered that under Anya's crumpled body a shoe, a trainer, had been found. The other had been flung along the corridor by the impact of her fall.

'How many times has Klaas been told not to leave his shoes on the stairs?' Ghita said. 'It's my fault. I always check, but I must have forgotten this time. I don't understand it.'

'But what did Klaas say? How come his trainers were on the stairs?'

'He's really upset. He won't talk about it. He's trying to comfort Olga.'

Pip knew the trainers hadn't been there, because when he'd gone up to the bathroom, the stairs had been clear. Surely Klaas couldn't have taken them off after that and put them on the landing? Why would he do such a thing? He had been in Olga's room when Pip had gone up. Surely he would have taken his trainers off there?

He remembered Klaas's words, *You don't know what I can do*, and his challenge to Pip to go and meet Spencer. Then Pip found himself wondering exactly how far the kid would go, even if an old lady stood in his way. He intended to find out. Nobody had asked him yet, and unless they did, Pip didn't intend to mention anything to the police.

9

Pip's first task when he returned to his rooms was to retrieve the information from the memory stick that Anya had given him. He had no illusions about her death. Although Ghita and Olga were convinced the fall had been an accident, he knew better. She was one more victim of the evil he was trying to destroy and who paid back all of his informants with the ultimate penalty, *death*.

All he could do was hope that the courageous old lady had not suffered too much in her exit, but it seemed unlikely. He had seen dead people in his time, and most of them looked peaceful – but not the Piper's victims. Anya's expression had been one of horrified surprise, mixed with agony.

What had she seen? Pip felt himself shiver, even though he was ensconced in his cosy, comfortable lodgings with the winter sun warming the room. He had been brave in his teens, in his twenties, and now believed that men in their forties, like him, didn't dwell upon the manner of their death, except in war or if they were unbalanced to a certain degree. He was waging a war of another kind, alone – and his own death was often on his mind. Would he die well?

He shook off these morbid thoughts and returned to his task with grim determination. He, too, had a duty to fulfil, foretold by the latest victim's grandmother, Eva Kirchma, the ancient gypsy; to rid the world of an immortal beast who strode through it, destroying the lives of innocent people. Yet Pip's fight was becoming more dangerous daily.

Would he have died if that cab had pinned him to the wall? Most people would. He had been hurt, but not seriously, because the vehicle had veered away at the last minute. He wondered why it hadn't come back, like pursuing cars do in gangster movies.

Was he indestructible? It was the weirdest thought of all. If any of his patients had proposed this premise for themselves, to Pip, the professional psychologist, it would have suggested they were delusional or bordering on insanity.

Yet, last night, he had seen the face of the driver of the supposedly driverless cab. It had been the face that haunted him; that of a man who resembled the criminal Walter Arvarescu, the music teacher who had disappeared with two children in 1952, and later, in 1988, had manifested as Diep Koppelberg, the manipulative paedophile, who had been hired by his mother as a music teacher for the family.

Simu Dalca had preferred to call these reappearances 'resurrections' rather than 'reincarnations'.

That morning, he was hoping that when he listened back to the last of the unfortunate Anya's story, he would finally be able to complete his account of the true root of the evil, and explain how it had begun with the Saxonian prince Nicholas, a devil-worshipping hostage at the Court of Charlemagne. Anya had said that it was all wrapped up in the history of the Holy Roman Empire. That much was no surprise to Pip, in light of the evil Popes pictured in the strange manuscript pages he had stolen from Eisenmann. Evidently, though, Diep Koppelberg, and all the Piper's other reincarnations through history, had no power over the Church. They could hurt only those who attempted to discover their secrets, like the unfortunate student Otto Werner – and look what had happened to him!

Now Pip was about to try to make sense of it all. He opened his laptop, ready to transcribe Anya's testimony.

<u>Dialogue 2. Compiled from fragments of an oral tradition related by (Black) Anya. Oxford. January, 2024. Recorded and collated by Philip Durrant, PhD.</u>

<u>The life and origin of the famous Nicholas of Saxony, a royal hostage, flute player, seer and magician who was first converted to Christianity by Alcuin and reverted to the Dark Arts.</u>
<u>This story has been handed down by one who knew him, a descendant of 'the Wicked Gypsy' of the Eastern regions, to his tribe and his descendants for posterity.</u>

Earlier in the day, Prince Nicholas had grasped me by the shoulder and beaten me with his stick, which had a huge male goat's head for a handle. He kept this stick in a locked chest far from the sight of his holy brothers, as they would have recognised it for what it was: an emblem of the Devil. As I cringed away, he snarled, showing his sharp incisors.

'Do not try to cling to my cloak tonight, little gypsy, nor spy on me. If you do, I shall conjure up a storm and make the wind blow so hard that it will carry your miserable pieces unto the end of the Earth.'

I crossed myself and crawled away. Many who knew the hostage prince suspected he was one of the tempestarii, *who ride on the clouds and consort with witches. I do not know if that is true, but he had many powers.*

I had been truly frightened all day, as I knew his savage nature, and at that time I believed that he could do such things. Yet I had also seen him pray in church with an expression that would suit an angel, and my heart had burned within me. At those times I said, O Lord, can this young master really be so bad? He is a servant of God, like us all. *In truth, I did not know then who he was, except I feared and loved him all at once.*

When the light of day was waning and the smell of summer was on the wind, I made up my mind. Like all of my race, I was curious, and desired new stories and sights to pass through the world. I suspected that Nicholas was going to meet the Princess Hildegarde, whom he lusted after daily. When he was kind to me, he often told me stories of his women, allowing me to revel in his secret thoughts. I was no priest, but I was his confessor!

In my heart I knew that something like that would happen that night. I had been near enough to listen to the heated whispers and the final lewd invitation that had been offered to the child princess. This, together with my knowledge of the date, and the fact that they would go walking that night through the forest gloom, filled me with both excitement and loathing. Where could they be going except to the devilish meeting? I wanted to be there to see what my master did. I knew in my bones that he wished her harm, and I had it in my mind once or twice to inform a lady who served the 'whore', as Nicholas called the Princess Hildegarde's mother; but to my shame I kept quiet to save my own skin, as I did not wish to go to Hell when he killed me.

Later, instead of creeping away to my small bed beside the hunting dogs, I watched him through the crack in the door as he prepared for his tryst. When he took off his cape, his workaday tunic and his shirt, I saw underneath that he was wearing a tight skin of red and yellow. Where he had bought it, I never knew, and yet I would have given my eyes for it, as it was covered in cunning patches that we gypsies love. It had been stitched to resemble a snake's skin, which is the sign of the Devil. It fitted every curve of his lithe body, a piece all in one, and where it began and where it ended I did not know. Nor did I know who could have sewn it in this manner. There are many clever needlewomen at the court, but which of them had the skill to do this I could not imagine, unless she was a witch.

I thought of the Princess and her girlish plumpness. Would she be hurt when he took her for himself? I had heard of the Devil wearing fish scales when he had intercourse with females. I had heard their cries before in the doing of that. I have lied to you, my fellow gypsies, because I have been to such meetings. But I have not taken part, only cowered amongst the bushes and trees, where my size allows me not to be seen. But back to Nicholas.

Over this skin, he slipped his best shirt, made of fine linen, not coarse like my thin tunic of the kind that peasants wear. He took a red tunic with its hood. A finely-tooled belt held his dagger, and over all this he threw his cloak. His boots were of a kind that I had never seen before, made of the finest leather that matched the skin next to his body. In my head I could see the serpent in him now, and I found myself sweating with fear. I wondered if the Princess would notice his finery. If she did, she would think he had dressed up for her and her alone. I marvel at the silliness of women when they are set such traps. But I watched on with eagerness, wondering if I should still jump up behind him, swing on his cloak and conceal myself. I decided not to, until he was in a better humour.

I saw him pick up his swan-bone flute and handle it lovingly. It seemed to come alive in his hand as he caressed it and put it to his lips. Yet no sound came out as he toyed with it. I shivered. If he played it that night then I would be done. Its plaintive voice drove me mad, and all the sense vanished from my head until I fell into a dream. No-one could play like him. The master of the monks, fat priest as he was, had threatened to smash it, but my master had concealed it so cleverly that the cleric could never find it afterwards.

Then, using a bone comb, he burnished his hair into beaten gold. Although I could not see much, I imagined by his manner that his strange blue eyes were sparkling. Sometimes they looked as if they were on fire, sometimes like a candle flame on which salt has been sprinkled. I have seen him in that mood when he has returned from the bed of one of his mistresses, but have never caught him in the act.

After this, he examined his sharp white teeth before the ornamented mirror that one of his aristocratic women had given him. All these things he secreted where no-one could find them, together with his most precious possession, the blasphemous Codex, which if it was discovered might bring him to execution. Only I knew what was in that Codex, because he had shown me. It was a record of his wickedness, written in a language I did not understand and illuminated by him alone. I am blushing now at the thought of it.

Nicholas had the opportunity to do all these things, because he lived apart from his fellow monks. On account of his fine work, he did not sleep with the other men but had been given his own cell. No-one could illuminate manuscripts like him, and if he had been one of the Emperor's own sons, he could not have lived better. In fact, I know that the Emperor was enamoured with him and admired his wit. But, as Nicholas often reminded me, he was a prince in his own country and one day he would escape this wearisome Frankish captivity. Maybe this was the day he intended to leave? I was waiting for that day, as I dreamed I could go along with him too, swinging on his cloak, because despite all his faults and terrible threats to my person, I loved Nicholas of Saxony. His brutish manners to me earlier did not matter, although it hurt me when I was excluded.

Indeed, once, as he held me up in the air after I was dizzy from his swinging around, I heard his menacing growl in my ear, 'One day, I shall exchange you for a black rat, Monkey, and watch the rat eat you afterwards, piece by piece!' Which was not a happy thing for me to hear – but I bore it because I could not do without him.

After he had left to meet the Princess, I was so sure of my master's destination that I made off quickly to the novices' quarters. That night, they all seemed to be asleep, except for one reprobate who was dressing himself in a hurry, hopping about trying to pull on his boot. He was another young Saxon who had been captured in battle, thrust into the font and held there by Alcuin of Tours until the boy, finding himself drowning, had renounced his Devil master and sworn he would be baptised a Christian.

Seeing me, he put a finger to his lips. I hurried forward and helped him to get ready, but he was not grateful, because he despised me. Then he threw on his cloak and I saw my chance. Usually, I would not have condescended to go with him, but I was so eager to see what my master was prepared to do to the Princess. And my legs were short! So I sidled up to him, smiling.

'Ah, little monkey,' he said, thrusting out his hand for me to kiss, 'you wish me to take you for a ride on my shoulder?' I nodded in a humble fashion and kissed his largest finger with my eyes shut. Otherwise, I would have bitten him.

'Yes, master, please,' I wheedled. A moment later, I was hoisted up. Yet, once outside in the windy night, he looked up at

me – and tossed me off. As I crawled to my feet on the grass, he snapped,

'Do you think I would take you to the forest on my shoulder, you ill-gotten midget of a gypsy?' he growled. 'Get away from me.'

I made an obscene gesture in reply, but then, as he strode away, I turned and ran behind him as quickly as one of the palace hunting dogs; and, taking off with a light bound, I clung to the back of his cloak, burrowing in. He could not get at me, nor could he leave his cloak behind for fear of severe punishment. Thus, swearing words Christian men should never utter, the godless novice was forced to take me where I wanted to go, and where he was headed – to the devilish celebration on the Eve of Mary Magdalene. As I jogged along on the novice's back, I would have been even more afraid if I had known what I was about to see.

I heard some snatches of music as I rode near to the place my master had planned for his tryst with the child princess. The notes could not be mistaken when we approached the glade in the forest, where the Emperor slaughtered his hunted and exhausted beasts on a great flat stone resembling an altar. The Emperor had ordered a little chapel built there. It was where he gave thanks to God for a good day's hunting the boar. But if he had known what blasphemous rites were performed there by his holy monks on high feast days, he would have had the edifice razed to the ground. I had seen enough times the way he hunted, and I was sick of it. Yet, sometimes I believed I yearned for a taste of fighting and blood, like all men do at some time in their lives. But then I remembered I was a little gypsy, all of whose kind have other matters on their mind, like taking advantage of wives left at home and goods to be stolen.

My master must be in a good mood now, *I thought, as the music slipped down the wind, melting it like honey dribbling into a pot to be licked.* **Peace,** *cried the wind and the flute together.* **Quiet, I shall not harm you.** *Maybe he did not wish the Princess harm, but I knew he was enchanting her, and soon her eyelids would droop and she would slip into a sleep more sound than if she had drunk the deadly juice of wolfsbane. I* *knew, because he had worked his charms on me before.*

I was almost disappointed as the novice came to a halt on the rim and sat down exhausted, looking from side to side for other wicked fellows, who no doubt were lurking somewhere in the bushes. All his enthusiasm to reach his destination seemed to have been blown away by the wind. I jumped off, but not before I had cut two pieces of wool off his garments to stuff in my ears, so that I should not also succumb to the music of the flute. Leaving the sacrilegious fellow to drift off, I carried on, safe with my deadened ears, and positioned myself so that I could see the spectacle.

The two of them were seated on the stone, as I had thought they would be, and she was leaning against his chest, her pretty little head with its braids drooping in sleep. I myself yawned at that moment, and I knew that if I thought of the meaning of the melody I would follow the rest of the congregation into oblivion. But I had superiority over all the folk who had gathered that evil night to make merry and to sin. I would not be entranced.

I yawned again, then hunched my shoulders in fear and ducked as he swung the flute in my direction. Did he sense someone was watching him? If he did, I was finished. All at once, his music must have changed, because the Princess was waking in the manner of a child, stretching her pretty limbs and smiling up at him as if he were a god. But I knew he was the Devil. I felt pity for her then, because he leaned down and kissed her, not on her mouth but on her neck and her breasts, and she did not try to stop him, but lay bewitched by his spell.

I knew it was time to unstuff my ears. When I did, I was almost deafened by the clamour. Grunts, sniffles and even screams of frustration as the bushes around me came alive. Those who had been sleeping also, were now flinging off their clothes and standing naked, both men and women, shaking their heads from side to side all the while. One shirt was flung so hard that it stuck and hung over the bush into which I had crept to take shelter. The loon to whom it belonged turned himself into a raucous pig as he jammed the animal's mask upon his head. I could see the mark of a collar round his neck, and I knew he was a runaway slave. A few yards away, a fat priest I knew from the chapter was disrobing himself hurriedly and fastening on the two horns of a bull, while his private parts jiggled about. I was sickened by his hypocrisy. There was an air of expectancy all around, as if the gathering was waiting for some great potentate to arrive; but I believed he was there already.

The wind too had risen from its knees in the low bracken and was gathering force. Both men and women ran out and took each other's hands and began to dance, their backsides, great and white in the moonlight, aimed toward my master and the Princess. They were chanting a mixture of prayers and psalms and lewd songs from the alehouse. I looked down at my own small body and decided I would not show if off that night. It was too good. Anyway, I needed to keep my clothes on in case I had to make a quick getaway. At times, I confess that I would have liked to have joined that merry, magic circle that swayed in and out in a rhythmic step, feet beating time in unison.

I craned my neck to see what the couple in the middle were doing, and gasped. My master had the Princess lying naked across his knees. Even I was shocked for a moment – I who, at my age, have seen every type of degradation and lewd behaviour. We gypsies have a sense of decency that those men and women lacked. I looked round, and I could see a child near me watching; a young fellow, eyes staring out of his head, goggling like the huge, fat frog he held in his hand. Around his neck was strung a coin, and I knew he had been paid to keep the frog for the master of the night. More children, tiny boys and girls, appeared now, driving a host of frogs from the muddy pool fed by the stream that trickled through the glade, to join the unholy spectacle. Too late for them – the children I mean – while the frogs were croaking, sensing what torture was to come. I blushed for the littlest and their lost innocence, because I am not all bad. Meanwhile, their godless parents danced before their eyes in a growing frenzy.

I withdrew from the bush and climbed into a tree, which was tall and slim, but leafy enough to hide me and strong enough not to bend beneath my weight. From there I could see it all. How I wished I had not looked! He was on her like a beast – and then I almost fell from the tree because, to my horror, on the farthest side of the ring, I saw her wicked mother, accompanied by her ignoble ladies and her confessor, all dancing naked and oblivious to what was happening to the poor Princess. They were all dancing in memory of Mary Magdalene. The bile rose in my throat, because I knew that the Princess's whore of a mother had been my master's mistress too, many times.

It was then I decided I had to do something. I am sure the Wicked Gypsy, my ancestor, felt like that in Bethlehem. He had been one of the dark King's slaves and had broken away in the hope of stealing the Christ-Child from his manger. Babies like Him brought gold in the slave markets of the East. But he did not succeed. It is said he repented of his wish to steal when he gazed into the bottomless depths of the Holy Boy's soft eyes and saw the hope of his own resurrection. All at once, he became a better man, replacing the Holy Child in His cradle carefully and thus saving mankind in his own way.

I made the sign of the cross and dropped from the tree, ready to force my way through the dancers to that great stone, that unholy altar, where my master was raping a helpless child with all the violence he could muster. I am not all bad, you see.

What I witnessed then was so terrible that I can hardly describe it; I hope it will remain as a warning for those who come after me, never to dabble in Devil worship. As I completed the first part of my mission, weaving my way through the dancers, I found myself glancing here and there. I am a male, and I confess to sinning myself by staring at those enchanted servant girls displaying their private parts so freely. Once or twice they tried to pull me into the ring, but I resisted.

As I began to climb up the great stone, I heard a shriek that would burst one's heart, a scream that would make most blood freeze within the veins. Above me, my master's little victim was being rent in two. I knew she was struggling against him, but at that very moment, I was face to face with his goat-headed staff. Leaning against the stone where it had been placed, it had come alive – and was watching me. From its gaping drain of a mouth, obscenities and foul threats poured. My heart almost stopped when I saw it growing larger. It seemed then to me, not to be a staff at all, but an opening in the stones, from which peered the *blazing eyes of a great creature, a rat so big that I nearly lost my senses! In my mind, I knew it was the rat that my master had promised would eat me! Being so small, I could not have fought against it, but I climbed on up the stones to the top and caught hold of one of the Princess's ankles and tried to pull her away from her attacker.*

The growl I heard from above me then was terrifying – while from behind, the awful chattering of many rodents assailed my unlucky ears. Next moment, I was caught by the scruff of my neck, and a powerful hand swung me up. The roar that accompanied it almost blasted me away. Above, the storm had broken, and I felt harsh stinging as small stones were whipped up by the wind and ripped at my face. I knew the earth was against me, and Hell too, as one moment later, I came face to face with what I had thought was my master.

The figure wore a devilish mask – or maybe it was his face – because whatever or whoever I saw above me was a monster. His eyes, like darting flames, were burning mine. Beneath them hung bags of old blue skin that must have seen an eternity of wickedness. His teeth were long and sharp, and I knew then there would be no pity for me in the world, because I was destined to be his next victim. Like the staff below, he continued to grow until he was huge, and as the thunder bellowed, my smarting eyes were dazzled with the yellow and red hue of a sinuous snake, which split open, letting the shell of my master fall away and crumple like a dead chrysalis on that foul altar of stones and leaving me to face the Devil himself. Moments later, in front of my terrified eyes, he rose and wreathed his coils above me, until a black storm cloud descended upon us all, cloaking the entire company. The shrieks and moans of those below me were vile to hear, but it was not their Devil master they were calling on, but their own true God to deliver them.

I think I fainted then, but when I came to, the Princess, bleeding from her ordeal, sat huddled on the stones, while my master lay silent at a distance. His swan-bone flute, which had enchanted her and the rest of the company, was lying beside him on the stones, with the goat-headed stick as its companion. Yet, in my half-deaf ears, I could still hear the faintest scrabbling that told me that the horrid rat was somewhere near. Many of the frenzied worshippers who had danced were staggering about now like drunkards, while others were kneeling in fear. I saw one or two on their hands and knees creeping away; but the Princess's mother and her ladies lay in contorted positions around the altar, like ugly wooden dolls. It was as if I was coming out of a nightmare. I truly saw it all, I warrant you – and I would swear that on the Holy Book before the Pope in Rome.

I gabbled my own gypsy prayer, because even though I was almost crazy with fear, I wanted none of the hypocrisy of those sinful Christians who had changed so quickly into penitents. My eyes kept glancing at my master, as I truly thought he might at last be sorry for his crimes. However, I was wrong. Instead, he rose and drew himself up to his full height, then approached the Princess, who lifted her tear-stained face to his. Her expression was one of staring horror, as if she too had changed into a girl child's stiff plaything.

I could see there was no remorse in the way he treated her. I knew then he had accomplished what he had set out to do, and the filth within him had fed his lust. The filth he had harboured had left this prince as he had always been, haughty and cruel, while, in comparison, little Hildegarde resembled a broken, tortured angel. As he approached her, she pointed her trembling childish finger at him. The ladies below had now risen, including her mother, who had her arms stretched out to Hildegarde, imploring her. But, to my mind, that woman should never be forgiven for her unnaturalness in watching her child treated so cruelly. They stared on, but dared not approach, as Hildegarde commenced to curse her conqueror.

'In the name of God, come no nearer, Brother Nicholas. You have done me great harm,' she screamed. 'I cannot make you sorry for your sin. Only God can do that. But you will pay for it until this world ends.' She made the sign of the cross, and others below her hesitantly followed her example.

'What care I for your cross?' he replied, his face hard set in wickedness. 'You and your Christian tribe have done me great wrong, and this is my time for payback. My master has always

been the Devil, and he dwells in me as you say your God dwells in you. He loves my wickedness, which I shall practise to the end of time.' He sneered, and I was disgusted by his blasphemous words. The air bristled with his anger as he faced the invisible line between them.

Princess Hildegarde turned away and addressed the silent crowd below. 'Listen to me, my people!' she appealed. 'I came here on this night in my sixteenth year as an innocent child, and now my purity has been violated in the most brutal way.'

To him again. 'I curse you, Nicholas, for my shame. I vow that, from now on, you will wander through the world forever. Whether or not you perpetuate your evil by committing other crimes like this, I shall never know, because I shall be dead within a week.' The people gasped. 'I shall have grown old, because I have no taste for life on this hateful earth. My great father Charlemagne shall hunt you down and bring you to justice.'

Back to the crowd. 'All of you, listen well. Today is my sinful mother's birth date.' She pointed a finger at the crouching whore. 'To her shame, I was conceived out of wedlock, and made that sin mine, although I am innocent. I charge you that this shall never be spoken of, except by married women, who must warn their daughters of the rapacious beast that lives within an evil man.

'Good men and the weak, who by virtue of their sex can never suffer a woman's misfortune, may only behold their females' anguish and learn from it. Hereafter, if a boy shall be conceived of an evil mother with this birth date, let him be crippled in leg or mind and be only a bystander, as this gypsy slave has been, with no care for the victim.'

She stared at me in disdain. I wanted to tell her that I had tried to save her, but there was no reason in her. God had taken over her tongue as the curses fell from her lips.

I saw my master sneer, as she told him, 'I pray you will never father a child; and if you do, that boy shall be your scourge and downfall. And from this day, if a girl is made to suffer like I have, rather let her grow old and wither, as I shall, before she falls into the hands of other wicked men. Every 36 years, which is your age, you will remember what I have said. That on this day I cursed you with my dying breath, and bade you wander through the world until you face my God on the Day of Judgement. Then and only then may you taste his mercy or his vengeance.'

With this, Princess Hildegarde fell to the ground and lay motionless, leaving the people trembling for several moments until they ran madly from the place, knowing that if they were rounded up by her father and his men they would face the most horrible tortures.

I stood, uncertain what path to take, as I had been singled out by the Princess and there would be no mercy for such as me. Then I felt cold, hard fingers catching me by the scruff of the neck.

'Come, you disobedient little gypsy,' my master snarled. 'This is no place for either of us.' A moment later, I was off my feet, then was being dragged along until I was half senseless, because the manner of his flight bumped the wind out of me. He did not offer me a ride on his back, nor did I wish it, knowing that I had seen him split from man into monster. It would not have surprised me if he had begun to fly like the **tempestarii.** *I knew now that Brother Nicholas was no ordinary being, that he was no mortal. All I kept wondering was when he would turn from prince to demon again and devour me whole.*

Others of my race will tell more of their tales to an eager listener, of how Nicholas the Flute Player and I wandered the world together, East, West, North and South, as he forced me to witness his many wickednesses and his ability to shift his shape at will for his own ends.

Yet I escaped from his slavery and took with me part of something he held so dear, which I had coveted for ages; the thing he loved most on this earth, his blasphemous Codex, in which he had set down all the sins he had committed. In spite of its content, I loved his art. No mortal man could illuminate the letters so; letters that I had never understood, with pictures the like of which I had never seen, reviling the Christian faith he hated.

And he did not die! But I could see in his eyes that he was tiring and searching for the date of the end of the world, so that he could free himself from the Princess Hildegarde's curse and, finally, when evil triumphed, rest in the arms of his master, the Devil in Hell.

As for me, after an eternity of wandering with him, I became grizzled and old; yet Nicholas remained the same golden-haired, blue-eyed man in his full powers, until I grew jealous of him and stole the only thing he loved in this world, that impious work of his – or, at least, some of the pretty pictures that spoke clearly of his evil – and placed them where he could never enter, the shrine in the great Dom in Saxony that houses the bones of my own tribe's first masters, the Three Wise Men; a shrine revered and guarded by my tribe for centuries.

Maybe that day when I risked my life to steal them, I was hoping that they might be discovered by good men, who would follow the Piper's trail and destroy him. You see, I had remembered the stories I had heard about the promises revealed in those deep, unfathomable eyes of the baby Christ-Child when he had gazed at my own ancestor, the Wicked Gypsy, as he tried to steal Him from His cradle.

I am a thief too, but I know my place. And soon, like the small Princess, I began to wither away; but not before I had related this story to the seers in my tribe, in confidence of that Child's forgiveness of this great sinner and the hope of my redemption.

10

Pip's computer chair creaked as he turned away from the transcript. He sat, leaning his arm on his desk and stroking his forehead with his hand. When written down, Anya's story seemed more fantastic than when she had told it. Now he thought about it, it was amazing how it contained elements of literature and tradition. There were figures that any modern watcher of television or film could recognise, or indeed any scholar of myth. The never-ending journey that the characters undertook; the monster that was determined to defeat the hero; and the trusted companion – all in these few pages of dictation.

In the Marcu Papers, Sacha Marcu had discussed with Robert, his charge nurse, how the schizophrenic women who were referred to him at Burbor Hospital all experienced the same visions. They had talked about the *collective unconscious* and Jung's belief that all people were born with the same myths and images in their minds. Here, Anya's recollection of the tales of her ancestors displayed the same mythical elements; the primary one in this case being the *immortal self*, the man who cannot die. In this case, the monster she described was Nicholas, the flute player, the Grandsire of Arva, and the Devil who lived inside him.

Pip felt his hair prickle on his neck. According to the little gypsy's account, Nicholas was searching for a way out, so that the Princess's curse could be broken. He needed to know the date of the end of the world; and, when he discovered it, he intended to write it down in his Codex, part of which was said to have been hidden in the shrine of the Three Kings in the great Cathedral, the Dom in Cologne, Germany. Why was that place chosen? Could it still be there? Could the gypsies still watch over that shrine? He thought of his adversary, Eisenmann. Did he know this? Was this where he had obtained what Pip had stolen from him? He had to do some more research! The whole thing was mind-blowing.

Here he was now in another Piper Year; and sooner or later, he was going to meet his monster face to face. The shape-shifter was after him still. It appeared to him, asleep and awake; it had left blood on his book; it had sent its awful rat companion, Snipe, to gnaw at the pages; and it had driven a driverless cab down an Oxford street to kill him. If he had told all this to a doctor, he would have been sectioned as mad. But he knew he wasn't mad: it was all true.

He rubbed his forehead hard. It was no good trying to rationalise. He had been handed Anya's story, of which he had to make some sense. She had paid for it with her life, so that he could move on. What had he learned from the narrative? Did it matter who the narrator was, who had ridden on the Piper's back or been carried in his cloak, and who had presented himself more like a talking monkey than a human companion?

Pip didn't feel any better for thinking it out. He had a horrible feeling that Anya's little gypsy might be *a child*. A child who had accompanied Nicholas wherever he went, had been a witness to his evil and learned evil from his example; a small being who had spoken with a voice meant to represent all abused children. He shook his head. That might be too clever. Too academic. But what had Simu said about children? *Only children stand between two worlds. Children are the visionaries.*

'Clever,' he muttered. 'But where am I with the Princess's curses …? They have to make some sense.' He paused and went into the kitchen to make a drink. 'You need more help, Pip. You're getting slow,' he said out loud. 'You need Simu back! But it's your fault he's dead! Send me some help, Simu,' he prayed, as he filled his mug with coffee.

He went back and sat down at the computer again. The curses … He looked into the black liquid in his mug, and Simu's face stared back at him. Pip squinted. He wasn't given to praying but … he closed his eyes. He could almost hear Simu's voice. *Curses. They are part of the Arvan tradition. The secret of the marriage bed.* Pip felt a glimmer of light. The ideas were coming.

'Now … what did the Princess say …' He turned and found the place on the screen:

'Today is my sinful mother's birth date.' She pointed a finger at the crouching whore. 'To her shame, I was conceived out of wedlock, and made that sin mine, although I am innocent. I charge you that this shall never be spoken of, except by married women, who must warn their daughters of the rapacious beast that lives within an evil man.

'Good men and the weak, who by virtue of their sex can never suffer a woman's misfortune, may only behold their females' anguish and learn from it.'

'You idiot,' he said to himself. This was making sense now. The 'Little and Chosen', the Grandsire's future victim, had to be conceived out of wedlock, and her mother had to be born on 22 July, the Feast of Mary Magdalene. The men were those Arvan villagers who watched helplessly as their wives and daughters suffered. That was why they did not try to intervene or make their wives tell them what was going on and stop it if they could. Even Simu Dalca, an educated man, had been at a loss how to do so; but he at least had been trying. Or maybe he had known more than he had told Pip? At that moment, Pip didn't want to think about it, as he was wrapped up with the unravelling of the Princess's curse. How much more would he have learned if Simu's life had not come to an end? He took a deep breath and plunged on. He couldn't leave it now!

'Hereafter, if a boy shall be conceived of an evil mother with this birth date, let him be crippled in leg or mind and be only a bystander, as this gypsy slave has been, with no care for the victim.'

Claudiu Basa, the old recluse with the deformed leg, who used to watch the girls 'go up' to the churchyard. His mother had been born on 22 July! *That's what Fr Joseph told me in the riddle,* realised Pip. *I can't prove he was conceived out of wedlock though. Come on, Princess, give me more.* His excitement was growing.

'I pray you will never father a child; and if you do, that boy shall be your scourge and downfall.'

This was all making sense now. The child in this particular case could be construed as Eisenmann, who was the product of Anya and the German tourist, Nicholas, who raped her. A boy child that had survived; a child that resembled the Piper as her grandmother, Eva, had seen him. A golden-haired child of angelic face and physical beauty, but an evil boy, who was not deformed or an outcast like Claudiu Basa, but who was conceived of a gypsy and possessed the nature of the Piper.

Gypsies were allowed to watch what was going on, but never to take part in the ritual. Nicholas's rape was pure revenge, because if he were the Piper, then he knew that he had been recognised, once masquerading as the blond Nazi officer who had rescued Magda, Anya's mother, from her rape by one of his brutal soldiers in the second World War, and once years later as the German tourist. This rape went against the conditions of the curse, as gypsies were exempt from the Arva ritual, in which they could not take part and only watch. The boy who had resulted from this unlawful coupling, and whom Anya had sent for adoption, had proved himself to be his father's son. Pip, like Marcu, had discovered this in the demonstration of Eisenmann's preternatural powers, which he certainly would not hesitate to use to further his evil aims.

Like the little gypsy before him, Eisenmann was bent upon stealing the Codex – some of which he had already possessed until Pip took it from him. It stood to reason that Eisenmann now wished to recover the rest – and discover the date of the end of the world.

'And from this day, if a girl is made to suffer like I have, rather let her grow old and wither, as I shall, before she falls into the hands of other wicked men.'

The Piper's child victim in 1988 had turned into an old woman and died within a week; a further example of the curses' power. This had been recorded by the late Inspector Valentin, who had seen this phenomenon himself.

'Every 36 years, which is your age, you will remember what I have said ...'

And every 36 years, the monster of Arva, with his choice of names, either Piper or Grandsire or Nicholas, returned.

Pip went over his evidence again.

Arvan women must have heard the old stories about the Princess's curses, which they had retained in their cultural memory. What these simple villagers had not known was when the cycle started. Simu Dalca, the husband of one of them, had discovered part of the story, as had the brilliant young psychiatrist Sacha Marcu, the village doctor Baescu and the police detective Inspector Valentin, who had all, unknown to each other, been following the same trail.

Now Pip was certain that he did understand the 36 year cycle. Its beginning coincided with the founding of the Holy Roman Empire in the year 800. To Pip, as a historian, it seemed that the notorious corruption of the mediaeval Church began with the worldly bargain made between Pope Leo III and Charlemagne, in which Leo crowned Charlemagne Emperor, and in return Charlemagne and his Empire protected the sinful Pope from his enemies. The Church by its nature and early precepts was in conflict with the Devil, in whatever shape he appeared; although it had also proved itself historically and religiously to be closely allied to many of his evils.

From an historical point of view, Pip knew that the little gypsy's story of the happenings at the Court of Charlemagne could be viewed as entirely untrue, as the gypsies did not arrive in Europe until around 500 years later! They had been living in the Middle East before that. But where the little gypsy's story itself originated from he was not sure.

The village of Arva had been founded in the Middle Ages, around 1376. That was the date written upon the glass case he had seen in Diep Koppelberg's filthy lair in Sunny Mead. The date that Browning had chosen for his poem *The Pied Piper of Hamelin,* the source of which was a work of 1605 by a man called Verstegen. An account that Eisenmann had read!

Walter Arvarescu, the schizophrenic paedophile, had boasted that his *alter ego,* Nicholas, the Pied Piper, had been able to steal away every child in Hamelin, except one who was lame, and lead them into Koppelberg Mountain, never to reappear.

36 years later, Diep Koppelberg, who appeared to be Arvarescu's reincarnation, had forced Pip to enter into the mediaeval world of the Piper of Hamelin in a vision in his Sunny Mead lair, where Pip had taken on the nature of the lame boy who was left behind, and also to face the only rat that had not perished in the massacre. Nicholas had boasted then that he considered Hamelin to be his greatest triumph.

Pip had discovered that one of the legends that had sparked off the story of the Piper was the migration of the blond-haired Saxons to Transylvania after the plague of 1384. He had also found several other legends about the loss of the Hamelin children; one in particular that fitted the wanderings of Nicholas the Piper as ordered by the Princess Hildegarde.

The strongest evidence of a legend based on truth was the depiction of the real historical event of the Children's Crusade, which Diep Koppelberg had shown Pip in another of his vile cases in the Sunny Mead chalet.

It was in 1212 that a mysterious golden-haired boy called Nicholas, with the blessing of the Pope, had persuaded thousands of children to join him in a siege of Jerusalem, to win it back for Christ from Moslem hands. The Crusaders had undertaken this journey earlier and had lost their battle for the city. Nicholas's persuasion resulted in a useless pilgrimage, the consequence of which for those thousands of little victims was a terrible and merciless death. However, the boy, Nicholas himself, survived and turned up in Rome to report back to the Pope. Little else is known.

As all legends have an element of truth to them, the present facts about Arva remained what Pip and Professor Dalca had worked out between them:

There was a serial killer on the loose, who turned up in the village once every 36 years to commit the crime of raping a helpless girl in her sixteenth year. Each time, the result of the rape was the victim's accelerated ageing and subsequent death as an old woman.

The identity of the killer had never been discovered.

No explanation was known for the ritual.

Nor for the mysterious prolonged death that followed.

Nor for the fact that, when examined, the victims showed no trace of human semen but evidence of animal blood.

Sceptics would have scoffed at the idea that the crimes were all carried out by one and the same man, who would have had to have been some kind of time traveller. But, from his research, Pip was able to say with some confidence that this was indeed the case. What scared him most now was the thought that he might not survive long enough to reach the point of discovering something that would be of great significance to all mankind: *the date of the end of the world*. The idea seemed nonsensical, but he *was* on the trail – and finding the rest of the Codex had become to him a possibility, because he had part of the precious book in his possession. Pip had to continue, and the little gypsy's strange account, as related to him by Anya, was another stepping stone in his efforts. Where should he go next?

Later, an unexpected idea came to him. What about Klaas, the 17-year-old 'genius'? Maybe his apparent instability was only a front, and he knew a great deal more than he was letting on? Pip needed to speak to the kid's one-time school friend, Spencer. From the way that Klaas had spoken, Pip's instincts told him that Spencer wasn't going to be a friend to Klaas after all. But he had other things to do first. First and foremost, to read the mysterious message that Simu had left for him in 2007.

He plugged the memory stick into his laptop and ran the program to open the file he found on there. As he waited for Simu's words to appear on the screen, he thought of Anya. She had been faithful to her son to the last, and had given Pip the memory stick as Simu had asked her to, even though she must have wondered if the day would ever come.

Pip had chosen earlier to review Anya's story first – to transcribe it while it was still fresh in his mind – but it bugged him that he hadn't yet looked at Simu's message. He had always been patient, though, ever since he had spent all those years in a wheelchair. Patient and painstaking.

Again, he thought over Anya's words, *We have only a little time. This is the beginning for you and the end for me.* Anya had done her duty. They were hopeful words, though. Perhaps this meant he was close to reaching his goal?

He smiled as Simu's message finally appeared on his laptop screen and he began to read.

Dear Pip,

I remember when you and I began to call each other by these pet names. I think it meant that there would be respect and friendship between us, as proved to be the case.

I have much to tell you in this document, which I hope will never be needed, as I prefer to explain to you face to face. I should have told you this a long time ago, here at my home. The night that we had the power cut, before we started to try to unravel some of the secrets of my village. Do you remember? Emilia had to bring us in a branch of candles. Little did I know then what her fate was to be, although I suspected that she would go the way of the other women of Arva. But at least she was saved from the worst of that, as she died before she was incarcerated in Burbor, for which I am very grateful.

Now to something you may find hurtful. I guessed a long time ago how you felt about my daughter, but although it pains me to say so, you were never the suitor I would have chosen for her – although eminently more so than the boy Anton that Emilia had set her heart upon. He is a good boy, but is simple and uneducated and has little ambition or intelligence. You are just the opposite, but you would have been too old for Ghita, and you have an ambition far from the ordinary, which I shall discuss with you now. You might also have led her into danger.

Given my great grandmother's certainty that you are meant

to be the 'saviour' of us all, blasphemous as it seems (and when have I cared about blaspheming, given my own background?), it would seem you have been chosen to rid us all of an evil far beyond even your own comprehension. Indeed, you have taken on the Devil himself, and what father would wish a husband like that for his daughter? But that has not happened, and as yet, no harm has come to her. But come it will, sadly, in the shape of children she bears. Prepare yourself now, Pip.

She does not know my feelings about your friendship, but she is well aware what it is like growing up and becoming a woman in the village of Arva. Indeed, she has told me she intends never to have any children, in case a daughter of hers has to go through the torment of 'going up' in her sixteenth year.

Believe me, Arva has the strength to draw her would-be victims back to her, wherever they may be in the world. The old customs never die, and they are ingrained as much as religion. Ghita sees them as a burden no child of hers should have to bear. She has made her choice, but I tell you solemnly, she must not waver from it, because if my Ghita gives birth to a girl, THAT CHILD WILL BE THE GRANDSIRE'S VICTIM.

Pip stared at the screen and could feel his heart thumping in his ears. He swallowed and read on.

I have deliberately kept this from you, Pip, and now I'm sorry. I didn't trust you enough in the beginning. GHITA WAS BORN ON 22 JULY, AND SHE IS DESTINED TO BE THE MOTHER OF THE LITTLE AND CHOSEN. If she brings a female child into the world, in 2024 that child will make her way to the churchyard in Arva village. There is one other thing, which Ghita does not know, and which will be almost as terrible for her. As it is decreed, she will be forced to watch and suffer the brunt of the Grandsire's anger, whatever form that might take, when he realises his victim has gypsy blood – as I am sure he will. He will destroy the child, and her mother too – if the other conditions are fulfilled.

It may be a heavy burden, and I have no right to ask you, but in the name of our past friendship, please do all you can to prevent this happening, Pip, if I am not there to do so. I beg you to do this for me, if I am not able.

Your faithful friend,

Simu Dalca.

Pip stopped reading. He felt sick, horrified at what he had learned. Ghita had been born on Piper Day, and so it followed that Olga could be the Piper's next victim. Pip couldn't believe it for a few seconds, and then his first thought was that he had to do something to stop it.

His shoulders slumped, his brain trying to compute a solution. Ghita would never let her daughter be hurt – and this was Oxford, not Arva. Yet did the location matter? So far, that was something that had never entered into the equation. He knew from his own experience that the Piper, after his rising, could appear anywhere in the world. He might hunt Olga down in his rage. Clearly he knew all about Pip, because he was stalking him. Why shouldn't he turn to Olga now, especially when he'd been cheated?

Pip couldn't bear the thought of anything happening to Olga. At that moment, he realised that he must be so deeply in love with Ghita that he felt the same about her daughter, even though he didn't know much about her, or about either of their lives since 2007. The enormity of the realisation hit him hard. He knew that he had to stop the Piper once and for all – and this time he would be brave, even if it meant his life for theirs.

Pip had never been a person who wanted or even needed sympathy. He'd had too rough a start in life, and when he'd been in the wheelchair after the accident, he'd had to look after himself and be independent as far as he could. This whole feeling about Ghita and Olga was different – a tenderness toward them, and the urge to be protective. It was a good feeling, because he knew he'd been more than selfish in demanding information from others that would probably lead to their deaths.

Then anger took over for a while. How could Simu have

withheld this from him? Was that what Ghita wanted to discuss with him? She had married Anton, and surely she must know the Arvan 'secret of the marriage bed' now? If she did not, it was her father's fault again, as he must have known Anya's story, and yet still persisted in keeping his secret.

A few minutes later, Pip softened again toward the man who had been his mentor and friend. Simu had had the best excuse. He hadn't lived to see his granddaughter, and had doubtless wanted to spare Ghita the massive shock of learning about her gypsy heritage. It had come as a shock to Pip himself, and he was an American and knew little about the gypsy question. Many ordinary Romanians reviled the Roma, who had consequently been consigned to filthy, poverty-stricken camps outside their cities. Might that have happened to Ghita eventually, however eminent her father was? Simu was dead now and couldn't protect her, as he had her mother and her grandmother.

At least in Oxford, Ghita and Olga couldn't be connected to Anya and her infamous background. Or could they? *More and more secrets breeding lies*, thought Pip, and his respect for Simu drained away again.

The Professor had decided too late to give Pip the information. Had he been afraid himself that he had learned something that should never be disclosed to a man? Could he have been that superstitious? Or had he been afraid that it would become public knowledge that he was a gypsy and the son a former prostitute? It wouldn't have been pleasant, but if only Pip had known before about the woman he loved – and he did love Ghita – they could have discussed the dilemma before all this mess happened.

Why hadn't he ever asked Ghita that simple question everyone asks, *When's your birthday?* He wasn't sure why. Perhaps he had been going to, but had been too afraid of the answer. Or perhaps he hadn't bothered, because she was past the age for 'going up'? Maybe he was as bad as Simu, who had never trusted him enough!

He thought some more about the other conditions of the curse. His heart lifted at once. Olga had to have been born out of wedlock to qualify! Simu couldn't have known, when he wrote his message, that Ghita would marry Anton. Then again, was it possible that Olga had been born before they got married? Or could Ghita even have been unfaithful to Anton? She had admitted that their marriage had not been a happy one. Possibly Olga hadn't been Anton's daughter after all. In which case, she could still technically have been born out of wedlock. The idea shook him. It looked distinctly possible that Ghita's unfortunate daughter was indeed destined to be the Piper's next victim.

Pip was close to losing hope now. He would have to try to find out from Ghita that exact circumstances in which Olga had been conceived and born. He could feel himself sweating. 'What a fucking mess,' he swore. 'And you left me to do your dirty work, Simu! You said you loved Ghita, but it doesn't feel like it to me. Isn't it better finding out you're a gypsy than risk losing your only daughter to some murdering beast?'

He needed to see Ghita anyway. She and Olga were very upset about Anya, and there was still the funeral to come. He had offered his help, which Ghita had declined, saying repeatedly, 'Poor Anya. I don't even know whether she wanted to be buried or cremated. I suppose being cremated is the best. I'm sure she wouldn't have wanted to be buried here in England. I have thought of taking her ashes back to Cluj. Olga is very keen to see Romania.'

Pip knew it wasn't his place to get involved in their business, and that he deserved no influence, given his cowardly behaviour. But he would watch over Ghita and her daughter from a distance – and wait for July.

There was only one other way that Olga could ensure she was safe, which sounded so sick that he couldn't possibly suggest it to her mother: she could lose her virginity. *Grandsire likes only children!* He had always hated that phrase. It was a shitty idea to think of, but a real possibility, however much Ghita disliked Klaas. He had only just met the guy, but he felt that Klaas couldn't be satisfied by his studies alone. He was a virile young man, and Pip remembered the way he'd heard the pair of them laughing late into the night he'd stayed at Ghita's. Now, in spite of himself, he was hoping they had been in bed together. Having sex with Klaas might be the best thing Olga ever did, and damn her coming exams!

Pip phoned Spencer James's mother the next day, but it seemed that Ghita had got there first and she was expecting Pip to ring.

'We've talked it over with Spencer,' she said, 'and he said he'd be fine with it. But don't expect to get much out of him, Professor. He's a teenager! His dad's given him an ultimatum, not to have anything more to do with Klaas, if possible – which might be awkward, given their music commitments. It was all that boy's fault, getting him to drive, and now Spencer has been cautioned and he's on the police register. I do hope you can help. Our Spencer is usually so sensible.'

'Please try not to worry, Mrs James. I shan't be with him long – and I do have a lot of experience with teenagers,' reassured Pip, thinking all the time how devious he could be to get his own way. He didn't want to think of the possible consequences, though; and, of course, that was entirely unprofessional. Yet he was pretty sure that whatever Spencer James could tell him couldn't be anything that would cause the kind of repercussions his informants had suffered before.

'Thank you,' his mother went on. 'I am so relieved, and we're actually a bit flattered that you want to talk to Spencer.'

'Why's that?' Pip asked, inwardly sighing. He knew what was coming. He was right, because Mrs James's tone changed, and she became positively gushing.

'I was *so* surprised to find out that Ghita knows such a well-known author *and* a professor at Norris, of course. Such a good college! I *have* bought your book.'

'Not quite *at* Norris. I'm a visiting professor. Just until the summer.'

At that point, Mrs James revealed her agenda! 'I do have some hopes for Spencer to have a shot at Norris after his gap year! He's predicted excellent grades. History is his best subject.'

'I'm afraid I have nothing to do with admissions,' replied Pip firmly. He then politely extricated himself from the conversation, after eliciting a promise that Spencer would be brought over to his rooms the following day.

Afterwards, he phoned Ghita, thanked her for her input and promised that they would get together after he had spoken to Spencer.

'Reporting back so soon,' she said, sounding in control again and not the woman who'd clung to him when they'd discovered Anya's body. 'I'd better tidy up, then,' she added, which was a feeble attempt at a joke.

'Not on my account …' The rest of the conversation was triviality, but ended on a note of detectable urgency from Ghita.

'Have you spoken to Klaas yet? About seeing him? He's here all the time now Anya's gone. You will come to the funeral?'

'If you want me to.'

'I do, and to travel in the car with us. With me, Olga – and Klaas. Evidently, my daughter can't do without him. I don't like it, but I do have some sympathy for the boy. Olga says he's been beating himself up about the accident. He told me himself he was desperately sorry for causing Anya's death. He seems to mean it, and I've begun to feel guilty that I've been blaming him – and spying on him.'

'I'm not sure spying on him is a good idea,' Pip answered. 'Just think of Olga. It'll do no harm for him to come, if she needs him. Now, are you sure you want me along with you?' Being near to Ghita was what he desired most of all, but knowing he was keeping secrets from her didn't sit well with him. He only wanted to come clean – about everything. But he couldn't see the way to do it – yet.

'Of course I'm sure, she said. 'In a way, I feel you're taking the place of Tăta. For old times' sake?'

He grimaced. Ghita wanted him to take Simu's place. To give her a shoulder to cry on. He was willing to try, but he felt as guilty as if he had left his own trainers on the stairs instead of Klaas – and knew that, indirectly, he had killed Anya, like he'd killed everyone else who'd furthered his quest. Trying hard to make his voice normal, he answered, 'Okay, thanks. It's a privilege. Just let me know the arrangements. Don't forget now, take it easy.'

'By the way,' she said, 'can we meet tomorrow in Waterstone's at lunchtime? Twelvish. I've got Anya's death certificate.'

'And ...?

'I don't want to discuss it right now. I feel choked up.'

'Right. You'd better have a rest, then.'

When she'd hung up, he hoped she wouldn't want an answer to her earlier questions. He wasn't ready. He had to think of how to present Simu's information without appearing an arsehole. What would she do if she knew that Pip suspected that although Anya's death appeared to be an accident, she was most probably murdered by someone or something supernatural? And what would be her view of him if he added that the kid she was taking with her in the funeral car was most probably connected with Anya's death in a far more direct way than simply being careless with his trainers? At that point, Ghita might be scared to death or think that Pip had gone mad.

11

'Anya's death was an accident, as we thought, but …' said Ghita, as they sat drinking coffee the following lunchtime, '… but it says on her death certificate that she'd had some kind of stroke owing to her blood pressure. When I asked the doctor to explain, he said she'd probably already lost her balance when she tripped on the trainers and fell down the stairs. We're all a bit relieved about that. Poor Klaas. He was sure we'd all blame him for killing her. I don't like the boy, but he is really upset about it.'

'I bet he is,' said Pip. 'Did he actually say "killing", though? It's a strong word.'

'Yes, but …' Ghita leaned forward. 'Olga let slip that some years ago at St Willibrord's he was involved somehow in the suicide of a boy named Edward, and a lot of the other pupils seemed to blame him for it. She knows the details, but she refused to tell me. She is so upset about Anya that I didn't press her. If I had, I might have said something I'd probably regret later. I've a feeling she was winding me up, actually. She was never like that before. She's so stroppy now!'

'As you said. But don't you think she should be making her own choices what to tell her mother by now?' He knew straightaway he'd said the wrong thing.

'What? At 15? I don't think so,' retorted Ghita. Her eyes sparked. 'You've never been a father, so how would you know?'

He held up his hands, warding off her anger in a mock

gesture. 'Okay, okay. I agree that I don't know much about kids, but I heard that some even have sex at 13 these days and don't tell their parents.'

Ghita made a face at him. 'What? Would you want that for your daughter? That is, *if* you had one.'

'Not that I'm likely to,' he replied, shaking his head.

'No recent relationships, then?'

The thought that she might really be interested in the answer gave him some hope. 'Not that I can think of. Peace?' She sniffed in response, so he added, 'I'm sorry. I didn't mean to meddle. I thought I was helping.'

'Why do you say that?' she countered.

'Just thought I might be,' he replied, still hoping. But any reassurance from her as to her interest didn't come. 'Anyway, the last time we spoke properly you said there was a question you wanted to ask me.'

She considered his words. 'More than one.' He braced himself. 'You look worried,' she added.

'I suppose I am. I'm not used to giving advice – except to my students, these days, I suppose.'

Ghita stared into her coffee, then rammed home what Pip had been dreading. 'In the last note I received from my father, he said he had something to tell us both. Do you know anything about that?' Her eyes were glistening, and he thought she was going to cry, but fortunately she controlled herself. 'Have you any idea?'

'Ummm ...' Pip cleared his throat. Should he lie again, and simply point out that she knew Simu didn't make it to the airport in time to talk to him? He needed to think quickly.

'You're annoying me,' said Ghita, her eyes flashing in temper now, as he remembered them.

'I always did, didn't I?'

'Not always.'

'And that's what you want to discuss? Your dad?' She nodded her head curtly in response to his words. He could see she was getting more annoyed. He cleared his throat again and continued, 'I expect ...' Now the opportunity had arrived to come clean, he knew he couldn't tell her yet.

'I don't need "expect". I want the truth. What were the two of you working on really?' she asked.

He looked at his watch. 'If I started to tell you that I'd be here all day, Ghita – and I have an appointment with Spencer James tonight about Klaas – as we agreed.'

'Don't try to change the subject, because you're only going to tell me more bloody lies!' The forceful answer hit him in the gut. 'Short of time or not, you're going to have to tell me about the memory stick that Anya wore!'

'What?' That took him unawares.

'Got you,' she said. 'I know about it, Pip. Do you think I'm an idiot? She carried it round her neck for years, and she couldn't even use a computer. It's only because I'm honest that I didn't take it off her bedside table when she was asleep. I knew it had to be from Tăta. I asked her once whom she intended to give it to and she replied, "Someone will turn up, Ghita." That made me really angry, because I knew what she meant. Her confidence made me sick, actually, considering I'd lost my belief in you a long time ago!'

'That's cruel,' he said, 'but I know I deserve it.' In a strange way, it made him feel better when she despised him.

'You deserve a lot worse than that, Pip, and yet ...' She stopped and breathed in deeply.

Don't cry, Ghita, please, he begged inwardly, *because if you do, I'll never have the courage to tell you the truth.*

Her eyes were glistening again, but she shook off the pain. 'I knew she had given you the memory stick, because it wasn't on her body after she fell. Also, I knew it was a put-up job between the two of you when I came into the kitchen that day after work. "Wandering about in Oxford" indeed. You're a good liar, but you've had plenty of practice, and if it wasn't for you helping me with Klaas, I'd kick you out now. Don't hang your head like that, Pip. I hope you're ashamed of yourself.'

He didn't answer.

'I asked myself so many times why my dad would give something to my great aunt, whom I'd never met, that he wouldn't give to me. Once, I thought it might contain her will, but now I know she made alternative arrangements for that. As it happens, she left everything to me – and it's a fair amount – apart from a decent sum to go to Olga. She obviously went and found a solicitor of her own, because the address, with a note saying to get in touch with him when she died, was in the top drawer of her dresser, almost as if she knew what was going to happen to her.

'The irony of it is that her solicitor told me she'd added a codicil to her will, saying that if the time came and she still had the memory stick, then it was the property of Professor Philip Durrant, an American psychologist, and must remain with the solicitor until every effort had been made to find you. I felt such a fool when he told me, so I said that you'd turned up and it had been handed over. I think you're probably going to have to verify that with your signature.' Pip nodded.

'It's as if she or my dad didn't trust me. That's how secret it was – and I want to know why. What was on the memory stick that I ought not to know, Pip?'

After that tirade had ceased, Ghita gave a juddering breath, then added, 'Well, I know I shouldn't be hurt like this after all these years, but I still am! It's like the two of you have betrayed me.'

Pip knew it was too late to defend himself and lie any more. He went to take her hand, but she snatched it away, fixing him with hostile eyes.

'Please don't think that, Ghita,' he pleaded. 'Your dad did it for your own good.'

'What do you know about my "own good"?' she burst out. 'I needed both of you, but I've managed very well on my own.'

'I know I'm a shit,' he said, 'but don't blame your father. Please believe me, I've been agonising about this for a while now. I was going to tell you everything, but I thought, what with the funeral and all that …'

She made a disdainful noise. 'I'm waiting,' she snapped.

'It's not something I can rush through.' He was the desperate one now. She was glaring. 'I'll explain it all very soon, but I can't right now, and I have an appointment tonight. What about tomorrow evening?'

She sat for a while, and he could see she was trying to contain herself, before she answered, 'Okay, I'll go along with that. But remember, I'll know if you're lying. Whatever that memory stick has on it, I want to know every tiny bit. I deserve that after what you've put me through. I'm not going to forgive you. I'm up to here with secrets and lies. For Christ's sake, I grew up with them, and I don't want my life and Olga's to be like that now.'

She turned her head away from him, then settled back and drained the rest of the coffee. He dared to catch her hand again, and this time she didn't pull away. He held it tightly, to give him strength as well as her.

'I swear I'll tell you everything tomorrow evening, Ghita. I'll bring over my laptop and you can see for yourself.'

'Right. What time?' she asked.

'Sixish?'

'Fine by me. Let's hope you don't disappear for another 17 years!'

He didn't dare smile at her sarcasm.

Spencer James's father dropped his son off as agreed. The kid looked as though he'd been having a hard time. Also, he seemed the wrong kind of guy to be friends with Klaas. But then, Klaas had said, "He doesn't like me." Klaas had indicated too that Spencer was scared of him. That figured, given Klaas's attitude even to Pip.

As he looked at Spencer, Pip wondered if there was any particular reason why he had been enough of a friend to Klaas to be used by him. Why, for instance, had Klaas let Spencer travel with him and Olga, and even drive his powerful and expensive car, when he must have known the kid couldn't handle it?

There might be an entirely mundane answer: dynamic good lookers often make friends with mousey, plain ones. It has something to do with ego, making the bright, handsome guys look even better by comparison. Somehow, knowing Klaas, Pip had a feeling that wasn't the case here.

The boy's head was hanging down, and he'd evidently arrived under duress. His father had a brief chat with Pip, while Spencer stood there dumbly. The boy had a hooded jacket, but the hood wasn't up like Klaas wore his. Short brown hair, neat jeans and T-shirt, all perfectly clean and pressed. No sign of a rebellious teenager here.

Both Dad and Mom have had a go at you, thought Pip. Luckily, the father didn't ask to be present for what he referred to as 'your interview'. His last words to Spencer were, 'You co-operate with the Professor, Spencer. And speak up!'

Spencer nodded, and after his father had gone, remained standing awkwardly in exactly the same place, until Pip motioned to him in a friendly manner to take a seat.

After offering a drink, which produced a quiet 'No, thanks,' Pip started to make headway with this seemingly typical English private school boy. Straightaway, Pip told him that everything they said to each other was strictly confidential.

'You can't tell even my mother and father?'

'That's right. I won't be preparing any report on this! This is a friendly conversation with nothing off limits. I've spoken to Klaas, and he assured me you'd tell me the truth. I don't know what he meant by that, but he definitely wanted you to. You do know why you're here, Spencer, don't you?

'Honen said that?' The use of the surname was a marker for Pip. This kid didn't like Klaas – but that was what Klaas himself had said!

'Sure. And in my professional capacity as a psychologist, nothing that happens in this room will be ever spoken of to anyone else.'

At this point, Pip handed over a leaflet confirming that a meeting between a patient and his psychologist was confidential. Spencer read it all carefully, while Pip waited. When the boy had finished, Pip said again, 'You do know why I wanted to speak to you? Klaas and I had a long talk about some things that I can't disclose, and I wanted verification of certain points. And he gave me your name.' Spencer nodded. He looked extremely miserable. *Things don't look good*, Pip thought. 'Are you all right with that?' Spencer nodded again.

'As long as you don't tell *him* anything.'

Pip indicated the leaflet.

'Okay.' The kid was sweating. 'Can I take off my hoodie?'

'Feel free. It's hot in here.'

Spencer complied.

'Okay now?'

'Yep.'

It was Pip's turn to nod. He went over and fetched a bottle of Coke from the fridge and a glass and put them down on the table by Spencer.

'Thanks.'

'So, tell me, how long have you known Klaas?'

'A long time,' replied Spencer. He seemed to have woken up. 'I can talk about anything?'

'Sure. That's what we're here for.' This looked more promising. There was an artlessness in the kid that Pip liked, but also a recklessness that hadn't been apparent a few moments ago.

'And you won't tell my parents?'

'No.'

Spencer looked round the room, as if noting everything. 'This is a good college,' he said.

'Yes.'

He leaned forward. 'I used to think I'd like to come here. Everybody in the sixth form would, but I'm not smart enough. My mother's mad on me trying, but I haven't a hope.'

'Okay.'

'But there's another reason why, if I were smart enough, I wouldn't come here for anything in the world.' The words were forceful. Pip lifted his eyebrows. 'You know why. Because ...' He hesitated. Pip waited. 'Because *he's* here.'

'You mean Klaas?'

Spencer dropped his gaze and stared at the floor. Then he

lifted his face to Pip. His eyes were screwed up like a little kid's who doesn't want to see anything bad. 'I – hate him,' he said. 'Honen knew I'd tell the truth … I'd have to say it. To tell you … because …' he swallowed, 'because … he wants me to, because … then he's going to pay me out.' He opened his eyes and stared at Pip. They were full of fear.

Pip realised that this kid was terrified of Klaas. He was sweating even more now, so Pip leaned over and offered him the Coke, which he took this time.

'What have you done to him, Spencer?'

'That's it. I haven't done anything, but he just … I know something will happen.'

'To you, you mean?'

Spencer nodded. 'He wants me to tell you what he's like, so he can have his own back. That's what he does. I'm scared as shit to say anything, but he knows I have to, because I'll be …'

'Just as scared if you don't tell me?'

'Yep.'

'Has he done things to you before?'

'It's not like that, sir. He has only to *think* and … it happens.'

'You need to explain a bit more, Spencer. You're saying he has only to think about someone getting hurt, and then they do? How do you know what Klaas is thinking? Has he told you? '

'You'll know too, if you have anything to do with him,' replied Spencer, ignoring the question. 'Sorry. I didn't mean to be rude. Sorry.' The boy was shaking.

'Was that why you didn't want to come?' Spencer nodded in reply. 'Okay. Tell me some more about Klaas.'

'You won't understand, sir, but … I wish he and Olga weren't together!' The words rushed out. Pip hoped it was a simple case of jealousy, but inwardly he knew it wasn't going to be.

'You like her?'

'No, not like that. And he doesn't either! He's …' Spencer took another swig of Coke, this time straight from the bottle. 'Sorry, sorry,' he said. 'I should have used the glass. Mum would kill me!'

'Do what you like, Spencer. Take it easy, and tell me what you mean about Klaas and Olga.'

'I don't know what I mean, except he doesn't go out with girls.'

Pip hadn't been expecting that! 'So Klaas never had a girlfriend at school?'

'No, sir!' replied Spencer. 'He's ...'

'You mean he's gay?' No answer. 'Have you evidence of that yourself, Spencer?' The kid looked scared now.

'I can't say. I don't know what he does to girls, but I know what he did to us.'

'Us?'

'Yep. Us boys. Not in *that* way.'

'What way, then? Please tell me, Spencer.' This was looking bad.

'I'm telling you the truth. He ... he ... killed ... I don't want to tell you.' Spencer put his head in his hands. 'I'll probably die anyway!'

'We're all going to do that sometime, Spencer, but not now, hopefully. It's all right. Calm down.' Pip waited. But he had to find out about Klaas for Ghita's sake, and now Olga's too. He was also worried about this kid who was now staring into space in front of him. This was serious. He had either just listened to evidence of a murder or had an abused child on his hands.

'First of all, if you're talking about the suicide, I know about it already, Spencer. But if it wasn't really suicide, that's a different matter. Are you afraid that Klaas will kill you after you've told me?' he asked. No answer. 'Have you had any thoughts about harming yourself? Because it would be best if you told me now, Spencer.'

'Maybe.' The words seemed to have been wrung out of the kid.

'Okay, first, I have to tell you that I think you need to talk to a doctor about this.' Spencer jumped up. 'No, listen. I don't mean right now. We'll talk about that later. Come on, sit down. I hope to be able to help you anyway. But I do need to know about Klaas and what is troubling you.'

Spencer sat down again and hung his head. *You poor little bastard,* thought Pip. *I don't blame you for being scared of him, but as for topping yourself, that's a different matter.*

Spencer looked up. 'I'm thinking now that … I think that … I shouldn't have got Klaas into trouble.'

I have to keep this conversation on track, thought Pip. *I don't want any cop-outs.*

'How did you get him into trouble?'

'After the concert on New Year's Eve. He made me drive his car. In a way, I really wanted to. But I shouldn't have, because we got stopped by the police, and Klaas – he pretended to be nice to me, but he was seething, and since then, I keep dreaming about it, thinking he's back at school and he's going to get me.'

'When he told you to drive, were you too scared to say no to him, Spencer?'

'Yes, I'm pathetic.'

'That's the last thing you are. I think you're very brave, coming here and telling me all this. Courageous for getting it off your chest. That's what I want you to do; and I am sure if you do, things *will* get better. It's the best thing to talk about it. Most people bottle it up. Was that what happened to Edward? Wouldn't he talk to anyone?' Pip shot the question at him. Spencer looked at him.

'How did you know that?'

'I know a lot about this kind of thing. If you let it get worse, it builds up, and then it becomes too bad. What really happened to Edward?'

'He was my friend. He was a good kid. I was the one who found him. Hanging! He hanged himself.'

Pip let Spencer cry. Tears of raw grief. He felt so sorry that this kid had spent so long worrying about some kind of fantasy that he had built up around Klaas, who was superior to most in every way and, unfortunately, played on that. *That's what you get off on, Honen, is it,* thought Pip. He felt grim. *I'd like to give you the benefit of the doubt, but at present I can't. Well, you won't be trying it on me!* Hopefully, Klaas hadn't actually put the noose around the kid's neck!

Spencer lifted his head and sniffed, then wiped away the tears with the back of his hand. 'Edward was my friend, but he … was really into Klaas.'

'You mean he loved him?'

'Suppose so. Anyway, he had all these thoughts about him all the time. He told us, and they did things together. No, not things like *that*. They … they, played games. Klaas took over his mind, sir! Edward used to tell us about them. You should have seen his face. At first, we wanted to join in. Crazy things they imagined together. He said they even dreamed together. I used to laugh, but then I got scared. It gave me nightmares. I began to believe it was true, even though it couldn't be.

'Honen's head was full of stuff; stuff other kids couldn't imagine. Edward said he did, that they shared it. He told us about some of the things he'd dreamed, where Klaas had come in with him and they'd dreamed them together. Edward changed. He got nasty like Klaas if we didn't believe them. The things they said, they weren't funny. They said they'd flown out of the window, then crawled up the wall again – like Dracula. We were all scared, but we couldn't admit it to each other. It was bad.

'And we didn't share a room with him, did we? Not like Edward. It was like he was hypnotised all the time. His eyes, they were scary. Like when kids do drugs.'

'Do you think it was drugs?' asked Pip. He needed to break in, because he could see Spencer was becoming increasingly agitated.

'Nah, not coke. Some of the kids do it, and we knew it wasn't that. Edward asked me one day if his head had got bigger. It was horrible. He couldn't do anything without Klaas. Nothing. And then Klaas dropped him. He said Edward wasn't good enough to keep up or something. I tell you, he did Edward's head in. He just couldn't keep up,' Spencer repeated. 'And then, he killed himself. He said to me "Do you think I could get a rope over my head?" I thought I should tell the housemaster, but I was scared. But he did it. His face was all blue. His neck was horrible.'

Spencer stopped. Pip waited. Then the boy looked up. 'I had never seen anyone dead before. It spooked me. It was horrible how Edward looked. I'll never forget it.' He shook his head, as if to shake the image out. 'They said at the inquest it was suicide; that he'd been under pressure from the exams. But I can tell you, Honen murdered Edward, just as though he'd actually put that rope round his neck.'

Silence followed, and Pip let Spencer settle. Then the boy added: 'When we're at our concerts, I'm so worried. I won't be able to keep up with Honen, and now he keeps being nice to me, even though he's left the school. I'm scared, because he knows that I know he did it, and that I'll tell someone about him – and now I have.

'I have to see him all the time, when we perform together. And when we do, I think I'm making mistakes, because he's so good at it. I don't want to do it anymore. I want to tell him to piss off, but I'm too scared, and now he's got Olga thinking the same. I know he's telling her all kinds of rubbish. She's only 15, and she's brilliant. That's why he likes her. Edward was like that. Brilliant. It's like Honen's looking for someone like himself. To take them over. Olga's not like anyone else in my year. She's different – and now he's got her.' Spencer's repetition was accompanied by more tears. 'She never had a boyfriend before. I want to do something about it, but I can't in case he …'

All Pip could do was listen to the flood of words, which were followed by more sniffling. 'I understand, Spencer, and I think I know what you're going through.'

'It's not because I fancy her, sir. She's not my type. I only like her. Can *you* do anything about it?'

'I'm not sure, but at present, I'm a bit worried about you, Spencer. Have you ever told your Mom and Dad how you feel? This is bullying, you know.'

'No way.'

Pip had been expecting that. 'I think we should talk again soon, and you can tell some more about Klaas. I don't want to upset you any more today. But just one thing. Did Honen or Edward ever mention anything specific about their dreams?

Apart from Edward saying that he thought his head was getting bigger.'

'There was one thing. They talked about murders. A long time ago. But not here in England. In a forest and a church. They always talked about a churchyard and a tomb.'

'And you don't know where?'

'No. I don't want to think about it.'

'I agree. Now, try not to be scared of him. You have told me now. That means someone else knows besides Klaas. He wanted you to tell me. Now I know it might start to get better.'

'You think so?'

'I do. Your dreams are your own, Spencer, and there are ways to control them, which I know and I can tell you. Just remember that. Someone is on your side now. As I say, I think we should meet again. I'm a visiting professor here, and I have some time. Would you like to do that? To let me help you?'

Spencer nodded. It was the first time Pip had seen him look happy. 'Do I have to pay for it?'

'No, I'm not going to charge you.' Pip hadn't meant things to get this serious. It had been some time since he'd practised as a psychologist, but he still had a licence. He felt he had an obligation, since he had asked to meet this kid for his own ends. But he had to speak to the parents first.

'Okay,' said Spencer, 'but what am I going to do when I see Honen?'

'I think you're overestimating his powers, Spencer. I shall be seeing him before I see you. Remember, he can't hurt you, because I know. And he was the one who suggested you talk to me. If he does say anything, tell him to get in touch with me instead. That gives you the upper hand. You can only hurt yourself by thinking too much about this. I'll explain to your parents. And don't worry about Olga. I'll be talking to her mother. Try to take it easy. Get some rest. Think of something else, and maybe decide that you don't want to play music with him anymore. Do you have to?'

'I dunno, but I could ask to be in another group.'

'Do that then.'

'You're not going to tell my parents what I've said?' The kid looked really scared.

'No, as I told you, what we have talked about is confidential,' replied Pip. 'You'll be fine. I have to say something to your parents, but you don't have to worry about that.

'Have a think about when we can meet again, then ring me. Here is my card. Then we'll talk some more. But I don't think you're going to be troubled much by Klaas now, because getting things off your chest like this does a lot of good. You've been really helpful to me too.'

'What about me going to the doctor?'

'Let's see how things go. But who do you see usually?'

'The one at school. I'm a weekly boarder now.'

'Even better. Have you the number?' Pip wrote that down. 'Right, you give your dad a ring now and I'll have a word with him when he comes. And try not to worry.'

When Mr James arrived and Spencer was sent to sit in the car, Pip explained in his own way. Mr James seemed extremely receptive, which Pip had expected.

'It's so good of you to try to help our Spencer, Professor,' he said.

'It's no trouble at all,' replied Pip. 'I'll report back to you, of course. I'll also speak to Olga's mother. But as far as I can see, your son is very sensible. I could refer him to the school doctor if I feel there's a risk of depression, but I hope it won't come to that. I've offered to see him again, and we're going to meet in about two weeks' time, if you're agreeable. No charge to you, of course.'

'Wonderful,' replied Mr James. 'I am so pleased to make your acquaintance. My wife has read all your books!'

'Great,' said Pip. 'Let me give you my card, so you can check my credentials.'

'No need.'

'Yes, there is.'

After the man had gone, Pip shook his head. He thought if he ever had a kid, he wouldn't let his son or daughter get to the point Spencer James had, seemingly without noticing. But Pip had seen it all before, too many times. All he wanted to do now was report back to Ghita, and after that to get hold of Klaas, who was going to be more of a challenge than Spencer. In fact, Pip felt worried, even disgusted, at the callous behaviour displayed by that 17-year-old kid. Yet, inside, he wanted to know as much as he could about the 'powers' that Klaas had intimated he possessed and had been willing to try out on a classmate – and seemed already to have turned on Pip himself. What the hell did Klaas think he could do?

The symbols of the church, a tomb, a forest in a foreign country with which Klaas was apparently obsessed, were both interesting and unsettling. Spencer thought that what Honen and Edward had been doing was sharing their dreams. But these sounded more like visions. What kind of visions was Klaas having? As far as Pip could tell, Klaas was now seeking someone who understood the nature of his experiences.

Pip recalled Dr Marcu's initial bewilderment at the fact that Arvan women all shared the same patterns of behaviour, which the psychiatrist believed was something rooted in their psyche. Now Pip had been set a similar puzzle: that the cycle of the Arvan ritual, which involved a tomb, a church in a far off country and a predator, seemed to be Klaas's territory as well as his own. Was it possible that a boy who shared Pip's nationality also shared elements of what he was seeking? After everything that Pip had witnessed, he was disposed to keep an open mind.

Maybe Klaas was not the callous bully he seemed, but was only driven in his quest? Something had drawn Klaas to Edward, whose mind he had searched almost as a testing ground for his powers. However, Klaas had chosen badly, and the boy hadn't been up to it. Edward had been expendable, and his resulting suicide had been akin to the result that Pip himself had sadly witnessed in the many people he had used to further his own search.

The most amazing thing was that Klaas had now found another contact with his imaginary world: Olga who, although she didn't know it, might be the link to something Klaas needed. Could Klaas have been drawn to Ghita's family, and to him too, for this very reason? The thought was mind-blowing, but one Pip was ready to consider, come what may.

Yet one of the things that worried Pip most was Klaas's dark side. Unlike Pip, who had felt intensely guilty when he realised that all the friends who had helped him had died, Klaas seemed to have shown no remorse over his behaviour toward his young victim.

Pip couldn't wait to meet Klaas again and question him, but his first duty was to see Ghita and tell her what she had deserved to know for a long time. How he was going to tell her what her birth date meant, and the truth about Klaas, was another matter!

He wouldn't have been human if he hadn't gone to bed with his problems on his mind. It took him a couple of hours finally to get to sleep, because he started to remember the blood that had appeared on his book, and the rat, real or imaginary, that had climbed up from the floor onto the bedclothes to lick it off. That was why he had slipped a clean sheet under the duvet, giving him the fresh smell of the new linen for comfort.

He had never been scared of rats before, except one in particular, the malevolent Snipe, the rodent that had been the object of his teenage nightmares and had haunted his visions. He knew remembering that rat was a bad sign, because although his tired, half-shut eyes registered only darkness, his already-sensitive ears picked up a scrabbling noise somewhere, which faded as he fell asleep. *It's here again*, he thought; but then he told himself it couldn't be!

Later, waking up with a start in the dark, he thought he heard the rat noise again. He tried to kick out his legs, and they wouldn't move. A cold feeling slowly replaced his bed-warmth, and he could feel himself trembling with fear. Then one of the worst of his memories hit him. *Fuck, I'm paralysed again!*

The sweat broke out on his forehead and trickled down his nose. He tried to reach up to wipe it away. No success. He was bound up, imprisoned in a case or something, like a caterpillar in a chrysalis. 'Christ,' he swore out loud, 'what's happening to me?' He could hear his voice leaving his mouth like an echo. In a lightning flash, he imagined the great rat crawling over him, licking and biting his helpless body.

His eyelids now had broken free from their sticky night prison. He blinked, but he could see only dark. *I'm blind!*, he screamed inside, but then his eyes adjusted and he recognised shadowy objects. He *could* see. He dared to look down at himself to see what had happened – and breathed a sigh of relief. He was wrapped up in his bedclothes! His sheet had shrouded him into immobility – and his duvet had contributed too.

He wiggled his shoulders, trying to get out, but the sheet held on to him like a straitjacket. He was fully awake now. How had he got himself into this fucking mess? It was ludicrous because, however much he struggled, he still couldn't move. The more he wriggled, the tighter the bedclothes grew, and the more painful they became. It was like tying a looped scarf round your neck and pulling one end through but not stopping.

He stopped. *This is crazy! I'm like a little kid. Like a …* He was going to say *poopy!* When the realisation hit him, it really spooked him. The poopies. Those grotesque wooden dolls in their strange cases that the girls buried around Grandsire's tomb in Arva. Why had he thought of them?

Immediately after, his ears were scraped raw by an inhuman sound. One that he'd heard before, and that played games with his brain: the horrible, god-awful noise that he had imagined filled his ears when he was deaf – like when his siblings were playing their music downstairs at home and he was able to hear them, even though he couldn't hear anything! When he was crippled!

Christ, am I dreaming? Is this a dream? The scrabbling had begun again. There was only one way to find out.

'Move yourself!' he said. His intelligent brain told him there wasn't enough room on one side of the bed, but enough on the other. But he couldn't reach it, he couldn't roll over. He tried to free his arms, but the bedclothes had assumed a life of their own and were dragging him down. 'I'm going mad!' he said, because they seemed to be fighting against him.

The scrabbling had turned now into squeaking footsteps on the age-old floorboards of the ancient college. Pip's breathing had shortened and his heart was working overtime. Then the sound of his heart drowned out every thought. He looked up into a face he knew so well, surrounded by bright hair, illuminating the darkness like an evil halo. The staring eyes were fixed on him while, below, the rat bite on his cheek oozed blood! The unearthly vision twisted up the corners of its mouth, revealing sharp incisors. It bent over him and snarled:

'Remember me!'

Pip had no speech to answer, no movement to remonstrate, no power to run. He was the apparition's prisoner. A tiny remnant that was left of his intelligent brain was urging him to hold on, reassuring him that this was just an illusion; but even that defence was useless, as then his visitor's eerie face changed, like a grimacing hologram, from Koppelberg to Arvarescu to Eisenmann – and finally transformed into the mocking face of Klaas Honen!

Pip was panting with fear as the face faded away. Worse still, his breathing halted in his chest as tiny feet, turning and twisting, pattered across his neck. He shivered as a wisp of fur passed close to his ear. Then all was silent as he lay trussed up for what seemed imminent execution.

He didn't know how long he waited until the sheets relaxed and he could breathe again. He looked round through screwed-up eyes at an empty room. No trace of his night visitor remained, only the bedroom door creaking in a cold draught. He shuddered, praying the vision would not return. Then his stomach heaved and the old nauseous feeling overtook him. Throwing the bedclothes aside, he tore himself from the bed and made a crazy dash to the bathroom.

Later, after he had put on his dressing gown, switched on all the lights and poured himself a stiff drink, Pip sat down by the fire, thinking that this apparition had been the worst he could remember. Medical professionals, who had never experienced a vision or the feeling of an evil presence, explained them as hypnagogic illusions that could be manufactured by a waking nightmare; but this was of little satisfaction to Pip. He knew that this *thing* – the Piper, the Grandsire or any alias it cared to use – was gradually gaining the upper hand. He had been scared out of his mind this time. He felt that soon the apparition was going to hurt him badly, and that this had been a further warning.

His professional knowledge was no use to him here. The fact was that this recurrent presence had the power to terrify him, to transform itself; and as Pip grew weaker, it grew stronger, drawing its strength from his fears. That it should have changed its face to Eisenmann's, whose blood ran in its veins, he understood, but that it should have displayed the face of some crazy teenager, who had no knowledge or real experience of what he'd gotten himself into, was doubly frightening. Of course, Klaas had been on his mind, but many other things scared Pip now as well. Why should the demon have used the boy's face?

An even more unnerving possibility was that, somehow, Klaas might be allied with it. He had known Klaas for only a month, and once or twice it had flashed through his wary brain that the 17-year-old might perhaps be another reincarnation of his ghostly stalker – although he had none of the usual physical characteristics.

Pip trusted no-one and nothing anymore, except perhaps Ghita. In that red dawn, he could see only one solution, one way he could test if his theory might be true: play along with Klaas, discover what he could and try to thwart whatever plans the kid's subconscious had for him.

He got up and walked over shakily to the window. Looking down into a deserted quad, he decided that he would tell Ghita about her ancestry and why her father had hidden it from her, but would not reveal the facts behind her birth date or the story that Spencer had told him about Klaas. Pip was sure he could manage Klaas himself, because he was in possession of facts that, as yet, the kid couldn't know. That way, Ghita would not be terrified, and Olga would stay safe in a few months' time. But he could never tell Ghita about his visions and reveal the coward he remained.

12

It took some hours for Pip to recover after his bad night. Feeling that he wanted the normality of being with other people, he headed for the Dons' Common Room, which possessed all the academic atmosphere of his Institute back home, if not its modernity.

The room was huge, but low-ceilinged, and still felt cramped, with its muted lights and diamond window panes. Added to that was its lack of warmth. Owing to the building's listed status, it had no double glazing, and it was no surprise to find ice on the inside of the panes after a particularly frosty night. But it was the sort of thing Pip had expected to find when he first came to an ancient college like Norris.

Frustrating his wish to spend time with his fellow dons, the room was almost empty. There was an elderly man wearing a clerical collar, who was hunched by the largest radiator. He had headphones on, listening to his MP3 player, drumming his fingers in time to whatever music it was playing and seemingly oblivious to the world. Two other earnest young men were engaged in animated conversation in a far corner. They, though, were the only occupants; and the bar, although open, was empty too, except for a barman polishing glasses.

Pip took a seat at the bar and ordered a soda. He didn't want anything stronger, preferring to keep a clear head. Although he had hoped to bump into one or two of his colleagues, he realised that he should be welcoming some quiet time to plan what he was going to say to Ghita later. He needed to think it through. But he'd taken only one quick swig from his soda when he saw that he was being approached by the clergyman, who had taken off his headphones and was carrying his beer.

Pip sighed and hurriedly transferred the rest of his soda to the glass. He didn't do God! But he stood up and indicated the empty seat next to him. The man, in spite of his age, which Pip judged to be around the late sixties, had keen blue-grey eyes under hooded brows and a copious amount of pure white hair. He introduced himself in a dry, precise manner as 'Reverend Matthews, ex-Chaplain to the college, and one of the present Fellows'. Then it was Pip's turn. He was brief.

'Ah, yes,' was the response. 'You're the American writer. Interesting. I have actually read one or two of your books.' The word 'actually' said everything to Pip, who had expected no more. He gestured enquiringly at the MP3 player and learned that the clergyman had been listening to the college choir's latest recording. *At least that's something to talk about*, thought Pip. But he soon discovered that the Reverend Matthews had another agenda, and it was not proselytising.

'I'm very pleased to meet you at last,' he said. 'Indeed, I was hoping I would. Sooner or later, we see everyone in the faculties here.' He settled himself and leaned forward. 'I've heard something today that is unsurprising but has made me curious. Although I'm not at liberty to disclose details, I gather that we're losing Klaas Honen. You know him?'

Pip nodded. 'Yes.'

'I understood you'd met him already,' added the Reverend.

'I have, but only briefly.' Pip frowned.

'Well, I understand he has been to see the Provost and has deferred.' Pip lifted his eyebrows. 'He has abandoned his academic work here – for a time, at least. You may be interested to know that I have put two and two together about his departure. Forgive me if I speak where I should not, but I feel I must.'

Pip was puzzled and somewhat apprehensive as to what was coming. The Reverend continued: 'Klaas threatened to leave Norris once before, for what he called personal reasons, but the Provost prevailed then. The boy's mother was contacted, and I believe they all met to discuss the matter. Several weeks later, Klaas returned. Maybe now he thinks he has a very good reason for needing time out again. He is very young.

'He has been called a genius, and I am disposed to think that those who gave him that accolade might have been right in some ways. Let us say that in all my years here, and there have been many, I have never encountered anyone like Klaas before. As to what he may become in the future, I have no idea.' He paused for a few seconds, then added, 'Given his youth, his deferment won't make the slightest difference to him in the long run, but the Provost is unhappy again. I suspect he had been hoping for a brilliant result in the Finals. The lad's been something of a crowd-puller since he started. He was only 13 when he was accepted. I think the Provost saw him as his own Ruth Lawrence. You've heard of her?' Pip nodded. 'A mathematical genius, and I believe a first for Oxford in taking such a young student.' He smiled. 'But, no, Klaas is quite different, and he has no need of a chaperone.'

At this point, Pip was trying to imagine Klaas having a chaperone!

The Reverend shook his head and continued, 'He was a strange child. Stood out from the rest from the beginning, with that golden thatch. What a mop.'

'Pardon me?'

'Sorry, you're American. Golden hair, and a lot of it. Corn-coloured, but I would say bright gold.'

'He's dark now.'

'Yes, but dyed. And he shaved his head at one time. I believe he wears contact lenses to change the colour of his eyes. Never seen him without them myself. These modern youths. But give him his due, he has done very well academically – although he hasn't been popular.'

'Is that a prerequisite for Norris as well?' At the start of the conversation, all Pip had wanted to do was to get away from this garrulous old man and think about the news that Klaas was leaving the college, but now that he had learned that the kid had changed his appearance, he was infinitely more curious about what the Reverend had to say. His training as a psychologist told him he shouldn't appear too eager to listen to this harangue against a student. Otherwise, he might be giving the old fellow fuel for his suspicions, whatever his agenda. But he felt compelled to say, 'The boy is not my student.'

The clergyman picked up his beer glass and took a long drink, then shook his head and answered Pip's earlier question. 'I take both your inferences. One, Norris is an extremely friendly college, as I am sure you've discovered. Two, I am telling you this for a very good reason, which I hope will be received with appreciation in the knowledge that I have your welfare at heart!'

Pip bridled at this, but he also knew that, in academic speak, this meant that it would be advantageous to listen well. After all, the Reverend was a Fellow, his senior, and Pip was only a new boy, even though he also happened to be a visiting professor!

'I knew Klaas from when he first began his studies,' Matthews went on. 'He liked to take me on. Needless to say, it didn't last long. Klaas made his views on God and His Church quite clear. But any religious views are accommodated here in the college. You look puzzled, Professor. I don't teach anymore. Occasionally I preach.' He had a wry smile on his face. 'I have a great deal to do with the choir – and people's troubles.'

'Where is this getting us?' asked Pip directly. He couldn't bear the patronising tone anymore. 'In fact, I'm beginning to feel quite uncomfortable discussing Klaas Honen.'

'I'm sorry, but I thought you'd welcome it, given your interests. It seems that Klaas has found his role model in you.'

Pip got up. He wasn't sure whether the Reverend was being sarcastic or insulting. 'Forgive me,' he said, 'but I'm short on time.'

The don looked up. 'Please sit down. Maybe *role model* is the wrong description. Sorry if I've offended you. I won't be long, and I've no axe to grind. Believe me, I'm sincere.

'I confess now, I have been wanting to meet you, and for that reason have been frequenting this bar more than usual. This may sound ridiculous to you, but I have been coming here every day in the hope I would see you. To warn you.'

'Warn me?' Pip sat down.

'I have talked with Klaas recently.' At these words Pip's mouth went dry. What had the kid been saying? The Reverend continued, 'If there were a prize for radicalisation, Klaas would win.'

The word 'radicalisation' meant only one thing to Pip – and he didn't like it. 'For God's sake …' he said.

'I don't mean in the political sense,' came the reply, 'because Klaas does not subscribe to any faction or group. He has only one aim, himself and his needs, and in the past I was a prime target for him, being an expert in theology and also a mediaevalist. We had many hours of discussion, which in my capacity as a clergyman I felt I could not refuse. I discovered he wanted to test me, to see if I had the potential he is seeking. I realised after a while that I was not the man he was looking for, but I continued to draw him out, because I was hoping –'

'What is he looking for?' broke in Pip.

'Someone to join with him in his rather unorthodox methods of research, which, as a churchman, I could never approve of. You see, Professor, I think he has decided now to test you too. I also realise he is a very troubled young man, who possesses a unique personality, coupled with a power he does not understand. He senses whom he should approach. Luckily, I have the Lord on my side. I do not know who is on your side, but I need to tell you that the power Klaas wields is not …'

'Usual?' Pip wouldn't say *normal* – as yet, he had never found anyone who fitted that description.

The Reverend nodded and replied, 'Let us say my interest in the supernatural is entirely from one perspective, Professor. Do I have to explain?'

Pip shook his head. 'You mean God?'

The Reverend smiled. 'Yes, although I do not rule out others having a different belief.'

'In the Devil?'

'It is good to hear you say that,' replied the old man. 'You've not declared your faith to me, which you probably would have in your penultimate sentence if you subscribed to mine. As for the other, at least you have acknowledged its existence.'

'And you believe that Klaas worships the Devil, or …'

'I keep an open mind. I have been the buffer that, so far, has stood firm.' Pip frowned, wondering what else was coming. 'I can see that you do not understand yet, but soon you may be approached by Klaas. I beg you not to join with him. Yet if you believe yourself his match, take care – although I suspect no good will come of it and he will discard you. Naturally, I am not speaking academically.'

'Of course not. But to be frank, I find this conversation unsettling and intrusive.' Pip had had enough. Matthews inclined his head. 'But before we part, I wish to know what he has said about me?'

'Ah, Professor, you have fallen into my trap. He is a reader of your books. You have a staunch admirer. He spoke with me only briefly of your meeting with him in Oxford, but I recognised the signs. I do not know if he will try to use you, like he did me. Yet I feel something is brewing, and that you could be his next victim. I suggest prayer as a remedy.' His pale face had reddened now, and he seemed congested as he spoke, then coughed. Klaas had certainly gotten to him. Pip realised this was the time to put an end to the conversation.

'Strange words, Reverend, but thank you for your concern,' he said. 'As an applied psychologist and a professional author, I have experienced such approaches before. However, I do value your advice, and I shall keep it all in mind if necessary.'

'Good man,' the Reverend said, withdrawing his handkerchief and wiping his forehead. 'Forewarned is forearmed. Should you ever need my help in any area, you know where to find me. I wish you well – and God bless you.'

At that point, the old man put his hands on the table for support and slowly got up from his seat. He nodded and walked off without shaking hands, leaving Pip to think hard about what he had said.

Strangely enough, all Pip could think of at that moment was his shock on hearing that Klaas had dyed his bright golden hair and wore contact lenses to hide the true colour of his eyes.

Later that evening, Pip was sitting on the couch beside Ghita, while she stared into the distance. *She can't look at me after what I've just told her*, he thought. *It was bad enough this morning, speaking to the Reverend, but this is worse.* He cared so much about Ghita and wanted to earn her respect again. As he'd dreaded, the news he'd imparted looked like being a major setback to their relationship – if it still existed. He watched her breathe in to compose herself, then pick up her coffee and begin to sip it in a deliberate manner.

'Please, Ghita,' he said, 'you wanted me to tell you.' She turned sideways and looked at him in such a strange way that he flinched. 'You're mad at me?'

'You're amazing,' she replied – and it wasn't a compliment. 'What would you feel if you'd just found out that your father had lied to you all his life? That he was really a gypsy. I'm a Roma,' she added, 'and he didn't tell me. And Anya was my grandmother, not my great aunt. It's unbelievable. But the problem is, it's the truth. And you, who meant so much to me a long time ago …' She shook her head, unable to continue.

'I'm sorry. I know I don't deserve it, but I care for you just the same, and I need –'

She turned on him. 'You need? What? When are you going to grow up?' she raged. 'Do you think I still care for you after all you've done?' He closed his eyes in misery. She caught hold of his arm and shook him. He sat in shock. 'The worst thing is,' she went on, 'I still *do* care, and I can't help it, but you keep on bringing me more and more grief.' She put her head in her hands.

Pip didn't know how to answer, nor dare to comfort her, and cursed himself for being so feeble. She lifted her head, and tears had brightened her eyes. 'No, I'm not going to cry,' she said, 'and if I do, I won't be crying for us, but for me and my bloody useless family.' He was hard-pressed to hear what she said next. 'I don't care about being one of the Roma,' she muttered, then raised her voice. 'I care that Tăta didn't trust me enough to tell me. I can see why Anya went along with it, but it's like being betrayed by both of them. Did my mother know?'

'I don't know. I was shocked when I found out, honestly. When he took me to the gypsy camp and told me.'

'Yeah, you've said all that. I don't want to hear any more excuses. I feel like an orphan. I *am* an orphan.' She sniffed.

'Come on, Ghita,' he said. 'You have Olga – and me.'

'Thank God I have her,' she said, and her voice wobbled. 'Would you leave me alone, please? I want to wallow in self-pity.'

'You want me to go?' he asked. No reply. He sighed. 'Okay, I will.'

He started to get up, and she pulled him back. He looked down at her, helpless to know what to do, and she said, 'You stupid, stupid man.' She was openly crying now, and all at once she was cuddling into his chest.

He was taken by complete surprise when she turned her face up to him; and, in spite of all she'd said, his long pent-up love for her overcame him. He put his head down and kissed her on the lips.

'There,' she murmured, when they finally broke apart, leaving both of them breathing heavily. 'That's how I really feel.'

'Thank you,' he said, 'that was nice.' A little voice inside whispered, *You've burned your bridges now. Please don't tell her about 'the secret of the marriage bed'. It'll spoil everything! She couldn't stand that. Be careful!*

'You are hopeless, Pip Durrant,' she said, 'but that's enough for the moment. Olga might come in.'

'Are you going to tell her?' he asked.

She looked him straight in the eyes. 'About kissing you? I don't think so. That she is half gypsy? That Anya was her great grandmother? Yes. I don't intend to let her wait all her life before she knows. Don't worry; I shan't need your help on this one.'

'You are the most …' He shook his head. 'The most …'

'Honest? I couldn't be as good a liar as you.' There was no sarcasm this time, but a flatness that made him feel like a heel again.

'I deserved that.'

'Yes, you did,' said Ghita. 'And I need to ask you something else. Something I've always wanted to. I think I mentioned it earlier. It'll stop me imagining things. What were you and Dad working on? Why was it a secret?'

'A biography!' He was quick to reply.

'What?' She looked puzzled. 'Whose?'

'A mediaeval figure.'

'Somehow, I thought it might be about our family. Is it someone I know?'

'Nobody knows a lot about this historical character.'

'Oh, right,' she said.

'I'll tell you all about it eventually,' he promised, 'but it's held up a bit at the moment. I've come to a dead end.'

She regarded him. 'I hope you'll tell me. I'm interested in things like that. Maybe you'll get a book out of it?'

'Maybe.' He was going along with everything she said, because he didn't want her to figure out the truth.

'I hope so, for Dad's sake. Sorry to keep asking questions, but they are important to me.'

'I understand.'

'I'm glad,' said Ghita, with the hint of a smile. 'God knows, I have plenty of other things to think about that are more important. For one thing, did you find anything out about Klaas? My big concern is for Olga right now.'

'No, but I'm working on it,' he lied. *For Christ's sake, Ghita, leave it there,* he prayed, knowing he'd got off lightly so far. The only thing that lifted his spirits at present was the knowledge that he and Ghita might make it after all – as long as he was careful and he didn't let her know the truth about her birth date and what could happen to her daughter.

What Pip had to do was meet Klaas again as soon as possible and discover what he was about. Whoever or whatever he was, and whatever real interest he had in the Dalca family, Pip swore to find out. And if Klaas did turn out to be a threat, he wouldn't succeed as long as Pip was there to prevent it.

Pip's head was still full of Ghita when he phoned Klaas's mobile early the next morning. There was no answer. A moment of panic ensued. Might he have left Norris already? But ten minutes later, Klaas returned his call, and they arranged to meet that evening.

Klaas yawned as he lay back in the most comfortable chair he could find. His enthusiasm and urgency seemed to have disappeared. He looked like any student of 17 who had only just crawled out of bed at his mother's nagging. He yawned again, which affected Pip the same way and made him feel annoyed.

'Yeah, you got me up,' drawled Klaas, 'but I couldn't miss this, could I?'

Pip looked at him, then glanced away, conscious that he was staring at Klaas's hair and eyes. He breathed in to calm himself.

'I don't know what you think you might miss, Klaas, but remember you were the one who begged me to see you a few days ago. I might not be your tutor, but I can still show you the door if you feel like that about it.'

'Tell you what I do want. A coffee.'

Pip would have told him where to go at that very moment, but Klaas was so unpredictable that he might just have done that.

'Right – but you can make the next one,' he said, making light of it.

He had the uncomfortable feeling that Klaas's eyes were watching everything he did in the kitchen; and when he re-entered with two mugs, the kid was still watching him.

'Coming up,' Pip said, handing the mug over.

Those almost black eyes were still fixed on him, but the psychologist in Pip noticed that the stare was lacking something, and it was nothing to do with his eye colour. To Pip, it meant only one thing: that Klaas was concentrating in a big way. He was processing information – on Pip's speech and body language. Pip had one brief moment to try to remember where he had seen eyes like that before, but although his mind embarked on a frenetic search, he couldn't grasp it. Where had he seen such unblinking eyes that resembled a snake's?

'Lagophthalmos,' said Klaas suddenly. 'Those morons at school couldn't even say it. Even the idea spooked them. They were scared. They used to wake up and accuse me of watching them while they were asleep.'

'Lagophthalmos?' It was the medical term for a condition where a person doesn't blink. Again his mind was directed to a work area he hadn't encountered for a very long time. The absence of blinking was a subject he had been interested in. It was a marker for several conditions.

'Don't worry,' replied Klaas. 'I've always been like it. I have mild ichthyosis as well. Olga told me.'

Pip's stomach turned. Klaas had snake-skin disease? It manifested itself often in a scaly skin – a condition that, at its best, could be cleared up with the right creams. He thought how shocked Olga must have been when she'd first spotted it – assuming she'd seen Klaas with his clothes off!

'I thought it had cleared up,' added Klaas. 'I'd forgotten it, but Olga is very perceptive. As you are, Prof. Don't get het up now.'

'That's the last thing I am,' lied Pip. He felt disturbed that the kid seemed to be reading his mind, but most of all that Olga was tied up with him.

Klaas smiled. 'Okay, so let's carry on with the business. Why am I here?'

'You know that, Klaas,' answered Pip. 'You're here because I asked you to be, and I'm very interested in your earlier proposal.' Klaas yawned again, and Pip erupted, 'For fuck's sake, haven't you had any sleep?'

Klaas didn't answer for a moment, then straightened himself in the chair. 'Only messing,' he said. 'Sorry.'

Pip shook his head. 'Why do you need to be so offensive? How can we possibly work together if you behave like that ...' he saw Klaas's wicked eyes sparkle, '... or like a little kid? I have other claims on my time.'

'This is what I suggest initially. We have five or six sessions to discuss your problem.' Klaas grinned. *You little bastard,* Pip thought. *You think it's* my *problem, don't you?* But he kept his cool.

'Great. Can we start today? Do I have to lie on the couch?' mocked Klaas.

'Grow up,' growled Pip. 'One more crack and you're outta here!'

'Yes, sir.'

He knew that he had Klaas's attention then; but where the boy's mind was, Pip had no idea.

'After you left my rooms last time we spoke, I made a few notes. But first of all I have to give you some guidelines. Otherwise, I can't treat you.' Pip was keeping his voice calm. He produced a single A4 sheet of paper and handed it to Klaas, who stared at it. 'It's an agreement that we both have to stick to.'

The student's eyes swivelled up and down the sheet, then he handed it back.

'You're meant to sign it if I'm to take you on. It's a safeguard,' said Pip.

Klaas raised his eyebrows. 'I should have brought one of mine for you to sign,' he retorted.

'Cut the crap. Either you sign this or ...' Pip paused, ' ... or we're finished before we start. These things have to be done properly. I'll sign it after you.'

Klaas appeared to take no notice as he read out the list of headings in the simple agreement Pip had drawn up between them: 'Code of Conduct; Confidentiality; Sessions; Emergency.' He looked at Pip. 'Nothing about payment? Thank you for being so generous, Professor.' His thanks were followed by a sarcastic grin. 'Referrals; Complaints; Credentials. Very impressive.'

Pip gritted his teeth. He was beginning to understand why Reverend Matthews had said he had never met anyone like Klaas Honen before. That would certainly be true if Klaas turned out to be another re-incarnation of the Piper. That sounded crazy, but Pip knew such things were possible. He needed to discover what this kid could do, and if he was even human.

'Okay, I'll sign,' said Klaas, taking out a very expensive pen. 'I'm going to enjoy our collaboration, Prof. In fact, I can't wait.'

Pip watched Klaas's slender musician's fingers produce his flowing signature on the pathetic little document. At that moment, as his own hand in turn trembled a little on the signature line, Pip began to wonder just what he had taken on.

13

'First of all, I'd like you to tell me something about your parents,' said Pip mildly. He resolved he would keep his anger in check, as he'd handled plenty of cocky kids before. His initial query wasn't rewarded.

'Off limits,' was the muffled answer. Klaas was chewing gum.

'Would you mind spitting that out, please?' Klaas's eyebrows lifted in a black squiggle. *Strange for someone who has bright blond hair,* thought Pip. *Dyed as well, perhaps?*

Then Klaas threw his gum with perfect accuracy into the wastepaper bin. 'I've noticed you have a slight limp, Prof. When did you get that?'

They regarded each other. Pip was not going to be drawn by the kid's question. He normally limped only when he was tired – but the fall outside Ghita's had been so heavy that he was lucky he hadn't broken his weaker leg. The last time he'd had a check-up, his doctor had diagnosed a touch of arthritis.

Pip realised that this was a bad beginning with a client – he had to call Klaas that now rather than a patient – who was ready to employ the 'question answered by a question' technique to annoy him. Klaas's opener had also been a reference to Pip's own past, which he had kept hidden from everyone. His disabled years.

'Good of you to notice,' he flashed. 'Are you surprised I'm limping, after the fall I had? And thanks for ejecting your gum across my room in such skilful fashion.'

The corners of Klaas's mouth twitched. '*Touché*, Prof.'

'I think we can drop the Prof now. You can call me Pip.'

'Suits me. I'll use either.'

'Now, back to your parents. You remember you can tell me anything, because this is confidential,' Pip said. 'I can't get a full picture of your problems until you open up.'

'Sure, but I've nothing to say. My mother is a minor diplomat at the American Embassy in London and I never knew my father. She gives me everything I want, because she can afford it, and she never expects me to be grateful. She doesn't dote on me and I don't feel much toward her, except some relief that she noticed my prodigious talent at an early age. I have no siblings.' He frowned. 'I wouldn't have wanted them anyway. They wouldn't have understood me.'

'Wow, that sure is a barren description of your family.' Another point for Pip's armoury. A young man with no father or siblings, and no mother fixation.

'I have her purse to call on when I need it,' said Klaas, as if he was reading Pip's thoughts.

'Good for you. So you've always managed on your own?'

'I don't understand that word. I've always been held back.'

'Why's that?' Pip asked.

Klaas shrugged. The way he was staring at Pip between each question was almost hypnotic, so Pip had devised a way of looking down at his notes and then back up at him to ease the awkwardness.

'No-one understands me,' Klaas said.

'In what way?' Pip came out with a stock question.

'You can do better than that, my new friend,' retorted Klaas. 'We might be sitting here all night if I had to answer that one.'

'So you feel I'm your friend now, not a therapist who is trying to help you?' asked Pip.

'I feel you are interesting and may be of some use to me.'

'What do you see in me that interests you, Klaas?'

'Would you like me to play the psychologist?'

'I think not, because then you wouldn't be able to try to

make me angry.' Pip's civility masked his real feeling, which was an instinctive wariness bordering on fear. He told himself that whatever happened between them, he had no intention of backing down. He had faced his unearthly stalker, Diep Koppelberg. He had faced Eisenmann, a half-child of the Devil. He would outwit Klaas Honen.

'You have a fine brain, Klaas, but you lack imagination.' Klaas's unswerving eyes held Pip's own, like glittering marbles. 'I have my strengths also,' Pip continued. 'A fine imagination cannot be measured, because the one who has it, can guess what another is thinking.'

'Bravo, Pip,' said the student, sitting back and clapping his hands. 'You should have been an actor, or maybe a lawyer.'

'I stick to the law, Klaas, but I couldn't dispense it. And neither could you. Instead you have made mistakes. You have set the world against you. You may think you live in your own world, but around you the ordinary world goes on, and you are compelled to be a part of it – if you are a human being.' He leaned forward and stared into Klaas's face. 'However much you despise what is around you, Klaas, you have to be a part of it in order to survive. I sense that you are hoping to find someone like yourself. Have you ever thought that even ordinary people desire that? Olga, for instance.'

'Olga isn't ordinary. She understands me.'

'Has she been able to prove that? Has she been a good choice? Because, by your own direction, I've completed some inquiries. Spencer told me that Edward was no use to you.'

Klaas unwound himself from the chair and walked about. He turned. 'What if I have already discovered that I am quite different from anyone else? I have already said something about that. '

'Yes, but not enough. We have not started well, Klaas, going through this farce of teacher and pupil. You talk in riddles. You know, I'm as sorry for you as I'm sorry for all who do not possess what you think you have, but would not understand it if they did. You're here because I am interested in what makes you think you're all-seeing. That would make you godlike.'

Pip waited for a negation, but it didn't come. That was what he had been hoping for. That was why he had led Klaas to this point. To find out what the kid wanted from him, as soon as possible.

'How do you know I'm not?' snarled Klaas. His mood had darkened. Pip prepared himself for the onslaught that would surely come if this boy of 17 was indeed one of the Piper's *alter egos*.

'I'm almost sure,' replied Pip, preparing his own attack. 'Why do you want *me* to discuss it with you? Do you imagine I have a brain like yours, perhaps? I may have or I may not, but I am not a Spencer, nor an Edward, nor even a Reverend Matthews.' Klaas's expression registered no surprise. 'I believe you know that. I'm not expendable like them.'

Silence was Pip's reward.

'Do you think you're immortal?' asked Klaas.

Pip was relieved. He would have expected a quick attack if his fears were well-founded. As for the simplicity of the question, he didn't know quite what to make of it. Did the kid believe in immortality, or perhaps re-incarnation? If so, was he going to try to prove it, just as Pip himself was in relation to the Piper? Was this what the kid wanted from him – because he'd read *The Last Vision*?

'Let's say that my beliefs have changed over the years, owing to my profession and my experiences. My soul has nothing to do with you, Klaas.'

'So you believe you have a soul?' asked Klaas.

Pip nodded. 'Do you?'

'Kind of.'

No mention of any divine being or the Devil, thought Pip. 'Then we're in agreement about something, Klaas,' he said, 'which is a more positive beginning. The question is, from what source does that soul originate?'

'Brain power.'

'Not a supernatural being, then?' Klaas didn't answer. 'A machine? What do you want your brain to do for you, Klaas? Isn't it powerful enough already?'

'I need someone else.'

'You mean another machine, not a person, to join with you? What for? I expect you have been following the latest research in psychology and psychiatry?' Klaas nodded. 'And now you want to know more. And you think I can tell you. Why me?'

'You've been listening to that old idiot, haven't you? The Reverend doesn't have what I am looking for, even though he spouted religion at me.'

'But he is no fool, otherwise you wouldn't have approached him. He suggests personal prayer as a remedy.'

Klaas's response to that was a gesture of contempt.

'Okay. So, hopefully, this is third time lucky now.' Pip counteracted the gesture with humour. 'Here's another question. Is it because of *The Last Vision* that you've approached me?'

'You said you needed some help. You were looking for someone to help you in your quest.'

'I did, but the quest in my book is not quite the one I have spent my life pursuing – although I do resemble its hero in some ways.'

'You mean you want to test me?' asked Klaas.

'And how could I do that?' Pip looked into eyes that had changed. Eyes that were now alive with hope that matched Pip's own. Klaas had entered his trap. He had to show his hand. 'You prove to me that you are different from the others you have met and I might consider it. So, I repeat. Why did you choose me?'

'Because I have seen you before, in my visions. I was tired of waiting for you to turn up, so I tried other people first.'

'Waiting for me to turn up?' repeated Pip. 'How could I? I didn't know you wanted me. I'd never heard of you. I'm here now, though. Where have you seen me in your visions? What was I doing? Remember, Klaas, it's no good telling me things that anyone would know.'

'I have visions all the time. I have always had them.' Klaas was leaning forward in his chair with his eyes fixed on Pip. 'Give me a chance to show you, Professor.'

'I'll give you a chance,' said Pip, wondering what this smart kid was going to come up with. 'Do you want to write it down?'

'No, it's all in here.' Klaas tapped the side of his head.

'Okay, give me some pointers.' Pip really wondered what was going to happen. He was even beginning to feel a bit excited. 'Can I record this?'

'Suits me,' replied Klaas.

While Pip fetched his microphone, Klaas went and lay down on the couch and closed his eyes. Pip looked at him. Was this a joke, perhaps? He didn't know. He decided to play along.

'Right. Would you like to start now? Where have you seen me, Klaas?' His own mind was putting together some possibilities. Klaas still had his eyes closed, and under his eyelids Pip could see eye movement that resembled REM sleep. 'What are you looking at, Klaas?' Klaas wasn't asleep, as the soft question was answered.

'A small village. A path leading up to the church. It's always the same village.'

'And this is your recurring dream?'

'One of them, yes. But they're not dreams! They're visions. I told you before. Leave me alone. I want to get it straight in my head.' Klaas closed his eyes again.

What the hell is he doing, thought Pip. *Is this how he thinks he's supposed to act?* He could have put a stop to the session right then, because it seemed that Klaas was using his imagination to dream something up instead of answering truthfully. What could this kid know of visions! Pip felt angry. Persecuted. A man who'd had his whole life made hell by inexplicable happenings.

Then he remembered what he was meant to be doing. Finding out how Klaas ticked, rather than judging him. Pip was a professional, and he owed that to his patient at least. He thought of his own visions. He didn't know how he looked when he was having them. How they worked. Perhaps Klaas was having a waking dream, like the absences schoolchildren sometimes have when they stare through the window and cannot be roused.

He wondered if the boy was attempting to use telepathy. He had noticed several times that Klaas appeared to have an uncanny ability to read his mind. The pseudo-science had made enormous progress over the last ten years and produced persuasive results. Then Pip ditched his self-examination and concentrated on focusing his mind on his patient rather than his angst.

Then the bombshells began to fall.

'Where exactly have you seen me, then?' Pip asked.

'I have seen you on the path near the churchyard.'

In spite of his earlier resolve, Pip felt a shiver that made his senses quiver into life. 'I'm a ghost, then?'

The mocking answer didn't put the boy off. 'No, you're not dead. You're standing – in the – the ruins of a house. You pick up – the picture of a cockerel.'

Pip leaned back, trying to blot the memory from his mind.

'And you pick up a stick, a big stick like a club. You walk around, and you are lame. You don't know what to do and – animals are shrieking.' Klaas put up his hands and covered his ears. 'They're pigs. And you're the farmer. You – you – you're scared, and then you can hear things like ...' He sat up with his eyes closed and his head inclined, as if he was listening. 'I can hear them now ...Feet, feet, little feet, a child's feet running, running. You drop your stick. Yes.' Klaas was breathing deeply as if to calm himself. 'She has blood on her! Blood!

'The squealing of the pigs is loud and – the child has pigtails and blood, blood, lots of blood on her apron. You're really scared. What have you done?' Klaas's dark eyes were wide open now, as he asked Pip, 'What have you done, Professor? Did you murder someone?'

Pip was shocked. Klaas got up and stared into his face, then tottered. Pip pushed him back, and he flopped onto the couch as though the life was draining from him. He sat still, set as though he couldn't move. When he spoke, it was in a flat tone. 'I do bad things too, but I can't help it.'

'Can you see Edward?'

Klaas shook his head.

'Olga?'

Another shake.

'Lie down again, Klaas,' ordered Pip, and the kid complied. It was as if he had put himself into a trance or was hypnotised. 'And you were there when this happened?'

'No, but I could see you.'

'What did I do next?'

'That's all,' breathed Klaas. Then he yawned and lay down on his side, facing Pip with closed eyes. Pip knew how he must feel after a vision – if it had been one. Totally worn out.

Pip stood up to calm himself. He went over and looked at Klaas, touched his shoulder. The boy yawned again and shook his hand off. Soon, his breathing changed, and Pip knew he was asleep.

Pip returned to his chair. He couldn't feel elated; he couldn't feel anything except a sense of horror. This was nothing he'd done. It was the most amazing example of what? Parapsychology? This kid could see into the past. He had seen Pip in 2007 outside the churchyard in Arva, when he had been standing in the ruins of Claudiu Basa's house. He had heard the pigs screaming. Most amazing of all, not only had Klaas done that, but he had entered Pip's own vision when he had seen the Little and Chosen, the Piper's victim, running down the path, her pigtails sticking out behind her, the blood on her apron.

Then Klaas turned over and murmured, 'What shall I do?'

'What you are going to do, Klaas, is keep calm,' Pip said, although he wasn't certain if the boy could hear. 'I haven't murdered anyone, and I'm sure you haven't either.'

If you're reading my mind now, Klaas, Pip thought, *you'll know I'm not being entirely truthful. I have seen off people who were my friends, and many of them. I could have stopped it happening, given up the search for the Piper, but I didn't. As for you, Klaas, you're like me: responsible too, but indirectly; for the loss of Edward, your friend who hanged himself, and of Anya, who tripped over your trainers and fell down the stairs. If you are as bad as you say, you knew she was a danger to you, and you killed her. Oh, yes, I understand that much, Klaas. We are both as bad as each other.*

Then Pip jumped as Klaas opened his eyes and called out, 'Why was there blood on that girl? Who was she?'

'No more questions. I have to think about this.'

'*Were you there?*' Klaas persisted. 'I'm not a kid to be told to shut up.'

'No, you aren't, and that's why you should,' snapped Pip. He hadn't meant to, but he was still in a state of bewilderment. Nor did he intend to give away his position yet. 'I'm going to look at the evidence and make a judgement later about what I've heard. I'm a scientist, and I don't take everything at face value. If you don't agree with my methods, we can just call it a day!'

Klaas glowered like the spoilt child he was, not the amazing being he had proved himself to be. The boy might have powers that were extraordinary, but he was still very much a 17-year-old hothead. 'Do you believe me?' he asked, and looked seriously angry.

'I'll look into it and tell you later,' replied Pip, who had recovered himself. 'Lie down. I'm going to get us a drink, and then we'll talk some more. Just lie down,' he repeated. He went into the kitchen, but as he waited for the kettle to boil, his hands were shaking.

He tried to remember if he had ever told anyone about the vision in the churchyard, but he was sure he hadn't. He needed to discover what else Klaas Honen knew about Arva; but when he came back with the two cups of coffee, he found that Klaas had gone to sleep again.

Still staggered by what he had heard, he put Klaas's coffee down beside him on the table and began to drink his own. He felt like lying down himself. He couldn't see a way out of it. The idea that someone had intruded into his mind filled him with both dread and awe. Who was this kid?

He tried to make sense of what had happened every way he could, but it defeated him. Again, he assured himself that he had never told anyone about his visions, which were private and had always been a secret source of worry. The boy could not have known by any normal means. Where did his power come from? Had he tried the same thing out on the Reverend? On poor little Edward, who had not even had adult defences?

Pip went through every writer's fear then. Had he let anything slip in his books? Perhaps in *The Last Vision*? But, again, he was sure he hadn't.

His theory that the boy was using telepathy was clearly flawed. The vision in question was the last one Pip would have thought about consciously. But as for his subconscious, Pip was not the master of that, even though he'd tried for many years. Somehow, Klaas must have tapped into it. But why choose that special vision? This led him to the question, what did Klaas want to do next? What were his motives?

Half an hour later, the boy was still motionless. Having Klaas Honen asleep in his room was not something that Pip wanted. He understood that the boy could have been affected by the process, but he had not been under hypnotism, or drugged, or in any kind of trance. Also, he had only been relating what he had experienced.

Finally, Pip could not decide if he was excited or appalled. From the time he had started to work on the Marcu Papers so many years ago, he had come to take the paranormal into account. It had lived uncomfortably beside his previous scepticism, and he always had to pinch himself whenever he faced something that could not be coincidence – an abstract concept in which he'd never had confidence.

He couldn't believe that a 17-year-old boy had presented him with the prospect of joining in an incredible adventure into the unknown. Yet, conducting paranormal experiments with Klaas might allow Pip to become powerful too; powerful enough to take on his old enemy. The whole concept was mind-blowing. Pip's eureka moment. "In 2024, science had uncovered hitherto-hidden secrets of the cortex. It could now observe the working of the human brain in many areas, and uncover the mysteries of sleep and dreaming. In a recent controlled experiment Pip had read about, a psychologist had viewed the interaction of two brains and begun to see the subjects' dreams, alone and together. In other words, a man could walk in another's dreams, but as to entering into their own self-induced imaginary visions, it had been unthinkable up until now."

The downside was the worrying possibility that, if Klaas was sound, both of them were being manipulated by some unknown force. More frightening still was the idea that Klaas might *not* be sound. This was his dilemma.

Added to all this, what was Pip going to tell Klaas about Arva? He had to give the boy some explanation. He could lie and say he did not know the place, nor why it could be important to Klaas, but it would not be long before the boy's brain would work out the deception, and then Pip would lose his credibility.

Pip had been chosen to save Arva from its monster. He had been told that by Simu Dalca and by Eva Kirchma. Had Klaas been sent to fill in the blanks? Would he lead Pip the right way or on a more murky path? Which way should Pip turn?

He opened his note page on his laptop. He had to weigh up the risks. It could be dangerous to both Ghita and Olga if he enlightened Klaas as to the background of the family he had sought out and allied himself with. It could also jeopardise Pip's own quest for the Grandsire. From where did Klaas draw the power for his visions? God or the Devil, was the Reverend's suggestion. But, if so, which?

Pip considered some further facts. This was a Piper Year, which demanded the correct ending on 22 July, with the sacrifice of a child victim, innocent of her parents' sins. That victim was apparent to Pip. Given her mother's birth date, it had to be Olga. Could the small amount of gypsy blood in her veins save her? How much did she require?

Pip's close friendship with Olga's mother and his knowledge of the secrets must have been given to him as a blessing and for a purpose. Had they been given to Klaas in a similar way, but by an opposing power? Was he a vessel for the Evil One? Was that the reason for his obsession with Olga? If Pip allied himself with Klaas, who would be there to protect Ghita and Olga? At this point, he had no idea, only hints and suggestions.

He closed the notes on his laptop. There seemed nothing more he could do at the moment. He had to stay calm, be careful and try to stall for time. Then he sat in his chair and dozed, waiting for the teenager to wake up.

When Klaas did wake, he was a boy transformed. 'I did it,' he said, strutting around. 'I could see by your face, when I told you, that you believed. When can we do it again?' Gone was the arrogance, replaced by a fierce earnestness that caught Pip's middle-aged nonchalance and slashed it, reminding him how he'd been at 17. He almost went back on his word and blurted out how he felt, but he needed to show a professional face to this wonder boy.

'Okay,' he said, 'I grant it was fairly extraordinary. But next time, I think we should do it under controlled conditions.'

'You are the end, man!' Pip winced inwardly at Klaas's derision. 'You know what happened, but you want to check and check – and try to catch me out.' He thrust his face close to Pip, who loathed himself at that moment, but knew caution had to be observed.

'No, I don't want to catch you out, but important things are at stake.'

'Like your international reputation?'

'Hardly. You wanted my help. I am offering to go along with this. I am going to work with you and see what we can come up with together.'

Klaas withdrew, and his instant 17-year-old deflation was plain to see. 'Oxford is shit,' he said. 'Where's all the euphoria?'

Pip almost laughed at the boy's histrionics, but contained himself. 'You'll get that, Klaas,' he said. 'You have plenty of time. I'll sort it. But you're leaving Oxford, aren't you? That's awkward.'

Klaas shrugged, and Pip could see he was considering his situation. 'I'll probably tell the Provost I've changed my mind again. I don't like to disappoint the old man. Oh, and by the way, when you asked about my parents, something I said wasn't true.' Pip frowned. 'I told you I didn't know anything about my father, but I did have a photo of him.'

'Did?' replied Pip, swallowing back his disappointment at the thought of not being able to see Honen Senior's face.

'Yep, but the shit never came back to see me once, so I smashed it and the frame.'

'Oh!'

'Now you know what it feels like to be disappointed, Prof,' he grinned, revealing a set of perfect white teeth. 'I can't show it to you, but I can tell you the guy was an ugly bastard.' He grinned, noting Pip's discomfiture. 'Fill me in when it's all going to happen. I'll go see the Provost tomorrow. And he won't be cheated of his Double First. Thanks for the experience. See you.' His cockiness was an irritation Pip could have done without at that moment.

Klaas grabbed his jacket from the back of the door and slipped out of the room. Pip sighed with relief and went to the window. He watched Klaas hurrying across the bright moonlit quad. To his horror, he saw the boy's shadow divide into two and follow him, as if this was entirely natural. Pip craned his neck to check that what he was seeing was right. There was no doubt. Klaas Honen had two shadows.

Pip's scientific training tried to provide him with an explanation. Maybe another light source could be causing the phenomenon? Several lights were on in the upper windows around the quad. Some were very bright, others less so, but none was obviously the cause. He quickly took off his glasses, remembering that he suffered slight double vision. It made no difference. He glanced up at the moon, which was full, its brilliance not obscured by any strip of cloud that could conceivably account for the effect.

As Klaas disappeared into a doorway, Pip turned from the window. He had grasped for some explanation and could find none. Given what he had experienced in the last few hours, together with the manifestations of the past, he realised with an unwilling but still open mind that he was ready to suspend disbelief.

Perhaps Klaas's second shadow indicated that some presence, invisible to the human eye, had attached to the boy, or was walking beside him? If that was so, what danger was the kid in? And, indeed, what danger was Klaas to Pip?

Pip opened his eyes into the strange half-darkness before dawn. He had been lying awkwardly, and when he moved his position he felt a sharp pain in his leg. He was cold too. He groaned, then put a tentative arm out of his duvet and reached for his mobile to check the time. He dragged his hand along the top of the bedside chest. His mobile wasn't there! He grumbled. It was always there. Then his fingers connected with it. But after the usual fumbling to turn it on, its screen remained dark. He swore. He must have forgotten to put it on charge. Had he slept late?

Then he remembered that it didn't matter, pulled the duvet over his head again, yawned and snoozed. He'd always had a habit of sleeping on one side of the bed, even when there was no-one to share it with. Then a noise disturbed him. He pushed his head out of the duvet's warmth and saw that the curtains at the window were rustling.

Although it was still dark outside, the room seemed lighter now. He sat up and, in an almost heart-stopping moment, saw a hunched shape crouched on the chair at the end of the bed; a thing with a luminous glow at the centre, like a glow-worm when brought into a house.

Pip went rigid, hunching back with only the duvet for protection. A familiar tingling sensation circulated round his veins, while the hair on his scalp prickled with fear. His unearthly visitor didn't speak or move.

You're still dreaming, shrieked his terrified mind as it tried to reassert control. Pip stared at the spectre as its glow brightened, illuminating his shocked, white face.

'Go away,' he gibbered. 'You're an illusion.'

He could hear his voice echo, producing an eerie reverberation in the little room. Still the creature sat immobile, but out of the corner of his eye, Pip saw the curtains rustling more and more, as if an animal was roaming up and down upon the windowsill. He shuddered. Had the apparition brought the rat with it, as before?

In that small moment of inattention on Pip's part, the thing on the chair crept round to the empty side of his bed and slipped in beside him to savour a human's warmth. As Pip realised what it had done, he tried to throw himself out, but he couldn't. It was like he was lashed to the mattress, or as if he was paralysed again. He could feel the wraith's presence, although through his screwed-up eyes he could see only the hollow void of its absent face. He was lying beside Death.

God save me, he prayed. *I'm going to die*. He thought he could feel old flesh then, next to his crawling skin. In his head, he kept screaming, *It's only a nightmare*. He could hear its creaking laughter as it tormented him with its growing presence; and all the time, it was sucking his strength from him, transforming into a brightly-glowing naked human form. The stuff of his early visions. The author of his teenage horrors. A bony old man with a gaunt and haggard face covered in rat bites!

'Koppelberg,' he gasped, before he passed out in the wraith's emaciated arms.

When he came to, the thing had gone. He felt his body all over with shaking hands to see if it was intact, then very slowly inched off the bed. He flopped out onto the floor, pulling his duvet behind him. He lay there shivering as the light of another winter's day welcomed him back to the world. When he found the strength to go to the bathroom and glance fearfully in the mirror, he almost fainted at what he saw. Plastered in dried blood on his forehead were the bold words: HE IS MINE

He decided right then and there that he would have to move from his rooms, which had been desecrated by such evil. 'I'm not staying here,' he said out loud. 'I can't face it anymore.' With a heaving stomach, he hunted for a face cloth and began to scrub off the blood from his forehead.

Later, when he was feeling better, he dropped the cloth into a plastic bag and sealed it. The blood was useful evidence. It couldn't be his; he had no sign of injury. He could hand it over to his old school friend, Clyde, who also worked at Norris and had a full lab at his disposal, where he could get an analysis done.

The warning he'd been given by his horrific night visitor had firmed up his suspicions. If he persisted with his plans, then he would end up in a further life-and-death struggle with his unearthly enemy, with only Klaas Honen at his side. It was a daunting prospect. Could he trust Klaas? Allow himself to believe that the boy's powers could afford him a hitherto unavailable weapon against the evil he faced? Or did the warning mean that Klaas was actually the servant of that evil, and was drawing him into the abyss? He remembered Dalca's affirmation that evil was still alive, and that children could be changed by demonic possession. Pip's meeting with the terrified parish priest, Fr Joseph, had provided confirmation of that.

Pip wished then that he could fully believe in God and the precepts he had been taught as a child. As yet, he didn't know if there was some great unseen being who could help him. Maybe he had enough faith to survive. At least he could see Klaas had some humanity, even a sense of bewilderment as to his powers, and perhaps, after all, some remorse for those who had suffered because of them.

'Simu,' he said out loud. It was the nearest he came to prayer. 'If you were here to guide me, what would you do?' Seconds afterwards, he thought of Olga. Why, he didn't know, but he felt he owed it to her and Ghita to take the risk of trying. It seemed extremely important to him then that he should become a hero in their eyes at least, even though he felt a coward himself.

'I will take the chance,' he said. 'I'll go along with the boy and hope for the best.' He knew that his choice wasn't entirely pragmatic, but born of an excitement that came from the prospect of contributing to a unique scientific venture that had been launched over thirty years earlier by a far-seeing President of the United States. Billions of pounds were still being spent by the scientific community on research into the only thing it felt it couldn't fully understand: *the human mind*. Pip had worked only on the psychological fringes of this so-called BRAIN project when he was at the Institute, but he had the right to conduct his own experiments – and now he had both the chance and a suitable subject.

After he had made his decision, he spent what was left of the night in a living-room chair, rather than in the bed that had entertained such horror. When he finally dragged himself up, he made coffee and began looking for something he had discarded a long time ago when he had thought he no longer needed it.

He found the small silver cross and chain, which his mother had given him before he first went to Romania, in a small box alongside two pairs of cufflinks that he never used and a few other trifles. Why she had felt the need to give it to him was still a mystery, but she had – and he felt he needed it now. Whether or not it would ward off evil, he couldn't be sure, but it was the only talisman he possessed. Strangely, it gave him a little comfort, coupled with the knowledge that his own intelligence must carry him through the next stage of his enterprise.

He picked up his mobile phone and sent Clyde a text message, asking to meet him in the Dons' Common Room that evening; it was going to cut into his time with Ghita, but he really needed to see his friend – and not just to arrange that blood analysis!

14

When he arrived at Ghita's, Olga was there too. He could tell that the two of them had been arguing, but in spite of that, Ghita looked extremely pleased to see him. His heart lifted.

To his surprise, Olga rushed to him and embraced him as if she'd known him all her life. 'Pip, come and help us. Mother's mad at me. I want to know what you think. Tell him, Mother!'

Ghita lifted her eyebrows, while he looked from one to the other. 'I don't want to get in to this,' he said.

'You solve other people's problems, don't you?' implored Olga.

'Not anymore. I've given all that up.' He glanced at Ghita, and she threw him a look that plainly said, *Don't you dare tell her you're my spy.*

'Well, I know better,' replied Olga. She turned to her mother. 'Pip's made Klaas really happy. I know you'll help us, Pip.'

He grimaced. 'What's up?'

He heard Ghita expel a slight sound of annoyance. 'Don't be silly, Olga!' she said, giving her daughter a fierce look. 'Pip has enough to do without involving himself in our problems.'

Pip was watching Olga, who seemed like a sulky child rather than a sophisticated young woman She flopped down onto the couch and began turning over the pages of a magazine.

'I'm going to make us some coffee,' said Ghita. 'Maybe you should tell Pip what you've just asked me.' She turned to Pip. 'We've had a few words,' she explained. Olga snorted. 'Just make her see some sense, please,' was Ghita's parting plea.

When the door closed, Pip faced Olga. She smiled up at him from dark, carefully-made-up eyes. Her mood had changed, and she had returned from little girl to artful teenager. He couldn't help thinking how much she resembled her mother when they had first met.

'Come and sit down here,' she said, patting a cushion. Then she shoved away a pile of books. 'I'm not very tidy myself, but Mother's worse. This place is a mess. I wish Anya was here – not, of course, just for tidying …' She stopped.

'I know,' he said with sympathy. Then he sat down beside her and waited.

She turned, and her expressive eyes stared into his. This time they smouldered with indignant anger as she blurted out, 'Mother won't let Klaas come and live with us. It would be really good for him with his Finals coming up – and he'll pay a massive amount for Anya's room! He told me he would. He said it would be the best place for him to study now, and I want him here, of course. He can help me with my revision, but Mother doesn't understand that. She thinks we're sleeping together, but however much I tell her we're not, she won't believe me. She feels guilty, because she's a Catholic. She never goes to Church, but she's worried about what other people will say. Who cares? What do you think?' She stopped, evidently waiting for his input.

To give himself time to compute the information, he said, 'Well, I was your grandfather's lodger, you know.' He realised that he'd made a huge mistake as soon as he'd said it, because she threw her arms round him and hugged him, then jumped off the couch, ran over, opened the door and yelled down the corridor.

'Mother, leave that! Pip thinks it's all right!'

'Hey, hold on,' he sputtered. 'That's not what I said.' He knew what he had done when he heard the mugs clattering as Ghita brought them in. She looked at him. Her cheeks were red and her eyes were angrier than her daughter's had been.

'You think it's all right?'

'No, I didn't say that. I said … I only said that I'd been your father's lodger once.' He could see how cross she was.

'Well, that was helpful,' replied Ghita with sarcasm. Olga was shifting impatiently from one foot to the other like a child again. *That's all she is*, thought Pip.

'Don't just stand there like that,' Ghita told her. 'I'm not going to change my mind unless someone persuades me it's a good idea. And I don't think anyone will. Do *you* want coffee?'

'*No!* You don't understand. I'm going upstairs.' With that, Olga stormed out, leaving Pip to face Ghita's wrath. The atmosphere smouldered between them as Ghita slapped down the tray in front of him and sat on a chair by the fireplace.

'Is this mine?' he asked, indicating one of the mugs. She didn't answer, so he left it where it was.

'How could you say that about having been our lodger?' she cried. 'She thinks you're on her side.'

'I'm not. I hadn't thought about it. What she said did give me a shock, though.' His tone was placatory.

'How do you think I felt? They've cooked it up between them. He has plenty of money. He could stay at any hotel, any flat, anywhere, but –'

'He wants to be with Olga. And he *is* friendless – except for her.'

'You know that? He's told you?' Pip nodded. 'You sound as if you're in favour. She's only 15, Pip.'

'I realise that,' he said, 'but really I'm not qualified to say anything, Ghita. It's not my business.'

She looked hard at him. 'I suppose no more than anyone else?' was the reply.

'What do you mean? I've only just met her – and you again, for that matter. I can't pronounce on matters between you and her.'

'Playing the psychologist card again!' She shook her head in disgust.

He wondered if he should go over and try to comfort her, but he didn't know how. He sat where he was. 'I'd like to help,' he said, 'but I don't have any experience of girls – in that sense.

From what I can see so far, Olga's not the kind of person that's going to jump into bed with any boy. Maybe he's just her friend? She says so.' He hoped that might make Ghita think.

'You're evidently in the boy's good books,' retorted Ghita. 'You'd better tell me what's been going on. Just what has made you Number 1 with Klaas? He hates people. What have you been up to?'

He could see it was going to be a long night, but he'd already thought of a few points in favour of the idea of Klaas moving in with Olga and Ghita – and they weren't conventional. He couldn't say that at present, though; he could only think it.

A sudden idea struck him. 'What about this?' he said. 'Have you another room?'

'Yes. The extension. It's a mess. Why?'

'How would you feel about having two lodgers?'

'Two!'

'Yeah. What say I move in as well? I could have Anya's room and we could put Klaas downstairs. We could tidy up.' He looked at her, and would have been hard put to describe her expression. 'Don't look like that.'

'I … I …' She was silent then.

'I could keep an eye on him. We'd both pay well,' he said.

The thought of him appointing himself as effective guardian to Klaas and Olga was ludicrous, but at least, given what he knew and also feared, he'd to be on hand if something happened.

'What about your rooms at Norris? It would be so cramped here.' Her voice had gone quiet.

'I'll keep my rooms open, so if it goes wrong then you can get rid of me. At present, Norris doesn't suit me. I need to be nearer the libraries when I'm writing, and I'm not used to college living. Most of us will be out all the time – and you know, Ghita, this is the best way to find out what's happening between Klaas and Olga. He'll be right downstairs.'

She ignored the last sentence and said, 'To throw them together, you mean!'

'Well, we do have experience of that ourselves,' he admitted, half-smiling. 'But we're adults now. Have your coffee.' He handed her the mug, feeling like Machiavelli, and added, 'I'll tell you about my progress so far.'

'I need this to get over the shock of what you've just sprung on me,' she answered, stretching out her hand for the coffee.

As he gave her the mug, he made sure that their fingers didn't touch. He didn't want her to suspect that the idea he'd broached was only for his own benefit.

After all had cooled down and Ghita had promised to think about his proposition, Pip gave her a carefully-edited account of what was happening between him and Klaas:

'We've agreed to meet for a few sessions and he's been quite reasonable. He's a very difficult boy of outstanding intelligence. He has had a pampered background but has never experienced a real family. I don't think that he means Olga any harm; in fact, he seems very fond of her. According to her, they aren't doing anything they shouldn't, and although I haven't broached that with him yet, I most probably will. He needs a lot of understanding. At least Olga seems to think he's happy with how it's going. I don't think you have anything to worry about at the moment.

'Oh,' he added nonchalantly, 'and just think about what I said earlier. If I moved in, even for a limited time, it would be all to the good.'

They were doing the washing up that had been left from breakfast, and he put down the tea towel, feeling ashamed that he was able to look her in the eye.

'And you have no other reason to want to move in?' she asked. They were facing each other.

'I would be lying if I said I didn't have some ulterior motive,' he murmured. He put his arms round her, and she didn't stop him, only looked startled as he blundered on. 'I'm ashamed about how I've let you down in the past, but I'm still very fond of you, and I want to make up. In any way you'll let me. I know

I'm not good at relationships, but I do care for you a hell of a lot.'

'Just stop there,' she said, withdrawing slightly. 'I'm no fool. I know you want to go to bed with me. I've seen the way you look.' She went over and sat at the kitchen table.

He followed, sat opposite and waited for the worst.

She continued, 'Well, I've been alone a long time now – for many reasons, not all to do with you. In fact, I'd almost given up hope of ever seeing you again.' Pip had the grace to look shamefaced. 'Let's just take it slowly, like we had to when we were kids. Just say I'm following the Government's pronouncement on the avoidance of promiscuity?'

Then her eyes became mischievous and she flashed him a look that he remembered; a tinge of the 19-year-old Ghita he'd known and loved for so long. 'But don't give up, Pip,' she added. 'I like you around, and you'll keep me alive.' He felt scared at that comment, and must have looked it, until she explained, 'Yes, I sometimes get depressed thinking of the old life in Arva, but don't we all? It's the future we should look to. At present, my future is Olga.' She reached out and took his hand. 'It wouldn't be setting a very good example if we were running upstairs every time we wanted to, would it? I know I'm giving her a hard time, because I love her – and you're getting the same.'

Pip took a deep breath, thinking this must mean she still loved him too. He was very scared. Not only because he was crazy to be near her, but also because he knew he was about to deceive her again. 'So,' he said, 'you'll consider me a fit person to have as your lodger?'

'Yes,' she replied. 'And I'll talk to Olga about having Klaas as well. I suppose she told you I need the money? That's not quite true. I need company like she does. We'll both keep an eye on them. And no,' she added as he moved toward her, 'don't you kiss me.'

'It was you who started it last time,' he reminded her. 'I was only being spontaneous.'

'Hah! The day you're spontaneous, I'll be amazed,' Ghita

retorted. 'That's what annoyed me about you when we first met. You were so serious and careful. A young man who worked out every move before he took it. The typical research student! Maybe you're doing that now? If so, hopefully it won't be to our detriment. And, by the way, you'll have to tell me soon about the biography you and my dad were working on.'

All Pip could do then was smile, but inside, he was quaking, because he knew he couldn't come clean; if he did, this new-found 'relationship' with the love of his life would soon be over.

Secrets bring terror, and the result of terror lasts for a very long time. It doesn't go away.

After leaving Ghita's, Pip returned to the Dons' Common Room to keep his appointment with his old school friend Clyde. The room was lively in the evening – very different from when Pip had been there last and met Reverend Matthews.

No sign of the old guy, Pip thought with relief. He saw Clyde by the bar and made his way over. They shook hands and found themselves a free table in one of the darkest corners.

Once they were seated, Clyde leaned toward Pip like a conspirator with a government secret to sell. 'Your message said you wanted me to help you with an experiment with a patient. Sounds very intriguing!'

'Well, he's not a patient really, more a buddy.' Pip couldn't believe he'd just referred to Klaas as a buddy! 'The two of us are trying something out. It's a private experiment.'

Clyde looked at him and grimaced. 'I'll have to keep a written record of all the details, I'm afraid, just to cover myself in case things go wrong.'

'What could go wrong?' Pip had a sudden worry that Clyde was looking for an excuse to back out.

'Nothing, I'm sure, but this is not entirely above board. You see …' he paused, and Pip waited for the get-out, '…the rules say that the labs can be used only by college scientists engaged on official projects.'

'I wouldn't want to put you in an awkward position,' said

Pip, 'but we're … Well, it's a bit difficult to explain.'

'I thought it might be,' replied Clyde with a sigh.

'Oh, well,' replied Pip. 'I can see your point, but I'm disappointed. I'm a psychologist, as you know, and here on sabbatical, including lectures, but my buddy …'

'Who is this buddy then?' interposed Clyde.

'He's a student here at Norris.'

'Well, that's something,' Clyde sniffed.

'You might have heard of him. Klaas Honen.'

Clyde looked astonished. 'You mean you're conducting an experiment with Honen?'

'Yeah. Is it that bad?' Pip was taken aback by Clyde's reaction.

'For God's sake, man, do you know what you're doing?'

'I don't get it.'

'Everyone wants a crack at him.' Clyde looked excited. 'He's the best mathematician we've ever had here. How did you get him?'

'Yep, he's an amazing mathematician,' Pip replied coolly, though his mind was reeling. Klaas had led both him and Ghita's family to believe that he was a historian! He realised it would not be a good idea to let slip to Clyde that he had been labouring under this misapprehension. He should have checked up. 'You might be surprised to know, he has a very strong interest in medieval history and the psychology of the mediaeval mind, too.' It was the best Pip could do on the spur of the moment.

'Wow! I can tell you something,' added Clyde. 'Whatever work you're doing with that kid, in whatever subject area, it's liable to mean publication later on. Do you know how many of our colleagues would like to be in your shoes? You lucky bastard!'

'Thanks for that,' said Pip, who was inwardly smouldering that Klaas had been deceiving him.

'In the circumstances, I'm sure the Dean would be happy to let you use my lab for your extracurricular activities. What exactly are you doing?'

'It's difficult for me to tell you exactly,' replied Pip slowly. 'Um … It's a new project. I can't say much about it, but it's tied in with other things. You know I'm a mediaevalist at present.'

'You're a lucky man, as I said before, Durrant,' noted Clyde. 'I'd heard you were approached by the BRAIN project in the early days. Do you still do work for them now?' He was keen as a ferret.

'Not now,' Pip said. 'I did a long time ago, but then turned to something that interested me more.'

'Cool,' replied Clyde. To Pip's relief, he let the matter drop then, getting out his laptop and consulting a spreadsheet. 'So, there are vacant lab dates here, and here. I can make the first, but not the second. It's still a month off, though.'

'Well, if that's the earliest, I'll take it,' replied Pip, getting out his phone. 'Excuse me while I make a note of the date. Memory's not that good anymore!'

'Ha, ha! I certainly don't believe that,' said Clyde, who was looking at Pip in a way that embarrassed him. 'Well done again for getting something sorted with that kid. I'm beginning to suspect you might have had something to do with him giving up the idea of deferring.'

'No, no,' denied Pip.

'Hmm, well, if you say so. Anyway, what exactly will you want me to do in this experiment? I'm looking forward to seeing that boy in action.'

'I just want you to hook us both up simultaneously to that equipment you're using to monitor test subjects' brain activity. Then simply record the data and, when we're done, hand it over to me – not to Klaas. Being senior, I get first shout. You understand?'

'Of course. Well, great.' Clyde finished off his drink. 'I'm relieved we could work something out. Look forward to it. You have a very willing helper here. Now, work to do.' He made to get up, but Pip held up a hand to detain him.

'Hang on a moment. There's something else. Would you be able to get this tested for me?' Pip produced the stained cloth.

'What is it? Blood?' Clyde squinted at him with an unsure

look on his face.

'Animal,' Pip said. 'You probably remember – I like to keep pet rats.'

'You should go to a vet, if there's something wrong.'

'Too expensive. Quick as you can?'

Clyde frowned. 'I'll see what I can do.'

'Thanks, I owe you one,' replied Pip.

'Rats!' said Clyde. 'Always rats. You're a madman.'

'I know.'

They shook hands again. Pip watched his friend lope away. The first thing he was going to do now was confront Klaas. Then he realised he was being hypocritical. Hadn't he once misled Simu into thinking he was working as a psychological researcher, because he had wanted to know everything Simu could teach him about Arva? A mathematician, eh?

He softened a little. At least Klaas would be familiar with labs and with what that kind of research entailed. Pip couldn't wait for the next month to pass until the lab date came around and he could have his next session with the boy. In the meantime, he had a move of lodgings to sort out.

Clyde had thought he was a lucky guy, and so he was. Pip felt as pleased and excited as he had 17 years earlier, when he had engineered an invitation to go and stay with the Dalcas. He was a lot wiser now, though, than he had been then.

Less than an hour later, Pip stood outside the gate of Klaas's halls, calling him on his mobile phone.

'What are you doing right now?' he asked. 'I have some news. I have the lab booked. And I need to talk to you.'

'No-one comes to my room,' was the gruff answer. 'Besides, I'm too busy to see you.'

'Like I was when you turned up at my door? I'm on my way up – unless you tell me you have a woman tucked away in there.'

'Come up, then. Staircase B, Room 7,' he growled.

Pip grinned and replaced his phone. As he paused at the foot of the staircase, he wondered why Klaas had been reluctant to let him come up. Had the boy been studying, or was something else going on? Consumed with curiosity, he started to run up the staircase. Then he halted as his weak leg let him down. He swore and limped on.

The corridor leading to Klaas's room was empty and silent. Pip frowned. The excitement had been replaced by a nasty little shiver of apprehension that ran along and under his shoulder blades.

As soon as he knocked, the door opened, and Pip gasped at the sight revealed. He had seen a room like it in a recent television thriller. Every inch of the wall was plastered with cuttings, prints and photographs of every kind – but, as far as he could see, no faces. And there was no sign of Klaas.

'Hi,' Pip shouted, 'I'm here.' Silence.

He walked forward, and the acrid smell of the laboratory assailed his nostrils, although he could see no scientific or mathematical apparatus. One of the walls was singed, as if there had been a fire at one time or another. It was the strangest room he had ever seen – and, given the other troubled teenagers' rooms he'd visited in his career as a psychologist, that was saying something. No women, no porn, no pop groups, no books, nothing but paper; so much paper, and so many photographs. Before Pip could go and take a closer look, there was a noise behind him. He jumped, then twisted round, and realised he was looking into the lightest of light blue eyes. Wolf-like. The old memories shook him.

'No contact lenses,' said the kid. 'It's my day for dyeing. And for washing my hair.' He grinned.

'What?'

'And maybe doing some piercing. My mother hates it. I had a phone call. She might be coming to visit. See?' Klaas thrust his face near Pip and motioned to his nose. It was full of what Pip first took to be tiny enlarged pores, but then realised were holes.

'You do that yourself?' Pip was trying to regain his cool. He hadn't known what to expect, but this … 'And just to annoy your mother?'

Klaas ignored the question. 'This is my own research,' he explained, gesturing to the walls. 'Maybe you recognise some of the places?'

'I was just going to look when you startled the shit out of me. And what are you cooking?' It was his attempt at a joke.

'Getting rid of some things.'

'Like what?' Pip was imagining bodies steeped in acid.

'Nothing that matters,' was the answer. 'So we can't have supper.'

'I haven't come for that,' replied Pip. 'I wanted to know why you lied to me – telling me you were a historian, when you're actually a mathematician?'

'Oh, that. It's easy. I forgot. I'm a philosopher too. Good at the classics as well!' He looked at Pip, and was suddenly serious again. 'I wasn't lying. I'm equally good at history. And that is what I need you for.'

You sure have a way of making people want to punch you in the mouth, thought Pip. 'I told you before that you were offensive. You're being that now. And I'm not going to put up with it. I don't want to be used. When you come to your senses, I'll see you again.' He turned toward the door.

'I don't want you to go,' replied Klaas.

'Then be civil.'

'Come and look, please.'

Pip relented and approached the pictures, only just managing to stifle another gasp as he took them in. He knew that countryside so well. It was burnt into his memory. Romania. Klaas was at his shoulder.

'You know where all this is, don't you, Prof? That's why I want to work with you. I've spent some time building up this collection. It started with dreams and then visions – and I need to go there. But I don't want to go on my own. I need to be with someone who knows what I know and feels what I feel.'

'What do you feel?' asked Pip. 'Where did you get this lot from, anyway?'

'I feel quite mad sometimes,' reflected Klaas. 'Oh, I got them from books, newspapers, wherever …'

When Pip looked carefully, he could see that some of the oldest-looking pictures were engravings, hand done, and very skilfully.

'So you draw, too.'

'Unfortunately, I do most things,' replied Klaas.

'And where does your degree come in the list?'

'Low at the moment,' he admitted, 'but I'll pick up. I have exactly two months until the exams. According to my tutor, I should do fine if I work hard.' He laughed. 'By the way, thanks for changing Ghita's mind for me.'

'You know already? But –'

'Let's put it this way: I do now. Gotcha, Prof.'

'You won't be bringing this lot,' retorted an annoyed Pip.

'Nope. I'll burn it all. Don't need it anymore; and, anyway, it's all in here.' He tapped his head. 'Plus, why would I want it, now I have you?'

'What makes you think I know these places?'

'Instinct. And I've seen you there, in my visions. I even have a shot of that path where you picked up the cockerel. Here, have a look.'

Pip forced himself to. Yes, there it was, the stony path winding itself down from Hell. But he didn't admit it. He was preoccupied with wondering why Klaas wanted to go to Arva – and not alone. Did he even know it was Arva? Because Pip couldn't see the name. Klaas pointed out other things. Ghita's house on the square; the bus stop; but not the church, nor the churchyard! Why was that? There was no doubt this was no ordinary student, nor ordinary human being perhaps. But did Klaas realise what he was?

'I want you to come to my rooms again, Klaas, before ...' He stopped.

'Before *we* move in,' said the other.

'We?'

'Yes, I know you're coming too. That you have the hots for Ghita.'

'Shut up,' said Pip.

'No offence meant. I can tell you something to pass on to

Ghita, though. I don't have feelings like that for Olga.'

'What feelings do you have?' asked Pip.

'I dunno. Maybe I want to protect her. But I don't want to hurt her. Never think that, Professor. But she and I – we were meant to be together. I feel that inside. I need to be with her.'

'I don't think I want to talk about this right now,' replied Pip. All he wanted was to go somewhere quiet and consider the implications of what he'd just seen.

'Suits me,' said Klaas, going over to the door. 'Look after yourself now, Prof. Don't hail any more driverless cabs.'

Klaas grinned, but Pip didn't appreciate the joke. He felt sick to the stomach. He knew that what he ought to do was go back to Ghita directly, report what he had seen and tell her that no way should she take the boy into her home. He had a very bad feeling about it; and if something happened beyond his control, he would never forgive himself. But he didn't do it, because he was determined to go to Arva himself and be there on Piper Day, as he had always intended. If Klaas Honen wanted to come with him, so be it.

A few days later, a blond and handsome Klaas became a lodger in Ghita's house, followed very soon by Pip. As Pip observed the changed hair, the now blue eyes, he couldn't help wondering if Klaas was shedding a disguise, and why he had felt he needed it.

One chilly winter's evening the following month, Pip was sitting with Ghita on the couch, reading in front of the gas fire. He had just thought how well the two of them were getting on and was contemplating putting his arm around her.

'I was expecting trouble, you know, when Klaas came here,' Ghita said, 'in spite of what you promised. But it has all worked out wonderfully. He is no trouble at all. So polite. He's kept to every rule I laid down. You're the trouble.' She smiled at him in the old way.

'Me? What have I done?' He pretended to look appalled, but he knew what she meant. The heady days of their relationship hadn't gone; now it seemed she felt the same.

'Nothing. I worried about Olga being with him, but I hadn't quite expected what my feelings would be toward you.'

He put his arm round her now. They didn't speak for a while. It was pure bliss for Pip, who had managed to push the lies away for the time being.

'What are your feelings toward me, exactly?' he asked.

She looked up at him and said, 'Just what they were before. How do you feel about it?'

'The same. Older and wiser. I was an idiot. Crazy enough and scared enough not to come back ...'

'Scared? Of me?'

'Not of you; but there might have been serious implications if I'd stayed around. You remember how you said it would be better if I left Arva, because of all the trouble I was causing?'

'I didn't say that,' she frowned.

'You did. You also implied that I brought bad luck to people.' She shook her head. 'Anyway, I remember; but it wasn't because of that I stayed away. I was scared because the final day, before I went to the airport, I called on someone, who I believe was shot immediately after I left his house.'

'Shot? Did you have anything to do with it?' she said.

'No. But I was worried that the police might think I did. You remember I had problems with them before, when they came to see me? Besides, this man let me have something, which I shouldn't have taken out of Romania. I was young, I was an American, and so I didn't feel I could come back.'

'What the hell was it?'

'Some pages from a book. A very valuable book. I wouldn't have been given a licence to take them away.' She looked shocked. 'I haven't sold them or anything. The originals are in my bank, and there they'll stay until I discover the proper way to return them.' Pip was amazed by the way he was able to bend the truth.

'Some pages from a book! Are you telling me this was the

reason you stayed away from me for 17 years?'

'One of them. Another was not wanting to go against your dad. He would have wanted those pages to stay in Romania too. More to the point, he wouldn't have wanted me to be with you. He was as scared as your mother that we might marry. We couldn't help it if we fell in love, but I would have had a hell of a job to convince him. There are more reasons, which I can't tell you just now, but I promise I will – soon.'

'For God's sake,' she said. 'I could have twisted him around my little finger.'

'You're so stubborn!' he said. 'Believe me, in this case, you couldn't have.'

'So, what have you still to hide, Pip Durrant?' she asked.

'I'll tell you everything soon,' he repeated. 'But I need to go to Romania first. I want to put things right. To replace what I have taken. I have an instinctive feeling that this is the right time.'

'Romania? When?'

'Not until July.'

'And you think you'll be okay? You're hopeless in a crisis. What about the police? They won't have forgotten.'

'They don't know anything about the book. It was a secret between the man and me. Besides, since then, I've discovered that he acquired the pages illegally.'

'This sounds like something out of your fiction,' she said. 'Are you sure you're telling me the truth?'

'I am,' he said. 'I can show you some photocopies I made of the pages.' He was gambling on her not taking him up on this.

'Has this anything to do with what you and my father were working on? The biography?' Pip nodded. 'Well, why didn't you tell me this before?'

'I wasn't quite sure how to.' That at least was the truth. 'Another thing …'

'Another!'

'About Klaas this time. He's developed a great interest in Romania, and he wants to go with me.'

'Klaas? Does he know about the book?'

'No. That is between me and you.'

'So what's his interest in Romania?'

'We've been talking about things in his past that have made him want to go there. I believe that both his parents came from there. Let's say he's on a kind of ancestry hunt. Strangely enough, their roots are centred on the Arva district.'

'I've never heard of any Honens. It's a German name.'

'Neither have I, which is interesting.' He couldn't believe she'd swallowed it all and hadn't kicked him out. She remained seated, staring at the fire.

'We could all go,' she said. 'Anya was desperate to go back this year. I don't know why. Olga and I could do it in her memory, like a pilgrimage – and I can scatter her ashes. Pip, you're a marvel, but I could kill you as well. All these years staying away from me because of some pages of a book! Where is the rest of the book, anyway?'

'I'm researching that now. As the man I met was from the Arva area too, there's a possibility that one of the archaeological sites there might be a starting point. Klaas is helping me on the project; but why, he doesn't know yet. A fresh eye is always good in these things. Anyway, we've been laying off since our last session together so that he can get some real time in revising for his Finals. And I have another two psychology lectures to prepare.'

'One thing though, Pip. I don't fancy July,' she said. 'It won't be a good time to go nosing around Arva.'

He knew she was remembering. 'I know what you mean, Ghita, but it'll be all right now. I've checked. All the old traditions have been subsumed into a cultural festival. The church has been razed to the ground and the graveyard has been re-sited. I saw it on the internet. They even have a fair there in July.'

'They never caught Grandsire then?'

'No.' He stiffened.

'As for fairs,' she shuddered, 'I don't like them.'

'Nor me,' he replied, cursing himself for going too far and reminding her of things she didn't want to remember.

'It's my birthday on the twenty-second,' she said. He swallowed, as his mouth had gone dry. 'Olga's is that month, too.'

'Olga was born in July? What date?' He became nervous even at the mention of that month.

Ghita smiled. 'She was actually due on my birthday, but she didn't come until a couple of days later. The twenty-fourth.'

Pip was calculating. If Olga had been born on 22 July too, then the conditions of the Princess's curse wouldn't have been met, because she would have been too old for the Piper to take. The curse had stipulated that it had to be a child in her sixteenth year. But as she hadn't been born until 24 July, she was very much in danger.

'I really want to go in July,' Pip said, 'but I'm not sure Olga should go too. She'll be waiting for her exam results then, won't she?'

'Hmm, that's true,' acknowledged Ghita. 'Oh, I hope she'll do well.'

'Remember who's helping her,' he soothed.

'I know, but ...'

'Klaas being here is stopping her going out at night, isn't it?' Ghita nodded. 'So ...' he added.

'What I said earlier, I did mean it.'

'That I was trouble?' His eyes were full of fun, but inside he felt bad.

'No, that we get on well, as we've done ever since you turned up at home in Arva and I thought you were – just hopeless. No, stop it, Pip, we can't behave like teenagers when he have two in the house already. Remember?'

'Yes,' he sighed. If only he was not still carrying his burden of lies. At least he'd told her some of the truth.

'Maybe, when we go on holiday,' she teased.

'Oh, you've made up your mind to go, then? We'll have to mention it to the kids now.'

As she disappeared through the door, he thought that he and Ghita were already behaving like a couple; which, unfortunately, they weren't – at least, not as far as having sex was concerned. Was that what was happening upstairs? He had heard Klaas go up a couple of hours earlier, and the two of them laughing when he had come down. However, it couldn't be, according to Klaas, as he'd told Pip he didn't feel like that about Olga. What did the guy want from her, then? The kind of tantalising life Pip was living with Ghita? Perhaps he really was just a true friend to her, as he claimed. Even her soul-mate. Maybe he was gay? He'd said he wanted to protect her. But did he know from what?

15

On the day of the controlled experiment, Pip and Klaas walked over to the lab, despite Ghita's offer to take them. 'The walk might clear my brain,' Pip had said, joking.

'Let's hope it doesn't,' had come the reply from Klaas.

With Pip, the boy's humour appeared to be confined to sarcastic or mocking repartee, yet there must have been more to it than that, as he could be frequently heard laughing with Olga. The young woman had set off on her bike to St Willibrord's at least half an hour before they left the house, and had seemed in a particularly happy mood. When she was happy, so was Ghita, and so Pip had enjoyed a less frenetic morning than usual.

As they walked, Klaas was yawning a lot, which Pip hoped might be a good sign; but he really had no idea how things would go, in the limited time Clyde had been able to secure for them in the lab. Pip had been thinking about that, and about what would happen if Klaas did manage to induce a vision in both of them.

When they reached Norris, Klaas suddenly veered off down a side path. 'Sorry, gotta go.'

'Go where? You know what time it is.'

'Stay cool, man,' was the annoying reply.

Even the sentence seemed false. 'Cool' was still in the vernacular, but whether or not it was ever used in Klaas's and Olga's circle was another matter. Klaas had said it like he expected Pip to understand.

'I won't if you don't turn up!'

'Thanks, Pip,' he replied. 'I hadn't that in my mind, but I have now.' Klaas had a wicked grin on his face as he headed off, leaving Pip standing there looking angry.

'He's behaving like I'm his parent now!' Pip growled to himself, smouldering inwardly. Then he had an uncomfortable thought. Was Klaas going off to do something that might help him induce the visions? As he considered the possibility, he began to become more agitated, going over in his head the kind of drugs he'd known in the past that induced hallucinations. His knowledge wasn't up to date, as he didn't work in that area. He had no idea what kids were into now.

Klaas's persistent yawning really spooked him in retrospect. Maybe the boy had taken something before he left the house? He'd been yawning like that the night they'd shared the vision, too.

Pip relaxed at little. That couldn't be the answer. While Klaas could in principle have given himself a drug-induced vision, he couldn't have accessed a past experience of Pip's like that, no matter what hallucinogen he had taken.

Pip was sick to the stomach as he walked down the upper corridor of the science block. The whole building was strangely quiet. Evidently most of the serious young students at Norris were at lectures, or with their tutors, or in other laboratories, worrying about the coming examinations. Pip knew one who was not. He sighed.

Switching his mind briefly away from Klaas, he concluded that his own weakness had something to do with what he imagined, or even feared, could happen in the lab. His visions had never been pleasant experiences, and he expected that this one, if it could indeed be provoked as Klaas claimed, would be no different.

He wondered how Klaas was feeling, and he thought he knew, because the kid was so full of his own importance. Pip had met one or two men he had rated as brilliant scientists, but had found them to be rather humble. Klaas didn't know the meaning of that word.

Pip felt as nervous as if he was entering a laboratory for the first time. He didn't need the key code to get in, though, because Clyde was hovering in the doorway.

'Jeez, you look pale,' he said. 'You're not sick, are you?'

Pip shook his head. 'Nope, only preparing myself. I'm grateful to you for doing this.'

'It's fine. Where's the wonder boy?'

'On his way. He had to go somewhere.'

Clyde looked at his watch. 'He should hurry up,' he warned. 'We don't have all day.'

'Exactly my sentiments,' replied Pip, feeling as if he would like to strangle Klaas.

'By the way,' Clyde added, 'I have your cloth here. You want to get rid of that rat.'

'Have you got the results of the analysis, then?' Having been preoccupied by the coming experiment, Pip had almost forgotten about the blood sample.

'They came in a couple of days ago, and I just glanced at them,' said Clyde. He held out his hand. 'Ten,' he demanded. 'The lab guys might be my friends, but they don't do anything for nothing. Bastards!'

Pip took out his wallet and handed over the note. 'Cheap at the price,' he replied, laughing, which lightened the atmosphere. As they were still waiting for Klaas, he sat down on a stool and looked over the lab report. A bit of medical jargon, and then just what he had expected to see, but hoped he wouldn't: haemoglobin, but not in the human band, probably rodent. He shivered.

Clyde looked over his shoulder, rubbed his hands and repeated, 'I'd get rid of that rat, if I were you. What have you been giving it? Blood thinners?' He looked at the clock and sighed. Seconds later, though, they saw Klaas's golden head approaching through the wired half-window, and Clyde went to open the door for him.

The boy was wearing jeans and an expensive shirt and looked every bit the serious young man. He smiled in a polite manner and shook hands with Clyde, but then glanced at Pip, who realised he had taken out his contact lenses again to reveal his true eye colour. He couldn't have looked more like the perfect student, but Pip wasn't particularly fond of blond-haired youths with wolf-blue eyes.

'It's great to have you here, Honen,' said Clyde. 'First time in my lab. Everything's ready.' His deference to Klaas sickened Pip.

'Okay, Clyde, let's go,' replied Klaas, like he owned the laboratory, which seemed a living thing itself with its computers' green and blue lights winking, all under his spell.

'First of all, I have to have your phones and any other gadgets you have on you, please. Switch off and place them in here.' He waited as their mobiles and other electronic devices were placed in different baskets.

'I'm clean,' said Klaas.

'And me,' added Pip. Clyde then locked the baskets away.

'Sit, now,' Clyde said. 'It might take some time to get this set up, as I don't have an assistant this morning. I assumed you wouldn't be keen on that. Now I'm going to place some headgear on your craniums, with electrode sensors attached. The gear will house a wi-fi transmitter. No wiring harness is necessary. Okay.'

They sat while Clyde fitted them with rubber whole-head caps, to which he attached electrode sensors. The mood had sobered and there seemed no need to speak. It was then that Pip started to regret what they were doing. Klaas seemed to have misgivings too. His face under the cap looked smaller, wan and pointed. The mocking smile and air of arrogance had disappeared.

'The recorder is all set up to take the data,' explained Clyde. He indicated two doors. 'Our two rooms both have beds in – twin beds in one, a single in the other – but you don't have to use them if you'd rather not. They each have a couple of chairs too, if you'd prefer to sit.'

'Can we walk around while the process is ongoing?' asked Pip.

'Sure, the wi-fi will allow that,' replied Clyde doubtfully.

'Sounds good.' replied Pip. 'I shan't be going to sleep.'

Clyde shrugged. 'Okay. You're the psychologist. I'm only recording the data and handing it over to you straight after. Now I just have to switch on. My job is done. The computer takes over then. The bonus is that this process usually allows me to see some nice, or not so nice, images on my screens. I have seen some things, boys. Wow! Not always, but sometimes. But if you say you won't be dreaming in this experiment, then I believe you. So Clyde doesn't get to have pictures. So what?'

'You can stop the experiment, though, if necessary?' asked Pip.

Clyde frowned. 'I guess so.'

'I would rather have the single room,' said Klaas. 'I like my own space. Is that okay, Prof?' Pip nodded. He wasn't surprised.

'Be my guest,' said Clyde, indicating Room 1. 'Carry on.'

Pip entered his room – Room 2 – but ignored the twin beds, feeling happier taking the chair. Clyde's voice came through a speaker.

'Is everything all right in there?'

Pip nodded. He felt nothing, except perhaps a warm tightness around the skull – which must have been an effect of the headgear – followed by a cold sensation running through him, like the one that sometimes comes immediately after the injection of an anaesthetic drug. He felt uptight, so he made a conscious effort to relax and be mentally open to receiving whatever images Klaas might try to send …

Then, he opened his eyes to a darker world that he did not recognise.

Pip stayed very still for a moment. The room around him now looked dingy and cold. In front of him on a table lay a large book. He didn't remember a book having been there before. He looked up at the lights, but they didn't seem to be on, and there was no window. No way of seeing outside.

The book looked as though it shouldn't be in a lab. It was obviously ancient. He fixed his mind on an almost lost memory, which raced up to him on call. 'That's it,' he breathed. 'I was looking for a book.' Could this be the Codex? It had a worn and heavily marked cover, as it should have if it was a thousand years old.

He stepped closer to the table, and the room opened out into a large study. He opened the ancient tome, thinking he ought to be using gloves. He saw that it was written in unrecognisable Latin, like the stolen manuscript pages. Then he heard a man speaking in a quavering elderly voice, in a language he realised was Latin too. Another, younger man answered in a commanding tone, again in Latin.

Pip looked up and saw the two men, who were now standing on the opposite side of the table. The young one was bending over the ancient book. He wore a wig that obscured his face, and had on a long velveteen coat of green, brocaded with gold. Pip turned his attention to the other figure. The older man was looking straight at him, but Pip knew he hadn't even noticed him, as his eyes were staring into space. Then he too looked down at the vellum pages of the book, lying open before him. He was wearing a skullcap, a frayed frock coat and a sash of red. Also on the table was a long, dust-covered curly wig, thrown carelessly down. The large hand of the young man was near the old man's head, pointing something out.

Pip could sense an air of tension and anticipation wafting through the shadowy room. He realised he must be invisible to the two men, but still he could feel the presence of danger. Looking down again at the book, he saw that many dates were inscribed on the vellum pages, lines and lines of them, and his head became giddy as he cast his eyes back and forth across the rows and up and down the columns.

The table had many other interesting, unusual objects upon it now: a brass telescope mottled with age; a silver metal cone – no, a prism; a grindstone with two handles; a great globe in a carved wooden stand. 'The tools of thy trade,' Pip whispered. Then he quivered with fear as he heard a fierce growl come from below the table. One thing he hadn't noticed before was a great copper urn there; and, bedded beside it, a small terrier dog, which was baring its teeth at him.

'*Tace*, Diamond,' snarled the bewigged young man in the green, gold-braided coat – and the dog subsided. Around the dog were quantities of discarded documents and books, even one flung into its makeshift cradle. It snapped at the book and tossed it aside with contempt.

The animal exuded such an air of evil that Pip moved back sharply and fell into a great curtain, which impeded his escape, flopping into his face and giving him a mouthful of dust. Then he became enmeshed in the curtain's thick tassel cords. The dog growled at him and bared its teeth again. He put out his hand to soothe it, and it bit him savagely. He yelled, but no-one seemed to hear him. He sucked at the bleeding bite, and the blood tasted vile, so he spat it out, while the dog regarded him fiercely.

Struggling free, he discovered he was now under the table, crawling on his hands and knees like vermin. He knew the men were above him, and became irrationally scared that they would find him. So he crouched there, like some small animal, his lungs still choked by the dust from the curtain. The dog was hunting him again; its ears were pricked and it was snarling.

It thinks I'm a rat, thought Pip, and he nearly fainted when he looked down at his hands. He had no nails, only sharp claws. He lifted one hand to his face and felt whiskers. Then he moved the hand low around his back and touched – a hairless tail! He screamed inside, *I* am *a rat*. He sat back on his two hind feet, and saw nearby a burner with a pan balanced on it and a three-legged stool beside.

He climbed up onto the stool and remained there, frozen with fear, watching the men. He was quivering all over. The old man's beard was long. Pip felt that he could creep into it and be safe. He moved with stealth toward the great being, and could see his face now. The vestiges of Pip's human memory stirred. He had seen something like this scene before – in a painting.

I'm in an oil painting, he told himself. *None of this is real.* He stretched out his clawed hand and scratched at the canvas. *I'm inside – and I'm trapped!*

He panicked, but found he couldn't get off the stool. He bent forward, reached out and caught hold of the nearest thing he could find – the serge of the old man's coat, which fell in folds. He swung there for a minute. Then, catching hold of the old man's broad leather belt, he crept up under his elbow until he was seated in the crook of his arm. He looked up into the old man's face and blinked as recognition grew. The unusual nose, the bushy white brows and the bright, intelligent eyes, which reflected Pip's features – *his real features* – as the old man moved his head and looked down again, concentrating, scanning the pages and pages of dates, his finger moving all the time, until suddenly – it stopped.

The old man jerked his head round to his young companion, whose shadowed face was bent over the pages. The dark, cruel face of the young man came nearer to Pip, nestled in the old man's arm. Both of them were entirely oblivious to his presence.

'*Hoc est date. 2060,*' the old man cried in triumph.

'This is the date,' breathed Pip. '2060.'

His eyes looked into a dark corner of the room, where a tall glass case was standing upright, propped against the wall. It reminded him of those he had seen in the Piper's lair when he was a child. Particularly the fifth and last one, the one that had been empty – not shiny and bright like the fourth, where the man in spectacles and the smiling child had come alive.

'The end of the cycle. The end of the world,' Pip said in wonderment. 'The Piper's last case. I understand now. It's the way out.'

He hunched himself up and squeezed out of the fold of the old man's coat and onto his arm, which was motionless, as his hand and finger were poised over the date for all eternity.

Then Pip felt a great weight on his back, crushing his spine, as a deft hand with hard, cruel nails clamped on and he was turned over to lie prone. He screamed, his little red mouth with pincer teeth wide open in agony, as he was drawn up toward the young man. He felt himself brush against the soft wig as he passed the cruel mouth with its sharp incisors and lips with turned-up corners. Then he found himself looking into eyes he knew so well, hard blue and wolf-like.

He screamed again.

'Nicholas!' commanded a mighty voice – and Pip was thrown with great force into the nearby glass case, the door of which snapped shut behind him as a sudden gust of wind caught it. He felt all around the walls of his prison, trying to find a way out, then noticed through the glass that there were now flames leaping up in the room outside. 'I shall be burned to death like Simionce!,' he screamed.

He saw the fiend of a dog standing over the burner, which it had tipped over onto its side. The great study, now empty of humans, was being consumed by a fire that gobbled the books and withered the papers and caught the tablecloth and crept over the table, destroying all before it. Then everything went dark!

When he came out of his terrifying vision, Pip was trembling so much that he could not move. He lay on one of the beds, where he must have fallen as if paralysed again. 'The last,' he gasped. 'My last vision. The last case.' He looked across at the window, where Clyde was peering in, a worried expression on his face. Pip tried to move, but his leg hurt. He must have fallen awkwardly on it.

He knew Clyde wouldn't come in to get him, so he made a massive effort and dragged himself up, then staggered across to the door and flung it open.

'For God's sake, man,' groaned Clyde. He was paler than Pip had ever seen him. Not at all like his usual self. 'I shouldn't have done this. I felt in my bones it was going to be a bad experience. The computer went mad and ...' He opened his hands in a gesture of pure bewilderment and disbelief.

Pip realised he couldn't see Klaas in the lab. 'Where is he, Clyde? How's the kid?'

'He wasn't any less rattled than you – or me – when he came out of it. I think – I think he realised he'd bitten off more than he could chew. But he was still cocky.' Pip raised his eyebrows. 'He legged it, after I ...'

'I'm sorry, Clyde,' said Pip. 'Really sorry. You mean you got upset …?' He broke off when he saw Clyde's expression.

'Upset? No, that wasn't it. I was telling Honen what I saw on my screens. In fact, I saw it twice – from both of you.'

Pip felt his stomach turn. He was scared for Clyde then; for what might happen to him. He told himself he shouldn't have asked his friend to help. He and Klaas should have carried out the experiment alone.

Clyde put his head in his hands. 'The data is all there, including the video, recorded on disk. I was going to look at it, but I didn't, in case –' He broke off, then sat up straight in his chair. 'What are you doing, Durrant? Do you know what you've let loose?'

Pip had never heard Clyde say anything like that before. He'd always been cool, measured and unflappable. Just a normal guy. Pip realised that he must have witnessed something on his screens that he had thought he never could. Something that had scared him half to death.

'You just take that crap with you, buddy,' Clyde added, pointing to the data disk. 'I'm going to forget I saw it – if I can.'

'For God's sake, tell me what you saw,' demanded Pip.

'I saw …' Clyde opened his hands in a gesture of absolute resignation. 'I mean – I think I saw – God – and the Devil! And the noise …' He leaned back in the chair and closed his eyes. 'The mind of God!' he whispered to himself.

To hear Einstein's famous words coming out of his friend's mouth really threw Pip. Whatever was going on with Clyde, he didn't know, but he was beginning to feel just as scared. 'Get a grip of yourself,' he urged him. 'What do you mean, God and the Devil? You can't have seen that on your screens. I didn't, and I was in there. You were watching us.'

Clyde bent over and put his head in his hand again. 'Don't ask me anything else,' he said, without looking up. Then he reached into his pocket and produced a bunch of keys. 'I'm not going to touch any of that stuff anymore,' he said, glancing toward the computer. 'I want you to take the data disk, close everything down, then lock up. You'll find my pigeonhole in the lodge. Hand in the keys there.'

'Clyde!' protested Pip. 'We can talk about this. I might be able to … After all, God and the Devil …?'

'No, I'm not going to talk about it,' he said. 'I have to try to get it straight in my own head now. The only thing I can say is that, before today, I didn't even believe in *them!*'

When he said that, he didn't even look like the Clyde that Pip knew. Fear did strange things to people, and the thought of what his friend could have seen was scaring Pip too. There was so much he could explain to him – assuming Clyde ever spoke to him again. 'I'll call you?' he said.

'No, I'll call you,' replied Clyde, in a tone that implied it was improbable he ever would.

At least he's still alive, thought Pip. He watched Clyde walk out of his precious lab without another word. Then he sat back in the hard chair and stared at the computer. What the hell had it recorded? And had Klaas seen the same things as Clyde? All he knew was what he himself had experienced. He had in his head a very clear picture of his vision, and he also remembered the date he'd seen revealed. And he knew now who the two men in the painting were.

Never in all his life had Pip imagined that he might be transported into the presence of the greatest scientist the world has ever known. The older man had been *Isaac Newton*, and his young companion the noted mathematician *Nicholas de Fatio*, who had been close to him and helped him with his work. Pip also thought he knew what work they had been engaged on. In 2003, a report had appeared in the media that Newton had predicted the date of the end of the world. It had been the first time the general public had been made aware of this prophecy, previously known only to a small group of scholars. The report had stated that Newton had calculated the date using the Bible, but Pip now realised that it must have been the Codex instead. What he didn't know, though, was whether or not the painting he had seen in the vision really existed.

Now he had to look at the computer data. And, after what Clyde had told him, he had to view it alone. At that moment he felt the same mix of excitement and apprehension he'd had on first opening the Marcu Papers. He waited to compose himself, at least to show some semblance of being a professional. What could Clyde have seen that had scared him so much? Something that had turned a level-headed atheist into making a declaration of belief in God and the Devil. Whose responsibility was that?

Pip considered his own position. It was Klaas who had suggested the idea of showing off his powers, and now he had performed a feat that Pip had never thought he could. He had induced a vision in Pip.

The important question was, had Klaas's own vision been anything like Pip's? If it had been the same as Clyde's … Pip grimaced. Maybe Klaas should be made to see what damage his power had caused? Maybe it would teach him a lesson?

However, it was Pip who had involved Clyde. It was he who had insisted on a controlled experiment. The major problem now was that the controller seemed to have gone crazy.

Pip told himself he knew his responsibility as psychologist to a patient he was treating. He should ring Klaas to see if he was okay. Maybe the kid had been as scared as Clyde; but, somehow, Pip felt that would not be the case. Luckily, there was no need for him to ring, as Klaas did so first. The boy wanted to come round and see the data. That indicated how upset he was, Pip thought.

'Give me ten,' replied Pip. 'I'll not tamper with anything. Then, depending what's to be seen, we'll compare notes. I'm going to write my own now.'

Surprisingly, Klaas agreed without argument. Maybe he had learned his lesson? Pip shook his head. If he was anything like Pip himself had been at 17, he wouldn't have. But Pip kept his word. He wrote up his experience first. Then, trying to put Clyde's scared face out of his mind, he sat down to watch the video recording.

He was in for a shock. There was nothing to see on either screen; and, when he checked, no data recorded either. Pip twisted round and round in his chair in sheer frustration and disappointment. The computer had obviously gone haywire. *It had lost the lot.* Pip wondered if there might be a back-up copy retained somewhere, but only Clyde would know that. Of course, it was possible Clyde had wiped the data himself! Pip felt completely empty and deflated.

However, Clyde had always been honest, and Pip trusted him. No, some other hand must have been responsible – and Pip was almost ready to believe it wasn't a human one.

Klaas could come and see the damage for himself. Maybe the wonder boy had the skills to bring the data back? Maybe the computer was waiting for him to come over? It was such a ridiculous thought that Pip shelved it for the time being. He turned to his phone and read over his notes of what he had experienced. He hadn't recorded everything – for example, his short and violent career as a rodent, and the date that had been indicated by Newton. Could Klaas have picked those things up? He doubted it very much. That would have been a three-way journey into the subconscious, which as far as Pip knew still hadn't been done – although doubtless it figured somewhere in the BRAIN project's research. He wondered what Clyde had been working on before he came to Oxford, and made a mental note to ask him as soon as they were speaking again.

As he finished reviewing his notes, Klaas walked in. The boy was paper-pale, which made his blond hair look less striking. The effect was almost albino, yet his eyes remained that startling light blue and stood out from his chastened expression. However, he was not the brash kid who had bounced unannounced into Pip's university rooms a few weeks ago.

'May I?' Klaas asked, gesturing toward the data disk. In fact he remained the ultra-polite undergrad he had been an hour or so before. 'Have you looked?'

Pip nodded and thought, *Best let him find out for himself.*

A moment later, deft hands revealed the blank. 'For fuck's sake,' Klaas exclaimed, turning round, 'what did the Professor see then that made him such a kook?' Pip raised his eyebrows. 'Yeah, a kook! He was spouting all kinds of weird things!'

'I know what a kook is! I think you should show –'

'More respect?'

'He said you legged it!' No response. 'Clyde is a dedicated

scientist, by the way, and a fine mathematician.' Pip felt he'd said enough. At that moment, he was really angry with the kid. Why did he bother about Klaas's feelings? Then he recovered himself. 'Did Clyde tell you exactly what he saw?'

'No, except he was like a crazy man when I came out. And you? You're his friend.'

'He said …' Pip considered the words, then decided to give them verbatim. 'He said he saw God – and the Devil.'

Klaas showed no expression of surprise, just sat down at the computer again. 'I might be able to retrieve the data,' he replied.

'Is that what you want? To see *God and the Devil* too?'

'They would be preferable to what I did see.'

Pip felt cold trickles of fear strike him. He replied, 'I've made notes of my own vision, anyway. I can copy them to you if you like. If you don't trust me. They're timed and dated.'

'I trust you,' replied Klaas, his fingers skimming and tapping on the keyboard.

'So what did you mean when you said you saw worse?'

'You mean what could be worse? I don't believe in God or the Devil,' replied Klaas.

'That's what Clyde told me, but that's what he said. What did you see?' Pip repeated.

Klaas started again, ignoring Pip's earlier question. 'Looks like someone did a good job on our controlled experiment. You sure you didn't wipe it yourself?'

'Don't insult me,' replied Pip. 'You didn't answer my question.'

The boy leaned back. 'I made notes too.' He flicked open his phone. 'Here, you can look.'

'I shall afterwards. Carry on talking.'

'Amongst a heap of other things, I saw my father!' he said.

'You saw your father?' repeated Pip.

'And he was just as ugly a bastard as he always was,' growled Klaas. 'That's why I smashed his face in the photo. Did you see my father too?'

'No.'

'So this whole experiment has been a heap of shit.'

'But how could I have seen your father? I don't even know what he looks like. You said there were no more photographs of him.' Klaas didn't reply. 'I'm waiting.'

'I can trust you?'

'Of course.' Pip sat down.

'I saw a painting,' said Klaas. Pip swallowed. 'An enormous oil painting. I'm not good on paintings, and I was just searching for it on the internet before I rang you. There's no record of anything like it. I guess it was just in my mind.'

'What did you see?'

'Two men. One young, one old. Standing beside a table. They were looking at a book.'

'Can you describe them?' Klaas went on to describe them perfectly. 'And you didn't see me?'

Klaas shook his head. 'Did you see me?' he asked.

'No,' replied Pip. He was tempted to add, 'Not in human form, anyway,' but that wouldn't have been fair, and might have led Klaas on to the subject of the rat. 'What else?'

'A dog. A horrible little terrier. Its name was Diamond.'

'How do you know that?'

'I heard the young one say it. In Latin. I'm good at Latin. He told it to be quiet.'

'Did you see the young one's face?'

'I can't tell you that, but it wasn't my father.'

'Why can't you tell me?

'I couldn't see it, for fuck's sake!'

'Okay. Let's go back to Diamond. You looked the dog up?'

'It was Newton's dog. So I guess the old one was Isaac Newton, and the young one ...' Klaas shrugged.

'That was Nicholas de Fatio, a young Swiss mathematician, who worked with Newton for several years. Then they split up,' said Pip with some satisfaction.

It was the first smile that Klaas had produced that day, and probably the kind he kept in reserve for Olga, because it looked completely sincere and boyish. 'You saw all this too?'

Pip nodded. 'There was more,' he added. 'Anything else in that room?'

'Yeah, something weird. A big glass case with a rat in.'

'A stuffed one?'

'No, it was squawking and screaming and scratching to be let out?'

'Why?

'Because the dog was watching it and tearing things up. And – I guess I might as well tell you now …'

'Go on …' Pip could hear his heart thudding.

'The dog …' Pip saw Klaas's Adam's apple working as he swallowed. 'The little beast had a human face, and it was my fucking dad!' He closed his eyes and breathed in.

'Klaas …'

'Don't speak!'

They sat in silence until Klaas looked straight at Pip and asked, 'Now where are your notes?'

Pip handed over his phone. He put his hand on Klaas's shoulder as he did so and said in a quiet tone, 'I apologise. Obviously you do have powers. And I would like to work with you. I have something I want to show you; but not now. I think we've had enough for one day.'

He sat and waited as Klaas read through his notes. 'Wow!' He looked like an excited kid again. 'Is that everything, Pip?'

'I could ask you the same thing,' replied Pip, 'but I think we should leave it for now. You've convinced me – and I've a feeling that might have been the last vision, or one of the last, for me.'

'I wish I could say the same for myself,' replied Klaas, handing back Pip's mobile.

'Okay. Let's get back to Ghita's, shall we?'

As they walked side by side in silence, Pip remembered how long it had taken him to tell Simu of his own background and the agonies he'd been through to save his family from Diep Koppelberg. Also, the supernatural happenings that had continued in his life until he went to study with Simu in Romania. Conversely, Simu had hidden from Pip things that would have been important for him to know; and one of the last had come too late, when Simu had been killed on his journey to the airport to tell him. They had played their cards close to their chest, and had both suffered for it. Here he was doing it again, and he had no doubt that Klaas was behaving the same way. However, it was too early to come clean completely. Although Klaas seemed to be changed, Pip knew that could be deceptive. Pip had to follow his instincts and continue to be careful until he was sure beyond all doubt that the boy was on his side.

Pip took the dog's behaviour in the vision as a warning of what might happen to him if he continued with his research. He was intrigued that Klaas had seen the face of his father on the animal. He had no idea what that meant. Whether or not Klaas had seen or heard the date on the parchment, foretold by the greatest scientist who ever lived, was also unknown. If he had, and if he was evil, then with his superior powers of intellect he might now possess the means to rise and become a kind of anti-Christ, and so effect the destruction of the world.

Pip really needed to know who Klaas's father was. Even more personal to him were the lives of the two innocents he loved, Ghita and Olga. He had to save them, like he'd had to save his twin brother and sister from Koppelberg. They had to come first, and if it turned out that Klaas Honen had allied himself to such evil, Pip had to find out before it was too late.

As they walked on, Pip's mind was occupied with questions. Had Newton come into possession of the Codex, the Piper's blasphemous Bible, in those years when he appeared to have abandoned science and taken up the study of alchemy and magic? And why should Pip have been shown that date in the vision? Had it been to indicate to him that the 36-year cycle that the Piper followed had been set down in his Codex before Newton's birth? Or had it been a warning that he could not prevent the Piper from killing Olga in 2024? Or, most frightening of all, could it have been a prophecy that he, or whoever came after him, would be unable to avert the destruction of the world itself?

And what of Nicholas de Fatio? Pip could not say that the mysterious Nicholas whom he had seen in the vision was an instrument of the Piper, but it seemed likely, given his name and appearance.

Again, Pip began to wonder if Klaas was the conduit of evil. Whoever he was, Pip was determined to find out, dangerous or not.

16

Later, when Pip had had time to think things through, he phoned Clyde's mobile. There was no reply, but he left a voicemail. When he heard nothing back, he walked over and spoke to the secretary of the Science Department.

'The Professor has gone off sick, I'm afraid,' the secretary told him.

'Do you know what's wrong?'

'No, I'm afraid not.'

'Sorry to hear that. If he calls in, please say Pip Durrant left him a message and that it's vitally important I see him.'

'Someone else is handling his work at the moment, Professor. I can give you the number.'

'No, thank you. It's a personal matter, and very urgent that we make contact. If he should call into the office, please pass on my message.'

At that point, Pip felt very worried. He decided to leave things as they were for the present time, but he was determined to speak to Clyde. After all, if anything happened to his old friend, he would feel responsible.

By then, he'd also decided what to do about Klaas, but he couldn't do it at Ghita's.

'Ghita, I'm going to be tied up for a couple of nights,' he told her when they met in the kitchen over breakfast. 'I won't be in for dinner.'

She looked up from what she was doing and replied,

'You've already had enough of us, have you?'

'Hardly, but there are things over at the college that I need to use for one of my lectures, and also I have another session with Klaas. You know I can't conduct that here, don't you?'

'Of course. He seems to be in a strange mood at the moment. Whether or not he's told Olga what the matter is, I don't know, but something's up. Have you upset him? He's not been right since the last time you had a session.'

Pip laughed aloud at the question. 'I thought you wanted me to find out about him? I told you before that you've probably been seeing the best side of him. Klaas might be brilliant, but he's also a teenager – and under pressure from the Finals.'

'I know that, but … Oh, I expect I'm being silly, but there's definitely something wrong. Woman's instinct.' She tapped him on the shoulder as he drank his coffee.

He looked up at her. 'I'll do the washing-up.'

'Stick it in the dishwasher,' she ordered. 'I know Anya hated the thing, but it's necessary with us all.'

'Okay.' What a strange relationship they were having; so near and yet so far.

'I must get off,' she said, packing her books. 'Kids!' she added, with a sigh. 'Don't upset him any more, Pip, otherwise he might return to what he used to be.'

'He's still that, Ghita, and people only change to a certain extent.'

'Always cheerful, aren't you,' she retorted.

'Pressure does strange things to people.' He was thinking of Clyde. 'I used to think my Finals were the worst time in my life, even worse than …' He stopped.

She lifted her eyebrows and cut in, 'And were they?'

'No.' It was the most truthful thing he'd said for ages. 'Gotta go too, after I've had a word with Klaas.'

A moment later, the door opened and Olga appeared. She snatched a piece of toast.

'That's cold,' said her mother. 'You should make some more. And why are you up so early? You're on study leave.'

'I have a revision class,' replied Olga, 'and anyway, what's the use of staying here? Klaas won't talk to me. What are you doing to him, Pip?'

Pip shrugged.

'That's what I said,' pronounced Ghita.

Ghita picked up her briefcase, and a moment later departed, calling back, 'Bye all!' Olga followed her out of the door.

As he saw them off, Pip felt guilty that he might have encouraged Ghita to take someone into her house whose mental state was not to be trusted. He knew it would be his fault if anything happened to her or Olga. It was not a good feeling.

After he'd finished his breakfast, Pip knocked on the extension door. There was no reply, so he rang Klaas. Once again, no response. So he left a message on his mobile: 'I don't know what you're doing today, but I think it would be to your advantage if you joined me. I have something to show you – and also I owe you an explanation. I'll be in my rooms this morning. Say around 11.00? You can call it one of our sessions if you like, but you will find this one particularly interesting.'

Later, as he walked down the street and passed the insignificant-looking little driverless cabs, he thought, *Klaas is going to have to show his hand sooner or later, and I'm going to make that sooner if I can.*

He picked up a newspaper as he went, and stopped walking, shocked when he read the headline.

Professor Found Hanging in Garage

Clyde Wilson (50), Assistant Professor of Physics at Norris College, and originally from the US where he worked for the American Defense Department, was found hanging in his garage …

Pip had to read the words again, as the letters danced up and down in front of his eyes through a mist of sudden tears. Clyde! His old friend! And Pip had probably caused whatever had happened. He leaned against the railings for support. Several people looked at him. A couple approached, but he waved them away. He felt his legs shaking. When he had managed to recover a little, he went back to the house. Klaas was eating his breakfast. He looked weary and unkempt, his blond hair stuck to his scalp. He stared at Pip, 'What's up, Prof?'

'This!' Pip thrust the paper in front of him.

Klaas read the report quietly, then handed it back. He didn't speak at first, even though he must have known Pip wanted him to. At length he said, 'You're feeling bad?'

'Aren't you?'

'He wasn't my friend,' was the reply. That stung Pip.

'No, he was mine – and he did both of us a good turn. Don't you think you owe him something?'

'I hardly knew the guy.'

Pip stood without speaking, trying to decide if Klaas was deliberately trying to upset him. He remembered that this was how the boy had been when Pip had fallen outside Ghita's door after the cab had nearly run him down. Did Klaas not feel empathy? Or was it that he merely had no respect? No regard for the decent guy who had put himself out for them?

Who knew what torment Clyde had suffered to have been compelled to do something like that?

Then Klaas said, 'You're a bit over the top, today, Prof. You think Clyde's death had something to do with you?'

'Yes.'

'Don't bust a gut over it,' he replied.

Pip could have hit him right then, but managed to contain himself. Klaas jumped up, as if he knew what Pip was thinking, and walked over to the other side of the kitchen, his hand pausing over the percolator on the worktop. 'It had something to do with me.' The words were calm, deliberate.

'What?' Pip squinted at him as if he wasn't hearing right. The boy stared back.

'I told you I'm bad luck,' he said. 'You know I do things. I've proved that.'

'You're behaving as though you're crazy,' snapped Pip, approaching.

'You can put one on me if you like,' said Klaas with a

mocking smile.

'I'd like to, but I'm not going to. I only want to find out what makes you tick,' replied Pip, controlling himself. 'Why would Clyde hanging himself have anything to do with you?'

'Do you want a coffee?' Klaas poured one out, his hand hovering over another mug. 'And I tell you right now, you couldn't feel any worse than I do.'

Pip looked at the mug and then at him. 'What the fuck do you mean? A minute ago you showed me you couldn't care less. I've known that guy since we were at school together. He was an old and trusted friend. How could you care more than me? How long have you known him? And how could it have had anything to do with you? Is that why you've been pretending something's been the matter with you over the last few days?'

'I warned you about me. You know what I do,' Klaas persisted, and Pip's pent-up anger at his behaviour burst out in a tirade he couldn't help.

'I know you have an extraordinary gift, but you're not killing people. You have a complex. A young kid committed suicide because …' Pip was lost for words for a moment, then continued, '… because he felt he wasn't up to your standard. You behaved toward Edward like you're behaving toward me now. I'm trying to help you. Am I going to go out and hang myself? I shan't, because I have the experience that you don't. Clyde was a friend who was helping *us*, not only you. How do you think you could have killed him?'

Klaas's expression darkened. 'I knew he was going to do it.'

'How?' gasped Pip.

'He told me.'

'He told you he was going to hang himself?' Pip didn't know what to do with this kid standing there calmly lying and winding him up. 'He actually told you? Why would he tell *you*?'

'I came out of my room in the lab that day and he was in some crazy state. He looked at me and he shouted, "Get the fuck out of my lab. Don't you ever come in here again, you freak!"'

'Clyde said that. To you?' Pip was amazed.

'He pressed my buttons,' replied Clyde. 'I knew the signs. I've seen it before. It was unfortunate. I couldn't help it. Any more than I could Edward. They both said something like that to me, but in Edward's case –'

'I don't want to hear about fucking Edward!'

'All you want is to find out about me.' Klaas's tone had changed into the deep growl of an angry man. Pip remembered how he'd mimicked Olga's voice before.

'Don't play games with me, kid. Show some respect.'

'No, no, no,' replied Klaas in the same threatening tone. In that moment, Pip realised he had gone too far. *Never provoke your patient* had always been his maxim. 'Don't say anything like that to me. Don't threaten me!' He was facing Pip, and the voice was menacing. 'If you do, I can …'

In those seconds, Pip thought of Anya. Had Klaas threatened her? He braved it out. 'What can you do?' he replied, his voice hard and cold. 'You can't do anything, because *I know who you are.*' He couldn't stop himself. 'Did Clyde see the *real you* when he looked at those screens?'

Klaas backed away. He didn't retaliate. The atmosphere was thick with anger – and with danger. Then it lightened. 'If I am whoever you think I am, I can't help it.' The boy's voice was normal again now – a confused kid's – as if he were two different people in one. This was the time for Pip to press on hard.

'How many murderers have said that, Klaas? How many crazy psychos?'

'I have powers, and you know that, don't you? I didn't want Clyde to see what he saw. He saw the Devil – and God! That is what is in me. I'm scared of it too.' He backed up until he was standing by the kitchen door. He put his hand up and pointed to himself, 'I am split, man, all of me, right down to here.' He made a sweeping gesture downwards from his head. At these words, Pip recalled the account of the Piper splitting open in front of the little gypsy. 'Good and bad. I've always been like that. That's why people are scared of me. I've got something inside me. A killer!' His face crumpled. 'I'm sorry. Don't be scared. Help me, help me, Pip!'

Pip stared at him. 'You're asking me to help you, after you say you killed my friend?' He stood his ground. 'Why should I?'

'You kill people too. I can feel it. I sense it. In here.' He tapped his head. 'You're killing yourself with guilt. Don't kill us both, Pip. There'll be nothing left then.'

Then Klaas turned and collapsed, slithering down the door onto the floor. The room was quiet except for the faintest trail of a mocking laugh.

'Did you hear that, Klaas?' asked Pip. 'Did you hear someone laughing? Is someone else here?'

'Yes, I heard it,' moaned Klaas. 'I can always hear it. It's his song.'

'Whose song? Tell me, Klaas.'

'*His* song. I don't know who he is.'

The air was clearing. Pip felt he could breathe now. That whatever had just happened was over. He stood, not speaking. Klaas still had his head down, but then he lifted it up. He wore once again the defenceless, wan look Pip had noticed when Clyde had strapped on his helmet before the experiment.

'I might know,' said Pip, and he thought he saw those blue eyes change – perhaps in hope or recognition that someone might understand him? If anyone else had been there over the last few minutes, they would have been terrified, but Pip felt that the boy had prevailed again over whatever he possessed inside him.

'I want to ask you something, Klaas, and I want you to reply truthfully. I understand what you've gone through just now. Did this happen when you used to meet the Chaplain at Norris?' It was a possibility, and maybe this was why Klaas had been written off as dangerous.

Klaas nodded. 'I think I scared the old guy to death. Once or twice, I was worried he actually might die, but he didn't.' He breathed in deeply, as if a weight had been lifted from him by his answer.

'Did he offer to help in any way?'

'Yes. He asked me how I would feel about being exorcised.' The statement was followed by a faint smile. 'I told him I didn't think it was a good idea. That I was too far gone. He didn't reply, but told me that we were finished together. His beliefs didn't take account of mine. I think he pitied me.'

'Maybe he did. Come on.' Pip stretched out his hand.

In spite of the horror that Klaas had just admitted to, and the threats he'd made, Pip felt hopeful. He had been determined not to pity Klaas in the beginning, but the evil thing that lived deep inside the boy had not killed him, and had only terrified the Chaplain. Maybe it was not yet that strong? It was possible that, in spite of all Klaas's arrogance and seeming self-possession, the darkness that lurked in his subconscious mind had not yet taken hold.

If Klaas had been any ordinary patient, Pip would have looked for certain things. Experience had told him there was always an explanation within the patient himself, and this would prompt skilful questions about his background, birth and childhood – and especially, in Klaas's case, his angry, negative feelings toward his father. Instead, the questions that preoccupied Pip now were the boy's obsession with a place he had never seen, and his affinity to Pip himself. Pip possessed some paranormal ability, which he had not yet figured out, but Klaas's far surpassed his.

Could 13-year-old Pip from the United States and a disabled man, the late Claudiu Basa, from a little village in Romania have heard the same evil laughter back in 1988? According to the Marcu Papers, their author, a skilled researcher and psychiatrist, had heard such laughter too, as had a number of his women patients. Now, in the UK, in 2024, 17-year-old Klaas Honen had declared the same thing. Did Klaas perhaps carry some gene related to the Arva community? But that would not solve the puzzle. Pip did not carry such a gene, and neither had Marcu, as far as he knew. Perhaps Klaas was the link that joined it all together? It was only a supposition, but Pip needed to find out as much as he could about the Honens. Had they been from Arva, or had links to it?

Klaas had proved that he could do extraordinary things, such as when he had recounted Pip's vision on the path to Arva church, giving an accurate description of one of the child victims – which must be considered also as a true link to the village.

If Pip's research was sound – and he believed it was, based on the work that Marcu had done earlier and the information gained from his collaboration with Simu Dalca – then his desire to prevent another murder must be centred on Klaas. He felt certain that he had been meant to meet Klaas, who might through no fault of his own have been destined to deliver Olga as the killer's next victim. Unlike Pip, Klaas could, as yet, have no knowledge of the role chosen for him. From now on, Pip needed to keep him close. Klaas looked up suddenly and gripped Pip's hand, as if he knew what Pip had decided. Pip hauled him up.

'Let's sit down over there, shall we?' Pip said. 'My invitation for today is still open.'

Klaas looked like he had come out of a dream, and staggered a little. He sat on the couch, head in his hands.

'I will help you,' added Pip. The boy nodded. 'Let's have that coffee now and get off to my rooms. Then we can talk about what I think has been happening to you.'

You are brave, Professor – but very foolish, said a voice that seemed to Pip to come from deep within him. In that moment, he wondered if Klaas had heard it too. He had his answer right away.

'I heard something else then – did you?' asked Klaas, looking round.

'Yes,' replied Pip.

Klaas sighed. 'I need to go upstairs and get my things. Don't go anywhere, will you?' he said, and it sounded as if he meant it.

Pip placed two mugs of coffee and two baguettes on the table between himself and Klaas, then sat down opposite the boy. Both had their laptops open in front of them.

Pip leaned back. 'I'm going to get straight into this, Klaas. You've read my books, so you know something about my quest.'

'And your quest has ended in Oxford? Does this mean I have to help you with your next book?'

'Is that meant to be funny? There isn't going to be a next.' Klaas raised his eyebrows. 'Okay, so if you've really read it – and that must have been quick – what would you say *The Last Vision* meant?'

Klaas moved his chair nearer to the table. 'More or less the same as the rest.' Pip grimaced. 'I'm not trying to insult you, but it's obvious you want to nail a murderer.' Pip nodded. 'You're also looking for a certain book – an ancient book – and because you've killed off all the people who were helping you find it, you're looking for another mentor! But he or she has to be the right one.'

'Spot on,' replied Pip.

'I assume, then,' Klaas said, 'you're trying to tell me this isn't fiction?'

'It's fiction, but it goes deeper than that.'

'I didn't come for an English lesson,' replied Klaas. 'Come off it, Prof, I can see what's behind all this – but I don't know why. You really want to find both the mentor and the book – and you think I might be able to help you. But why? That's what I want to know. I have a week of exams to face.'

'Which you made quite clear before that you couldn't care less about. If I said this could all be about someone you know, would you be more enthusiastic?'

'Yes.' He looked at his watch, then stared hard at Pip. 'Give me some credit,' he added. 'You have my full attention. Are you going to tell me something interesting, or what?'

'To start with, I'm going to remind you about our agreement ...'

'Point taken.' Klaas tapped his nose with his finger.

'Okay. Well, the first thing you ought to know is, I already have some pages of the book in my possession,' revealed Pip.

'Wow. So it is a real book. How did you get them?'

'It's a very long story,' said Pip, 'but I have photocopies of them here, and the originals are in my safe keeping.'

'Then why didn't you mention them in here?' Klaas gestured to Pip's novel. 'Did you steal them?'

'In a way,' Pip confessed, 'and I'm not proud of it.'

'Cool,' he said. 'You have my admiration as well as my attention.'

'Good, so let's move on. They belonged to a businessman, who I believe had other plans for them.'

'A crooked guy?'

Pip nodded.

'So you saved them.'

'In a way.'

'You couldn't show them to anyone, because you were scared he might come looking for you?'

'Correct.'

'Can I see them?'

'Yes, but I have more to tell you. The rest of the book – it's called the Codex, by the way – is lost. How the businessman found these pages is a mystery I'd like to solve, but there's a legend attached to them.' Klaas was leaning forward. 'You may have heard about it. They are supposed to have been stolen by a gypsy from the book's author, an unfrocked monk, and hidden in the Cathedral in Cologne. The Dom.'

'I know it,' replied Klaas.

'You do? The legend or the Dom?'

'I remember my mom taking me to Köln when I was a kid and showing me …' he paused, '… showing me the shrine of the Three Kings. She said there was something about it she liked.'

'Is that so?' asked Pip, noting that he had used the German name for the city. 'I wonder what it was?

'Maybe I knew but – I can't remember.'

'That's unusual for you,' said Pip.

Klaas frowned. 'I don't dwell much on my childhood.'

'You remember your father, though!'

'Don't bring him up!' Klaas's tone changed.

'I don't intend to,' lied Pip. 'It was you who mentioned your mother.'

'Are you hoping this will lead to some kind of confession from me? If so, you can stick your story,' Klaas said.

'Don't worry, I'm not,' replied Pip. 'Back to the book. There is another legend about it, which goes back to the year 800.'

'The date of the founding of the Holy Roman Empire. Leo III was Pope then, and he was a bad guy. According to Einhard, the mob put out his eyes and cut out his tongue.'

'I could also argue that the mob *tried* to blind Leo and cut out his tongue, but he escaped. Charlemagne cared most of all for Rome, and wanted the city to retain its proud and noble position.'

'What planet are you on, man?' Klaas ignored Pip's correction and added, 'Charlemagne wanted that crown, and Leo was the only one who could give it to him.'

'You think so? You're remembering a lot now,' said Pip, thinking of what else the scholar, Einhard, had written in his *Life of Charlemagne* about the vanquishing of the troublesome Saxons, who had at last been forced to give up their Devil worship and adopt the Christian faith.

'I remember about Leo and Charlemagne because I'm a mediaevalist,' protested Klaas.

'What would you say if I told you that one of the pages I possess shows Charlemagne being crowned?'

'I've seen both of the original paintings of Charlemagne's crowning in the National Library in Paris,' replied Klaas. 'You're not going to tell me that bent businessman lifted the pages from there?'

'No, the Codex is something else. It was illustrated by the unfrocked monk, who made some additions at Charlemagne's Court.' He thought of his beautiful manuscript pages that had been adulterated by the replacement of the monk's face with that of Diep Koppelberg – the ultimate evidence of some supernatural agency at work. Many times since he and Otto had paid their visit to the bank vault in New York, Pip had wondered if Eisenmann had also been able to see Koppelberg's face in the manuscript pages. Back then, Eisenmann had been ahead in his search for the Codex, and after Marcu's dismissal had believed he had no rivals – until Pip had come along.

The time for testing had come again now, and Pip felt guilty. He might be putting Klaas at risk by doing this, but he wanted to find out if the boy could see in the photocopies what Otto and he had seen in the originals. He could not show him the originals themselves, of course, as they were still in New York.

'Why have we stopped the question and answer session? asked Klaas. 'Are you going to show me those photocopies, or not?'

'I'll fetch them now.' Pip went over and rummaged in his briefcase. He was in no great hurry to comply, but finally he placed the photocopies in front of Klaas. The kid stared and stared – then he pushed them away, an angry expression on his face.

'Is there something wrong?' asked Pip, hoping and not hoping.

'What the fuck are you up to?' Klaas asked. 'You think you're funny? Sooner or later, you're going to pay for this.' He was up from his chair and standing over Pip. 'How did you do it?' he demanded.

'Honestly, I have no idea what you're talking about, Klaas. What have I done?'

'You've tried to trick me,' came the ominous reply. 'Maybe you did that in the lab too?'

'What did you see, Klaas?' Pip persisted.

Klaas picked up the photocopies and thrust them into Pip's face. 'You and your fucking legends,' he said. 'I was beginning to believe in you. You have made a big, big mistake upsetting me like this. Don't ask me to do anything for you anymore! Watch your back from now on.'

'Stop that,' shouted Pip. 'Stop acting like a kid. Just tell me what you saw.' He went to grab the photocopies back, but he hadn't Klaas's speed. A moment later, he was sent crashing to the floor as the boy's fist connected with his jaw.

'Maybe I'll kill you,' Klaas snarled.

'Then you'll never know,' Pip shouted. Klaas stared down at him as he continued, 'I know what you want, Klaas. To find out about Arva. The village where you saw me on the path. Your research! And I can tell you all about it. But you have stop behaving like a madman and a thug.'

Klaas backed off then, allowing Pip to struggle painfully to his feet.

Pip didn't look at the boy's brutal expression. He was trembling inside and out, and remembering that he wasn't young anymore. 'Everything you have done so far has come down to violence,' he said, 'and it's got to stop. You have to believe I'm on your side.' Klaas was still watching him. Pip staggered to his chair. 'Did you see someone in that photocopy that you knew? Was that it? A face in a copy of a manuscript from a thousand years ago? I think you did, and I think you'd better tell me before it's too late.'

The atmosphere in the room, which had been sizzling with violence, now dropped into a quivering silence. Klaas took a step forward.

'Are you going to beat the hell out of me,' asked Pip, his voice unrecognisable to himself, 'or are you going to sit down and be sensible?' He could have laughed at himself, talking to this powerful young man as if he were a child.

Klaas sat down, then got up again and walked away from Pip into the kitchen. When he came back, he was carrying a towel, which he threw onto the table. Pip reached over and wiped his face on it, leaving traces of blood.

'Sorry, Professor. I hope I haven't broken your jaw.'

'And so do I,' replied Pip.

Klaas put his head in his hands and mumbled something. Then he looked up, and said, 'That monk, that monk, behind the throne was … was my … I knew him.'

'It was your father – again!' replied Pip. 'Somehow, I thought it might be.'

'How?' was the muffled reply.

'Because someone else saw the same thing. But not on the photocopy; he saw it on the original. So did I. I don't know your father, but I know that face too, and it made me feel like you feel now.'

'How could you know my father? He's dead!'

'That's what we need to talk about.'

'But this is crazy. My father's dead, and you told me that book is a thousand years old.'

'That's the kind of thing I've been trying to figure out since I was 13, but I didn't want to kill anybody – except him,' replied Pip. 'That's the difference between you and me – and I tell you, Klaas, it's a difference that worries me a hell of a lot.' Pip knew now that he couldn't hold back. He had to explain it all to the kid – and if he'd made a mistake, then he'd come out a lot worse than simply having a bruised face.

'You say your father's dead, which you have always believed. Maybe he is – but ...' he stopped. 'You're not going to punch me again?' Klaas shook his head. 'Your father might well be dead. Seeing pictures of him doesn't mean he isn't. Do you agree with that? If you weren't the brilliant young man I know you are, as a psychologist I could offer you the explanation that your subconscious mind needed to see the picture of your father and you made yourself do it. Wait, I haven't finished yet.' Klaas looked like he was about to explode. 'But that wouldn't explain why I should see the same image as you. In our experiment in the lab, although our experiences largely coincided, I didn't see that face on the dog.' Klaas's expression was twisted now in both pain and anger.

'I understand this is painful,' continued Pip, 'but it's better to review all the possibilities. Would you believe me if I told you I had seen the same face before I met you? Before you were even born? So where does that leave us? Both seeing the same face, which you have always believed to be that of your father.'

'We share the same visions.'

Pip nodded. 'But when I say I have seen him, I don't mean only in a picture or a vision.' Klaas was staring at him. 'I have actually met this guy. He came and lived in my family home for a summer vacation, way back when I was 13 years old. My mom hired him as a music teacher – and he was a demon on the flute.'

Klaas didn't miss Pip's inference. 'I am too,' he said. 'So – he might still be my father. It would make him pretty old now, but ...'

'According to his CV, the music teacher was 36 years old back then.'

'That's far too old!'

'Just so, Klaas,' replied Pip. 'I am now going to share with you something that might seem unbelievable – except to me and a small group of other people who are now all dead. One of them was Simu Dalca, Ghita's father, my loyal friend, who was a well-respected and eminent Professor of Mediaeval History at the University of Cluj. He died before his time, in suspicious circumstances – like most of my friends who were prepared to countenance that the man who came to my childhood home that summer might have been a thousand years old.'

He waited for Klaas's response.

'You mean this monk was a time traveller? Some kind of supernatural being? Was that why he was unfrocked?'

'He was unfrocked because he harmed a young girl, who then cursed him.'

Klaas screwed up his eyes.

'Yes, another of my legends. But this one is more than a legend, Klaas. It took me a long time to believe as well, but it is true. At one point, after I met you, I thought you might be influenced by the monk, or even allied to him or …'

'*Be him*?' said Klaas. They stared at each other.

'Are you, Klaas? If you are, then you should make yourself known to me now, because the game's up.'

'Are you fucking mad?' burst out Klaas.

'I hope you don't mean that.'

The mood relaxed. Klaas sat down. 'I want to know some more. I get from this that this monk, in whatever form he takes, is not a good guy.'

'Far from that,' answered Pip. 'I should say he is the worst guy I ever met.' They smiled at each other. Inside, Pip was still trying to assure himself that Klaas was to be trusted. He certainly seemed sincere. However, the Piper's methods had changed in some ways over the years, and he couldn't be absolutely sure yet.

'What did he do?' asked Klaas.

'He tried to steal away my siblings. He's good at that.'

'So he's a paedophile? Does he kill these children?'

'Yes.' They faced each other at the table. Pip surreptitiously scanned Klaas's face for any tell-tale signs of the Piper's features. He certainly had the same eyes, the same hair.

'That's sick! A child murderer, then?' replied Klaas.

Pip nodded. 'Yes, he's a serial killer.'

'But what about the friends who helped you? They weren't children.'

'No, but they knew too much about him – as do I.'

'So how come you're still alive?'

'I used to ask myself that, until someone a long time ago, who is now dead as well, prophesied I was invincible. But now things are changing.'

'How?' asked Klaas.

'I get hurt. That cab, for instance. I was expecting it to come back and finish me off. You said you saw the face of the driver too. Was that your father's face?'

'I was only kidding you. You looked so pathetic, just lying there in the garden. You couldn't even get up.'

'You were pretty smart, then. And heartless.'

'I was sorry afterwards. I picked you up, didn't I?'

'I've seen his face even more recently,' said Pip.

'The cab driver's?'

'Oh, yes, I've seen him a lot lately. Were you lying when you told me you are often visited by the mysterious hooded man?'

'No – but I've never seen his face,' replied Klaas. Pip raised his eyebrows, but nothing more was forthcoming.

'Also, do you know you have two shadows?' added Pip.

'No kidding! I'm unique, aren't I?' Klaas laughed. Then he appealed, 'I promise you, Pip, that I am not that monk.'

'Okay.'

'Tell me some more,' asked Klaas. He was calm.

'I shall, but it's going to take a long time for you to catch up with me. And as for that photo you had, which you thought was of your dad, maybe it was put there by your mother for a reason – for you to hate. Maybe she had a premonition that one day you would meet me, and wanted you to be aware that your family had at some time had dealings with this legend. You said you were Germanic in origin. The monk was a Saxonian, who had been forced into Christianity by Alcuin.'

'I know about Alcuin,' replied Klaas.

'Good. Now, if that photo really was of your dad, it means I should be very wary of you, Klaas, and I don't want to be that. I have no other explanation for his frequent appearances to both of us, except the supernatural.

'I have some ordinary news now, though. Most of my friends died in Romania – and this year I need to return there. I can't explain as yet why this year is special, except that my own studies and those of Professor Dalca all point to the fact that the monk will be coming back for another child. I want to be there when he does; and I intend to prevent him succeeding. I came to Oxford to further my research on this.

'Ghita also wants to visit Romania in the summer, to scatter Anya's ashes, so we plan to go together. Olga will probably want to go too – especially if you're with us.

'As for your own research, one thing I can tell you is that the village your mind has centred on is the one where I am going and where it all kicked off in the beginning. Like I said, it's called Arva.'

'You mean you think the monk might come back there?'

'Possibly. Anyhow, I think we should call a halt to this session now. I imagine you would probably like to follow up a few leads of your own from here. I am too busy just at present – as I think you should be.'

'You mean the exams?'

'Yes. I still committed myself to mine when I was your age – even though I had begun to understand, with the help of a shrink, what I needed to be doing. So should you. Your results will give you entrance into different circles, where you can further your own research.

'I don't think I have to warn you that it is best you keep

quiet about all this. You will not be believed, if you tell anyone.'

'Except by people like your friend Reverend Matthews,' broke in Klaas.

'Yes,' Pip said. 'You shouldn't have scared him. He is not my friend, but he is an intelligent man with a lifetime of research and wisdom to back him up.'

'Point taken,' replied Klaas.

'I believe you and I were meant to meet, Klaas, but as yet I don't fully understand why. We can cooperate or we can do the opposite. It's up to you. I'm willing to help you wherever I can, but I'll be upset if you betray me.'

Klaas shook his head. 'I won't.

'Thanks.'

'Arva's where Ghita comes from,' said Klaas.

'Yes, and that's where I first met her, at her father's house. There were happy times as well as sad.' Pip looked at his watch. 'Enough for now. Please don't say anything of this to Ghita – nor to Olga at present.'

'Sure.' Klaas's face seemed different in a way Pip couldn't describe. 'Shall we walk back to Ghita's together, Prof?'

'No thanks. I still have a few things to do and notes to make.' Pip opened the door. 'Good night.'

'Night.'

After Pip closed the door, he kept thinking about Klaas's expression when the boy had left. Finally, he decided what he had seen there could have been hope – but for what? He had gone as far as he dared, just in case.

'You look worn out,' remarked Ghita as he returned to what had become his home.

'Busy time. Research, exams, lectures to prepare.'

'Don't lie,' she said. 'I know it's more than that. When Klaas came in earlier, he looked like that too, and he was quiet – but in a different way, almost as though he was satisfied with life for a change. I think things might be going well between you?'

'Probably. Let's just say that, before, we were walking round each other like a couple of dogs, but now, I think we understand each other better.'

'Charming,' she replied. She looked round the cluttered room with a sigh. 'Oh, I can't bother with any of this tonight,' she said, moving a pile of papers away from the couch to an adjacent chair.

'Any of what?' asked a voice. Olga came in, dressed for bed in an old wrap over her T-shirt and leggings. She was yawning. Ghita frowned.

'Housework,' she said. 'I have a lot to do – and no Anya to help me.' She stared over at the mantelpiece.

'Don't look at that urn, please,' said Olga. She turned to Pip. 'Why does she keep it on the mantelpiece? I loved Anya, but it's gruesome. I can move some of this, if you like,' she added, pointing to the coffee table.

'I wish you would,' replied Ghita, 'but not Anya, because I like her up there.'

'Maybe she'll come and do some housework,' teased Olga. Pip frowned at her. 'Well, this place is a tip.'

'We're all tired,' replied Pip, 'but what about if Klaas and I get going on it tomorrow morning? We'll be in.'

Olga looked astonished. 'Klaas?' she repeated.

'Why not? He lives here as well. I think we should give your mother a break,' he replied, lapsing into Romanian.

'Why would you do that?' asked Olga, laughing.

'Because if we don't help her, then we won't be able to pay for the holiday!'

Ghita was frowning now. Pip knew it was with a mixture of annoyance and perplexity.

'Holiday?' cried Olga.

'Yes, your mother and I have discussed it. Subject to someone's good results, we're all going to go together.'

'I can't be bribed,' Olga said, but her eyes were alight with excitement. 'Does Klaas know?'

Pip nodded, and Ghita shot him an angry glance. 'We're all

paying for ourselves, Olga,' he added, 'except you of course. And we're taking Anya too.'

'Oh, God,' cried Olga, glancing at the urn.

'For the time being, though, you need to focus on your studies,' added Pip. 'Klaas and I can give you a break too by giving this place a clean-up in the morning.'

'You sound like you're my dad, but you're not.'

'Olga!' remonstrated Ghita.

'I don't care anyway,' Olga said, hugging Pip. He felt strangely pleased as her arms wound round him. 'I'm glad you're our lodger, in spite of you being such a ...'

'That's enough!' ordered Ghita. Pip wondered whether her sharp reaction was prompted by Olga's hug or by her intended insult. He wanted the girl to like him. He wasn't sure why. Probably because she reminded him so much of the Ghita of the past – and because he needed her to be happy to please the Ghita of the future.

'I'm going to see Klaas now,' Olga said.

'Isn't he upstairs?' asked Ghita.

'No, he's had his head stuck in his books for hours – and *he* doesn't need to.' A moment later, she was gone through the extension door.

Ghita looked at Pip. 'You are so ...' She seemed lost for words.

'You mean I shouldn't have told them?'

'Oh, I don't mind really. I'm afraid I'm leaning on you more and more. And so far, you seem to have worked wonders. I'm grateful.'

'How grateful?' he asked, smiling.

She shook her head, but she was smiling as well now. 'You know that I – I can't ...'

'You can't set Olga a bad example? I know. But perhaps you'll think about it?'

'Maybe,' she said, sitting down. He followed suit. Offering to be Ghita's lodger had been the best move he'd ever made. In fact, he wanted to spend what remained of the rest of his life with her – and at that moment, he was disposed to think she might feel the same.

He sipped a glass of wine and stared at the polished urn on the mantelpiece. He thought he could hear Anya's words when they had first met again after so many years: *So you have found her at last, Pip Durrant. She has missed you.* Pip felt that at last he believed Anya, and that things would come right between Ghita and himself; but whether or not he would be around long enough to enjoy it, after the events of the coming July, he wasn't sure. *Best things stay as they are until then,* he thought with regret. He had been alone too long to worry about love.

The sudden depression that had struck Pip the night before had lifted again by the morning when, wearing his oldest jeans ready for housework, he came down to find Ghita already dusting.

'Hey,' he said, taking the duster, 'we're going to do that.'

'No chance,' she replied, snatching it back.

'Why aren't you at work?'

'It's Saturday,' she replied, flicking the duster at him. 'And they've all gone out. Thanks for the offer of help, but …'

'I'm sorry.' He was full of remorse. 'I lost count of the days.'

She shook her head. 'And you're a professor!' she laughed. 'Olga's at another revision class and Klaas went out dressed-up – in a suit.'

'What?'

'I think he might have a date, because he was very cagey about it.'

'Are you sure Olga's gone to school?'

'Yes, she phoned me. She left one of her books behind.' She sighed, then smiled. 'Don't worry. I'm sure they haven't eloped. And I'm fed up with this already.' She threw down the duster. 'Coffee?'

'Great! And I can help you afterwards.' He smiled, trying to look cheerful, but a suit? Who was Klaas seeing? Then he added, 'I have to do some work in my rooms this afternoon, though.'

'You mean we're not going shopping?' He stared at her. 'Only joking,' she said, putting on the kettle, a mischievous look on her face.

Later on, Pip remembered what Ghita had said about shopping and wondered if it really had been a joke. He thought, *Maybe I'm not pulling my weight? She has to look after all of us.* He had no idea what a family of four ate over a week, but he thought it would be a good idea if he went out and got a few goodies to add to the larder. He was hurrying along to the nearest mall when he stopped, shocked.

Two people were crossing the road in front of him: Klaas – and a girl. The girl was even better dressed than Klaas himself, and was certainly no student. They were both laughing, and went over to look into a jeweller's window. Pip pulled himself into the doorway of a women's clothes shop nearby, earning the disdainful looks of several customers who had to push past him laden with their Saturday purchases.

Pip didn't want to snoop, but he was determined to see the girl's face, even though she was wearing sunglasses. A quantity of silky hair fell about her shoulders as she pointed out one item or another in the shop window. A silk scarf also floated about her shoulders, and she wore it like a woman who knew how to attract. Klaas was smiling, and Pip retreated further into the doorway so they wouldn't see him. Klaas's companion tousled his mop of bright hair and laughed. He didn't seem to mind, and Pip could tell they were exceedingly familiar. Then they went into the jeweller's.

Pip waited for several minutes longer until they emerged again, with the girl carrying one of the shop's glossy bags. He felt he could hardly breathe as they crossed over the road and walked up toward him. He had to make some move, so he pushed open the door of the women's clothes shop and loitered about inside until they came level with the window. They halted, and he felt as if they were looking straight at him.

The dark glasses were hiding most of the girl's face except for her pretty, heavily made-up red mouth and delicate pointed chin. She was petite and slim – the kind of girl most men would love to be seen with. They moved on down the road and, feeling the shop assistant's suspicious eyes boring into his back, Pip mumbled an apology, slipped out again and watched them disappear into the crowd. What was he going to say to Klaas? Was he going to grill him? For Olga's sake and for Ghita's, he felt he had to.

Half an hour later, as he set off for home after finishing his shopping, he was surprised to spot the girl on her own, still carrying the jeweller's bag and making for one of the car pick-up points. *So*, thought Pip, *he didn't go to see her off, then*. Klaas had told him he wasn't having sex with Olga; could it be that he had turned to a high-class escort girl? He could certainly afford it.

The girl stopped, and Pip watched her put her mobile to her ear. At that moment, how much he wished he could pick up her conversation! He shook his head. The thought that Klaas might be going behind Olga's back and paying for sex with this girl was enough to make Pip turn and go into the nearest pub. After a half hour and a couple of beers, he felt better and began the walk home.

The girl was about to end her long conversation.

'Yes, I told you, my darling. He is absolutely fine. Things are going just as we always planned. *Ja*, we have kept our promise. Everything is in place. All I need is to be near you. *Ich liebe dich. Wiederseh'n.*' Then she made another call, and several minutes later, a large Mercedes with smoked windows nosed its way from the direction of the edge-of-the-city car parks. The driver came round and opened the door, she wound in her legs and the car glided away.

An awkward conversation ensued when Pip returned to the house. Klaas was in the kitchen drinking a glass of Coke, and according to him, Olga and Ghita had gone shopping.

'I saw you with a girl in town,' Pip remarked in a mild tone, but he was up for another fight if need be. 'I know it's not my business, but I'm sure Olga wouldn't be happy.'

'Why?' Klaas put down his glass.

'The way you were behaving with that girl.'

'It is none of your business, but as it happens, that was my mother!' retorted Klaas. 'You said you'd like to meet her; now you've seen her.'

'I don't believe it.' Pip couldn't help it. 'She's far too young. She looks about 18!'

'Yeah, Botox. She's pretty fit, but I promise I share her DNA!'

Pip couldn't blame him for being rattled – but he still couldn't believe the woman was Mrs Honen!

'You said you didn't get on,' Pip reminded him.

'I was playing the dutiful son, and she the bountiful mother. She wants me to do well in my Finals; and besides, it was time for presents.'

'For her,' replied Pip.

'Were you stalking us?' Klaas narrowed his eyes.

'I saw you go into the jeweller's. She was the one who came out with the present.' He broke off, then added, 'What are you doing?'

Klaas was fumbling inside his silk-lined jacket. He produced a roll of bank notes and waved it at Pip. 'She gave me a couple of thousand bucks in American currency. She had set her heart on a little trinket, and I bought it for her. I wasn't being unfaithful to Olga. Here, take this,' he grinned, holding out the money. Pip stared. 'It's for the vacation. For Romania. I told Olga I wanted to pay for her and her mother, but I know Ghita won't take it from me. But she'll take it from you.'

'What makes you think that?' asked Pip. 'Anyway, I don't need your money.'

'You will. When I go travelling, I like first-class plane seats, a great hotel, nice places, nice things. Impress them, Prof. My mom can afford it. The Service pays well.' Pip raised his eyebrows and Klaas caught the inference. 'Diplomatic Service, I mean. What are *you* paid, anyway?'

'That's none of your business,' replied Pip. Evidently Klaas wasn't aware how much an international best-selling novelist could make. Money didn't mean a lot to Pip, who spent very little.

'And as for why Ghita will take it from *you*,' Klaas went on, 'both Olga and I know you have the hots for each other.' This time, Pip didn't remonstrate. 'Here, have it, for Christ's sake. I need to get rid of it anyway,' he urged. 'I've plenty.'

'Did you tell your mom you'd be going to Romania?'

'Yep. She seemed fine about it.'

Pip sighed. Whoever Klaas's parents were, *if* his mysterious father was still alive, then they knew his business now. He took the roll of money and stuffed it into his jacket.

'You might be disappointed at how I get on, trying to persuade Ghita,' he said. 'And your mom shouldn't carry so much cash around.' He was thinking that the cash was more proof of how much Klaas wanted to go to Romania and make sure Olga was with him as well.

'My mom can look after herself,' replied Klaas. Pip didn't answer, only grimaced. 'And if it had been a high-class hooker, like you were thinking, I wouldn't have been taking her shopping.'

'Don't you have work to do?' Brilliant or not, Klaas was too good at annoying him.

'Sure, Prof,' Klaas joked and, carrying the glass of Coke, he loped off to the extension.

Pip started to put away his shopping, thinking about why Klaas had become so biddable, and how he could persuade Ghita to accept his offer of paying for the trip.

'I don't think so,' Ghita said. 'For the third time, I don't want you to pay. I like to be independent.'

'I thought you'd say that,' replied Pip. Now was the time for guile. 'Please, Ghita, I owe a lot to your dad – and I still feel responsible for his death.' Her eyes flashed in indignation. 'My offer would be a kind of – reparation? You know he would have wanted to spoil his granddaughter as well as you. Come on; let's give Olga a great time. I can afford it. Think of all those books I sell, and no-one to spend the royalties on.'

He could see she was weakening. He wondered if he should add – but the words slipped out of his mouth before he could stop them, 'Besides, I need to make up for my cowardly behaviour all those years. Please take me up on my offer. I don't want anything in return – except your happiness. You deserve it.'

'Knock it off,' she said, 'You can pay. But remember, I'm not doing this for you. It's for Olga. She would like a wonderful holiday – and it isn't as though we have to fund Klaas, is it! It seems he's part of the family now.' She laughed, and he loved the way she'd said *family*. 'I'm beginning to wonder why I worried so much about him. He's a model lodger.'

'Yeah, I get it,' he said, sitting down and easing himself between the piles of books. 'I'm a bit more problematic.'

'I wouldn't say that,' Ghita answered. 'You just know how to handle people better.'

Pip was grateful for the indirect compliment, but reflected that Klaas had clearly managed to enchant Ghita – just like Koppelberg again. Pip, though, was resistant to the boy's charms. He'd still be there – whatever happened – although he was truly scared of what Ghita would say or do if she knew that he could be leading them into a trap, taking Olga to Arva on a day that could mean the death of her.

Pip still trusted no-one but himself, and was disposed to believe that Klaas had some ulterior motive. Anya had thought him dangerous, and he could still turn out to be the Piper's agent, reeling in his victim …

Pip just wanted the exams to be over – in fact everything in Oxford to be finished – so that they could all make their trip to Arva, and hopefully emerge unscathed from whatever awaited them there. Then he could try to begin his life with Ghita anew, with his conscience cleansed.

17

Cluj Napocka, Romania. 21 July 2024

Pip limped more than usual as he walked across to look out of his hotel window at the heavily overcast sky. He leaned on the sill and stared up at the clouds, oblivious of the green space below and the city traffic that roared alongside it. He reflected that the next 24 hours could well be the most important of his life. He had woken early that day after a restless night, trying to be optimistic, but his real mood was reflected by the weather forecast: hot but overcast, with frequent storms. It was a bad omen. In 1988, the last Piper Year, it had been just the same at his home in the US.

Later that day, he, Ghita, Olga and Klaas were due to visit Arva, a short distance away from Cluj, where he believed the Piper had taken the Hamelin children over 600 years earlier. It was there that, the following morning, he fully expected to have to intervene in the terrifying age-old ritual of 'going up', to try to thwart the Piper's evil intentions. If he failed, then Olga could be raped and murdered.

And that is what I have to face, thought Pip, *in the company of a 17-year-old boy whom I don't know if I can trust, and who is probably smarter than I am. At least he doesn't know all my secrets!*

Pip regarded the lowering clouds hanging over the city. As he did so, their dark shapes seemed to form themselves into faces, with expressions matching his own melancholy mood. He tried to pull himself together. 22 July was also Ghita's birthday, which they had come here to celebrate in spite of her earlier misgivings. That evening, they would all be attending the Arva fair – an idea that made Pip shiver, as he suspected it was just a modern take on an event that throughout history had been sinister, terrifying and murderous.

Klaas, though, seemingly couldn't wait to get there. The boy had done as brilliantly as expected in his Finals and was now fielding PhD offers from institutions worldwide. Olga had not yet received her exam results, but had worked very hard – with his help.

Then Pip thought about the stolen manuscript pages safe in his bank. His instincts told him that if the rest of the Codex was still to be found, it would be in the place the Piper prized most: Arva's church, or more precisely his tomb adjacent to it. Pip's recent research had shown that the church itself had been razed, on account of its sacrilegious malpractices.

Perhaps the Piper has found his book by now, he thought. *If so, does that mean he'll still be searching for the lost pages? Perhaps he's been waiting for tonight or tomorrow to make his onslaught?* Pip shivered again at the thought of the Arva fair. He needed to get away on his own at some point while they were there, so that he could snoop around a bit.

He felt the same guilt that had plagued him for years. Should he tell Ghita the significance of her fateful birthday and risk everything that he prized? He could not. He had considered informing the police of the danger, but he was still wary about having any contact with them – besides which, he knew that they would put his concerns down as the ramblings of a madman. At least he had managed to pass uneventfully through airport security, which he had been nervous about, given his past record in the country.

This last ten days in Romania had been a very different experience from the few months he'd spent there in 2007 at the University. He'd always been a loner, but this time he'd found himself thrust into the company of three other, very different individuals.

Klaas had hired an expensive Land Cruiser, which had been waiting at the airport for them and matched the five-star hotel Pip had booked with the boy's dollars.

Contrary to the impression Ghita and Olga had of his lifestyle, Pip was rarely to be found in a hotel for any length of time. On book tours, he moved from one to another without taking much notice of his surroundings, as long as they were reasonably comfortable – all that was handled by Larry, his agent.

Klaas, though, was clearly very much at home with expensive places and things; a young man who handled every situation and person he met with the kind of self-assurance that came only from having a privileged background.

They had done the 'tourist thing', as Olga had put it: driven through dark forests and wandered around eerie but magnificent castles while guides related fanciful tales of vampires and demons. Ghita and Olga had gone on several shopping expeditions too, while Pip and Klaas had either waited in the car or sussed out some museum or art gallery for a visit the following day. They had attended two concerts, a ballet and an opera, where Pip had watched Olga's eyes as they drank in the kind of tragedy of which she herself knew little.

Ghita had also taken Pip on a sentimental return visit to the University. They had even taken a curious peek into the now vamped-up post-graduate room that used to be Pip's; but they had avoided going back to the small room where, that one memorable night, they had slept together.

They had also until now avoided returning to Arva, telling themselves they would rather leave that till last. It was as if they were both afraid of dragging themselves back into a past that had not been very happy for either of them. Yet Pip felt that he and Ghita were drawing closer all the time; and he was also getting better acquainted with her daughter. One thing he had learned about Olga was that she had a very serious side to her. He suspected that her more typical behaviour as a stroppy teenager was simply an escape – although from what, he had yet to find out.

They were all having an early dinner in a restaurant near St Michael's Church and the University; one that Ghita and Pip had considered their favourite 17 years earlier. Ghita put down her dessert menu and turned to Pip.

'I wanted us all to go to the Arva fair together,' she said, 'but Olga isn't keen. She wants to go on her own with Klaas, while we stay here.'

'Yes, I think I'd feel better that way,' Olga told her. 'You've always hated fairs. Why spoil your holiday at the end? And I know Pip doesn't like them either.'

'Well, maybe so,' Ghita replied, 'but we wanted to show you the countryside – point things out. We came from that village, Olga. I know you don't remember, but ...'

Olga turned to Klaas, who was still eating his bowl of the local stew. All that day he had been wearing a red T-shirt and yellow shorts – which, in spite of their bizarre appearance, were apparently designer! He had a white cashmere sweater folded over the back of his chair. Everything about him fitted and was immaculate.

His persistent charm, his powers of persuasion and now even the colour of his clothes, thought Pip. *All exactly like Koppelberg.*

Olga was frowning. 'Klaas already knows everything there is to know about this area.' She must have noticed her mother's surprise at this remark, as she added, 'He has a marvellous guide book, and has been looking everything up on the village webpage too.'

Pip had studied the webpage himself, and found little useful information there. He suspected that the real history of the place had been left out on purpose, and guessed that Klaas's knowledge actually derived from his own research, as he called it.

'To be honest,' Olga added, 'I'm not really sure I want to go the fair myself now. Maybe we could just go to the hotel spa instead?'

'That's booked for your mother's birthday tomorrow,' Pip reminded her, 'but we could certainly do something else this evening.'

Klaas spoke up then. 'Honey, you'll love the fair,' he said. 'You want to see some old cultural customs? Fancy dress? You were dead keen before. Remember? Come on,' he wheedled.

'I still don't want to go.'

At this point, Pip wondered if Ghita had said something to Olga about the past. Or if Klaas had … 'What kind of cultural customs?' he asked the boy.

'See, Prof, you don't know everything. It's all in here.' Klaas waved his ultra-modern mobile at him.

Pip was determined that, whatever was decided, he was not going to lose sight of Olga, not even for a minute. But he knew that would be particularly difficult at a fair.

Klaas stopped eating to stroke Olga's back with his sensitive fingers.

'I suppose I'll go,' she said, 'as long as you'll take care of me.' She looked up at him.

Ghita glanced at Pip, then said, 'And we're definitely coming too.'

'Well, okay,' conceded Olga. 'I don't think I'll be going on any of the rides, though.'

'You used to love them!' Ghita exclaimed.

'Maybe when I was a kid,' Olga replied. 'But I don't feel like it now.'

Ghita made a face at Pip, who shrugged his shoulders. He felt worried.

Finally Klaas finished his stew and sat back. He looked round. 'I've a surprise for you all. We can stay over. I've already organised it.'

'Stay in Arva?' Pip hadn't bargained for that. He'd hoped to be away from the place before midnight, after he'd sneaked a quick look at the tomb – which, judging from a picture he'd found online, had been left undisturbed, save for having been fenced off.

'Stay over?' repeated Olga.

'At an inn,' confirmed Klaas.

'You were lucky finding any rooms free, with the fair on,' commented Pip in a calm voice, knowing that Klaas hadn't been lucky at all: American tourist dollars were exactly what any Romanian hotelier wanted. 'Arva didn't have an inn before, as far as I remember. What's it called?'

'I dunno. Something like …' Klaas wrinkled his nose ' … like Rux – Ruxandra's. Used to be a hiking lodge at the head of the valley, but the new proprietor relocated.'

A cold shiver ran down Pip's backbone. Ruxandra Sala and her family had been the owners of the Inn Sancipia: the place where all the Little and Chosen had always ended up after their horrific ordeal in the ritual.

'Are you all right, Pip? asked Ghita. 'You don't mind?'

Pip shook his head. 'No, that's fine.'

'It does mean I'll be able to get an early night,' Ghita added, smiling. 'As Olga said, I don't like fairs. But what about our hotel here? You're paying for all this, Pip.'

'The hotel won't care, Ghita,' cut in Klaas. 'They'll be getting their money regardless. This way, you and Pip can have a look around the village and see how it's changed, while Olga and I have a good time at the fair – even though she's scared of the rides!' He grinned.

'I admit I don't usually like fairs, but I'm still keen to see this one,' Pip said firmly, thinking, *No way are you taking her off on your own, Klaas!*

'No problem,' Klaas replied. 'Maybe we can fit in a bit of archaeology while we're up there too, eh?' Ghita gave him an enquiring look. 'Just a little research project we've got on the go,' he explained.

'You and Klaas are working on something together, Pip?' Ghita asked in surprise.

'I'd love to be in on that too, Klaas,' announced Olga, seeming to wake up.

'What? This evening?' Ghita regarded them all with puzzled eyes.

'It's a really interesting site, isn't it, Prof?' prompted Klaas.

'Yeah, it is,' replied Pip. He was beginning to fear the worst.

After their meal, they all returned to the hotel to collect some things for their overnight stay in Arva. Storm clouds were still gathering overhead, threatening a bad evening. As he packed his rucksack, Pip made sure to include a small but extra-powerful torch and a few other things he felt he might need, including a knife and even the small silver cross his mother had given him. He had slipped out and bought the knife secretly at a hardware store a couple of days earlier; if he had to jettison it before he returned home to England on the plane, he would.

Rumbles of thunder could be heard in the distance as they arrived in Arva and Klaas parked the Land Cruiser.

'Deserted,' Klaas said, surveying the empty streets and buildings.

'Where is everyone?' asked Olga. 'And where did all the traffic go! There were loads of cars on the road coming in.'

'They must all have stopped or turned off on the old church road,' Klaas replied.

'Why? Where's that?'

'The church itself doesn't exist anymore,' chipped in Pip.

'Why?'

'For goodness sake, Olga!' Klaas said impatiently. 'It was up there, where the fair is. There's a new church down here in the village now.'

Ghita glanced at him, then looked up at the sky and grimaced. 'I'm glad I brought my mac and umbrella – and yours, Olga.'

Olga looked up too. 'Those clouds are so strange! It's the middle of summer and it's nearly dark already.'

She was right. Night was falling too soon for late July, and

Pip fancied that the daylight had shrunk away from Arva in fear of what was to come, creating a bloody sunset that mingled with the coloured lights of the fair on the hill above the village.

Ghita stared up at Ruxandra's. 'This place used to be two or three cottages when I lived here,' she told Olga. 'They were quite pretty.'

Pip remembered one small whitewashed cottage in particular, where an aged peasant had sat outside smoking a pipe, accompanied by his wife in an old cardigan and skirt. The woman had jumped up with a little scream when Pip had asked for directions.

This inn looked very different from Ruxandra Sala's ancient hiking lodge at the head of the valley, which Pip had first read about in the Marcu Papers. That was where Ruxandra and her husband Gheorghe had discovered Anka Petrescu, the small battered and blood-soaked victim of the Piper, hammering on their door on the morning of 22 July 1988. This new Ruxandra's had garish modern fixtures and fittings, although the walls were lined with a plethora of old black-and-white photographs of the original: the lodge exterior, the dormitories, the eccentric washing facilities and even the hunting trophies of bear and boar heads. The brew turned out to be good, and the rooms were clean. 'Not like our five-star, but adequate,' judged Ghita as they gathered in the bar.

Olga had eyes only for Klaas that evening. She had even dressed up. She was wearing her best jeans, an almost transparent blouse and a necklace with matching earrings, and her hair was piled up on her head, only to fall in wispy curls at the sides, accentuating her high cheekbones. Ghita had demanded that she cover herself up with a sweater, on the pretext that the weather had turned cold; but even though Olga had agreed, looking sulky, the barman still kept staring at her in lecherous admiration.

'I'm going over in a moment to tell him she's only 15,' Ghita said.

'I shouldn't,' Pip replied, 'He'll get over it.'

'At least Klaas doesn't seem to have noticed,' Ghita added,

'which is a good thing.'

Ghita might have been reassured, but Pip was scared as hell. He saw Olga go and sit beside the boy, who didn't even lift his eyes, just clasped his hand over hers. When she took her hand away to sip her drink, Pip saw her massage it lightly with her other hand. Evidently Klaas had been exerting some pressure.

Pip looked at his watch. The steep, upward slope to the ancient church, which had once been the path to Calvary for scared little girls, would at this very moment be heaving with people: tourists pouring out of their buses; Arvan locals; and gypsies and their families arriving in horses and carts. All proceeding upwards to the fair. All that was left of the churchyard was the massive mausoleum, Grandsire's tomb; and within Pip's party, only he and Ghita knew that it was surrounded by the disgusting remains of children's buried dolls.

Pip went over to the bar to fetch some drinks. 'It's very quiet,' he said to the barman in Romanian. 'Where are the locals?'

'They won't come here.'

'Why not?'

'They do usually, but not on fair night.' He offered no more information.

'And the fair happens just once a year?'

'That's right,' replied the barman. 'On 21 and 22 July.'

'Why's that?' asked Pip, although he already knew the answer.

The barman frowned. 'You ask a lot of questions. No idea myself, but it's something to do with the Church. I don't hold with religion. Some Saint's Day or something.'

'St Mary Magdalene.' Pip jumped at this interjection from Klaas, who had come up to stand beside him. 'Make merry on the day of the sinner. Used to be lots of witches around.'

'Them I can stand,' said the barman, grinning. He was looking across at Olga.

'That's my girlfriend,' said Klaas. His voice was hard.

'You should tell her to keep herself covered up.' The barman looked at Klaas, then backed away. 'No offence, sir.' A moment later, he'd walked round the back.

'Moron,' snarled Klaas, a threatening expression in his strange blue eyes.

Pip put a hand on his arm. 'Calm down,' he said.

Klaas shook his arm free and returned to his table, but the atmosphere he left behind him was stained with anger.

An hour later, the four members of Pip's party were walking together up the hill to the beckoning fair.

'I'm tired,' yawned Olga. 'I think we should ride in one of those!' She gestured toward a number of carts of different shapes and sizes drawn up at the side of the path, where their owners were touting for trade.

'What about that one?' asked Klaas. He pointed to one that was bigger than all the others, with a dirty white tarpaulin covering hooped rings. The horse was smart and the small driver was standing quietly beside it, smoking a cigarette. He had thrown down a quantity of old sacks to protect his customers' feet from the mud that the horses' hooves had stirred up.

Ghita looked at Pip. 'Anton's father kept one of those,' she said. 'This all brings back the past – and I don't like it. I don't feel at home here anymore.'

'I don't either,' he replied.

'Look, it's got a little flat-bed attached at the back,' added Klaas to Olga. 'You and I can sit on that while Ghita and Pip ride inside.'

'Shall we?' asked Ghita, but Pip was already speaking to the driver, who quickly climbed up on the wagon and started to roll back the tarpaulin.

'Now we can all see each other,' Pip said.

They clambered on board, and soon the cart was jogging on up the hill, Ghita and Pip lost in their memories.

As they reached the second-highest point, the place where Basa's farm had stood, Klaas called out, 'Hey, Prof, was I right?'

Pip ignored him.

'What does he mean?' asked Ghita.

'Just a joke to do with our research,' Pip told her; but as he spoke, he thought he could glimpse that vision again. The cart trundled on past the place where he had picked up the faded picture of the once-bright rooster, the disabled man's rotten boot and the angel figure half-buried in the earth. Then a distant flash of lightning brought Pip back to reality, and he saw Olga snuggle tight into Klaas for support.

From then onwards, the Magdalene fair assailed their eyes with glaring, tawdry spotlights powered by hidden generators. Deafening bursts of raucous music and excited shouts made conversation difficult, while their noses were assailed with delectable smoky smells like chestnuts and hot dogs, together with the sour nearness of unwashed rural humanity.

They wandered around without aim, taking in the sights and browsing various stalls, Pip trying all the time to keep Klaas and Olga in sight, which made his head ache. What he really wanted to do was leave this all behind; but he was sworn to save Olga if need be.

Someone thrust a leaflet into their hands and they stopped to look at it. 'Folk dancing,' Ghita said. 'Oh, Pip, I hate this sort of thing. I really do.'

'Well, Olga seems to have cheered up,' he replied. 'Let's follow them. Come on.'

'What did Klaas mean about there being an archaeological site up here?' As she hurried along beside him, she collided with a man muffled in a tattered coat and wearing a black chimney-pot hat over his ponytailed hair. His long beard and side-whiskers gave him a wild aspect, and his appearance was made even more bizarre by the fact that he was carrying a stick from which hung a cluster of rag dolls, which he waved in Ghita's face.

'Buy?' he asked, jiggling the dolls and grinning. Pip pushed him away. Ghita was trembling.

'Rag dolls,' she gasped. 'I hate dolls.'

'Understandable,' he said, gesturing at the man to leave. He watched him back away, then switched his gaze to look for Olga. She was nowhere to be seen. He was beginning to panic as the crowd heaved behind them and carried the two of them along. He briefly caught sight of a mop of bright hair glinting through the dark press of humanity. Klaas! Then it disappeared again. But he could see Olga now. She was laughing, throwing her dark head back and shaking it in time to the sudden music.

What the hell is she doing? Pip thought. 'Come on, Ghita, they're over there.' Grabbing her hand, he pulled her behind him, pushing on through the crowd. He heard curses and yells of indignation as he fought his way right to the front. He was near Olga now, then gasped. What was she wearing? A black headscarf and apron!

The music overtook Pip then, creeping into every pore, filling every sense. It flowed up and down through his body in a senseless beauty. He forgot everything. He hadn't heard it since … He struggled to think, and then he knew. The student party all those years ago on Halloween.

Revellers of all kinds were moving with the sway of the music, their feet squelching in the mud, laughing as if they were drunk. Some were even videoing the proceedings on their mobiles as they tottered backwards and forwards, left and right, forming an involuntary circle.

Then the spotlight picked out Klaas playing a flute, accompanied by strangely-dressed local musicians following his every lead. He had borrowed a cloak to accentuate his actions. Flashes of yellow were revealed as his body twisted and turned. Around him, small children had formed a fluid ring. Some in national dress, others in black headscarves like Olga, holding up their matching aprons as though waiting for rewards to be thrown into them. Girls were appearing now in flimsy clothes, then boys joined them and took their hands. The boys were in traditional Arvan garb, with ridiculously tall black chimney-pot hats. All were dancing to the music of Klaas Honen's flute. Then someone threw him a whistle, and he seized on it, as if all that mattered in the world was that he played his wild music, enchanting all who heard him.

Pip felt sick but he, too, was entranced. Once before, when he was a child, his deaf ears had sensed when his pets had gone mad, as downstairs his family had played their violins in accompaniment to Koppelberg's flute, the precursor to disaster. Centuries earlier, a Piper had played in Hamelin and stolen a town's children away. And Pip could do nothing about anything as he swayed to the Piper's music, spellbound.

Then suddenly Klaas stopped playing, threw the pipe back into the crowd and ran over to grab Olga. He spun her around three times, drawing her into the middle of the circle, where they danced together, their backs facing the local musicians, who continued playing. Pip came to then, and thought of the little gypsy's account of the Devil worshippers' dance. He was sweating, but he could not move to go in and pull Olga from Klaas's arms. He watched in horror as the frenzied children withdrew small animals from their apron pockets and let them run squeaking round and round the circle. Small rats; guinea pigs; hamsters; even small snakes slithered there. The children laughed and laughed, keeping in step with Klaas and Olga.

Ghita was hanging onto Pip's arm, her lips moving silently. Her imploring eyes searched his face as she willed herself to act where he could not. She came to reality with a little scream, then ran inside the circle and dragged Olga out of Klaas's arms. The music ceased and the crowd moved away, turning into a muttering, cursing mass, as Olga fought against her mother, while Klaas stood silently behind them.

Pip ran over to the boy and yelled, 'Who the fuck do you think you are? The Pied Piper?'

Klaas shook his wild, bright hair out of his eyes. 'I got carried away! Did you see all those little guys?'

'You mean the kids' pets? Rats, mice, snakes?'

'Wow,' said Klaas. 'Maybe I should be a performer, not an academic.' He yawned. Pip's wanted to shake him, but desisted. 'It was great while it lasted,' the boy added. He took a deep breath and moved over to Ghita and Olga, who was crying. 'I'm sorry,' he said.

'I'm not,' Olga replied. 'I didn't want the music to stop. Nor you to stop.' She turned angrily to Ghita and Pip. 'Why did you make him stop?'

'Where did you get that flute from?' Ghita asked Klaas. 'You shouldn't have made a show of my daughter.'

'It was wrong,' Klaas conceded. 'I'm sorry. I guess the whole local culture thing got to me. I felt I needed to jump into that circle. And somebody handed me the flute and the whistle.' He looked contrite.

Pip somehow doubted that he was really sorry – or that he had simply got carried away.

They had a hot dog each afterwards and coffee. 'Shall we go back to the inn now?' asked Ghita. 'I've had enough.'

'So have I of the fair,' Pip replied, 'but … I must do one or two other things before we leave. For one thing, I want to go and look at Grandsire's tomb.' He checked his watch and couldn't believe it was already approaching midnight. 'I think we should stick together,' he added.

Ghita was shocked. 'How can you think of doing that now?' she asked.

Olga put her arm around her mother, comforting her. 'I don't mind,' she said. 'I'm sure it won't take long.'

'We won't have another chance,' Klaas put in. 'The grounds will be locked again when the fair goes. Please, Ghita, it's part of our research. You remember?'

'All right,' Ghita gave in. 'I've a bad headache, but I'll come.'

Keeping Olga and Klaas in his line of sight, Pip followed them across the muddy ground leading to the black shape of the tomb. Behind them, the distant fair lights bobbed and twinkled in the gloom, making the raised area the four of them were about to enter seem like an ominous alien world.

When they were within ten metres of the large stone obelisk that stood above the Grandsire's tomb, they encountered a circle of low bushes that had grown up around a wire mesh fence.

There were wooden benches positioned at intervals around the outside of the enclosure, and Ghita sank gratefully down onto one of them. 'I'm not going any further,' she said.

Just visible within the bushes was a placard on which was printed a brief history of the place. 'This is really creepy,' said Olga as she read. She looked up at Pip, while Klaas held the torch. 'It says it was once a place of pilgrimage! Which saint? Mary Magdalene?'

'No saint really,' Pip said. 'That's all over now.'

Klaas swept the torch's powerful beam through the fence, revealing that to one side was a pile of litter that had probably been blown there by the wind, while to the other lay a huge broken cross, propped up by heavy stones. Olga joined Klaas as he peered in at the cross. 'That was mentioned on the placard,' she said.

'Yes, it was broken off the monument in a storm,' Pip explained. 'They're bad up here in summer.' He pointed to an enormous pile of logs nearby. 'Last time I came here, there were two big forest trees standing just over there. I expect that's all that's left of them.'

'Wow, must have been some storm!' Olga exclaimed.

Klaas appeared uninterested, loping off around the perimeter of the enclosure. When he was beyond the pile of logs, he shouted back, 'Look over here. Pumping equipment, Prof – and a generator.'

Pip went over and looked. The carelessly dumped machinery lay in a small heap. 'The tomb floods,' he said, thinking of the terrifying events he had experienced there long ago.

'I can't see any way into the enclosure.' Olga's tone was uncertain and a bit shaky. 'There's a gate over there, but it's got a chain on it. The tomb itself must be private.'

'Not to me,' said Klaas. 'Hey, here's a gap in the fence.' He started pushing the wire mesh aside, and soon he had his leg through. A moment later, he was on the other side.

'I wonder why all this equipment hasn't been stolen?' mused Olga.

'People are too scared,' replied Pip, panting a little as he went through after Klaas, and cursing himself for being unfit.

'Legends,' explained Klaas. Pip glanced at him.

'What kind?' queried Olga as, after a moment's hesitation, she too squeezed herself through the gap in the fence.

'You should ask the Prof,' he replied.

Pip smiled reassuringly at Olga, wondering what to tell her. As he did so, he noticed that the black headscarf she was still wearing was now being tugged at by the wind. She caught his glance.

'Mother said this souvenir was ridiculous when I bought it,' she admitted, 'and she was right.' She started to untie it.

'No, don't do that,' said Klaas. 'It looks good, and it'll protect your hair in this wind. Otherwise, you'll look like one of the *anemoi*, and I'll be one of the *tempestarii*!' He looked up to the sky and stretched his arms out wide to either side of him, allowing his own mop of bright hair to be blown about by the wind, which was becoming stronger now. Olga looked puzzled by the unfamiliar terms he'd used.

'Wind spirits,' explained Pip.

'Stop being a fool, Klaas,' she said, adjusting the wayward scarf and the matching apron. As she did so, Pip saw for the first time that both garments had white embroidery around the edges, depicting rows of dancing poopy dolls. He shuddered involuntarily.

'That apron will help keep you clean when we start digging, as well,' joked Klaas. He held out his hand to Olga, but she shook her head nervously. A moment later, he was off round the rear of the tomb.

'I don't think you should go inside, Olga,' Pip said. 'Why don't you go back through the fence and stay out there with your mom? You can huddle together to keep warm.' He could see through the fence that Ghita had her arms folded and was rubbing them with her hands. She kept looking over at the tomb, then up at the sky, where the storm clouds were still just visible in the failing light. She had already put on her mac and raised the hood. Pip knew she was as scared as he was, but for her own reasons.

'Yes, please stay here, Olga,' Ghita called across.

'No, I want to go with Klaas,' shouted Olga. 'He'll look after me.' And with that she pulled away from Pip and ran off after the boy.

Pip hated to abandon Ghita outside, but no way was he going to let Olga go into the tomb alone with Klaas! He made a gesture indicating to Ghita that he intended to follow them, and then did so, feeling like a heel.

He soon caught up with the two teenagers. Klaas was crouching by the tomb's arched stone door – the Arch of Darkness, as it had been described in the Marcu Papers. Olga was holding the torch for him as he rubbed away some dirt to reveal a faded carving at the top. 'What do you think about this, Olga?' he said, pointing to the carving. It was the figure of a child with crutches, and its hands were stained dark red.

'Ugh, gross,' she said. 'What's made the hands that colour, Pip?'

Pip shrugged. 'Rusted iron?' he ventured.

'There are kids like that carved all around the top of the tomb,' said Klaas. Olga made as if to go and look, but Pip put a restraining hand on her arm. 'But what's different about those kids is they're all dancing – just like the ones on your scarf and apron. Boo!' He made a scary face at her and she jumped back. Then he pulled her to him. 'Don't be scared, babe. It's just something to do with the folk tales of the sick people round here.'

She laughed, but her face gleamed white in the torchlight. Pip said nothing. He didn't dare. All he had to do was stick with them. At least it stopped him from thinking about the last time he'd examined those little figures himself, and Eisenmann had jumped out at him.

'Let's go inside,' said Klaas. 'Archaeology, remember?'

'Suits me,' agreed Olga bravely.

Klaas started shoving at the door, but didn't really need to; it yielded quite easily, and he almost fell down the flight of stone steps beyond. Olga gave a little squeal of alarm, but the boy quickly righted himself. A moment later, he took the torch from her and began to climb down. The flight was steep and carried on around a dog-leg corner hewn out of the rock.

'Wow!' exclaimed Olga as they rounded the corner. Pip and Klaas simply stared, lost for words. The steps had led into a huge cavern. Pip shook his head. It was like no mausoleum he had ever seen before. The shelves on the walls housed no sarcophagi, skulls or bones; they were all completely bare. There were signs, though, that someone had been excavating here. The walls had even been shored up with steel scaffolding in several places where the rock had been gouged out and desecrated by picks.

'What do you think they're digging for?' Olga asked. Klaas glanced at Pip, who shook his head. Olga sighed. 'Well, if you won't tell me that, can you at least say what you two are looking for? I want to know!'

Pip sat down on a heap of stones. 'I – all we know is, there might be something precious in here.'

'Treasure?' Her eyes sparkled like those of a little girl about to hear a fairy story.

'Kind of,' said Klaas. 'A book.'

'What?'

'It's a thousand years old,' he added.

'This is fun!' Olga said, turning to Pip. 'Whose is it?'

'Not sure,' lied Pip, 'but whoever finds it will be handing it over to a museum!'

'Oh, I thought we might make a lot of money.' She looked crestfallen for a moment, then suddenly cried out in alarm. 'Klaas!'

Pip looked round to see that Klaas had climbed up some of the scaffolding and was now hefting a pick he'd found there. At that moment, Pip thought he could hear once again the all-too-familiar sound of faint, mocking laughter. He put a hand up to his forehead.

'Are you okay?' Olga asked, sitting down on the stones beside him. Just then, a massive peal of thunder shook the ground and, to Pip's horror, he saw the scaffolding tilt to one side and almost collapse. Klaas had to hold on tight to avoid being thrown off. Then another peal hit the cavern, and another. Realising that the storm must have broken, Pip jumped up from the stones, while Klaas clambered back down to the ground.

'Go back up and find a safe place,' Pip told Olga. 'Your mom will probably have taken shelter already!'

'Okay,' cried Olga, but then the ground started shaking again, and fragments of rock began to be dislodged from the cavern roof. Small avalanches fell around them as they crouched protecting their heads. Olga screamed, 'It's an earthquake,' and held on to Pip.

'No, it's just the thunder,' he lied.

Klaas moved to put his arms around Olga, but then suddenly let her go and ran across to a large pile of stone slabs that had been toppled over by the tremor. Next moment, he had crawled under three of the slabs that had come to rest in a rough arch shape.

'Come out of there, you idiot' yelled Pip, craning his neck to see what the boy had spotted. He and Olga watched as Klaas backed out, covered in dust, struggling to drag something after him.

'Come over here – help me!' he yelled, but another rock fall forced them back.

Pip could feel spots of rain hitting his face now, and he realised that cracks must be opening up in the roof. 'The whole place is breaking up, Olga,' he warned. 'Get out of here!'

'No, I'm not going without Klaas!' She squared up to him defiantly.

'Over here!' screamed Klaas again. There was a brief let-up in the rock avalanche, so together Pip and Olga ran across to him.

At Klaas's feet stood a sturdy wooden chest, which must have been dislodged from a well-camouflaged hiding place. Pip and Klaas exchanged a glance. They both knew that they had to get the chest open and see what was inside.

Above them, the storm was increasing in intensity again, and Pip's instincts told him that sooner or later things in the cavern would get even worse. But Klaas was sitting back on his heels, tousled, dirty and grinning, seemingly oblivious of all danger. He took out a heavy chisel that had been concealed in his coat.

'It's the Codex ...' he breathed.

'Perhaps,' Pip panted.

A moment later, Klaas started hacking at the iron catch that held the chest shut, and soon it began to give. Then he was lying on the floor, trying to prise the lid open with the chisel and his fingers. Despite his best efforts, the catch refused to yield. He put his eye to the crack, turned and looked up at Pip, and there was an expression of triumph on his face. 'I think it's a book! But I can't be sure.' He resumed his hacking with the chisel.

Then the whole cavern was rocked as a bolt of lightning forked down from the sky above and struck the tomb directly. Klaas was blown onto his back by the huge blast, but quickly pulled himself up again, still clinging on to the precious chest.

'We can't leave it!' he shouted.

Pip looked at Olga. 'Go,' he yelled. 'Get to the steps.'

Olga turned and ran, but she was thwarted by another blast, which sent her flying. Shoving the chest aside, Klaas ran across to her. When he reached her, she was only just moving.

'We'll have to leave it,' shouted Pip, joining him. All he wanted to do was to get Olga out of what might otherwise turn out to be their own tomb. Klaas shook his head, turned back and continued his work, while Pip ministered to Olga.

As the thunder continued to growl in the sky above, suddenly the half-darkness of the cavern was dispelled by a strong electric light. Like people rousing from a deep sleep, Pip, Olga and Klaas all lifted their heads and stared across to the far end of the mausoleum. A small door had opened up in the rock wall, and a tall, hooded man in a cloak was coming through it.

'Grandsire!' The word dried in Pip's mouth.

'I don't think so,' Klaas muttered, 'unless his ghost has taken to wielding a gun!'

The man strode across the floor and pulled back his hood with his free hand.

'Eisenmann!' Pip groaned.

'You thought you could steal my property again, upstart?'

Pip was too shocked to answer. Klaas was tense beside him, while Olga was still lying barely conscious on the ground.

Eisenmann shook his head. 'And now you'll pay the price.' He advanced a few more steps. 'This time I shall have what is mine. And *you*, boy, have found it!' He turned to Klaas, who struggled to his feet and faced the gun barrel.

'No, Klaas!' screamed Pip.

'You're dead, you bastard!' snarled Klaas.

Eisenmann was grinning. 'You were taught well,' he growled, 'and you have done well. Fetch me the chest. Put it here.' He pointed in front of him.

'Fuck you!' shouted Klaas, taking one step closer to him, then another.

'No, Klaas! He'll kill you!' Pip crept forward on his knees, reaching out a restraining hand, but Klaas pushed him back. 'He isn't your father ...' Pip's shocked mind reeled as he considered the possibility. Maybe Eisenmann *was* Klaas's father? Had it been his face, and not Koppelberg's, that the boy had seen in the photocopies of the manuscript pages? If so, Klaas was the Piper's grandson ... All this passed through Pip's mind in an instant as Eisenmann and Klaas stood facing each other.

'My *dead* father,' Klaas said. His tone was dangerous. 'Why should I let you have the chest?'

'Come, boy, do as I say. It belongs to us. To you and me. It contains something very precious. We can be masters of the world. That's what you want, isn't it?'

Klaas only stood there. 'How would you know what I want?' he snarled. 'I needed a father!'

'Klaas, listen to me. He doesn't care for you,' shouted Pip. 'He wouldn't have treated you like that if he did. Don't go near him. He'll kill you. Listen to me! All he wants is the chest!'

Pip's voice echoed eerily around the walls. Then suddenly it was drowned out by a deafening roar as the tomb was rocked by another direct lightening strike. Temporarily dazzled by the blinding flash, Pip could still see just enough to register that Eisenmann had fallen backwards, clutching at his chest. The gun slipped from his grasp, and Klaas grabbed it with a deft hand, a look of triumph on his face.

Pip quickly checked himself and Olga over and found to his relief that they were both unscathed. They sat up and stared at each other. Eisenmann was lying face upwards at a distance, motionless, arms outstretched and … Pip looked away. The lighting had hit the German, splitting his body wide open.

Suddenly Klaas let out a shocked exclamation, caught hold of Pip's arm and turned his attention back to the corpse. To his horror, Pip saw that a column of thick black smoke was emanating from Eisenmann's torso and pluming above him, like a waterspout as it rises. When the smoke reached the roof, it started to spread out across it and billow through the rest of the cavern. Pip, Olga and Klaas all began to cough.

Pip grabbed hold of the two teenagers and pulled them toward the steps. His trembling hands had regained their strength and more. He didn't stop to wonder whether the dreadful smoke was a natural phenomenon caused by the lightning strike or, instead, a supernatural one – he was only terrified it might choke them all to death! He could hear Olga murmuring with pain as he pulled her along. Klaas, who seemed to have recovered from his shock now, was shuffling along on his own.

Pip's breathing was worsening, but eventually he and his two near-exhausted companions managed to reach the precariously balanced pile of stone slabs from beneath which Klaas had pulled the wooden chest. Pausing there to rest for a moment, Pip and Klaas looked back to see that Eisenmann's wrecked body was now wreathed in the acrid smoke. Then, unbelievably, it started to twitch with movement, and they heard moans of human agony.

Klaas made to go back, but Pip grabbed his arm hard. 'No! You can't help him now!'

Klaas pulled his arm free, started to move across to Eisenmann, but then halted, as both he and Pip spotted the flickering light of flames coming from that direction. The black smoke suddenly parted, and they stared open-mouthed as a mottled zig-zag thing started to rise up from the German's body. They watched it grow and grow until they recognised the form of a brightly-patterned snake, fluid but ascending vertically. The flames that licked around it resembled a tight tunic of harlequin yellow and red. It was an inhuman thing, emerging from a crackling human chrysalis.

What remained of Eisenmann's body was burning, without and within. The fiery snake thing that rose above it suddenly lunged forward, threatening Pip and the two teenagers with the twin fangs that protruded from its smooth, pale, leering mouth.

Pip's reason had almost deserted him now, and his body was pouring with sweat as the cave grew hotter and hotter around him. His inner voice screamed, *Wake up! We're all going to die!* When he opened his eyes again, the smoke had wreathed itself cloak-like around the snake, which was rising higher still.

'Oh, God, save us,' Pip prayed, feeling for the silver cross he had hung around his neck. All he could think of just then was the legend that Anya had recounted to him of the little gypsy seeing a demon emerge from its evil master's bisected body.

Klaas had now slipped down to the base of the stone slab against which he had been leaning. His eyes were wide open and staring, as if he was in a trance. A moment later, a dark shape bounded toward the fire. Then it turned, and they saw that it was a great black rat with its mouth wide open. Suddenly it hurled itself right into the fire, and they heard it shrieking in agony as it was consumed.

Pip fell to his knees. He had to protect Olga! 'The cavern is burning up,' he screamed. 'We've got to get out!' He managed to drag the girl across to the bottom of the flight of steps. Then he remembered Klaas, and looked back. The boy was still slumped at the base of the stone slab, the wooden chest beside him. Then came another peal of thunder, followed by a further fall of rocks, one of which struck Klaas on the forehead.

Propping the still-groggy Olga against the wall leading upwards to safety, Pip turned and fought his way back through the evil-smelling smoke to Klaas's side. The boy seemed to have been stunned into immobility, but Pip seized hold of him and, with a tremendous effort, managed to get him over to the foot of the steps. Then, pulling a dizzy Olga to her feet, he forced her up in front, while he dragged Klaas along behind.

'Go on, Olga, you can do it!' he urged. But he soon realised that she couldn't. When she reached the dog-leg turn in the steps, her strength gave out, and she collapsed to the ground. Pip let go of Klaas and slid down beside her, tilting her head up toward the stream of clean air blowing in from above. Then he fell back against the steps, exhausted, his lungs heaving. He thought he could hear the sound of faint, mocking laughter again, along with the murmur of voices, which he assumed were also in his head. He glanced back into the cavern and saw that the wooden chest was now completely engulfed in smoke and about to be consumed by the flames. He bent his head in misery.

At that moment, a dark shape appeared above him, caught hold of Olga by the shoulders and dragged her up and away. Pip's last thought as she disappeared was, *He's got her! And it's all my fault!* Then he passed out.

18

Pip woke with a start and stared about him. Transparent white curtains blew about a large window that reached up almost to the ceiling. He looked away, his tired eyes drooping against the light. He felt bruised, but at peace. He drifted, then came to again. He sat up and looked around. White. Was he dead? He felt over his face, and there was something protruding from his nose. He panicked and tried to pull it out, but a soft hand prevented him. He hadn't the strength to fight back.

Then a familiar face hovered above his. He put up a hand to touch it, and felt the warmth of humanity again.

'You're awake,' said Ghita. 'You mustn't pull out the tube. It's oxygen for the smoke inhalation.'

He began to remember, and started up in alarm, then flopped back onto the bed, his strength deserting him. 'I failed you,' he said, drowsily. He felt her hand again.

'No, you saved Olga – and Klaas!'

His senses returned. His mind was all over the place. 'Where …?''

'You're at the University hospital in Cluj. It's the drugs, Pip. You'll be okay soon.'

He closed his eyes. When he came to again, he saw Ghita sitting beside the bed. 'You're back!' she said, smiling. There were so many things he wanted to ask her, but he could barely speak. It felt like he had a football in his chest.

'You inhaled too much smoke,' Ghita explained, seeing his discomfort. 'Olga is fine, and Klaas is in the next room. What a lot you are!' she added. 'I come on holiday to celebrate my birthday with three people, and all of them end up in hospital! Luckily, I'm okay, but I'm not sure if you are.'

Pip frowned as he detected in Ghita's voice a note of worry, tinged with something else he couldn't quite define.

'I had to fetch the emergency services,' she went on, 'and now there's a policeman outside who wants to talk to you.'

Pip caught his breath. He shouldn't have been so stupid as to return to Romania! But he'd had to. Then he remembered that Eisenmann was dead and Olga was alive.

'He's a detective,' Ghita said. 'I told him you were my partner. You don't mind, do you?' He stared at her in surprise. 'No? I'll let him in, shall I? You can explain after.'

Pip nodded in agreement. He understood now.

'I'll wait outside, until you're finished.'

He nodded again, and already his befuddled mind was trying to figure out what he was going to say.

Even if Ghita hadn't mentioned it, it would have been obvious that the policeman was a detective. No uniform. No gun. At least, none that Pip could see. Everything about him was unprepossessing – a man who would never be noticed in a crowd.

'May I sit down?' he asked.

Pip indicated his approval.

'I'm Detective Inspector Korac. I shall be recording our interview.' No question of seeking his approval there. The man's face was deadly serious. 'We have had dealings with you before, Professor Durrant.'

'When?' Pip croaked.

'2007. Seventeen years ago. You must like our country.' Korac smiled wryly. 'Shall I remind you of the circumstances? Several sudden deaths of people you had been involved with. All of which you managed to explain away very well.'

'I was exonerated.'

The detective ignored Pip's answer. 'Shall I list them for you? Chief Inspector Valentin, a retired detective, hit and run. Fr Joseph, a parish priest, suicide – poor fellow. And Robert Riparu, a hospital nurse, a very unusual case of rabies. Three men with strong connections to Arva; none native to the village itself, but all respected members of the community.'

'That's all in the past,' replied Pip, who had been waiting for Eisenmann's name.

'It is relevant though. Your name came up in those investigations – and here you are, bothering us again!' He stared coldly at Pip, who avoided making eye contact by feigning tiredness. The detective pressed on regardless.

'How exactly did you come to be in a fenced-off area of one of our cultural heritage sites in the middle of the night?'

'I can explain that,' Pip said, his voice gradually returning. 'I am here in connection with Oxford University. I was researching some Arvan history that I found particularly interesting.'

The inspector nodded. 'I gather you were meeting a friend of yours; a Mr Honen, an American businessman. At least, that's what his son says.'

'*His son?*'

'Mr Klaas Honen. He's in this hospital too, as I am sure you are aware.'

'Yes. How is he?'

'I'm not a doctor, but he seemed perky enough when he gave me his statement.'

'What else did he say?'

'I'm not obliged to disclose that, but I can tell you that he claimed you were there with his permission.'

'His permission? Why would I need his permission?

'That whole plot of land belonged to his father, who is now deceased, making Mr Klaas Honen the new owner.'

'What happened to him – Mr Honen Snr?'

'He burned to death in the fire, I'm afraid. A blackened

corpse was found that Mr Honen Jnr confirmed could only be that of his father. He said you two had arranged to meet him at the tomb on 22 July to conclude some historical research. You have friends in high places, Professor. Also, you seem to have a knack of getting out of trouble. So far, you have escaped our grasp. But there is another matter I want to raise with you: that of some missing manuscripts pages.' Pip waited. 'Mr Honen Snr reported them stolen after you left a meeting with him – although he later withdrew his complaint.'

'Mr Honen reported them missing?'

'Sadly, a little too late for us to be able to prevent you from taking those protected historical items out of our country. He was very upset at the time, but then decided to let things drop. I believe you made it up with him and continued working together?'

Pip nodded in confirmation. Now he understood why he had never been able to find any trace of Eisenmann in all the intervening years; the German must have assumed the new identity of Honen almost immediately after he left.

'There's something I still don't understand,' he said. 'You mentioned that Klaas had inherited the tomb site from his father, but I'd have thought that Klaas's mother would be the beneficiary.'

'Sadly for the young man, he is now an orphan. His mother's body was discovered in the mausoleum as well. Also burned. She was in the blocked-off passage that led to the site of the old church. A fast-track dental records check confirmed her identity as Mrs Sigi Honen.'

Pip had never known there was a passage from the tomb to the church! He realised that Eisenmann and Sigi must have been hiding there when he and the two teenagers had entered. Could all the parish priests throughout the ages also have been aware of its existence? Maybe that was one of the reasons Simu had hated the Church so much and seen it as complicit in the child murders.

'Are you all right, Professor?' asked the detective. Pip nodded, but his head was aching and his breathing shallow.

'Some other ancient inhabitants of the tomb also perished, incidentally. Rats!'

'Rats?'

'Yes. Hordes of them were found clustered around Mrs Honen's body. Hopefully none of the buggers escaped!'

Pip nodded, thinking of the huge rat he'd seen. Had Snipe disappeared forever now into the fire – or returned to the Piper, his rightful master?

'Anything else you can tell me?' Pip asked.

'Actually, I was hoping for some clarification from you,' replied Korac.

'I can't help. I've told you everything I know.'

Korac switched off his recorder. 'A wasted journey,' he noted sardonically, 'and once again I have nothing to charge you with! Maybe you've suffered enough to keep you away from Romania now? Then I shall say goodbye, and I hope for your speedy recovery. But,' he leaned forward and stared into Pip's face, 'should you ever be tempted to embark on any more dubious activities here, Professor, I warn you that we'll be keeping a very close watch on you.' His dark eyes searched Pip's face. 'And if you want to remove any other historical items from this country, make sure you remember to apply for a licence first. Do I make myself clear?'

'Perfectly,' replied Pip. 'See yourself out.' He closed his eyes and waited until he heard the door bang shut. A few minutes later, it opened again and Ghita returned.

'He didn't look particularly happy when he emerged,' she said. 'Why did he want to see you? Breaking and entering a public monument?'

'No,' said Pip. 'He was only checking on my health and seeing if I could tell him anything about how the fire started.'

Ghita laughed. 'And no doubt he raised the subject of the two dead bodies they found in there?' Pip stared at her. 'I always know when you're lying. Olga has already told me a lot about what happened. She's still very upset. Later, when both of you feel better, then we'll have to talk. I have something important of my own to tell you. It didn't feel right before, but now I think it's time.'

'Whatever Olga has said about that night,' he told her, 'rest assured I would never intentionally lead her into harm's way.'

Ghita sighed. 'I hope I can believe that. At least, I shall try.'

Several days later, Pip left Cluj hospital. He had spoken to Klaas before he was discharged. The young man had a brilliant future ahead of him, and had inherited a fortune from his father, but still Pip pitied him, as he had now lost both of his parents and was left with no family at all.

'I'm *the* Honen now,' he had said. 'The big boss, expected to fill the shoes of a man I've always hated and believed to be dead. I still do hate him. But I know my mother would have been glad to die with him. He pulled all her strings. I can see it now – I was a pawn in some sick game they were playing. I'm free now. He'll probably roll over in his grave when he knows what I intend to do.' He looked down at Olga, who was sitting close to him.

The girl smiled up at Pip. 'And I'm going to help him,' she said. Pip nodded, but inside he was hoping that she wouldn't.

'I ought to say thanks for saving Olga – my soul mate,' Klaas told Pip, clasping the girl's hand. 'Thanks for saving me, too; but I'll be my own saviour from now on.'

'Olga ought to be your saviour!' retorted Pip. 'But not until she's old enough to make her mind up properly!' He shot Klaas a warning glance. 'Anyway, where are you headed?'

'I haven't a choice,' he joked. 'I'm moving in to the old homestead. And I expect you to come and visit me! I'm being picked up tomorrow and flown home for the funerals, which have been arranged by my father's business attorney. He's ready to shape my future as head of Honen Inc; but he's got a shock in store. As soon as the dust has settled, I intend to wind the company up. I didn't even know that much about it until a couple of days ago. My mother always told me it was owned by some distant relative of my father's. Another of her lies!'

'What are you going to do, Klaas? You can achieve anything

you want, you know. Now even more so than before.'

'My PhD. And I shan't be accepting any offer from the Department of Defense to fry my brain! I shall keep on with my own research, and that means I'll be in touch with you a lot.'

Olga had been looking at him, taking in his every word. It was quite clear that she adored him, but it still worried Pip.

'Would you mind leaving us alone for a few minutes to talk over some things, Olga?' Klaas asked.

'I don't want to, but I will,' she replied with a smile.

When she'd left the room, Klaas turned to Pip. 'Olga will tell me if you're behaving yourself,' he said. 'And do something about Ghita!'

'You should mind your own business!' Pip replied. 'Anyway, what do you want to talk to me about?'

'A lot of things!'

'Then you'll have to wait,' Pip replied.

'Okay. Cagey as usual. But you're going to have spill those secrets some time. One thing – did you see the same thing I did?'

'In the tomb? I saw a lot of stuff. Do you really want to talk about it? Because I don't.'

'Why?'

'Because I truly believe it would be painful for you,' Pip replied.

'Family emotions! Off limits.'

'Then we're quits.'

'I have a theory,' said Klaas. 'We had a vision together.' Pip's eyes narrowed. 'What was with the rat and the snake, Prof? You'll have to spit it out one day.'

'Maybe I will, maybe I won't.' Was Klaas really blocking out his father's horrific death by imagining it had been a vision? Pip doubted it. More likely, he was just angling for more information. He offered the boy his hand. Next moment, he was enveloped in a strong hug, and stood still with shock.

'You'll have to explain one day,' Klaas whispered again, then withdrew. 'I'm still part of the family.'

'We'll see.' Pip lifted his eyebrows. Then he put his hand

into his jacket pocket and handed Klaas a roll of bank notes. 'I owe you. Two thousand bucks. Here – but thanks for the offer.'

He left Klaas standing outlined against the sunny hospital window.

'You will definitely see me again,' the boy called after him. 'It's not over yet, Professor.'

Pip smiled, lifted his hand in farewell and went out without looking back. Olga was waiting outside. She caught the door to stop it swinging shut.

'Will you tell Mother I'll be back soon?' she asked Pip. 'Klaas and I have lots of things to say to each other.'

Pip nodded. 'Be careful, Olga,' he said. *She seems to have grown up*, he thought.

Oxford, August 2024

It was the evening of the Sunday following their return to the UK. Olga was upstairs playing her music when Pip settled himself beside Ghita on the couch with an open bottle of wine and two glasses. To make room to put them down, he had to push aside two dusty piles of books.

'I can't believe I left the place in such a mess when we went to Romania,' said Ghita, sighing.

'I can,' he replied.

Inside, he felt nervous. Ghita had told him she wanted to have a serious talk. If she quizzed him hard about what had happened in Arva, he knew he might end up having to make a damning confession: that he had used her daughter as bait, knowingly leading her into a trap that could have resulted in her being murdered. He needed to come clean about some of the secrets he had been keeping, and had rehearsed it all during his wakeful nights. He wanted to tell Ghita that, because Olga had gypsy blood, she had never been destined to be the Piper's victim. But he had not been entirely certain of that himself, so the fact that the dramatic events of 22 July had had a positive outcome for them could only be put down to good luck – or perhaps to divine intervention. He recalled, somewhat uncomfortably, that in his weakest moment he had called upon God to help him.

As for Ghita, she had said that she was going to enlighten him as to her own secret that evening, after he had packed to return to his lodgings. She hadn't tried to stop him leaving; she'd just said that it was only fair that he knew the truth first. Pip thought she might be going to tell him that she was still married, or … he couldn't really think what else it might be.

To Pip's relief, Ghita didn't question him at all about their Arvan escapade. 'Here we go,' she said, sipping her drink. 'I have tried to tell you this so many times, but I couldn't. In fact, I thought you might have guessed? Sometimes you're a very stupid man, in spite of being a professor.'

'I think I might have worked it out,' he ventured. She sighed with relief. 'I think,' he began, 'you might want to tell me that you are still married – and that you've decided to go back to your husband, whoever he is.'

She stared at him, began to laugh, then sobered quickly. 'Now you really *are* being stupid,' she said. 'Olga is – your daughter!' It came out in a rush. 'Have you never guessed?' He could only stare at her. She waited for a few moments, then burst out, 'Well?'

Pip felt humble, amazed and idiotic all at once. 'Does she know?'

'No. I felt we should probably tell her together. What do you think?'

As he sat there trying to take in the stunning revelation, Pip's mind flew back to Koppelberg's chalet, where in the penultimate display case he had seen the comforting image of the guy carrying the little girl on his shoulders. He remembered that, afterwards, he had studied his own reflection in the bathroom mirror and thought that the guy had looked a bit like he would when he grew older, and that the little girl had had about her a hint of his sisters, Rose and Mel. 'I like you,' she'd said to him. 'When will I see you again?' he'd called. 'Not for a long time, Pip ...' they'd chorused. So often since then, he'd longed to see them again, and drawn strength and reassurance from their memory. Now, he'd finally found that man and that girl, and understood what they meant to him. *Pip and Olga.*

'What are you thinking, Pip?' Ghita asked. 'Are you sorry I told you? Are you angry? Are you sad?'

'Hush,' he said, brushing her hair back from her face. 'Not sad, but happy. Very, very happy.'

He and Ghita talked and talked. Afterwards, they went upstairs together with the rest of the wine and their glasses, just like he'd imagined them doing when he'd first gone to lodge there.

When Pip woke in the morning, with Ghita beside him, he thought of his future and theirs. His wish to be reunited with Ghita was finally fulfilled. She was the one he loved – and Olga too now. The other family he'd needed all these years.

Yet his other quest was still ongoing. Before he had left the hospital in Romania, he had spotted a glaring headline in the local newspaper:

GIRL ABDUCTED AT ARVA FAIR. LOCALS GATHER.

The accompanying report had sickened him. The Piper had found his victim after all. Once again, the locals had gathered at Ruxandra's, just as they had done at Sancipia for hundreds of years before. Again some poor 15-year-old child who had been raped, and who was destined to die very soon afterwards, had found shelter there until the police had arrived.

Pip had failed to stop the Piper, and yet he had not been defeated by him. Should he continue the search for the killer? Or would someone else take on the struggle? He knew another wanted to: Klaas Honen, in whose blood a devilish strand of the Piper's ran. He would fight Grandsire, his own grandfather, now Eisenmann had gone. But had the wooden chest and its probable contents survived to reveal the whole of the Piper's story and his secrets? Or had it been burned to ashes or buried under the rubble of the collapsed tomb? Whatever happened, Pip was sure that Klaas had sworn to discover that infamous book. Had the boy also seen the date that Isaac Newton had shown Nicholas? The date of the end of the world, when the Piper's curse would be finally lifted and evil would triumph, unless good men prevailed? Could Klaas cope with all this on his own without Pip?

Pip didn't know the answers to those questions; but, for the first time since he was 13, he felt that he was now free of the terrible quest that had become his destiny when the Piper had arrived in Sunny Mead to demonstrate the Devil that lies within Man.

Pip closed his eyes again. He could think only of Ghita now. With her, he felt safe; and, at that very moment, Ghita woke, yawned, and smiled at him.

About the Author

Helen McCabe is a highly regarded author whose love of writing and powerful imagination, coupled with a determination to succeed, have ensured a long and successful career. Her lifelong fascination with literature, history and research and an interest in the paranormal have enhanced Helen's immense gift for creative storytelling.

She graduated with Honours from London University, where she read English, and holds an MA degree in 18th Century English Literature from the University of Keele.

Her long career began with her first novel at the age of seven, with poetry published at 13 and read on the BBC. She started her true career as a novelist after becoming well-known for her short stories and serials in popular magazines. In 1995 her first full-length novel – *Two for a Lie*, about the 19th Century Princess Caraboo – was published, gaining much interest and critical acclaim. Since then, in tandem with work and family, she has written more than thirty novels in various genres, including historical, romance and more recently horror/thriller and crime. She also writes scripts for film, television and the stage.

Alongside her writing, Helen has worked in a variety of jobs, beginning as an assistant librarian and finally becoming a lecturer and teacher. She is a member of the Romantic Novelists Association, the Crime Writers' Association, the Horror Writers of America and the West Country Writers' Association.

Helen was invited to join Mensa, the high IQ society, in 1989.

Helen lives in Worcester and has three grown-up children and a grandson.

Her website can be found at www.helenmccabe.com.

Also Available From Telos Publishing

SPECTRE by STEPHEN LAWS
Something is stalking the Chapter, picking them off one by one,
something connected with their past, and with the girl they
used to know.

<u>SAM STONE</u>
KAT LIGHTFOOT MYSTERIES
Steampunk, horror, adventure series
1: ZOMBIES AT TIFFANY'S
2: KAT ON A HOT TIN AIRSHIP
3: WHAT'S DEAD PUSSYKAT
4: KAT OF GREEN TENTACLES

JINX CHRONICLES
Hi-tech science fiction fantasy series
1: JINX TOWN
2: JINX MAGIC
3: JINX BOUND (Coming Sept 2016)

THE DARKNESS WITHIN
Science Fiction Horror Short Novel

ZOMBIES IN NEW YORK AND OTHER BLOODY JOTTINGS
Thirteen stories of horror and passion, and six mythological and
erotic poems from the pen of the new Queen of Vampire fiction.

TELOS PUBLISHING
Email: orders@telos.co.uk
Web: www.telos.co.uk

**To order copies of any Telos books, please visit our website
where there are full details of all titles and facilities for
worldwide credit card online ordering, as well as occasional
special offers.**